THE END OF THE ROAD

MARTIN VENNING

mvenning.net

Matador
Unit E2 Airfield Business Park,
Harrison Road, Market Harborough,
Leicestershire. LE16 7WB
Tel: 0116 2792299
Email: books@troubador.co.uk
Web: www.troubador.co.uk/matador
Twitter: @matadorbooks

ISBN 978 1 8004 6557 2

British Library Cataloguing in Publication Data.
A catalogue record for this book is available from the British Library.

Printed and bound in Great Britain by 4edge Limited
Typeset in 11pt Adobe Garamond Pro by Troubador Publishing Ltd, Leicester, UK

Matador is an imprint of Troubador Publishing Ltd

For Matt – sorry you didn`t get beyond the Causeway.

and Simon –
pleasure to meet!
Regards
Martin Venning
Enjoy!

PROLOGUE

IT HAD BEEN A big week for Dr Desmond Kelly.

On the positive side, he had succeeded in his mission to pioneer the creation of a new generation of heavy-duty high-performance diamond batteries from nuclear waste, encased in recyclable plastic, that was destined to revolutionise the global manufacturing industry and clean up the environment.

On the negative, he had been diagnosed with cancer which, although not entirely unexpected given the tests he had undergone, came as a shock, nonetheless.

He was not naturally the collegiate type and these two significant outcomes had been realised without the active support of his peers and family. Both created a new dynamic in his life, or what was left of it.

The success of his experimentation with the catchily titled *Hyper Condensed Chemical Vapour Deposition* or '*HCCVD*' had taken research into the crystallisation of radioactive waste graphite to a new level. By, in effect, locking a Carbon-14 radioactive isotope into a manufactured diamond and linking it to energy-harvesting sensors, he had developed an energy source that would not need renewing for at least 5,000 years. Although the basic science was known, its application had been strictly limited to low-level energy devices such as hearing aids and heart pacemakers. His innovation was to introduce a step change in performance – a unit that could create significant multiple and sustainable heavy duty power generation – everything from heating homes to mobilising vehicles, ships and planes. Its basic raw material, derived from depleted uranium rods, was stored in potentially hazardous subterranean silos and with some 95,000 tonnes collected from its own power stations and those of its allies around the world, the UK was well placed to turn this innovation into a unique global industry.

While retaining its traditional brick-like look, this new battery was a complex piece of kit. Its precise make-up and manufacturing process was a trade secret, but he was confident companies around the world would bid for the production rights. The safety issues were significant. The core material would have to be encased on-site, prior to being transported for consolidation. But he was still some way off from that ambition. Tests had established the raw power of the product, but integrating it into vehicles and trucks in particular, was at an early stage. His real ambition for its application related to shipping – itself responsible for over 2% of global carbon emissions – but now he could not be confident about being alive to develop the marine application.

As anyone involved in nuclear research was aware, the power for good or otherwise with the technology was immense. The scientists engaged in it themselves formed a unique global community, seeking knowledge for the benefit of mankind, but constrained; often working under diverse political influences that did not always share their high moral or ethical standards. Members of this exclusive club would meet from time to time, sharing their research papers at international conferences, inviting comment and analysis, except when a breakthrough was achieved – when their masters got involved.

Kelly was caught in such a moment and faced a dilemma. Yes, he had achieved a milestone in power generation in laboratory conditions. He had taken out the cerebral insurance of de-linking and distributing elements of his research programme to a diverse range of institutions, who in themselves would not have the capacity to interpret the results. As of today, his paymasters would not know of his achievement or how to replicate his work as the formula for his discovery had not yet been documented. If he followed through and completed his records, he knew they would be seized upon first by the military, who were always looking for more efficient ways of killing people, and his true ambition of preventing excessive global warming would not be realised. And yet for him, time was short. He had received his death sentence and he had a matter of months or years.

From a personal point of view, despite his devastating diagnosis, Des had to admit to a fleeting moment of euphoria. After all, he had reached a seemingly impossible target, a milestone, perhaps ten years ahead of his own projections. He had to tell someone – an individual who knew of his research and who he trusted. That person, Dr Galina Rustanova of the Russian Academy of Sciences, presently on secondment at the US equivalent in San Francisco, would be his chosen confidant.

He had got to know Rustanova, as a result of assessing her work on the bioremediation programme, at Chernobyl in the late 1980s, and the pair had had cause to meet on many occasions since in different parts of the world. While their relationship had been, for the most part, platonic, Kelly had come to foster a real admiration for her as a scientist and an engaging character, capable of mixing humour with a dark sense of foreboding, so typical of her countrymen. She was attractive, too, in what he considered an understated way, with a trim figure, short sculpted blonde hair and intense eyes highlighted by the measured use of mascara. They had shared some memorable moments together; professionally, setting standards for nuclear inspections for the International Atomic Energy Agency and personally, over dinners from London to Moscow, Vienna and Jerusalem to Delhi. Although she was familiar to him, like a comfortable pair of lightly worn brogues, he had to admit he couldn't claim to know that much about her personal life. After all, why should he? All he knew was that she was in her early forties, married with a couple of children, had a flat in Moscow, and had binge-watched the US sitcom *Friends* as a way of chilling out. What he had shared in return, beyond the perennial strains about the vagaries of accessing funds for his research in the West, was limited to his two grown up children – Miles, a graduate trainee with Revenue & Customs and Abigail, an aspiring actress, recently hired to promote a new brand of yoghurt on TV – and his newly 'semi-detached wife', Sue, who had lost interest in him and his work but enjoyed the benefits of what had become a marriage of convenience.

Perhaps he had said too much. Anyway, what the hell…

He picked up his mobile and texted her a short message: "I've done it!", followed by a smiley emoji.

Message sent. It was the end of an exhausting day. Time to sign off, shut down his computer and make his way home to his comfortable, if slightly anonymous, residence in the Thames Valley. He paused, looking at his reflection in the glass panel which formed one of the boundaries of his personal space.

For a man of his age, he still had a good crop of grey hair (admittedly with flecks of white), and a freshly grown beard and sunken eyes gave him what he considered an unjustifiably moody look.

No, he didn't feel upset, just worn out. It was time to raise his game for the journey home.

As he started to swap his white lab coat for a more sober tweed jacket and anorak, his assistant, Dr Jakeman (Jake) Roberts, walked into his office.

"Glad I caught you, Des, just taken a call from my *alma mater* at Stanford. They are looking to set up a conference early next year on new commercial applications from industrial waste. They want us – you and/or me, 'someone' – to give a keynote on the future of the industry; probably nothing more than domesticating small-scale community nuclear power stations, AI, that sort of thing."

"Do you think we should do it?"

"Well, on balance, I think doing these things from time to time is a good idea. After all, you are not talking to a room of postgrads at Stanford. These are money men with deep pockets looking for the next big deal. If we impress, then it offers a shortcut to long-term finance without the normal bullshit commitments and form filling we get from the government here. It's also a great opportunity to show those guys that innovation is not defined by initiatives invented over there."

Kelly was preoccupied and, at that moment, not engaged.

"OK Jake, give them a provisional acceptance for now. We've got a bit more time to think through how we want to play it. I understand you'd quite like to take it on, especially as you could combine a trip with a visit to see your mum and dad in Oakland."

Roberts nodded, smiled, and moved towards the office door.

He hesitated, turning to Kelly.

"Des – sorry to be a bit personal – are you all right?"

Kelly fixed him with a steely look.

"If you have spent the afternoon studying a spreadsheet on micromovements of emissions from fifty-year-old contaminated rods, you get to look like me."

Roberts laughed.

"Yes, and I bet you will be coming to me to calculate the rate of absorption into storage waters in a couple of days."

"Careful what you wish for."

Kelly followed him out, closing the door of his glass-walled office and made his way past the four rows of desks occupied by members of his team, nodding to the one or two who were still focused on their screens.

"Night, Jake. Let's grab a coffee in the morning."

"Night. Hope you feel brighter after a good sleep."

"Sure I will. There's nothing a couple of glasses of Mouton Rothschild won't fix."

If only it was that simple.

Cocooned in his car for the drive home, Kelly normally had the six o'clock radio news on, but tonight he just wanted to close himself off from the world as much as he was able to do, heading south on the A34 towards Newbury. This was not a night to shout out at the latest mad utterances of the prime minister but was a moment for introspection and reflection on his predicament. Looking at his music selection, Mahler's '5th Symphony' seemed to capture his mood best, especially with a winter squall enveloping his windscreen and the cloudy day fading into night.

What to do? He would need to tell his boss, Sir Gavin Laidlaw, at the Lauriston Foundation, who would be duty bound to tell his partners at the Nuclear Decommissioning Authority, Ministry of Defence and their colleagues in the energy department who in turn would in all likelihood tell the Americans. Maybe he should issue a press release? That way they might all get to hear his explanation of his situation and not how it might get to be interpreted by other people. And what about Sue and the children? For her, it would be an inconvenience. She would probably seek reassurance that the pension was in place and want a date when he was going into hospital, either to make sure she had a reserve bridge partner in place or to make alternative arrangements for her dog to be walked in the evenings. He might get a more sympathetic response from Miles and Abigail, but they had their own lives – flats, lovers, hopes and fears, where his news would only be a passing footnote in their own experience. Strangely he was comfortable with that. He respected their independence and certainly didn't want them grieving his loss.

He had now reached the exit that led to his village. Home was just a few minutes from here. He expected Sue would be arriving about the same time, so whoever was there first would be expected to pull some dinner out of the freezer and get Milo the Rottweiler out to do his business.

So what was the answer? He remembered his Yorkshire father's words, "when in doubt, do now't". The stakes were high; once the information was released it was out there and he would no longer be in control. Frozen dinner prepared and eaten, message from the missus confirming the assignation with the choral society received, Milo's comfort restored, it was time to return to Mahler in the front room armed with a glass of claret, a quick look at the domestic CCTV footage and LinkedIn on his phone as well as the latest copy of *Private Eye* for entertainment.

*

The following morning he had a meeting with his doctor. The discussion was predictable. He was at Stage IV for prostate and his liver was under attack. Chemo was an urgent priority and although suffering a degree of discomfort he wouldn't necessarily describe himself as being in pain, due in part, he had to admit, to his permitted but liberal use of controlled drugs. So, to the big question: how long? Not much science on offer with this diagnosis. It all depended on how quickly he had treatment, the intensity of it and how his body reacted. A year, maybe two, but that was it. And what of the alternative doing 'now't'?

Six months at best. To Kelly, the alternatives didn't look great. The chemo would certainly force him to change his working habits and would make him feel a lot worse than he felt today. Given the advanced nature of his illness, it was still unlikely to clear him completely.

So he was trading a certain outcome for maybe a few more years of existence. Yes, existence was the right word; where although he would be alive, he would be unable to live it in the way he wanted. He had built his career on confronting problems and finding solutions. There would be no solution in this case other than to use his limited time to the full.

"I understand you are not keen on the treatment, Des.

Nobody is," his doctor observed. "Do remember, you may change your mind and then it will be too late. Take some time out today and think it through some more. Call me as soon as you're ready and I can make the necessary arrangements at the hospital. Have you discussed it with your wife? I thought not. You really should, especially if you are expecting her to look after you."

Des grunted noncommittally. Their relationship was already in 'special measures'. She was not the compassionate kind and he didn't wish to feel the chill of her indifference.

"Thanks doctor, I'll think it through some more and come back to you. Sorry, I have to run now. I have a review meeting coming up with my boss. Maybe I will bring this into the conversation if the opportunity presents itself."

The irony of his drive to his office in Oxford was not lost on him. The premises in the new wing of the Lauriston was only a few minutes' drive from the John Radcliffe, the likely venue for his treatment.

He was no nearer the pressing decision to take his peers into his confidence.

*

The sun was setting on what had been a glorious spring afternoon in Kaliningrad Oblast – Russia's most westerly outpost, a corner of eastern Europe retained by the old Soviet Union after the second world war, located between Poland and Lithuania. Stefan Zanowsky had embarked on a little 'off the record' tourism, having arrived at the bus station on the early morning service from Gdansk and spent most of the day being a sightseer, catching another bus from Teatralnaya Street in the city to visit Baltiysk and then the Vistula Spit – a thin strip of land offshore running southwest to northeast between the Baltic Sea and the enclosed waters of the Vistula Lagoon. Although requiring the obligatory 'on demand' visa, this was not an excursion for the faint-hearted. Cameras were frowned upon and care required selecting the background for the obligatory selfie. The locality was the nerve centre of Russian military operations on its western fringe, with the docks being a hub for some of the Russian Navy's most advanced ships and submarines. As a traditionally 'closed' community, the sight of foreigners still drew some attention, especially those instantly recognisable as being 'different' – from Africa and Asia in particular. But the locals had been quick to take on the mantle of welcoming hosts, offering informal cash exchanges between roubles, dollars and euros, wherever they saw an opportunity, while others were keen to offer specialist tourist guide services, showcasing relics from the locality's bloody Prussian past and extolling the virtues of their favourite local food and drink, *Stroganina* and *Pologar*.

The town itself was bordered not only by the Baltic Sea, but some four military airfields bristling with advanced weaponry, targeted at the West. By Russian standards, it was an odd place. Perhaps unusually for its size, it had all the trappings of Nordic prosperity, which made it a favourite posting for sailors and airmen with a range of shops, bars, restaurants and nightclubs. Away from the docks, it also enjoyed the benefit of sandy beaches and opportunities for birdwatching in nearby forests, especially on long summer days. Yes, this place could be regarded as a hidden gem, certainly on a par with some other towns on the more affluent northern seashore in Sweden and Finland.

Despite these distractions, Stefan's purpose was clear. He had a job to 'spring' a Russian nuclear physicist, specialising in marine propulsion, on behalf of MI6. It was a typical British assignment, characterised by little effective forward planning, masking as a cloak of complete deniability in the event of failure, but offering the prospect of some serious money on delivery.

Although it was beyond his pay grade to understand the circumstances and method of communication which had led to the opportunity, he had a name, address and the flexibility to make the necessary transport arrangements as he saw fit. He had been on the payroll of MI6 for some three years now, a sort of unofficial gofer or 'informal trade representative' as he preferred to think of it. A Polish national, he had solid networks across the Baltic states and beyond who had the capability to manage cross-border transactions without the need for paperwork.

Although he had just arrived, his preparation had begun two weeks previously. The logistics were reasonably straightforward, the challenge was the extreme scrutiny that would be incurred as a result.

The basis of the plan was to mean that his subject was going to disappear, leaving a message for his housekeeper saying his mother in Rostov was dangerously ill. He knew the information would be shared and checks would follow but that would still allow him sufficient time to do what needed to be done before the bad news became known. The next thing had been to smuggle a 'Stefan lookalike' into the country to take his place on the return bus to Kaliningrad. That, too, had been relatively straightforward. His brother, Grigor, had left the northern Polish coastal holiday resort of Krynica Morska and hiked the four kilometres north with his girlfriend two days ago – up the 501 to Piaskowa on the Vistula Spit, where the road ended and the route to the Polish border with Russia descended into thicket. This frontier had no means of crossing and considering it had been arbitrarily carved out of the strip of thick woodland running shore to shore for less than a kilometre, seemed to have little other than symbolic value. Symbolism was, however, important to the Russians. There were two big security fences, a cleared open corridor patrolled by soldiers with attack dogs and several rather rickety-looking scaffolded eight-story watchtowers with cameras. And yet, compared to other Russian frontiers in the region, this one was distinctly low-tech and best traversed by climbing a tree on the Polish side and locking a grappling hook on one of the rungs of a watchtower, between camera positions. Having picked his moment after dark and attached his line with care, Grigor was able to shimmy over the barriers, disconnect the rope, which was pulled back by his partner, and climb down to the shadows on the other side. The border crossing was completed in a little under ten minutes with the military observers oblivious to his passing. Grigor pressed north, back into the thicket running parallel to the seashore, for what seemed an age until he reached, first, the oddly abandoned concrete deck of the former Luftwaffe runway and then the holiday cabins on the southern edge of Baltiskya Kosa, the small fishing village on the northern tip of the Spit, facing Baltiysk across the narrow straight leading to the Port of Kaliningrad. He made camp and pitched his small tent under the cover of trees but with a clear line of sight to the village. It was a grey day. The leaden sky and the brisk wind would ensure anyone stopping by would not be attacked by the marauding mosquitos which frequented the locality on warmer days. Should he be discovered, there was nothing odd about a hippy in a tie-dyed T-shirt, jeans and sandals camping here. Although early in the season, such sights were commonplace this side of the water as Baltiskya Kosa was, first and foremost, a laid-back leisure destination, all about beaches, fishing and surfing, without the industrialised urgency of the military infrastructure on the opposite bank.

This calmer environment not only had attractions for visitors. Increasingly, those senior officials in the military machine, who preferred some distance and additional privacy between them and their day jobs, were buying up holiday homes on the Spit and taking the daily ferry into the dockyards.

One such was Professor Boris Ponomariev, Stefan's target, living at number 32 School Street. Grigor had arranged to meet Stefan at the general store on the quayside at midday. There was no showy greeting between the two, just a chance to surreptitiously swap jackets, sunglasses, passports, tickets and visas. The duty sentry at the end of the ferry gangplank had started to show a passing interest, but got distracted by a conversation with one of the deckhands. When he looked back at the two men outside the shop, they appeared to be sharing a cigarette – that was of no concern, just the typical reaction of a couple of bystanders hanging about waiting for the boat to start boarding. Grigor told Stefan where to find his backpack and Stefan told Grigor to pick up the tourist bus in the layby next to the Peter the Great monument by the Aquapark, just along from the arrival embankment. It would be delayed while the guide collected up the requisite number of passengers from around the famous star-shaped Pillau Fort complex before returning to Kaliningrad. It was a typical Russian tour, casual to say the least – nobody would give Grigor a second look – all that mattered was his documentation. Grigor told him where he had pitched the tent and went to the ferry; Stefan stood to watch the departure.

As the vessel departed the quay with its load of ten cars, two vans and a refrigerated truck, Stefan walked down Marine Drive towards the small flotilla of fishing boats, moored two abreast. Some were clearly laid up, their decks deserted, but those on the outer edge had men on them, some carrying pipes to refuel, others checking nets, loading ice into the temperature-controlled holds and stacking the plastic trays they were going to need to store their catches.

Stefan saw an elderly unshaven man with a pot belly and beanie hat walking towards him en route to the quayside shop.

"I'm looking for Igor," he said.

The man waved his hand-rolled cigarette towards the craft at the far end of the strip. Stefan could see a tall thin man, in a wool toggled jacket, shiny waterproof over-trousers and wellington boots, hosing off the front deck. He walked forward at pace and shouted a greeting.

The man looked up as if surprised, smiled and waved him to come over.

Stefan scrambled across the two vessels to reach him.

They had met many years before when both had labouring jobs in the Gdansk shipyard and had retained their friendship ever since, even though Igor's present unkempt appearance had proved to be a momentary barrier to recognition. Border restrictions meant stays were difficult, but meeting for lunch was easy and social media allowed them to keep in touch as their lives changed. Igor knew Stefan was into the 'import/export' business but knew nothing of his clients. In Russia, it paid not to ask too many questions.

Putting down the free-flowing rubber pipe, he enveloped Stefan in a bear hug, as if to ensure he shared his labour-induced fish aroma with his old friend.

"Stefan – good to see you again. Clearly, the years continue to be kind. I think you Poles have gone soft, now that you don't have to queue for bread like the rest of us. You should be careful about spending so much time on Facebook – you may look healthy but looking at porn will make you squinty-eyed!"

"I wish I could say the same, my friend. You look like you`ve spent too much time shagging and drinking in the Zolotoy Yakor nightclub across the water – although next time when you do, I hope you're able to take a shower."

Igor laughed.

"Well, that's the life of a sailor and why I have to go to sea to pay the bills… which reminds me…"

Stefan thrust a thick brown envelope into his hand.

"As promised, half now and the rest tonight. Hope you are ready."

"Yes, I will be ready, I packed the inflatable earlier on and will run a check on the outboard before I get fuelled up. I even arranged for my political supervisor to go on a date with Lyudmilla, the guide from the tourist office – although it will be expensive, it will be better for him than spending the night in the wheelhouse, moaning about his leaking roof and the neighbour's dog. Besides, it will give him something more interesting to talk about when he's out with me tomorrow night."

"When do we go?"

"An hour after sunset. Pyotr and Arkady are taking their boats out tonight as well, so stay off the quay until they've weighed anchor. I want them to go ahead of us. Hope you'll be kitted out properly. The forecast isn't great; the sea will be rough and, if it isn't raining it will be blowing, so don't eat a big dinner tonight unless you are going to provide some puke for bait. Oh, and don't forget to bring a decent bottle of vodka. I like your *Krupnik* best, makes me realise how much crap we drink most of the time."

"See you later."

Stefan smiled, playfully slapped Igor on the cheek, climbed back over the railings of neighbouring boats to the quayside and set off to look for Grigor's tent.

That part of the operation was not difficult. No one else had cause to be walking around there at that time, as most dog walkers stayed around the beach and dunes. Crawling inside gave him the opportunity to rest, think through his plan for the evening and to prepare.

Having checked arrangements, all he had to do was to wait for night to fall. Grigor would now be in the city having a beer, no doubt, before getting the late bus back to Gdansk. They would touch base at the end of the week.

For now, the question was how far away could he get from here without being discovered. Given the proximity of Poland, while being potentially the shortest route to safety, it would be the hardest. Smuggling some illicit amber momentos was one thing, explaining the presence of a revered nuclear physicist with your hand luggage was something else again. North-east Poland in some ways suffered the same as their European Union neighbour to the north – Lithuania. Although run by Western style anti-Soviet democracies, they were riven with Russian sympathisers and 'influence', to the extent that if he delivered his prize to his client in those places, they could not be sure of getting him safely into hiding. That is why the first base would be Sweden, and its

Baltic-island outpost of Gotland – unfortunately a relatively long and uncomfortable sea journey, but ultimately the most secure alternative.

Stefan could see why Ponomariev had chosen to live on School Street; his well-maintained white-painted wooden two-storey house was on the edge of the dunes with an enviable sea view. From here he could while away any private moments watching the variety of shipping, from naval frigates and car ferries to bulk carriers and fishing boats heading through the strait, mainly towards the Pregolya estuary and the Port of Kaliningrad, but also for some offering a route across the almost enclosed Vistula Lagoon to the small Polish port of Elblag. The physicist was clearly a member of the social elite that warranted such accommodation, and yet, he was about to say goodbye to this relatively comfortable existence. Heaven knows what his new life in Britain would offer, but Stefan reasoned it would need to be special to justify this pending one-way ticket.

He had made time to allow him to find Grigor's tent, collect the backpack and walk round the boundaries of the property, to check sight lines, potential nosey neighbours and any CCTV positions. Perhaps surprisingly, away from the military bases, Kaliningrad Oblast seemed relaxed by normal Russian standards.

He recalled previous discussions over the years with Igor, who, although born and bred in the Oblast, didn't really consider himself to be Russian but 'European'. Maybe it was a label that suited him when he worked in Gdansk. The term was meant to imply a degree of social sophistication not commonly found in the mother country. As a foreigner dealing with Russians and Kaliningraders, he hadn't noticed the difference. Maybe it was because the locals had a taste for wine and beer, not just vodka. When he'd taken on this job, Stefan had asked about family members who might wish to come or could be at the house when he called. He had been dismissed with the answer, "Oh don't worry about that," which had the opposite effect. This whole shaky venture depended on the professor answering the door personally and offering his co-operation. Reluctantly he had to accept that there was a possibility he would be making the trip across the Baltic without his special cargo but, more importantly, without the prospect of his fee for his trouble.

The question on his mind was answered when he rang the doorbell just after seven o'clock, dressed in a dry suit and deck boots with the backpack.

It was opened by a prematurely balding, wire-spectacled figure with a fair skin, goatee beard and a quizzical expression – this was indeed a professor personified, albeit minus a white lab coat. Dressed in brown checked flannel shirt and matching heavy wool sweater and jeans, this was a man who seemed to fit Igor's image of a 'European' who, at first sight, could have come from anywhere from Glasgow to Helsinki. It was the square jaw that gave him away. So many of his countrymen had that same look of a prize fighter.

"Professor? My name is Stefan. Winston sent me to collect you. May I come in for a minute? I have brought some over-clothes which may come in useful later on."

Ponomariev stood to one side and nodded to him to come in. The house's timber interior was painted powder blue and furnished in a simple Scandinavian style with a minimal level of fixtures and fittings, as he would have expected to find in a holiday rental.

"Is everything arranged?" he asked.

"Yes, I will take you to the handover point. What happens after that is between you and Winston."

"When are we going?"

"As soon as you're ready. We're taking a trip on a fishing boat, so you'll need a dry suit and boots. You are a Euro size 45, right? The stuff is in the backpack."

"Wait here, please."

Ponomariev took the backpack and made his way up the staircase. This would be the moment of truth. The moment when a couple of FSB goons leapt out from the shadows to arrest him.

He had been prepared for this and so had those he was working with. He and each of his associates knew just enough about their own contribution to the plan to fulfil their role but nothing more, so in the event of being compromised they could not implicate colleagues. The expected challenge didn't emerge and his walking 'consignment' came back down, the weight of his boots accentuated by their noise on the bare wooden steps.

He looked directly at Stefan.

The Pole saw a mixture of emotions in his pale blue eyes – emptiness and regret.

"So for now, Mr Stefan, I am in your hands. When we leave the house, I will keep my wool cap low on my face and the hood tied, just in case I see any of my neighbours."

Given the fact that it was now dark, and the light drizzle was increasing in intensity on the back of an easterly wind, Stefan thought it unlikely they would meet anyone out at this hour before they arrived at the quay, but he just nodded his acknowledgement.

The professor locked the door, being careful to leave a lamp in the hallway on, and stepped onto the narrow pathway, walking with Stefan towards the first of the sporadically sited streetlights; the whipping sound of the wind through the shadows of surrounding sedge tufts warning them of the perils ahead.

It was relatively quiet at the quay. The other two boats going out that night had already left, so it was down to Igor doing his final preparations and waiting for his unusual cargo.

Stefan introduced Ponomariev to Igor, who immediately gave him a lifejacket and took him below deck to a cramped cabin which had the benefit of a bed.

"The sea is a bit choppy tonight, so I suggest you stay here. There will be a bit of pitch and roll. If you feel sick, there are some bags to use over there and a piss hole through that door." That marked the end of his welcome speech. He left his passenger down below, shutting the hatch behind him almost as though he wanted to forget he was on board.

"You heard that?" Igor said to Stefan.

The Pole nodded.

"Get your lifejacket on. I'm hoping we can outrun the weather when we get to sea and things will calm down. You must know that I cannot take you ashore at the other end and we may need to launch your inflatable in unstable conditions, which could be dangerous. Now the other two have sailed and most sensible people have gone home, I have got my boys to pre-inflate your boat and test the outboard before we leave, in case the weather is too bad at sea. I don't think anyone has noticed but even if they have, I'll say I lost it in the storm. We will keep it lashed and tied to the crane during the journey which should be OK, as we won't be dropping nets until you've gone."

"Can I help?"

"You can keep me company in the wheelhouse once we leave. I just need to radio the harbourmaster we are on our way. Our journey plan is authorised to take us 200 kilometres north towards the Gotland Deep, the closest quality deep fishing we have. That's where Pyotr and Arkady have gone. I am planning to take you on a bit further and do the drop here, around fifty kilometres off Burgsvik. Then it's up to you."

"Are you being watched?"

"Normally I am required to take a commissar with me to ensure I don't go anywhere I shouldn't, but funnily enough I fixed him up with an expensive date in town tonight, so to avoid disturbing him I got him to sign the manifest earlier, before loading the inflatable. The authorities will just assume he's on board because of our headcount – he certainly won't want the harbourmaster to know he was out fucking in a warm bed instead of getting cold and wet with me. Otherwise, they'll keep an eye on the radar and give us a call on the radio if they want a chat."

"What about shipping?"

"The Baltic is a busy stretch of water. It's normal for the Russian Navy to keep a vessel out on active patrol – something like a corvette with a pop gun up front to scare off any smugglers and make sure we behave, but that's about it. They tend to be more concerned about coastal traffic heading east-west. The Swedes and the Poles have a presence out there as well, but try to avoid each other. Our route weaves in between established ferry routes from Kaliningrad to Ust Luga and Petersburg so we can stay out of sight for part of the journey."

Fishing boat B474 weighed anchor and headed north, following the same route as the other two who were around ninety minutes ahead of them, and soon found themselves battling the predicted heavy seas and driving rain.

Stefan had elected to stay in the wheelhouse with Igor and his bosun, Anatoly, while the rest of the crew took refuge in the canteen below. Time and again the bow dipped, confronting a wall of water which smashed down with what felt like the force of a truckful of rubble, before it seemed their vessel had launched itself up into the sky, only for the process to be repeated time and again. The only reassuring sound was the rhythmic knocking of the engine which gave them confidence about their momentum.

Stefan held onto the bulkhead as though on a fairground ride. Igor sat impassively in the captain's chair, his feet locked around its steel base which was bolted to the floor. Anatoly, clutched the wheel, keeping them on their forward trajectory.

"Hope you brought that bottle of *Krupnik* I asked for," Igor shouted.

Stefan smiled nervously, unzipping the top of the dry suit and extracting the bottle.

"Good man – this is probably the best way of passing the time when you are out in this."

The hours passed.

The bottle was shared around and seemed to disappear rapidly.

The radio crackled intermittently with calls from Pyotr and Arkady, reporting improving weather, bad jokes and general banter before a more sinister call from the harbourmaster's control centre.

"B474, adjust your navigation to 120 over 90. You are running wide of the corridor. Please acknowledge…"

The messaged was repeated.

Stefan looked to Igor. The bosun remained unmoved.

Igor took the microphone, opened the line and paused, sending a static message without speaking.

The line was quiet.

After a few minutes the message from Baltiysk was repeated, with Igor offering the same response.

"That's our warning signal. They won't be worried just yet. They will know I tried to respond and will just assume we are a bit fucked up. It does mean the start of the countdown to the drop."

As Igor's colleagues had predicted, they were outrunning the storm and it became sufficiently calm to walk outside the wheelhouse.

Stefan went to check on his precious cargo.

Although Ponomariev had a fair complexion, he wondered whether a human could look that white and still be alive. It was as though he had come out and left his blood in a bottle at home. He was glad be hadn't spent the storm time in the cabin; the window was damp with condensation and the confined space smelt of vomit.

"How are you doing?" he asked.

"As well as can be expected," came the reply.

"Don't worry, we haven't got far to go now and then you will be on your way to a better life."

Ponomariev confirmed what Stefan had suspected.

"I hope you are right. There was only one thing wrong with the one I left behind."

"Why are you here then?"

"I'm gay – hadn't you guessed? Living freely as a gay man in Russia is impossible. If I was not an expert in my field, I wouldn't have a job. I have been tolerated for years but I can't continue to live in this way, when I am harassed and sneered at, outside my home, at the shops, in bars… it's ridiculous in the 2020s. Now Vladimir Vladimirovich has decided to make us illegal, banning same sex relationships. It was the final straw, and if VV really understood his own country it might prove to be his final straw too."

The hatch door opened. Igor leaned through.

"OK guys, it's time to muster. Check your protective clothing and lifejackets and come up aft."

Igor's intervention had saved a longer conversation which Stefan didn't wish to engage in. He really didn't wish to know much about Ponomariev, only to deliver him to Winston intact and get his money.

On deck, Igor pointed on the starboard side.

"This is as close as I can take you. From this point, you're about thirty nautical miles from Gotland in that direction. I hear these days, the Swedes have quite a strong military presence so I doubt whether you will have to wait to get to their coast before being intercepted."

"The rest of your money is under the bed behind the bulkhead. I stuck it there to keep it dry. Thanks for your help and I will see you again soon, my friend."

A brief hug and Stefan and Ponomariev were stowed on the inflatable and lowered into the sea. The outboard sprang into life and the final stretch of the journey began.

The inflatable bounced over the now undulating waves.

With Stefan focused on the way ahead, Ponomariev looked back to the declining profile of the fishing boat, the last vestige of his former life in Russia.

ONE

IT WAS A BEAUTIFUL morning in Berkshire and the day was starting well. Sue had left already to take Milo for his morning constitutional around the village green. Des was in the kitchen doing toast and coffee on the run before making his daily dash to Oxford. Given the impending drive, he did not want to load his mind yet with the various pressures and responsibilities of the day. He picked up a copy of the satirical magazine he had started to look at the night before while waiting for his cappuccino to cool. Des was clearly an unusual person. He always started reading newspapers and magazines from the back. It was a bad habit that he`d picked up over the years, driven by his professional need to speed read often dry technical reports. In this case, his habit had brought him to the classified section with a collection of often humorous goods and services which never seemed to be available elsewhere. His attention was drawn to one small ad titled: *Eye Die*. It read: *Had enough? Want to disappear gracefully without fuss? We can give you the dignity and privacy you seek.*

For reasons he didn't fully understand it struck a chord. There was a box number for replies. On impulse, he picked up his laptop, found the page and typed a reply: "Interested. Tell me more," before noticing the time, snapping the computer lid down and grabbing his car keys.

His drive to the office was routine. Jams in the expected places on the A34, no news to speak of on the radio, banal drivel on the national popular music channel… no – Rachmaninov's 'Piano Concerto No 1' was a much better listen. It was a suitable backdrop to get his thoughts in order for the day.

He was sharper this morning. Despite the pressing need to go back to his GP, tell the family and his boss his situation, he knew for now it had to keep.

He had to stay in control as long as possible and that meant carrying on as normal.

*

Sir Gavin Laidlaw's office was a modestly better furnished goldfish bowl than his own – probably because it was situated three floors higher up the building. Apart from what looked like a standard chair, desk, computer screen, drawer caddy and adjustable lamp, this one sported a settee (which was far more uncomfortable than it looked), a coffee table and a wall-mounted TV. Probably the perk of the job as chief executive, Des thought. In the time he'd worked at the Lauriston (admittedly only for the past four years), he had never seen the TV on and wondered if it was kept as a distraction for his children when, occasionally during the holidays, they came in to see their dad. It was bright outside, necessitating the part-closure of the window blinds and consequently blocking the magnificent view north towards the Chilterns. There was no other visual distraction apart from the jazzy pattern of the carpet, which reminded him of an offcut from a Piccadilly Line carriage. Perhaps it was a visible demonstration of the frugal attitude of the management in directing most of its resources into its research activities. No – in reality, it was probably expensive and just in bad taste on the part of an interior design consultant. He had been momentarily distracted.

"Morning Des – you look a little washed out. Coffee?"

It was the start of the day; this was coffee number two. To his certain knowledge he had the prospect of another four coming up in meetings to follow. Given his condition, he knew he had to take it easy.

"A cappuccino would be good, thanks."

As befitted his position and interest, Sir Gavin was a man who liked a gadget. Des had failed to notice in one corner of his boss's office a small state-of-the-art coffee machine with a modest collection of mugs clearly calibrated to complement its ergonomic design.

His boss pressed a button. A small console lit up, followed by a series of clicking and whirring noises which seemed to defeat the possibility of their early dialogue. Frothy cappuccino in hand, Sir Gavin Laidlaw gestured to Kelly to sit at the desk. It looked like this was going to be a formal meeting, but at least his seat was close to the settee which he could admire from his perch.

Tanned and balding, dressed in a charcoal grey business suit, white shirt and plain pea green 'notice me' Dupont tie, Sir Gavin made himself comfortable in his black leather chair and peered over his gold-framed half-lens glasses.

"I do prefer meetings here instead of town, don't you? That's the great thing about Oxford – you have the time and space to think."

This seemed like a particularly abstract way of starting the meeting.

"I'm sorry we haven't got together in the past couple of weeks. I`ve been held up down the road with the Perm Sec in the Energy department – usual problem. They've buggered up their procurement on nuclear again. I keep telling him to keep the bean counters out of the way of decision making as they really don't get the scientific aspects, and as soon as they cock up the allocations, they get moved to somewhere else, where they can do more damage – like the Treasury."

Kelly smiled and resisted the need to comment.

"Des – you should know I have worked my way through all your reports on HCCVD. I tend to be a man who avoids excitement, but in your case, my enthusiasm rises by the minute. This work is truly ground-breaking and could prove to be the most important innovation not only in sustainable renewables but in starting to address our national millstone of radioactive waste storage. When will you be ready to move to the patent stage? It is critical to our future planning to ensure we keep track of this and avoid others, like the Americans, Russians and Chinese, getting to market before UK PLC."

"Have you reported on this in Whitehall?" Kelly asked.

"Not yet, I wanted to talk to you first to understand where you're at. But as you know, our funding review will start at the end of the month, and I want to put us in the strongest position."

"Well, I am aware others are looking at this too, although I'm sure we are ahead on proving the scientific application here, but we still have a little way to go with the testing and we must get through that before we look at patents. At the moment, we can't be certain we have fully assessed all the production and process issues involved, although our work does make a clear and strong case on handling the safety aspects – storage, monitoring and maintenance. I've developed the first generation of test units, which we will look to take into field trials in the coming months, and these are likely to involve military transportation and propulsion systems. I will prepare a prospectus for you to take to the MoD in the course of the next few weeks, but for security reasons it will be light on detail."

"OK, but you yourself know how all this will work?"

"Absolutely, I have it clearly in my head, although I still need to document a couple of the most sensitive elements."

"All right. Given the requisite secrecy involved, I want to you to keep me personally appraised with progress on a weekly basis from now on. Reporting can only be face to face, but if urgent, by the secure line. I will need to take this to London as soon as possible, even if we are short of a couple of essential elements. By the way, before you go – for your ears only, I have been offered some new relevant high-level expertise, recently arrived from Russia. He is being checked out at the moment. Looks like quite a coup for us. All other things being equal, I'd like you to take a look at him when he gets clearance. I think he has the potential to accelerate the delivery of your work and I suspect you may be feeling a little stressed at the moment? This chap might be able to share the load a bit. Anyway that's a conversation for another day. Keep me posted and send my best to Sue."

Des nodded and accepted his cue to depart. Heading for the lift, he checked the messages on his phone. Usual crap, but one stood out – from Denmark of all places – and he didn't recognise the sender.

*

With Kelly out of the door, Sir Gavin swivelled his chair and peered out of the part of the window that was not covered by the blind. Although looking into the middle distance he was not focusing on anything on the horizon but thinking about his exchange with Des. What was that all about? Scientists tended to be an eclectic breed and Des Kelly was a one-off, that was for sure, but all the same, he appeared out of sorts, distracted. Given his present run of research successes he was expecting him to be more energetic, enthusiastic. No, something wasn't right with him, but he couldn't put his finger on it. Given the nature of their work, all his team at the Lauriston had the highest levels of security clearance as a result of enquiries which penetrated deep into their personal lives. Although, in this age of data protection, he might not personally know all there was to know about any individual under his direction, his friends in the security services probably would. Desmond Kelly had a pivotal role to play in the future fortunes of the institution and Sir Gavin was aware of the potential risk to his own reputation if his 'star man' failed to perform.

His instinct for self-preservation told him he would need to keep Des under review. He had a meeting scheduled with his Defence Ministry contact, Gerry Bannan (who he thought was probably a 'spook' from MI6) at the end of the week, about this Russian fellow. It would be a natural opportunity to also raise the subject of Kelly. But he would leave it there. He might pick up some useful information closer to home. He stared at his online diary for the following week.

"Now there's a coincidence," he muttered under his breath. He saw he had a 360-degree peer review with Dr Jakeman Roberts, Kelly's number two.

*

Despite his audience with the boss, the morning had dragged for Des as he sat through a presentation on proton molecular reassignment and started to discuss its implications with two of his research team. The coffees kept coming as predicted, but the strange communication from Denmark was still rattling around in his mind. When his colleagues had run out of interesting things to say, he realised it was lunchtime and he would be leaving to take a look at one of his new pet batteries under test conditions in the laboratory at Harwell, a brief drive away.

His departure provided a short interlude when he would not be disturbed in his car, and no sooner had he got to his vehicle than he opened the email, which linked to a short video clip.

He saw a middle-aged man in a blue sports shirt, cream gilet and jeans, with a ruddy complexion, sitting in the sun on a sand dune talking to the camera.

"Hello, my name is Nils and welcome to my island home of Rømø in south-west Denmark. Thank you for reaching out to enquire about our unique discreet assisted euthanasia service which offers a personal and empathetic approach to help you reach the conclusion of your life. As I expect you know, this course of action is never as simple as those requesting it would like, and some of our clients have been surprised about the lengthy approach we take. And so to the bad news first. Working with us is not cheap but can be rewarding in some unexpected ways. The process normally runs over a six-month period and involves three visits to us here in Rømø in southern Denmark.

"Naturally, to protect our own commercial confidentiality and to ensure it is tailored to your circumstances, we do not publicise or promote the details of our programme but would expect to tell you personally what is involved as part of your first visit to us.

"All you need to do is to contact me via the phone or email shown on the screen at the end of this video. We can get you booked in and take it from there. The nearest airport is at Billund here in Denmark, but quite a few of our clients prefer the convenience of more frequent services via Hamburg in Germany, around two and a half hours' drive from where I am talking to you now.

"Come and stay. You'll need at least three days with us to begin with – enjoy our hospitality and learn about how we can help you complete your life's journey. I look forward to meeting you soon."

The camera panned away from Nils towards the sea before fading to darkness and the contact information.

He took a sharp intake of breath. What about that? He was talking about assisted suicide in such a downbeat, 'everyday' way in a tone of an insurance salesman or like the handyman selling that miracle cleaner that can put a shine on any surface or banish limescale.

He seemed both knowledgeable and friendly – the sort of 'ordinary Joe' you could imagine having a quiet pint with and sharing your innermost insecurities in that 'blokey' way. It was effective. This was no assisted dying for the frail or infirm. This was a full-on, organised conclusion for the fit and healthy. He would check out flight availability and make that initial booking.

But first, he intended to find out more about Rømø and to understand why it was the best place to end it all.

*

His afternoon at Harwell had proved productive. Checking the test configurations, he had heightened the extractive charge and conductivity to 12.9 volts, a level higher than most acid-based conventional batteries' plate design and acid densities. Ironically, given the diamond casing and conductive channels, the test product was arguably safer than many other battery specifications, requiring no special arrangements for storage and maintenance. The real test of the product was durability, but although it could be rigorously tested to check its behaviours for release of charge, the tests for continuity of supply were not yet proven. His approach was based on creating the extractive system outside the battery to control its function and although he was confident he had the right formula, the physical equipment needed for the task was cumbersome. Although colleagues at Harwell were assisting in the creation of the appropriate laboratory test conditions, it was still his preference to keep details of the extractive technology to himself, until he was able to present his findings to the Lauriston's Innovation Committee – the first formal step towards registering patents.

Time in the lab was limited and precious, as was the need to follow not only the site security procedures on nuclear materials, but his own personal criteria. The former were pretty straightforward, relating to what he considered long-winded and common sense health and safety rules. He had to remind himself that, as a result of the revolutionary diamond sealing method, his samples were safe enough to put on the mantelpiece at home, even if the product itself was visually bland and unappealing. His own security criteria were more stringent. This meant avoiding leaving a trail of evidence that would allow any casual scientific observer to understand the capability of the experimental hardware he had designed to extract the power. With this in mind, he took the essence of his discovery, an item resembling a small copper plate, away with him in his briefcase. To the uninitiated, it would mean nothing, but in reality this was the ignition key to the power source. It was in effect, a type of precision laser guidance casing which only he knew how to fit, and, because it attached to one of the outer interfaces of the battery, was not radioactive.

*

Beethoven's '7th Symphony' was his chosen musical accompaniment in the car on the journey home as he reflected on his situation. Years of research were about to deliver a stunning result that would have major implications across the world. For now, that knowledge and power was in his hands. The responsibility made him feel as though he was running up a beach pursued by a tsunami of demands that he would be powerless to control and would sweep him away. Yet he knew the discipline of mindfulness. The road home was the way to repackage his professional concerns and focus more on his personal worries. Given his diagnosis, the thought of visiting Denmark was not a negative one in his mind. It was clear the end was in sight. The man, his physician, who had delivered the knowledge was a long and trusted friend. At his age, he didn't feel the need for another opinion. Notwithstanding the money, he knew it was unlikely to reach a different conclusion. All in all, despite the regrets that everyone in the world harbours, he had enjoyed a full life and was appreciative of the opportunity to end it on a high and on his own terms.

On returning home, the house was empty, save for Milo who offered his own bark of welcome, he thought, quite pleased as his solo house guarding duties of the day had reached their conclusion. Des grabbed Milo's lead from the hallway and set out for their evening village walk. It was dusk and despite the background hum of traffic, known to all who live in the Thames Valley, his little part of it did seem like a rural idyll. There was no footpath down the hedgerow-garlanded lane to the village green, but no cars at that time to worry him. The village centre was particularly attractive. Lights on in a number of surrounding cottages promising a welcome to their owners returning home. A war memorial shaped like a mini obelisk, testament to the enduring heritage of the settlement and, to his right, the centre of community life, his local, the Dog & Duck. It was a route Milo knew well and although Des's progress was achieved at a steady walking pace, he had to allow for Milo's chosen spots for sniffing out where his friends from neighbouring properties had been, and inevitably leaving his own territorial mark for the benefit of others.

Given he had a lot on his mind, Kelly had more than the convenience of his pet as an excuse for taking the walk. He wanted a drink and this night, also the company that went with it. Had he not been preoccupied, he might have noticed a blue Ford Focus with two figures in it, parked by the entrance to the pub car park. In a way it was conspicuous – a Ford Focus parked in a place normally frequented by Range Rovers, Mercedes and Jaguars, but also because the figures remained in the car, not going inside to partake of a beer or the myriad of meals offered on the menu outside.

Had he been interested or paying attention he would have seen the two leave their car a few minutes after he had entered, walk past the pub and up the lane towards his house.

For the moment, his attention was focused on a freshly pulled pint of his favourite local brew, the aptly named Loose Cannon IPA. On these occasions, Milo was his usual drinking companion, having been bribed with the offer of a packet of crisps, which he munched on noisily at his feet.

"Busy day, Des?" enquired Bryan, the landlord.

"Yes, it's been a long one, fitting square pegs into round holes, so it's always good to get back home."

"Cooking tonight?"

"Not sure if I can be bothered, especially when you have the homemade meat and potato pie on the go."

"So that's an order then?"

"Saves time and probably much better than anything I could rustle up at home."

"Missus out again tonight?"

"Yes, it's Wednesday, that means the Madrigal Singers in the church hall."

"Oh, her life seems like a regular social whirl."

"Well, her social calendar helps me to keep track of the days, that's for sure. Anyway, it will be different next week when I'm away – she'll have to stay home to keep Milo here entertained."

"How do you guys manage? You never seem to be home at the same time."

"Oh, about eleven o'clock seems to work for us most nights – it's quite good really. Prevents us having to talk much and by that time, she's tired of Gilbert & Sullivan, so I can be sure of a good night's sleep."

"Ah well, I guess you'll be able to live it up a bit next week…"

Kelly looked surprised.

"…when you're away. Going anywhere nice?" Bryan ventured.

"Berlin."

"Berlin, eh? You know that's one of those places I`ve always wanted to visit, especially the *bierkellers*, but…"

"Your girlfriend prefers Malaga?" Kelly countered.

The landlord laughed.

"Well, if I don't fix it, she'll go on strike, then there will be no meat and potato pies for anyone."

At that moment, Kelly's mobile rang. He was about to ignore it but decided to check before answering. It was Sue.

"Des, where are you?"

"In the Duck with Milo."

"Can you come home right now?"

Kelly looked at his watch. It was just after eight o'clock.

"A bit early for you?"

"Er, yes. I decided to leave early. I've pulled over at the bottom of our drive. I've just seen a couple of people who I think are breaking into our house."

"When? Now?"

"Yes. My headlights caught them running up the far side of the paddock towards the back door."

Des pulled out his mobile to view the domestic CCTV. The infrared cameras at the gate and the front doorstep looked empty, as he would have expected.

"OK. On my way with Milo. Don't get any closer. Come down and wait in the car park here."

"Shall we call the police?"

"Not just yet – it will take them a while to arrive, and it might be a false alarm. If there are any arrests to be made, I will leave it to the hound."

Bryan overheard some of the conversation and saw Des's concern.

"Got to run. Duty calls. Save the beer and the pie."

He zipped up his anorak and was swiftly out of the door, the dog leading the way.

Walking briskly back towards the lane, he saw Sue's car turning towards the pub. He gestured to her to stay while he headed towards the house.

Although not late, it was now dark and he was limited by the diluted light from the lamppost on the corner of the lane, together with the torch on his mobile. As he approached his gate, he released Milo's muzzle and lead, telling him to run ahead into the darkness.

From Milo's perspective, any opportunity to run free was not to be missed and he raced forward down the drive towards the house.

Kelly couldn't be certain what happened next, as the courtesy light triggered by the movement detector by the front door failed to pick up the dog's bounding movement.

His pet kept him in the picture by emitting a deep-throated bark followed a few seconds later by a whimper and then silence.

He continued to stride forward towards the front door, guided by the light of his mobile phone. Despite this, his eyes were becoming accustomed to his surroundings and he was now able to clearly see his front door and the walls and windows of the house. He was surprised to see the place in darkness, as he was sure he had left a couple of lamps on in his absence to suggest it was occupied. As he started to walk round the exterior, there were no signs of a break-in, no smashed panes or forced window frames, and the heavy front door remained resolutely secure.

He called for Milo. Normally his call solicited a barked response, if not compliance. Not on this occasion. He continued past the paddock to the rear of the house. Coming round the corner towards the back door, torch fixed at an upright angle looking at the windows, he tripped over some inanimate object. He stumbled forward and avoided the fall by leaning into the wall but dropped his phone in the process. At that moment, twenty, maybe thirty paces ahead, there was a sudden movement, only given away by the sound of some breaking of shrub branches.

"Hey!" His shout was involuntary. What was he trying to do? Get somebody's attention? Call them over to help or reveal themself? Regaining his balance and the phone, he saw that the object that had destabilised him was his dog, which, despite being kicked in the incident, had not moved.

A few things were clear. There had been someone, some*thing* in the garden. They hadn't identified themself so it was clearly an intruder. The power to light up the property had been cut. It had never happened before, so it must have been tampered with and yet, look as he may, there was no sign of a break-in. Perhaps it was just someone 'casing the joint'.

Again, instinctively, he had no thought of alerting the police.

His focus was Milo, still not moving, but seeming to still have a beating heart. It was weird – as though he was in a deep slumber, perhaps a coma. He moved to the paddock, still secured, and opened it. This was his 'man shed', a workshop where he would spend his few leisure hours pottering about, doing everything from carpentry (his hobby) to reading. This was definitely a place where he was certain of being able to navigate in the dark. He was able to collect a big heavy duty torch from its resting place on a nearby table, grabbed it and went back out into the night to look at Milo.

Closer inspection of his dog led to the discovery of a tiny dart in his neck which he removed to examine. It seemed to have a phial of liquid in it which had clearly been injected into the animal. Carefully he wrapped it in a tissue and put it in his pocket.

Moving to the back door, he unlocked it and moved in through the kitchen to the cloakroom, where the main circuit breaker box was. Resetting of the master switch immediately brought the lights back on but he didn't stop there, going from room to room, then upstairs to assess the situation. Each room he entered appeared normal, like it always was. Basically tidy with nothing obviously out of place. But despite his slumbering dog, something seemed wrong, as if his privacy had been violated. He didn't have time to ponder. Two calls; one to Sue, that all was OK and that she could come home, the other to the vets to get an 'out of hours' home visit. The next job involved rolling Milo onto a rug he had brought down from the bathroom and pulling it through to the kitchen. Given the weight of the dog, the move had been more complicated and time-consuming than he had expected. Nonetheless, Milo was in position, under strong lights, by the time the vet arrived an hour later. Des stayed with Milo during the vet's inspection. Sue spent her time upstairs checking that her possessions were where she expected them to be. The diagnosis from the vet was as Kelly had expected; Milo had been injected with a sedative and would fully recover in the next six hours. So all there was to show for the past two hours of stress and anxiety was a tiny pellet fired into his dog's neck and a short power cut which hadn't even affected food in the fridge/freezer. What sort of story would he have to concoct to get the police interested? As far as they were concerned, an assault on a pet dog would not be high on their priority list. Maybe he had saved the day by arriving soon enough to prevent a burglary. There was nothing more to do that night. Sue had gone to bed with a brandy, but only on the basis that Des had double checked that the security chains were engaged on the exterior doors before he came up. The soporific effect of the alcohol worked for her. Des lay by her side staring at the ceiling, reflecting on the day and the possible challenges tomorrow would bring.

*

In the morning, Sue had things straight in her mind. Des had indeed foiled a break-in attempt and by implication nothing had been stolen and no damage done. Milo had stirred from his deep slumber and seemed completely normal, pestering Sue to take him out for his usual morning walk. Des had woken late after the excitement of the night before and had to dash off to work. There seemed to be nothing left to add, so Des would report the incident sometime during the day when he had a minute. They were agreed that would be the end of it – except it wasn't.

News of his heroics soon went around the office, thanks to Jake. Kelly had absentmindedly recounted the previous evening's events over coffee the following morning and research scientists appreciate a good gossip about anything totally disconnected with the day job. Had Des been party to the various conversations, he would have known his role, in surprising the would-be robber and chasing him away, was growing more impressive with each telling. The almost universal conclusion was that all were impressed with his actions, although, equally it was suggested that nobody thought he had it in him to act so bravely. By the end of the day, the story had even reached the ears of Sir Gavin, who failed to share in the general hilarity of his colleagues, although they would not understand the reason.

Before returning home, he fulfilled his promise to Sue and called the police. The response was as predicted – indifference, although a voice on the end of the phone did offer to send someone round in a couple of days to 'have a word'.

Sir Gavin's reaction was to put in a call to Gerry Bannan to recount the tale, and he concluded with the question, "Was that down to you?"

He noted the mock amusement in the voice on the other end of the phone.

"Come on, Gavin, you don't really expect me to respond to that, surely? I did tell you I would look into the Kelly situation, and it is ongoing. I'll tell you what's going on when I know more – probably in a couple of days. I think that will fit in in nicely with an update on the Russian chap I'm lining up for you to meet."

"I think he's already involved the police," Sir Gavin countered.

"Given the circumstances that's not surprising – maybe they'll turn something up. Keep me posted if you hear any more."

The exchange told Sir Gavin what he had already suspected.

Des had been subject to an MI6 house call.

*

The visit from the local PC occurred a couple of days later, fortunately in the early evening before it got dark. Long separate explanations of the sequence of events took place, including the presentation of the dart, before it was officially concluded that no offence, beyond a technical trespass, had occurred. But another tantalising clue had emerged; a footprint in a flowerbed towards the back wall of their garden. A picture of the tread was taken, together with a measurement of the depth of the imprint. The PC said he'd investigate further and revert with any new information. Des had visions of the police scanning their database for a one-legged felon capable of traversing a six-foot wall wearing a size 9 boot. The offer of an appointment with a crime scene investigator was made, who would make a routine inspection of the exterior and dust for fingerprints, but the Kellys were warned it was unlikely that anyone would be apprehended.

The visit provided some sort of closure for Des. The matter had been of concern but it had not happened before, no damage had been done, and now it had been reported that was the end of it. His attention turned to his forthcoming trip to Berlin. This was a meeting of the International Sustainable Energy Forum, a biannual get together of leading scientists in the field, sponsored by Maximum Power, the international oil and gas corporation, trying to plan an alternative carbon-free future without losing their shareholders or the value of their investment portfolio. Apart from the opportunity to network with 'the great and the good', as well as to review the latest international initiatives on everything from wind, wave, solar and steam, to shale, hydrogen and nuclear, he would present a paper on the progress of his own work at the Lauriston. Of course, the skill in these things was presenting sufficient evidence to be credible, but deliberately omitting the elements which could be regarded as being commercially confidential. This was a key reason why he wanted to resist Jake's Stanford invitation for the time being, until their position on patents had been secured. Berlin was more than putting his own work into context; but would also serve a personal ambition of giving him a few days to travel on to Rømø at a time when his absence from Oxford could be easily explained.

With so many of the Lauriston's HR operations being automated, his only duty was to make sure he had blocked his diary and booked leave – seven days to cover just four for professional engagements. He made his own travel arrangements. Flight to Berlin, train to Hamburg, hire car to Rømø and then on to Billund for the return to Stansted. The hotel was fixed as part of the delegate rate and he would email Nils regarding the Danish arrangements. With just two weeks to go, he would have time to finish his presentation as well as contacting other colleagues he wanted to meet.

It's amazing how time passes when you are enjoying yourself. At least, that was what he told himself. He was surprised at how quickly the days passed leading to his departure. He put it down to his detailed preparation and private documentation of his research on the performance behaviours of his diamond-encased battery. Domestically, all seemed to have settled down and Sue was organised with the care duties for Milo, or perhaps in reality it would work the other way. While he was away, she would be home outside office hours, although Des had no doubt his absence would only mean a change of venue for her 'active' social engagements.

His flight would depart at 11am, giving him comfortable time to get round the M25, although Stansted was not the easiest to negotiate internally.

Given the early hour he avoided the need to say goodbye in person, leaving his communication to a scribbled note on the kitchen table. If there was anything urgent, she would undoubtedly call. As a regular at this event, he had a pretty good idea about what to expect and was looking forward to meeting up with many of his peers, benchmarking his own work against international competitors and enjoying the company of some great people who he had so much in common with. Even so, this trip would be different, perhaps no less special than previous conferences, but given the circumstances, this would be his last international professional engagement, which would carry its own unique poignancy.

The logistics were working well. He got to the gate around ten minutes before it closed. He had avoided one of those dreadful interminable waits in an increasingly stuffy, sun-drenched glass-fronted corridor, surrounded by a mass of humanity – students, mothers with unruly kids, a few oldies discovering city breaks, and a group of lads with the smell of stale alcohol clearly preparing for a 'stag' adventure. Fortunately, he had a seat at the front, which promised the least disturbance on the journey and a chance to think about how he would manage to get to his accommodation.

He had settled on the S-Bahn and arrived at his hotel, the iconic Adlon, just after 5pm, located adjacent to the Brandenburg Gate at the western end of the Unter den Linden. For new visitors to this charismatic city, the Adlon was right at the heart of the capital, located close to the main embassies and the Reichstag. Although a contemporary building, it was constructed on the site of the original Adlon hotel, built in 1907 and for many years was part of the city's cultural heritage, especially in the Weimar period, until it was accidently burnt down in 1945 by inebriated Red Army soldiers celebrating their victory. Although Kelly was no stranger to his surroundings, he couldn't help but be impressed at the way the city had been reconnected following the collapse of the Soviet Union and, in some measure, rebuilt in the modern era. Away from the more obvious tourist attractions, there were precious few reminders of the former East German capital, except further down the road towards Humbolt University, a collection of neo-classical buildings renovated by Soviet architects, now largely occupied by state museums. Given the circumstances, it was understandable that its Nazi-inspired past had largely been demolished, either as a consequence of bombing during the war or owing to the lack of care and investment by the East German authorities. And yet, despite this selective airbrushing of history, what had emerged was a sophisticated, modern and liveable metropolis at ease with itself and open to all – businesses, cultures and ideas. Having checked in, he couldn't resist a walk, out towards the Brandenburg Gate and the Tiergarten beyond. It was a cool but dry evening. Beyond the phalanx of camera-clicking tourists from all parts of the world, gathering around guides at the base of the Gate, offering impromptu history lessons for those able to hear. The parkland offered a glimpse of how ordinary Berliners enjoyed their downtime – kicking footballs with their kids, walking home with their pet pups, feeding ducks, lovers whispering sweet nothings in their partner's ear – even a few brave souls enjoying a sort of picnic, sitting on rugs in a circle, beer bottles in hand. What would previous generations have made of this scene? Maybe, as for him, it would engender a strange sense of calm, optimism… of freedom, away from the day-to-day worries and humdrum of routine.

Understandably his mind was wandering until a voice he recognised called from behind.

"Desmond Kelly! Fancy meeting you here!"

Turning, his face lit up to see Professor Aldo de Leonibus, a research fellow from the European Nuclear Safety Regulators Group and an old friend, coming to greet him.

"Aldo, wonderful to see you! When did you arrive?"

"I got here yesterday. Although I'm early, I wanted to visit the Egyptian Museum behind the Cathedral. As an Italian, I have always wanted to see the bust of Nefertiti – the most beautiful woman in ancient history… I mean statue, not the…"

He gesticulated in the shape of an hourglass figure.

Both men laughed at the Italian's limited use of the English language.

"Have many arrived yet?"

"Yes, I've seen a few coming in and out of the hotel, but I guess we will get an idea of exactly who is here at the opening dinner tonight. I must say I am looking forward to your seminar tomorrow. Your presentation is oversubscribed already. HCCVD could become the big story of the conference."

"I don't know about that! There's plenty more on the agenda to get our members talking."

"But their proposals aren't sustainable like yours. You have the potential to deliver one of the most important energy innovations of the day as well as helping to clean up after the nuclear industry. There are many who want to see your vision for the future become reality."

Des smiled. "Well, that's a conversation for tomorrow. We

have a whole evening ahead of us to enjoy first. Food, wine, a speech from the Chancellor. There's even an 'oompah' band to welcome us and a short ballet performance to finish. That will inspire me to perform in the morning."

They wandered back to the Adlon, absorbing the atmosphere of the scene and anticipating the business to come.

TWO

THE EVENING BANQUET WAS in keeping with the elegant surroundings and justified the change into dinner suits. Kelly had been right. This was one of the few conferences for professionals in his field that was not to be missed. As far as he could tell, most of his peers were present and most he knew, albeit in some cases vaguely, as a result of assessing their research papers or visiting their laboratories on familiarisation visits. The event was certainly grand with the trademark order expected of the German hosts. Delegates gathered in a large hallway where drinks were served in the convivial surroundings of a modest trade show, with suppliers of scientific goods and services, as well as international prestige projects, jostling for delegates' attention. Given the general pessimism about the world economy, it was good to see sponsors from pipeline companies, geological services, data analysts and a few others vying for attention, but despite these apparent worthy commercial enterprises, there was one dominating commercial presence acting as main sponsor; Maximum Power, whose brand seemed to be stamped on most things in the vicinity – delegate packs, room decoration, internet services and more. They should have been called 'Maximum Opportunity', thought Kelly, as the host for the proceedings, a glamorous woman in black sequins, who he was told was the presenter from the German TV evening news, welcomed everybody to the city and acknowledged the generous support of Maximum Power in making the whole thing happen.

The scientific community, especially in the energy sector, had pretty respectable gender balance, and he was fortunate to have four women on his table, none of whom he knew.

As he looked at the table menu with the seating plan, he wondered what methodology had been employed to make the selections. Maybe it was like the FIFA World Cup draw with delegates seeded by group to ensure a mix of skills and interests. Never mind, he would use the time to get acquainted with those the organisers clearly thought he should meet.

He began with the woman to his right. Her table card identified her as Margarita Duarte. Tanned, with a black tied-back ponytail, dark brown eyes and a green gown, a veritable '*girl from Ipanema*', or so he thought, in a private, wild moment. She turned out to be a Chilean geophysicist running an offshore mineral exploration project out of Arauco.

"There's a lot of secrecy about what we do. It does wonders for your social life. We can't tell local people because we either get besieged with requests for jobs or attacked by fishermen for damaging the environment," she explained.

"It's a bit difficult hiding a rig, isn't it?"

"We're not at that point yet. We're based on a survey ship, so there's not so much for the casual visitor to see."

"So, what happens with your surveys?"

"My company is contracted to Max," (her friendly term for the conference sponsors), "so they get first refusal of anything we might find."

"That's a good position to be in."

"I guess you are right, I know they have similar deals around the Pacific basin and probably elsewhere. I think they must see the end is in sight for oil reserves so they need to scoop up options while they can. Then they won't need someone like me. I am here on my own time and expense to plan my next career move."

They swapped business cards and continued to make small talk until Kelly saw the chance to join the conversation to his left. The woman next to him had noted his interest.

"Well, Dr Kelly, I am so pleased we haven't had to wait for dessert before we had the opportunity to chat. My name is Eve Grainger, Head of Special Projects at Maximum Power."

Petite, with carefully styled bob-cut, light brown hair (out of an expensive bottle, he guessed) with gold teardrop earrings and a simple tan silk one-piece.

"Delighted to meet you. All this looks like a big commitment," he said.

"You may know, we aren't the new kids on the block. We've been in Europe for nearly twenty years now, but always had a low profile. In the last five years, we've decided to ramp things up a bit under our new chairman, Hector Birnbaum, following the acquisition of firstly, Dart, and then Flare Industries, which now makes us the number three marine mineral extraction player in the market. We decided it was the right time to put down a marker for the future, and let people get to know us better."

"So, you're still in the carbon business?"

She smiled. Her green eyes met his directly.

"For now, but you know how it is, in this game you follow the money and if people want something new, we won't be getting left behind. We are starting to look seriously at alternatives."

"So, what is the fuel of the future?"

"Are you asking *me*? I'm only a new business executive. I think *you* should be telling *me*!"

"Well, by the time your people have reported on all the conference workshops over the next couple of days, you'll be spoilt for choice."

"I am only interested in winners, Dr Kelly."

"Call me Des."

"Des. And my research suggests you could be one of those."

She had turned her body on her chair to face him. If the move had been a 'come on' signal to talk further it failed, for at that moment out of the corner of his eye he saw the one person he had come to Berlin to meet, who was crossing the floor some five tables in front of him heading for a comfort break, or so he had assumed. It was Galina Rustanova.

Kelly had been distracted. He made a hurried apology to Ms Grainger and leapt to his feet as if to follow her towards the bar and the rest rooms. In his haste he had failed to observe the general crush of people, feet, and tables between them, and was unable to follow her quickly enough. She had disappeared. Although spotting her by chance had been easy enough under the circumstances, she was one of many women wearing black, which made her harder to pick out at a distance. Having got as far as the bar, he assumed she must have gone to the rest room, so he waited as though he had been with her all the time. Surrounded by other small groups of delegates talking and drinking, Kelly decided to look as if he was waiting to get served, manoeuvring to ensure he never quite got to the front of the queue. He must have continued this charade for nearly fifteen minutes before he had to reluctantly conclude either that he had been mistaken or that perhaps she had gone to her room. He needed to know for sure, so he slipped out and went to reception.

"Excuse me," he asked, "could you put me through to Ms Rustanova's room?"

The concierge consulted his computer screen.

"What was the name again, sir?"

"Rustanova."

"Rustanova… Rustanova, no sir, we don't have anyone of that name staying at the hotel. Have you got another name for her?"

Kelly was now embarrassed at his impetuosity and not a little confused.

"Er, no, no, don't worry. Thank you anyway."

He stepped back, returning to the throng of delegates massing at the bar.

At that moment, he bumped into Aldo again.

"Desmond, what table did you end up on?" His Italian friend was starting to look the worse for wear.

"Twenty-three, sandwiched between a Chilean rig engineer and one of the sponsor's groupies. You?"

"You are clearly more important than me, my friend. I'm on table forty with one of China's state power station architects and a South African transmission expert. I think I have done enough small talk for the night. Why don't we get out of here and find a drink outside? I think I saw a really nice café bar a couple of blocks away earlier when I went to the Egyptian Museum."

"Why not?"

He could think of plenty of reasons 'why not' at that moment but, faced with the prospect of returning to the dinner or going back to his room to call Sue, a beer in some cellar bar in central Berlin looked like an attractive prospect.

*

At least that's what he decided at the time. In the cold light of day, he thought it hadn't been such a great idea. He had been really pleased to spend some down time with Aldo, who had recounted his frustrations supervising the closure of the Kozluduy Six reactor in Bulgaria, a job that should have been achieved in a matter of months but was now drifting into a second year. He'd talked of other things as well, ranging from his plans to buy a farmhouse near Arezzo, to his developing a close personal relationship with a Bulgarian female MP. Frustratingly he couldn't remember the detail (because he had not been paying attention) but realised he had shared his disappointment about failing to meet with Galina Rustanova earlier in the evening. He was now worried about having shown too much interest in her to Aldo, and surprised that mention of her name sparked an animated reaction from his friend, which was less than positive.

"Rustanova, Rustanova, don't get me started on her! One of the few leading figures of modern scientific thought in her country – even getting the Americans to start to take emissions and responsible energy generation seriously – and then she just packs it all in, quits San Francisco and goes back to Moscow with no explanation to anyone. I don't understand it. She worked so hard to get out of Russia and now she's sold us out and gone back to become one of the president's stooges. If she is here in Berlin, it won't be because she's interested in anything the International Sustainable Energy Forum has to say, she'll be on a mission for him."

He didn't have long to dwell on the point. That was then. This was now. His seminar had gone well. The room had been packed and the schedule only allowed a limited time for questions. The conclusion of the session ended somewhat chaotically with three-quarters of the audience filing out in an orderly way for a coffee break and to attend other sessions. What was left was a gaggle of animated delegates in front of the stage, engaged in their own conversations about his work, continuing to try to ask questions of him or get their photographs taken. The star of this particular show proved not to be a person but an object – a diamond brick containing a spent section of nuclear rod, the sustainable power source of the future. His presentation had focused on the science and showing a short film demonstrating how the brick was manufactured. The winning point was made by the physical presence of the brick on a table which was absolutely safe to have on the premises and authenticated by a Geiger counter check. Members of the audience were less interested in Kelly, but all wanted selfies with the brick and the Geiger counter. It was an excellent diversion. He didn't have to explain in any detail the level of charge which could be accessed from the brick, nor the equipment and process involved. That was for him to know and for the moment others to wonder. A security guard had taken responsibility for looking after the brick and marshalling its visitors. As he continued to engage in small talk with a delegation from India his eye was drawn to a figure standing some ten rows back, because this person was separate, appearing not to be part of a group or with colleagues. It was Galina Rustanova. For a split second he had not recognised her but wasn't sure why. Was it because she was wearing a pastel blue skirt and matching jacket, as opposed to the black evening dress of the night before? Or was it something more basic, the fact that she was smiling and looking directly at him. He held up a hand, gesturing her to wait, while he deftly extracted himself from his conversation and struck out through the crush to meet her.

He clasped both her hands and kissed them in what she clearly thought was a gallant manner. "Galina – I'm so sorry I missed you at the dinner last night. I think I only got to see you when you were leaving. So great to see you! This moment was my real motivation for coming here!"

She laughed – an action revealing the flawed, lined contours of her face. Kelly estimated her to be in her late forties, but well-preserved to his way of thinking. She had transformed from a vivacious blue-eyed blonde in the Scandinavian tradition to a more thoughtful, considered elegance, born of motherhood and life experience. To his mind, this was much more attractive, even sexy in its way. Her makeup was understated by Russian standards, and the tailoring of her jacket was clearly Paris-designer inspired, and probably original.

"Dr Kelly, you say the sweetest things. Did you think I'd come to Berlin and not make it my business to see you? I am worried about you and know we must talk. But not here. Based on last night I didn't want to sit through another of those dinners again, hearing about why Maximum Power and its Russian equivalent, Rosatomic, should be working together. It's boring and I've heard the same pitch already when I was in San Francisco. I see you are staying here at the Adlon. I will send a car to pick you up at eight tonight and we can go to one of my favourite restaurants."

Rustanova had the air of confidence that comes from spending time with high-powered people. She turned to leave without waiting for him to answer. His acceptance had been assumed. For the first time since he had arrived at the conference, Kelly smiled and hesitated, watching her departure and her measured high-heeled steps before being enveloped by what was left of the hard core of his audience still determined to get his attention.

His reason for attending the event being fulfilled, he was now able to give full attention to his personal agenda and look forward to the evening to come.

*

Kelly may have been away from the Thames Valley for a day but at that moment he certainly wasn't forgotten. Sir Gavin decided he wanted to find out more about his star asset's state of mind and saw Des's absence overseas as an opportunity to make his own enquiries. He left the office an hour earlier than usual and made his way south on the A34 towards Kelly's village. He didn't need the satnav to find it, and timed his arrival in the early evening to be sure Sue was in. Their domestic CCTV would log the time as 18.38. He knew, of course, their children now lived elsewhere, so the opportunity to have a frank one-to-one conversation with Kelly's nearest and dearest was not to be missed, although the welcome he received took him by surprise.

When Sue saw him on the doorstep and smiling in that benevolent way, she immediately became agitated and slapped him with some force across the face.

"Bastard, come to humiliate me?"

Her complexion was almost as florid as his own.

"No, I… I came to see how you were getting on. With Des away I thought…"

"You thought you could come round here and carry on where you left off?"

"I thought we could put all that behind us."

"Really? You persuade me to sleep with you, in order to approve Des's promotion and then dump me as soon as you'd had your way? You are lucky I didn't call rape."

"It wasn't like that. I was called into a secret government investigation and I knew my own private life would be checked out."

"Oh, so you thought you were the only man in public life with a secret between the sheets and I was not good enough even to admit to, and you certainly weren't going to the rock the boat with your wife. No, I really have to say 'bastard' is too much of a good word for you. You just dropped out of contact. Do you know what that feels like? Humiliation—"

Sir Gavin cut her off in mid-sentence by putting his arms firmly on her shoulders and kissing her. He felt her resistance but remembered how she had told him she liked a firm hand.

Sure enough, her body seemed to remember Sir Gavin's previous attentions and slowly responded to him. He had forgotten her latent passion and staggered across the threshold with her locked in his embrace.

The prospect of sex was exciting and more pleasurable as Sir Gavin was sure he was not going to be disturbed. In fairness he had told himself, quite honestly, a sexual encounter was not the reason for the visit, but why not? He was an alpha male and at his age was not going to refuse the offer. But even he had his standards.

He did not want to go to bed with her, especially the bed she shared with Des, but also because sex in a marital bed made the act of infidelity worse somehow – premeditated – especially when he knew the man he was replacing so well. It was like the difference between manslaughter and murder. An assignation in the bedroom suggested something more serious – not just sex, but an affair, a sort of perverse mental commitment. Affairs were regular assignations, compounded acts of betrayal. No, this was a one-off, a second one-off, based on lust and healthy spontaneity. He thought of it as a good old English romp with no recriminations, and a natural part of life. That's why, on this occasion, the hallway stairs were the best place to fornicate. She had brought him to attention quickly and expected to be fully pleasured in return as much as their fumbling efforts to climb out of their clothes allowed. Despite the drama of the moment, the action seemed to be over quite quickly, leaving him on his knees and her spread-eagled six steps above him. The obligatory awkward moment of embarrassment came and went with a muttered "Thank you" as both pulled themselves and their clothes together, Sue carefully stepping over the souvenir mark on the carpet Sir Gavin had left behind. His knees were now sore, so his attention soon turned to the living room and the opportunity to take a seat in an armchair, Des's favourite seat.

"I suppose you want a drink now?" Sue said sullenly.

"Tea is fine," he replied.

A steaming cup with the bag still in duly arrived.

"So why are you really here? Surely not to talk about old times."

"I'm worried about Des."

"I'm not surprised. With friends like you who needs enemies?"

"No seriously, I have been watching him recently. I think there's something wrong."

"Apart from the fact his boss is fucking his wife, you mean?"

"No, I'm here for a serious conversation. He seems… preoccupied about something and that attempted break-in the other night didn't help, I'm sure."

"When he realised that no one had actually burgled the house he didn't seem that bothered. I'm the one who's feeling violated, in more ways than one. Still, we will see what the police do with the evidence they collected."

"Evidence?"

Sue lit a cigarette and exhaled.

"Oh, some bloke came along to dust for prints. He created a

right mess, but didn't find anything, that is, until I pointed out a boot-print in the flowerbed. He certainly took pictures of that and measured the depth of the tread."

"Was that it?"

"No, there was also the dart in Milo's neck."

Sir Gavin looked surprised.

"Milo, your dog?"

"Yes. Des came back early and disturbed them. He set Milo on them in the dark and they shot him with a tranquilliser. Knocked him out instantly, otherwise he'd have caught them. After Des had got the vet round, they found and removed it. I'm not sure what Des has done with it, but I do know he kept it."

"And he's not seemed worried about work at all?"

"How would I know? Nuclear fission or whatever you guys do isn't a topic I know much about. Besides, we don't talk that much anyway… or share anything else for that matter. I have my own social life. But no, he's not looked worried to me, but he does like to pop into the Duck down the road for a quick pint when he's walking Milo. Maybe there's someone down there he confides in?"

"And you haven't had cause to worry about an attempted break-in since?"

"Again, no. When it happened, I caught sight of a shadowy figure on the drive when normally I would have been back first. That's when I alerted Des. If it occurred again when Des was away, I would go down to the Duck and get Bryan the landlord to come back here with me. I might even reward him for his trouble," she smiled provocatively.

"Well, if there's anything I can do," he said, standing up and heading for the door.

"I think you've done more than enough for now, don't you?" she said. "Shut the door on your way out. I want to let Milo out of the kitchen."

*

It proved a relative short drive from the hotel to Restaurant Einsunternull, a left turn one hundred metres beyond the Russian Embassy on the right side of the Unter den Linden, then straight up Friedrichstrasse to the junction with Hannovershestrasse for a seven-course fish tasting menu washed down with an unusually dry Domdechant Werner Hochheimer Domdechaney Riesling Auslese 2011. Great food, excellent company, and a top drop of wine in a dark cosy restaurant whose interior was in the style of 1970s kitsch.

That was easy for Des to recall but probably not for Galina growing up in Russia. The country of her youth was not noted for quality restaurants, but she and Des had 'form'. In recent years it had been characterised by their secret enjoyment of dinners in top restaurants around the world, made possible by their regular participation in international conferences and academic seminars. Their 'private fine dining club' had started as the result of a brief intense personal relationship nearly twenty years ago.

They were both very different people then, but Des held the memory close to his heart, and even now he could recall every minute of their first time together. They had met at Electric 99 conference, held at the Steigenberger Hotel in Vienna, having joined an 'unofficial' pre-dinner evening walking tour of the Graben district of the city, which took in both the Hofburg and St Stephen's. The casual amble through Old Vienna's grand central district was a great way for delegates to get to know each other personally, away from the stresses of the business day. Des attributed his meeting with Galina to his slow, some would have said dawdling, approach to the trip. The enthusiastic ones stayed close to their guide, listening intently to her paraphrased account of the centuries of Austro-Hungarian history. Des smiled to himself at the thought of being face to face with so much culture and classical architecture yet having one primeval thought on his mind – getting his 'leg over'. He had scanned the group to see if there were any likely ladies who might be the target of his attentions, but the few who were there seemed to stick together in some sort of subgroup. Most of them formed the enthusiasts who regarded this essentially relaxed activity as warranting the same amount of attention as one of the conference plenaries. Not so Galina; she had stood out as being one of the younger ones on the walk and appeared not to have come along with any obvious companions. She looked a natural candidate to engage in conversation. In fact, given her appearance, she didn't really look studious in that way you would expect a scientist to look. She dressed smartly and was clearly aware of how to show her figure in an engaging and subtle way. She didn't look Russian, with those trademark, slightly Slavic features. Besides, at that point, she had not spoken. She had ended up at the back of the group, not because of any attraction to him, but because of her interest in looking in the windows of some of the designer dress shops they were passing. Occasionally, she would look behind her as if trying to remember the location of the shop to allow her to make some future clandestine visit, armed with a credit card.

Des's opportunity to say 'hello' came when he encouraged her not to get left behind. He had joked about it being important to 'get fit, not get fat' because Vienna was one of the world's best cities to get lost in, especially as, in his estimation, you could only ever be one street away from a cake shop. Her earnest reaction gave way to quiet humour as she absorbed the joke.

"It looks like a wonderful city. I hope to explore a little before I go home."

"How long have you got?"

"Maybe one or two days. It depends."

"On?"

"Whether my bosses like my reports from the conference. The better my reports, the more flexible they will be."

"Who are your bosses?"

"Well, it makes a change when a man asks first who my bosses are before he asks my name. I already know you must be a scientist."

"Er… yes. Hi, my name's Des. I'm from England."

"And who are *your* bosses, Des?"

"I work for the Lauriston Foundation, part of Oxford University."

"I`m Galina and since you ask, my bosses are at the Novosibirsk Academy of Applied Energy Sciences."

"Oh." He paused.

"So that tends to finish any interesting conversation I may have."

"Are you here on your own?"

"In some ways yes, in other ways no. I am part of a delegation of scientists here from Russia. We all have different specialisms. But it seems I am the only one interested in seeing Vienna. It's such a pity. It is their loss."

"But you seem so young."

"It is true this is my first conference in the West, and before I came here, I was warned about the patronising attitude of their scientists, so they have been proven right. It is interesting to see how few delegates from European Union countries here are women. I think all of them are at the front of this group."

"Is the conference living up to your expectations?"

"I think so. We are here to seek collaborative opportunities to fund research projects and I think we are making some important connections. Maybe we could work with your Oxford Lauriston? You must tell me more about it."

"We can talk business tomorrow. Here is my card with my mobile phone number in case we miss each other. Tonight we can be off duty and enjoy the sights. You were saying this is your first trip out of Russia?"

"As a professional yes, but as a student I have visited London, Paris and of course, Rome."

Des didn't quite understand the reference to Rome, but Galina answered before he asked the question.

"Rome is the most beautiful place – history, food, people.

I think every tourist should visit the city at least once in their lifetime, or in my case, twice."

She smiled at him for the first time.

"Maybe you'll change your mind when you get to know Vienna."

"I don't think so. Here is too tidy, too neat, too… organised. A city should have a rough element, some grit as you would say. It is the grit which makes its character. In Russia, we have much grit."

She was definitely warming to their conversation.

"I'm sure there will be some grit around here somewhere. It's probably in one of the cellar bars. Why don't we see if we can find some? This looks a possibility."

They were now in the Langer Gasse, a few tens of metres behind their energetic guide and her groupies, at a place called the Bird Yard. It was dusk and she followed him down the steps to the cellar, which seemed to be welcoming the onset of night. Its dark walls provided the canvas for a prominent exotic, bold, street-art-like painting with a glow-in-the-dark factor to it. The subjects were a mixed depiction of flowers and animals, which acted to wrap the visitor up in some intimate, slightly edgy surreal world. If Des had been looking for some local grit, he had chosen well. This was not the Vienna stereotype of beer-fuelled thigh-slapping lederhosen-clad dancers, horn blowing and yodelling, more the sort of place for couples to congregate who didn't want to be seen out together. If these walls could talk, they would have an anthology of stories to tell, and Galina was about to add her own unique chapter.

They talked over a couple of Steigls and vodka chasers about everything and nothing. He couldn't recall the detail after all this time. Families and friends, hobbies and travels. It transpired that, although Galina was a native of central Russia, she felt like a second-class citizen because she lived east of the Urals.

"The further east in Russia you live the thicker they think you are. In Moscow they think of us as poor peasants. We are only good to work on farms or join the military. You don`t have such discrimination?"

"I guess we do, but it is more understated. After all we are just a small island on the edge of the Atlantic. We have this thing called the north-south divide."

"Isn't that about England against Ireland?"

"No, that's something different again. It's complicated. I suppose what it shows is that wherever you are in the world, prejudice is part of the human condition."

The conversation was starting to veer off-limits and Des detected Galina was starting to look uneasy.

"Time is moving on. Your colleagues will be starting to worry. Come on, let's get back to the Steigenberger."

Coming out into the cool evening they walked slowly back towards the hotel; this time Galina linked her arm into Des's.

"I hope you don't mind walking like this. I am told it makes you less likely to be targeted by thieves."

Des laughed.

"I'm not sure how many thieves would be out around here. I think we are safe enough."

She looked up at him.

"Don't be so sure. We have been told stories of Moldovans, Roma and Albanians running street crime here. We must be careful."

Des was not sure whether Galina's interest in conspiracy theories was a personal or national trait but at that moment he didn't care. The walk back could have taken ten minutes but they made it double that and Des was resigned to the evening's entertainment ceasing as they entered the lobby of the hotel. Galina seemed to tense up at that point, moving straight to the reception to check for messages. There weren't any. From a distance, her body language seemed to return to the positive. She moved back to the centre of the lobby where Des was waiting.

"I think we may have missed dinner. Are you hungry? I can order room service."

He wasn't certain if he was misinterpreting her signals.

"Are you sure you want the company?"

She lowered her voice, looking directly into his eyes.

"For your benefit, I was being polite. If we were in Russia, I would just ask you if you wanted a fuck."

It may have been some twenty years ago, but the moment was etched on his memory and still made him smile. To an extent they were different people back then, free of the responsibilities they now had.

The lovemaking was legendary. Like nothing he had experienced before or since.

Slow, sensual, starting the second her bedroom door was closed and locked. It was devoid of all initial nervousness and he could still almost smell the delicate mix of her perfume and body odour. The food came and stayed outside the door while the main course was being eagerly devoured inside. To Des she had the frame of a gymnast, taut with her muscles gently sketching out the contours of her body. She was clearly well-schooled in the natural arts, knowing exactly how and when to trigger his passion while his mouth examined her bit by bit. She moaned her acquiescence and panted her way to the conclusion, her bucking dictating his response.

Looking back, Des knew they must have been at it for hours as he remembered he only got showered and ready to go when she received a concerned call from one of her delegation colleagues. A rapid flow of Russian finishing with "*Da, Da*" had brought it all to an end. That and the sharp shaft of sunlight which flooded the room when he had opened the curtain.

He couldn't remember anything else from that conference, which meant it had either been very boring or his encounter with Galina had been so good. On reflection it had probably been both. His one regret at the time was that, in their hurry to get ready to rejoin the event, he thought they had not had the chance to say goodbye properly. Had that been up to him? His last sight of her in the bathroom felt so matter of fact, as though already she had forgotten the preceding night as 'one of those things', no more important than washing her hair or doing her makeup. He chose not to worry about it, anticipating seeing her in one of the formal sessions later in the day. And although he had kept a look out, he had not seen her again.

He didn't see or hear from her for another two years, by which time Des had put the whole matter out of his mind. After all, what had he expected? They had performed a trade, exchanging lovemaking services at a time of mutual requirement. That was that. He had been wrong to hope for anything more. After all, he was English, she was Russian – any further liaison was always going to be difficult, especially in their shared line of work.

*

Two years on and their next meeting was at a strategy workshop organised by the Baltic Sea Rim countries to discuss the construction of the underwater Nordforge pipeline project in Stockholm.

For Des it had been an unexpected, but pleasant surprise to see her, albeit at a distance. He wasn't sure it was the same for Galina. Her natural beauty was undiminished and as a result, it ensured she stood out in a crowd anyway. She had registered the presence of Des, slightly too late to avoid acknowledging him (as he thought) but was surrounded by half a dozen overweight men in various states of balding in badly fitting suits, preventing any opportunity for dialogue. These turned out to be representatives of St Petersburg City Council and she was there as their 'technical adviser'. Although she had nodded and smiled at him briefly, she seemed worried that he might overreact to her move and immediately dropped eye contact.

The business of the day was interrupted by a buffet lunch, when she had some space from her minders and approached him.

"Des, how good to see you again. I'm sorry I could not be more forward in my greeting, but you will understand my position has changed since we were last in touch. I have a new role advising the City of St Petersburg on energy policy now, which really matters to us as this pipeline will be an important currency earner for my country in years to come. How are things with you?"

The tone of this conversation seemed more distant than the last and she was clearly appreciative of the fact that he had not sought to raise the matter of their first meeting in Vienna.

Their exchange concluded with a suggestion of dinner again that night, but she was quick to manage his expectations.

"I'm afraid dinner will be just that, no extras," she smiled. "I am dealing with an issue that I could use a second opinion about, and I don't get many opportunities to consult an expert from Oxford University."

The arrangement happened. The dialogue rebooted, this time on a higher, more professional level, garnished with just a little discourse on their respective personal circumstances.

Des admired Galina's apparent rapid promotion. Even to the uninitiated, engineering a move from Novosibirsk to St Petersburg demonstrated outstanding ability or perhaps exceptional networking with the political elite.

She let slip that on her return from Vienna, she had met her future husband, who had some 'hush hush' job in the military and had a child. Apparently, he already had a son by a previous relationship, so she was now a mother of two, with a partner absent on military deployment and a contract as an adviser to the council.

"As you can imagine, Des, I have had to become even better at managing my time. How do you keep all the plates spinning?"

"I keep a lady of leisure who does all the domestic stuff, leaving me free to develop my conceptual engineering projects."

She laughed, probably because she realised Des understood her position and was not trying to make a pass at her. It was to prove the foundation for their lasting friendship.

*

Now they were in Berlin. Their exchange in Stockholm seemed fresh in Des's mind. Despite their history, they were comfortable in each other's company as old friends usually are.

Galina had been given the use of an embassy car and chauffeur for the night. Their driver was clearly multi-talented, doubling as a bodyguard, and kept a distant but watchful eye on proceedings from the bar.

Their conversation didn't seem to be affected by the long gaps between their meetings, and both seemed not to have trouble keeping it light, their family issues discussed in passing, alongside some general thoughts about future international collaboration, the impact of the uncertain market conditions on world oil production and what were the best bargains to pick up in the Berlin stores.

Des smiled as he remembered Galina's preoccupation with the high-end designer outlets in Vienna. He understood what she would think of as a bargain – perhaps 30% on a Louis Vuitton handbag – would be quite different from most other women's perceptions.

He had been interested to note her driver/minder's uneasy shifting body language when she took out her mobile to show him pictures of her children.

What was he imagining? Some public sharing of military secrets?

Again, Des was interested in what she chose not to show him – her house or her husband.

He assumed that was a step too far but could not be sure if that was the result of personal or professional censorship.

THREE

THEIR EVENING WAS DRAWING to a close, the wine and vodka chasers were taking their effect. Galina took the opportunity to strike.

"Des, are you all right? You seem… distracted."

She clearly knew him well.

He was starting to get used to being asked the question.

"How do you mean?"

"You know. Unless I've not been paying attention, I can't remember your texting me when we haven't been in the same city. And what did you mean, 'I've done it'?"

She pulled up his message from a month ago on her mobile and showed it to him, as if to jog his memory.

"Oh that. It was just a spur of the moment thing. I've been wrestling with a scientific puzzle for the past five years and I've suddenly found the answer."

"Puzzle? Answer? This must be to do with your diamond brick, right?"

"Right."

"Well, it is certainly an exciting project. Your presentation this morning was great. I can't think of too many occasions where the star of the show was an inanimate object, not a person. After today your brick is about to become the most famous on the planet!"

They both laughed at that.

"Come on Galina – don't tell me your people aren't looking at it, too. We all know what the potential is, but the question is how to access it. I sent that text because I have found a way of stimulating a consistent charge of 12.9 volts out of one of these. Nobody else has been able to generate that level of power from a compact sustainable unit like that. Your lot and the Americans haven't got beyond the sealing and storage elements of diamond containment."

"What makes you so sure?"

"Because you are still experimenting. Because if you had done it, your leader would be boasting about it. Based on the recent Leovalev paper from your colleagues at the Academy, you still have some way to go and the solution you are seeking may not come from the path you are following. I would also be surprised if you had got through your sabbatical in San Francisco without being asked about it."

"Des, this sounds like a riddle. You know me. We Russians like straight talking. Tell me what is going on."

Kelly leaned forward and connected with her gaze.

"OK, in a nutshell – I am dying from an advanced cancer and may have only months left. I have discovered how to generate huge power from an individual diamond brick – possibly the most important discovery of my career. The technology will have a massive impact on the way we live our lives. It will change global economies. It will offer new hope for global natural environments. The oil industry and the need for extracted fuels will disappear. Some countries will plunge into poverty. Others who have the technology will share unparalleled riches. There will be more and possibly catastrophic wars. The likes of Maximum Power will not exist in its present form five years from now. This is the start of a global energy revolution. But…"

"But what?"

"I won't survive to be part of it."

"So, your colleagues in Oxford will take it forward."

"Only if they know about it. Different members of my team know pieces of the story, but nobody else has the full picture or understands how the project interfaces fit together."

"But surely you will be documenting this..."

"Probably – I am undecided. It is ironic, I have been doing this work, but my own energy reserves are depleted. I am wondering if I can put together the necessary research in the time I have left or whether not to bother and go and make my personal peace with the world. What I have discovered should be a prize for the future of mankind. I worry that whoever gets this knowledge will adapt it for a more sinister purpose in order to strengthen their own political power and influence. Sometimes I feel excited by the knowledge, other times cursed and I can't see what to do. Nobody fully understands the scale of what I have discovered and I am sure, as we both know, there are some talented brains who will follow my path and get there in the end. But that could be at least ten years away and who knows what will happen in that time.

"So, the text was just me, celebrating an achievement that, for now, only I understand. The act of texting you was a release. I have a grown-up family that have their own separate lives, a loveless marriage and few friends who understand what I do. It is a hard load to bear on top of my diagnosis, and the act of contacting you was to share a fleeting, private moment of joy with someone who, I knew, once cared about me. It was a silly, impetuous thing to do, but even scientists are human – now and again. There was another reason also at that time. Ever since we first met, I have been attracted to you, not just in the obvious way, but because I loved your personality and devil-may-care attitude. I needed to experience that once more before I go, so I had hoped I might get to see you here, perhaps for the last time."

She reached across the table, putting her hand over his.

"What can I say, other than thank you for sharing your feelings with me. Your candour is a gift that I value."

She continued her light but firm grip on his hand.

"I can't properly explain but, when I met you, I recognised you would be an important person in my life. I was young and could not understand the difference between love and sex or how you could also share a deep love between friends. Sometimes that feeling grows with absence not togetherness. Somehow in my own darker moments, I have thought of you thousands of miles away and wondered how you would have approached some of the situations I have encountered. Just that thought has enabled me to be positive about my situation and prospects. So perhaps in reality, I owe you. You are one of the few people I have met who has offered unconditional friendship as well as, on occasion, useful professional advice. I am pleased to know you and regard you as a personal mentor. I feel shocked and upset but know there must be things we can do to make the situation right. Although we have a funny way of doing things at times, we take medical science seriously. I am sure we have the skills and technology to help you. I will make some calls in the morning."

"You are very kind, Galina, but that moment is past. I was warned to have chemo over a year ago. I put it out of my mind to focus on my work and have morphine tablets which ease the discomfort. I knew what I was doing and now I have to face up to the situation and deal with it, with the strength of mind and determination my colleagues would expect of me."

"What are you going to do?"

"The first thing is to conquer my fear. It is irrational, sucks up my personal energy and has no place in my life now. I don't want to die in my home or in hospital. I want my last moments to be unpredictable and stimulating and I think I have found a way of doing it. I have done what so many others do when they know the end is near. The second thing is to make full use of my limited time. I have made a list of things I need to get done. Meeting you tonight to reminisce about happier times and to find a way of rounding off, *closing* our relationship, was one of those items.

I couldn't be sure it would happen, but I am satisfied now that it has. Thirdly, I have to decide what to do about my research. Although I am done with it now, I need to ensure I leave it in a way that can benefit the greatest number of people who will follow me. I'm not sure what that looks like at the moment. And fourthly, *finally,* I want to pick the moment for my passing, which for many of my peers should be a surprise. On my way home I am calling in to a place in Denmark that offers a kind of low key assisted dying service. It might be something I want to follow up, at least a means of taking away the pain and adding the surprise element."

Galina looked at him earnestly.

"If that is what you want, you don't have to go to Denmark for that. Many of my countrymen, like my driver by the bar, offer that service for nothing, but normally it involves a brief but necessary element of pain. What do you fancy? A bullet to the head, a poisoned strawberry milk shake? Perhaps a dizzy attack followed by an unfortunate fall from the window of an office tower block? These are our specialisms."

They both shared the mawkish moment of humour.

She continued, "Seriously, don't assume you have run out of road, Des. There may be help out there you are not aware of. I have access to some of my country's best knowledge on the subject. I will find out and tell you all I know."

She nodded to her driver at the bar, who moved to pay their bill.

"Do you need a hug? I can stay with you at your hotel for an hour or so before I am expected back at the embassy."

"No, no Galina. If you were to come into the hotel I wouldn't want you to leave, and would probably embarrass myself by wanting more than a hug. Thank you for dinner. You had better get straight back to the embassy. It's a relatively short walk back to the Adlon from here and I could use some air."

He helped her into her coat, and they followed her driver out onto the street.

She turned to him and kissed him gently on the cheek.

"It is only polite to say goodbye. I am only saying farewell now to mark the closure of this wonderful evening with you. I will be in touch."

The driver took her signal to open the rear door of the limousine. It seemed to swallow her easily, a dull thud marking the act of closure.

He turned and walked towards Friedrichstrasse, unaware that in the back of the departing car his friend was wiping a tear from her eye.

He was also unaware of a man in motorcycle leathers casually walking behind him chewing a burger.

*

They had arranged to meet in what Gerry referred to as his 'liaison office' in Barton Street, located behind Westminster School and College Green. The small mews was a venue he preferred to use when having meetings with public or non-service contacts. A great place for an unattributable one to one. Even better for hosting those who, childishly, relished the prospect of visiting MI6 HQ the other side of the river. Such people tended to be time wasters or bullshitters, indulging themselves in the thought they were secret agents by nature of the fact that they were mixing with obscure civil servants from the MoD, in premises whose cumbersome security checks actively discouraged visits from outsiders. Barton Street was often used by his colleagues for staff interviews, briefings for members of the security and intelligence select committee or off the record exchanges with colleagues from the Met or armed forces on terrorism matters. He thought of it as 'the soft play area', a place of comfy three-piece suites and understated homely decor, devoid of formal office paraphernalia, meeting room desks and video conferencing facilities. It was the ideal place for a meeting with Sir Gavin Laidlaw. Gerry liked

Gavin. He had a military mind – tidy and punctual, economic with his language and not just analytical in the standard prerequisite of his profession, but intuitive. Who knows? Had Laidlaw's career panned out differently, maybe he would be in Gerry's shoes now. On second thought, probably not. Gerry recognised Gavin's one real weakness – his ego. Egomaniacs or narcissists never got far in military intelligence, they were too much of a liability. To them, leadership was about recognition, respect and reward. To prosper in MI6, you needed to be a corporatist, influencer, a process man, good at sticking to the script and following orders. All that and being an acidulous observer of detail and behaviour. Perhaps the one thing Gerry enjoyed most about meetings outside the service was a widespread assumption on the part of visitors that the intelligence services knew about every aspect of their background and lives when he met them. Part of the fun from Gerry's perspective was to see how open they would be in his company, and he noted Sir Gavin was a particularly complex character. Gerry had been ready for Sir Gavin's arrival for the past twenty minutes and had already planned how he intended to handle the encounter, so much so, that in the past ten minutes he had switched on the TV to see the Home Secretary announce the new immigration rules to Parliament. Of course, he had been consulted about the statement, but his interest was to see how she presented the strategy in public. Would she be 'softly, softly' and incremental, or go for the shrill 'fuck you' approach? It looked as though the latter was winning the day. Anyway, that was a distraction. Sir Gavin had arrived and was shown into the first-floor lounge one minute ahead of schedule. Gerry pressed the remote to switch off the minister as Sir Gavin crossed the floor.

"Gavin, thanks for taking the time to pop in. You've made my day. I'd rather talk to you than listen to the Home Secretary."

Sir Gavin smiled a little, but not too much. He wasn't sure what Gerry might read into his reaction. Gerry continued, "I understand how fraught these days in London become when you are not here every day. Never mind, you're looking well, so there must be health benefits to your pressured existence."

"I'm pleased we were able to meet here, Gerry. I've got to speak at a Parliamentary reception later on this afternoon, so at least I won't break a sweat crossing town."

"Exactly so. Do come and sit down. One of my people has just come back from China with some rare Da Hong Pao teas from the Wuyi mountains. It's ironic that they don't grow enough to export, but they are missing a trick with this stuff. It's really good, but a bit of milk I think takes the edge off the flavour. Try it and see what you think."

Gerry poured a cup carefully, using the tea strainer which was strategically located next to his cup and saucer.

"So, we have a number of things to discuss – let me begin with your Dr Kelly."

He picked up a slim dossier from the coffee table and looked as though he was consulting it, when in reality he already knew its contents.

"He's one of your stars, isn't he? All that stuff on hyper condensed chemical vapour deposition – HCCVD – will make the UK international market leaders as well as helping to save the planet. He certainly looks as if he will be important in getting the government to agree to your coming five-year settlement."

"He's done very well recently, and his research is helping us secure lucrative private funding as well; but as you know, we have to be a bit circumspect about this. The Americans, in particular want this technology now, but whereas our interest is really in civils like heating and light, I get the impression they are scoping military applications."

"Undoubtedly – it's their military programmes that will carry their budget, but I think we'd rather like the opportunity to combine this new technology with our own product first, just so that we can maximise the economic benefit. I'm sure you understand."

"Of course, but right now I have a bigger worry – the man himself. His research is excellent but the more sensitive aspects of it are not being fully documented. He seems to be behind on his record keeping. The value to us is in the record, and if it is not documented properly, we don't have control."

"Your point is?"

"His behaviour has become more erratic, insular… distracted. To me, he is displaying signs of being clinically depressed. I've tried to be supportive, to get him to talk, if only so that I can put in place the necessary support mechanisms to help, but he keeps closing me down. I'm trying to find out whether all is well at home and I'm not getting far on that, except for hearing about the ham-fisted way your guys started checking him out after we spoke on the phone a couple of weeks back."

"Excuse me?"

"Come on, Gerry, I know you moved as soon as I sounded the alarm."

"What do you mean?"

"A few days after we spoke there was an attempted burglary at Des Kelly's house. His wife even saw one of the intruders, albeit at a distance. Yet when Kelly himself went to investigate there were no signs of a break-in. All there was to see was a tranquilliser dart in his pet Rottweiler's neck and a perfectly preserved left boot-print in one of his flowerbeds. No self-respecting felon would countenance breaking into a house and not leaving a trail of theft and vandalism for the police to follow. There was absolutely no damage to exterior doors and windows and interestingly, according to his wife, no fingerprints anywhere. You guys are the only people I know that enter any premises you like but are well mannered enough to leave things as you found them. Anyway, according to his wife, Kelly has kept the dart as part of the evidence trail to find out who was behind it."

"Well, that's all very interesting, but not very relevant. I expect Dr Kelly lives in a nice house in a good neighbourhood so it can't be unusual to have local villains casing the place looking for an opportunity. It sounds like your man turned up at just the right moment."

"But what about the dart?"

"Dart?" Bannan looked surprised but not worried. "Oh, the thing that calmed his wild dog? Well, I wouldn't know about that. I'm not sure if we are in the habit of putting dogs to sleep and even if we do, I would have thought we would use a standard doggy treat. If we'd be likely to use a dart, it would be a standard proprietary brand not a piece of special kit. We all have budget disciplines to observe, you know. I am sure others who may have been interested in Kelly's house would arrive and be ready to take the same precautions. I note your information comes from Kelly's wife. I'd be cautious about that, Gavin; I wouldn't be sure you could rely on the word of a serial adulterer. No wonder you think Kelly's depressed… under the circumstances, can you blame him?"

Sir Gavin looked uncomfortable and shifted slightly on his seat.

Bannan looked at him quizzically.

"Don't go there, Gavin. If I decided to concern myself with the peccadillos of all the people I encounter, I would need my own resident shrink. All you need to know is that I am aware of the activities of Kelly's wife, not only with you but certainly two or three others. I have to say from what I have understood you are probably the most influential of the bunch and I think she'd agree. After all, she was the one who got you to put Kelly in charge of his department. Now it looks like you are being repaid handsomely.

"Notwithstanding those shenanigans, there are some other snippets which have come to my attention which may be relevant. Firstly, he keeps some eclectic professional company. In particular, he seems to be friendly with a lady who is definitely of interest to us – Galina Rustanova. Have you heard of her? She's now the number two in the Russian Academy of Sciences in Moscow and was recently on an IAEA secondment with her opposite numbers in San Francisco. Seems to have known Kelly for a number of years but I am not sure we understand their connection in the way that we should. Keep your ears open. If you hear anything let me know. The other thing is his medical records. We've turned up some correspondence from the local NHS asking him to attend an appointment for consultation which he never took up. It was over a year old so is probably not relevant anymore, but if he has a health issue, that may well be making him a bit more irascible than usual. Based on your reaction, I assume this is news to you? Well, I'll sniff around and see if I can find out more, but you should do the same. It's possible you could be without your star player before your next round of funding is fixed.

"So, as I read it, Gavin, at the moment you are in the driving seat on this one. We will keep a watching brief, of course, and if you get anything else, let me know.

"Anyway, if that part of our chat has made you feel a little… unsettled, I may just have the answer. One of the reasons I wanted to see you here today is that I have someone I'd like you to meet."

Bannan pressed a button on what looked like the TV remote. There was no response from the box on the wall, but his move did prompt the housekeeper to come into the room.

"Victoria, could you ask Boris to join us?"

A moment later, a blond-haired man with glasses in a sky-blue turtleneck and claret trousers entered the room.

"Dr Professor Boris Ponomariev – may I introduce you to Sir Gavin Laidlaw, Director of the Lauriston Foundation, University of Oxford? Boris has recently come over to us to build a new life, which, despite its many attractions, is not available to him in his native Russia. I think he has some very interesting skills and experience which will be useful to you in the months ahead and who knows, may also help Dr Kelly to realise his potential on our behalf. Naturally, he is feeling a bit new at the moment and we are concerned to help him to settle down. I'm not sure if the *kopek* has dropped about his absence in Moscow yet, but it can't be too far away and I expect their president will be a bit pissed off, which has its own security implications. So, for now, we are keeping Boris out of harm's way, but very soon, once we have completed our debriefing procedures, we would like him to get involved in your work. We are pretty sure he can make an effective contribution."

"Good afternoon, Sir Gavin, it is an honour to meet you."

"You too, Dr Ponomariev. I hope to have the pleasure of welcoming you to the Lauriston in due course."

"Yes, I would like that. I have always wanted to visit Oxford. I have heard of its dreaming spires..."

"There's some lovely country to explore, as well as some internationally significant research projects which I am sure would be of interest."

Bannan intervened.

"That's something for Boris to plan for in weeks to come. In the meantime, he is working through his debrief programme with my people, which still has some way to go, but I will keep you in the picture, Gavin."

"That would be good, Gerry. I hope you will excuse me. I really must make my way across the road."

He noticed Ponomariev looking perplexed.

"To our Houses of Parliament," he added, for Bannan's guest's benefit.

"That is something else you can enjoy," he added, "watching democracy in action."

The irony in his voice was picked up by his host but not the Russian, who replied, "I think I have much to look forward to."

"Indeed, you have," said Bannan.

*

Investigator Gennady Arbutsev was relieved to get off the phone from his FSB boss in Moscow. The shit was starting to hit the fan. Where was Ponomariev if he wasn't in Rostov? He certainly wasn't in the capital. Could he be ill or have stopped off en route? The name didn't appear on any passenger booking to Kaliningrad, either from Moscow or St Petersburg. It had been made very clear to him that he had twenty-four hours to find him or… or there would be consequences. 'Consequences' is a word that always sparks depression in the heart of a government *apparatchik*. It is a euphemism which is often associated with unfortunate and often terminal accidents, ranging from being hit by a bus or trapped in a house fire to an obligatory heart attack. The state seemed to have a long menu of terminal options to choose from and their increasingly innovative methods were often the subject of bar room conjecture.

How come Ponomariev had not been identified as a risk previously? It seemed mad upon reflection. He lived on his own and for a man of his age had no track record with women and didn't have much of a drink problem. He had been allocated a house reserved for the political and military elite with a degree of personal privacy. He had worked on a range of missile technologies for the past ten years and had developed five designs for ship-to-ship rockets and a new propulsion system for torpedoes. His time had been split between the naval bases at Kaliningrad and a secret site on the Barents Sea near Polyarny. His reports attested to his brilliance in design and calculus and his work rate recognised as giving Russia a lead in some of the major naval weapons classifications. Ponomariev had achieved a first in applied mechanics at Moscow State University and a doctorate concurrently from the Russian Academy of Sciences. He was known for his interest in white water kayaking and collecting stamps.

A search of his house in School Street had revealed little. A bed, clearly recently occupied by one person. A fridge half full of potted beef, milk, cheese and cabbage, a lounge simply furnished with nondescript abstract art and a picture of an old woman with a headscarf – presumably, the mother he'd gone to visit.

Of course, it had been tidy when his men arrived, and the last occupant had been kind enough to leave a light on to welcome a prospective visitor in the twilight hours. But it had not been left as it was found. There was no forensic crime scene investigation here, just a casual ransacking in the search for obvious clues – credit card receipts, personal letters, pornography, money, valuables. Drawers were emptied, clothes spread around the floor, a laptop computer confiscated. The instruction from Arbutsev was clear. Any evidence would be taken and, if there was none, the place had to be wrecked to make it easy to plant some if necessary. The point about planting evidence was never about establishing Ponomariev's guilt, a decision had already been taken in Moscow on that point, but Arbutsev had a time-limited option to avoid the inevitable finger of blame that would follow. He was clear that, whatever the outcome of Ponomariev's unexpected absence, he would make sure he could pass the blame.

Privately he thought his colleagues in Moscow were overreacting. Russia is a big place, after all, and unlike their opposite numbers in China, they didn't have a camera on every street corner. Kaliningrad Oblast was one of the harder parts of Russia to move about in undetected anyway, with the same level of border security applied to crossing into Russia proper as international frontiers. It was inconceivable that he had passed out of Kaliningrad without leaving a record, although there was one exception. From time to time, members of the military elite could get a spare seat on an air force transport flight back to Moscow at no charge, with no questions asked, as a favour, provided prospective passengers did not embarrass their hosts by overstaying their leave entitlements. In such cases, an extra name would be scribbled on the computer-generated manifest and the individual concerned would slip away through a military post room or mess without anybody being the wiser. Access to this service was a closely guarded secret known only to a select few, and especially not those connected with the FSB. Had this been the means of Ponomariev's escape? Surely he would have been more likely to take the train. If so, was he travelling under an assumed name? That too was a possibility if, in reality, he had been on an FSB assignment.

What was happening here? He didn't know. Perhaps this was just an elaborate game to trap him into a demotion for unwittingly upsetting some senior official. His mind was starting to respond to the likely plotting of his superiors. Had he upset anyone? Had he fucked someone he shouldn't? Had he been doing a little bit of informal import/export business on the side with his Polish neighbours? Whatever. His conscience was clear.

He gazed out of his second-floor window at the back of his office on the Lenino Prospectus which overlooked a line of well-drilled sycamores to one of the deep-water berths presently occupied by the destroyer *Admiral Chabanenko*. This leviathan, originally built at the nearby Yantar shipyard, was an integral part of Russia's northern fleet, visiting from its operational base further north on the Kola peninsula. This ship was one of the first beneficiaries of the updated P270 Mosquito – the supersonic ramjet anti-ship cruise missile which Ponomariev had helped to design. It was ironic that he should be looking at it when he took the call from his boss, Dimitri Nikitin, in Moscow regarding the fate of its principal architect.

"So what have you got, Arbutsev?"

The Baltiysk FSB man was keeping his options open.

"We've been to his house and are checking travel records now. We are finding out a bit more about him, having got hold of his computer. You know, it's weird, as though he had just popped out of the house. There wasn't much out of the ordinary, but we will see when we work through the evidence we collected."

That was code for forty-eight hours – about the maximum time he could spin out his report for.

But now was the opportunity to turn defence to attack.

"What's the word from Rostov?"

His boss was forced to concede.

"We found his old mother, who wasn't expecting him, but

has now got it into her head he's coming over, and keeps calling my man to find out when he is arriving, because she can't reach him on his home number. Silly cow – I don't think she is really all there! We are trying to research some of his old university mates here. It's possible he's been out clubbing and got into a bit of personal trouble."

He knew Nikitin was clutching at straws. If this turned nasty, he wouldn't be the only one to shoulder the blame.

"I'll come back to you soonest when I have something."

It was important he gave the impression of being in control. He had to get a lead.

Next on his list was to check out his work colleagues, bars and whorehouses. Best thing about Baltiysk was that it was a small place, so all the venues he needed to visit were grouped in a relatively confined area. Against that, based on a couple of initial interviews with two of his closest work colleagues, he was not hopeful of success. A picture was emerging of a man who kept himself to himself, did the day job and disappeared across the estuary to walk to the house in the dunes. The man didn't own a car, so that was another avenue of enquiry closed off to him. He would have to be patient, if only for another day. If nothing had turned up by then he would have to load some porn on this computer and find some mafia lowlife to fit up for killing him and throwing his body into the sea from the Ust Luga ferry.

But sure enough, patience was rewarded in an unexpected way. In amongst the legions of negative enquiries building up in the case file was a surprising entry from a housekeeper of a holiday let in the village just across the water. Apparently she had seen a small tent set up on the edge of the woods at the far end of the village. She had noticed it by chance when walking her dog nearby and had not paid any attention at first, as she thought it belonged to one of the itinerant surfers who would often arrive in the locality at this time of year. What had sparked her curiosity was that nothing appeared to have changed around the impromptu campsite for the past three days, which she thought surprising, as she walked her dog nearby morning and night. On the fourth day she had plucked up courage to take a closer look and was surprised to find it empty, with just an old crumpled Polish newspaper in it from the previous week. Try as he might, Arbutsev could not find any records of Poles with authority to stay in the vicinity. He widened his search to look at those with temporary visas who had been in Kaliningrad, or Baltiysk people who had cause to go the other way, either to Gdansk, Elblag or Bartoszyce. He found six names; each would be verified. The hours passed, six was whittled down to one – a day tripper, Stefan Zanowsky of Gdansk. Credit card checks would follow, and he would ask one of his colleagues at the consulate in the nearby Polish city to make further enquiries. At least he would have something to talk about the next time Nikitin called. The Moscow train records, and commercial flight listings were of no help. This was his only lead. And even if it could be established, what possible reason would Ponomariev have to associate with some bum from Gdansk? He certainly had not joined Zanowsky on the tourist bus back to Kaliningrad. Unless maybe bum was the word – could Ponomariev be into free love from whatever quarter it came? Maybe this Zanowsky had killed him because of some failed tryst. This far-fetched conjecture would probably help him to stay in his job until he could get some incriminating material onto the confiscated laptop. That would at least give his masters some reassurance that the situation was under control. Nikitin had listened carefully to Arbutsev's entertaining explanation.

"It is certainly a creative theory, but now you must ground it in some fact. We need to find Ponomariev dead or alive. I think you should first rule out the possibility he is alive, because, according to you, if this option is correct, he must be somewhere in Kaliningrad Oblast. He's not in Rostov or Moscow or even up north – that we do know. In which case, why would he hide? The other possibility is he has escaped. How is that possible? Where could he have gone and who helped him? I don't think you have exhausted all the possibilities there. Of course, it might be easier for you if you find his body, then we could return our focus to other pressing matters. Get on it and update me tomorrow." The call ended abruptly.

As far as Arbutsev was concerned the options were narrowing. If the Doctor Professor had escaped Kaliningrad it was not by air or land; sea had yet to be investigated. All ships leaving port in the past seventy-two hours – military or civilian – would be checked and instructions were duly issued, but there was still this Zanowsky guy to think about. Common sense made a connection with Ponomariev unlikely at best, but he had a feeling, a copper's hunch, there was some link that would explain the situation. It transpired there had been thirty-two ships out of the Pregolya estuary in the period, with destinations in other parts of Russia and the Baltic and a few further afield, such as Reykjavik and Luanda. These long-distance voyages were dismissed as being pointless for Ponomariev, but perhaps inadvertently joining one of the Arctic patrol vessels seemed more likely, offering the prospect of observing their weapons systems in operation in theatre. Just so that he could knock it off his list of targets, he had sent an investigator out to talk to the local fishing crews. He had remembered how bad the weather had been over the past few days and was pretty sure that Ponomariev would not have relished this as an escape route, especially as one of the ships' commissars would have reported if they were carrying an unauthorised crew member. The returns from all his enquiries were drawing blanks and the end of the day was approaching. He needed a beer or perhaps something stronger. He got his coat and walked out of his office towards the town centre and into the first drinking den he came to – the *Ded Pivko* bar.

Baltika beer in hand, he casually watched a group of off-duty sailors playing pool while still preoccupied with the mystery of the disappearing Doctor Professor.

"Don't worry, *tovarisch*, it will probably never happen." He looked up to see Vladimir Moscovoi, one of the fishermen's commissars, offering a brown-toothed smile through wild, black facial hair.

It would have been tempting to act as though he was surprised at seeing him, but that wasn't the case. Firstly, Moscovoi was one of the few people these days who still used the term *tovarisch* and those who did were the old-timers, who after some forty years still thought they lived in a Soviet paradise. Secondly, this would be the time for the fishing crews to do their drinking as they contemplated another hazardous night out on the waves.

It was quite a good job being a fishermen's commissar. You didn't really have to do that much, just check the charts with the skipper and make sure the crew behaved themselves on board. For the most part their job was to listen to the banter on board, make the tea in the canteen and report back any useful gossip to the harbourmaster's office. In that sense Moscovoi had common cause with Arbutsev. He regarded his weekly reports as an exercise in fiction, if only to provide him and his readers with a little light entertainment and to ensure he had absolved himself from any potential illegal activities on board. Officially, smoking and drinking were banned at sea, as were drug-taking and sex, but it all happened from time to time and Moscovoi was known to take an editor's commission to ensure the names of offenders were omitted from his reports, as the mere mention of names in the wrong context could mean a job would be lost or an already meagre salary would be halved. It was inevitable he would ask about his recent trips out on the B474 with Igor Poliarkin, but nonetheless, even by Moscovoi's standards, he was surprised at the vague response.

"Same old, same old," was the answer to his question about whether he had seen anything unusual.

"That's a bit of a surprise," observed the investigator. "One of my sources tells me you had a very expensive night out a couple of days ago with that woman, Lyudmilla, from the tourist office."

Moscovoi looked alarmed.

"Oh that, yes – I had to fit *that* around my other responsibilities."

"Responsibilities?"

"Yes, getting the paperwork authorised in the harbourmaster's office."

"So, you were able to do all that, fuck one of the best-looking available women in Baltiysk and get to sea in the space of a couple of hours? I've heard about quickies, but that is going some. You must tell me your secret. How did you get off with her, do the business and catch the boat?"

"Ah but the boat was over an hour late leaving port and she was tucked up by the time I left."

"Tucked up, you reckon?"

"You can ask her or ask Igor."

"My men have done. Lyudmilla is an airhead who will say whatever she is paid to say, and the skipper, Igor, backs your story because he knows what will happen otherwise. Are you sure you have nothing to add?"

The commissar took a long pull on his cigarette and stared at his boots.

"That's it."

"Looks like your skipper did you a favour. According to the port radar he was exactly one hundred minutes late leaving Tuesday night, so it looks like your story holds up – for now. Imagine my disappointment if I discover I`m wrong. Imagine the *consequences* for you..."

"It's getting a bit smelly in here. Must be the bullshit I just stepped in. Time I went to work in the fresh air."

The commissar finished his bottle with a flamboyant swig and headed for the door.

Arbutsev still had his doubts. He would keep Moscovoi as a reserve card if he failed to make progress elsewhere.

FOUR

KELLY HAD TAKEN THE ICE Bahn from Berlin to Hamburg – a relatively short two-hour hop – and changed onto the S-Bahn for the journey out to the airport to pick up a car for the drive north to Flensburg and the Danish border. He had occupied his time fiddling with his phone; checking up on the CCTV at home, answering some LinkedIn posts, including a couple of contacts he had met for the first time at the conference. Getting to the airport to collect the car had been the easy part. The problems started as he weaved his way through the congested streets towards the autobahn route 7. The passing countryside of Schleswig-Holstein, a mix of meadows and woods, was unremarkable, not helped by the leaden grey sky overhead. It had been a while since he had last driven any distance in Germany and he still had the idea that speed limits did not apply on a road like this. Clearly, he had failed to keep up with the times and certainly on this road there were speed gates every fifteen kilometres. If he transgressed, he knew he would be getting a letter from the car hire company, but fortunately he had avoided hiring a big swanky Mercedes and had settled for a more modest sporty Fiat hatchback, which despite his coaxing was never going to get over 100 kph. Never mind. For his purpose, it was fine. Driving north on this road still had an urban feel to it despite having left the city behind. He wondered how long it would take him to get to the border and if he'd be stopped. The answer to his question soon came to his attention when the speed limit dropped, the road widened for a short distance and a Danish police patrol car was parked next to the carriageway with a blue flashing light. A portly figure with a bush hat, dressed in khaki with sunglasses (a Danish policeman perhaps) stood next to the car, staring at the passing traffic as if he was waiting for a bus. This man didn't look to Kelly like a figure of authority. The Fiat bumped as it went over a ridge in the road. The signage changed colour and he knew he had arrived. It was amazing how the vista had changed in just a few short minutes. This was rural Denmark all right, but somehow the countryside looked richer, neater, and more prosperous. The effect was heightened also by the fact that the road became narrower and more congested as a result. He took the first exit off the main road, turned left and immediately drove into a picture postcard scene. Suddenly the landscape felt deserted, the traffic disappeared, and the road ahead was no longer the preserve of time-stressed commuters or logistics trucks. This was the territory of the most successful type of Danish business – the white-walled, red-roofed pig farm – their bacon the iconic symbol of their nation. Fortunately, Kelly was being guided by his satnav, which indulged him by speaking English. Despite having driven over one hundred kilometres his guide told him he still had ninety minutes to run. *Ninety minutes – if I blink I'll miss Denmark altogether on that timescale*, he thought. It was a further forty-five minutes before he picked up the first signpost for Rømø, another left turn. By now the trees had largely left the horizon and his vision was taken with an expansive view of land and sky. This place was starting to offer an odd juxtaposition of verdant desolation. A seemingly forgotten part of the world, featureless, overlooked. Yet it conveyed a sense of anticipation as though the grass and the hedges bordering the road were waiting for something to happen. Another odd experience was coming to a roundabout in this wilderness. It offered three alternative routes, but to the layman none offered any distinctive features to help the first-time visitor, except of course another sign pointing the way to Rømø.

Already he was starting to understand why Rømø was offering the services he was coming to find out about. Here was a place where time had not stopped, but was working to rule. Here, he got the impression that nothing happening in the outside world mattered. This place would just jog along in its own sweet way.

He sensed he was now close, arriving at the start of a long straight causeway with shallow sea and mudflats on both sides. Driving straight, it was easy to get the feeling there was no way back. He had now committed himself to his short-term future. Was this the beginning of the end or the end of the beginning? He was about to find out. Initially, for some strange reason, he drew confidence from seeing a petrol station. The first building on the island side. Already this looked like some sort of sophisticated buttress against the forces of anonymity and neglect. And then another roundabout and another left turn.

Journey's end was ahead – Havneby – where some three-quarters of the island's population were said to live. He decided to pick up the pace at this point. Navigation was no longer needed.

He just had to go on to the end of the road.

*

Sue had ambivalent feelings towards Des. She liked to have him around, but not too close. She was happy when he was either locked in a laboratory at work or in his 'den' in the paddock at home, provided he didn't get too involved in her busy and active social life. In fact, she would freely acknowledge that Des had an important role to play. Without his inflated income from the Lauriston she would not have the freedoms that she most dearly valued. So looking after the dog while he was away 'junketing', as she thought, was a small price to pay. But there was no doubt the unusual incident of the phoney break-in had unnerved her. Despite the attentions of Milo, she felt uneasy at being home alone. It wasn't just a matter of company. She was already well practised in solving that issue. It was more about feeling safe. It was difficult for her to invite friends or neighbours from the village, as some (perhaps understandably) chose to misunderstand the invitation, thinking there was more on offer than a civilised glass of wine and a chat. She had confided to some extent in Abigail, who was between engagements and would benefit from a quiet couple of days in the country. Maybe it was a family thing, but her daughter picked up on her anxiety.

"You can't keep on worrying about what might have happened," she told her mother. "If they were serious, they would have just broken in, stolen your jewellery, wrecked the place or whatever. Seems Dad arrived at exactly the right time."

"No, he didn't. He was in the pub and only turned up when he did because I called him in a panic."

"So at least he scared them off. There was more than one of them – right?"

"I couldn't tell. I definitely saw the silhouette of one of them, but I think there was another one as well."

"How can you be so sure? The only light you had was from the car headlights and that only made the night seem darker. Maybe it was that guy who used to be in the TV commercial skiing down a mountain to give the woman he admired a box of chocolates," she started to laugh.

Her mother was forced to smile.

"Now come on, where did you see that? On YouTube? You're not old enough to remember."

"Well, I might know more about it than you think. The chap who runs my agency says they are doing a remake for a new generation. He thinks boxes of chocolates are an outdated concept that manufacturers are struggling to keep alive. But I don't care if it's another job; after all, and saves me having to take my clothes off."

The remark had been calculated to get a shocked reaction from her mother. Surprisingly, it didn't.

"I don't understand how you make a go of being an actress. The only proper jobs are in TV series or films, and there can't be enough to go round."

"That's only one way of looking at it – there is always the theatre. But the growing area of work is product placement on social media. If I recommend beauty products on my vlog that is a sure way to get money in. That and the shopping channel on cable TV. Have you ever watched it? It's amazing how long those presenters can keep talking about vacuum cleaners, but people still watch it."

They made dinner together and continued making small talk over the TV news.

"And what about boyfriends?" asked her mother.

"What about them?"

"Are you going steady with anyone at the moment?"

"One or two, but no one I'm ready to bring home, just in case you were wondering. You?"

"What do you mean?"

"Come on, Mum, you've always been a bit of a head turner. Don't tell me you've not been tempted to look over the fence when Dad's away."

"Abigail! What a suggestion!" her mother feigned indignancy and paused.

"Maybe there have been moments." She paused again.

"But that is a bit like going shopping, isn't it? It's one thing to look in the window, it's another thing to go inside."

It seemed the time with her daughter was just the tonic she had been looking for.

The frivolity of the exchanges had lifted her mood, as had the shared bottle of chardonnay.

It was a quiet night in the village – nothing but the soft hum of the valley and the occasional squawk of a barn owl looking for a midnight feast.

The following morning it was time for the start of the daily routine for Sue but today Abigail came with her. These days, private time between mother and daughter was precious, especially when they didn't seem to have their usual disagreements. There was no more talk about her life in London or her 'bohemian' flatmates, just a moment to enjoy the peace and tranquillity of the countryside. When they returned home, Sue decided to make coffee before realising she had run out of milk.

Abigail grabbed her bag and headed for the door on her way to the village shop. It was just after nine in the morning.

Sue hadn't given the matter another thought. Hadn't even said goodbye. Milo was preoccupied with a bone on the kitchen floor.

The village shop was half a mile away and the route involved a public footpath which ran behind a neighbour's garden. The day was bright and clear. Her mother estimated the round trip would take no more than twenty minutes but after an hour there was no sign of her.

Gradually, Sue's sunny disposition gave way to panic. Where was she? It was only a small village. There was no prospect of her getting lost. She called her mobile, which just went to voicemail. She grabbed her coat and keys and set off in the same direction, retracing her route.

Her mind started to race. She really hadn't thought about what she was expecting to find. Could Abi have fallen over, twisted an ankle, perhaps broken a leg or even been hit by a car or just stopped to engage in a conversation with a neighbour? She took the shortest route using the public footpath. Nothing appeared out of the ordinary or out of place and no sign of anyone. Milo stopped periodically to sniff the ground but it was clear his interest was not trying to follow the scent of Abi, but the trail of other assorted dogs which had recently made the same journey.

She had to cross a main road to get to the village shop which was again deserted. Tying Milo's lead to a drainpipe, outside the front of the shop, Sue went inside, to be greeted by Mrs Harris, the proprietor, herself a village institution alongside the premises itself.

"Morning, Mrs Harris, have you seen my daughter, Abigail? She came down here about an hour ago to get some milk, but I think she must have got sidetracked or delayed."

"That's a pity. I'd have loved to have seen her. I don't think she's been in here for more than a year. If she'd been in, we'd probably still be talking, but not this morning, no, not at all."

Mrs Harris looked ready to start a round of gossip with her in the hope of picking up some juicy titbits to share with other local customers. The banter was a key feature which kept locals coming in, or so she thought. Sue Kelly was always a topic of interest to her, but right now, the object of her attention showed no signs of dallying. Instead, all she got was muttered thanks and a faint smile as she departed. She showed no interest in buying milk. Collecting Milo and now on the edge of the village green, she saw a postman emptying the box.

"Excuse me, have you seen a young woman – blondish – walking around here in the last hour?"

The postman looked at her and smiled.

"I'd remember if I did, but I've only been doing deliveries here for the last twenty minutes. In this job you don't get to see as much you'd think. I spend most of my time on the lookout for pets like yours." He paused, adjusting his distance to ensure he was out of Milo's reach.

"No, the only thing I have to report that has been out of the ordinary was some nutter in a van with blacked-out windows accelerating up the lane in the middle of the road when I arrived. God knows how he missed the front wing of mine. I didn't want to have to go back to the depot to explain that."

"When was that?"

"Over half an hour since. It was coming out of the village while I was approaching. Don't think they were expecting something coming the other way at this hour. I guess it was some tradesman late for a job."

The postman smiled and nodded, understanding that would be the end of the conversation. He collected his sack and threw it into the back of his van. Sue continued her odyssey towards the Dog & Duck. Bryan, the landlord, was opening the cellar in anticipation of a delivery from the draymen. He stopped to wave his greeting.

Sue and Milo walked over to meet him. A similar exchange took place, but this time with a slightly different ending.

"I'll have a word with Stuart, my odd-job man. He was down here earlier on and comes past your house on the way here. Maybe he saw something? If he did, I'll give you a call."

Sue had now exhausted all likely leads and set off back to the house. Outside she stopped and called Abi's mobile again. It went to voicemail once more. What to do? She'd call Des. Maybe he might have some ideas. Again, Des's mobile went to voicemail. Who else? Gavin. He'd be useless but would be a sympathetic ear and, at least, he did answer his phone. She endured the expected introductory platitudes culminating with the observation, "Maybe she has a friend – a secret friend – in the neighbourhood she wanted to see?" The inference was clear – like mother, like daughter, she was away sowing her own wild oats. Was he serious? "We're talking about nine in the bloody morning!"

Not many people she knew were looking for sex at that time of day. But it was clear the thought had crossed his mind. In reality, he had been smarting from Bannan's observations.

"I'll pop round later if you like, to see how you're getting on."

Patronising bastard, she thought.

There was only one person left to confide in; her son, Miles.

He had listened carefully to his mother and understood she was on edge. His words were the best tonic.

"Sit tight at home, Mum. If Abi is in trouble she will expect you to be there. If she hasn't shown up by tonight let me know and I'll see if I can get in touch with some of her friends."

It was difficult advice to ignore. She had run out of options.

Back home, Sue tried to busy herself with mundane housekeeping tasks – tidying up, vacuuming the carpets, doing the ironing – but these provided little comfort.

It was just after four when the phone rang. It was Bryan from the pub.

"Hello, Sue. I did say I'd catch up with Stuart after we spoke earlier, and he came back with something unusual. He was on his bike coming over this morning when he was overtaken by a black van with blacked-out windows. Got so close it nearly pushed him into a hedge. Anyway, a bit further on he saw the van stopped up ahead with its hazard lights on and what he thought was a commotion going on at the side. He half wondered if there had been an accident and was about to stop and help but a big bloke suddenly came towards him, gesturing him to pedal on past. So he did, but he thought he saw two other people fighting or struggling by the side door of the van, which was open on the nearside by the hedge. He thought it didn't look right, but didn't want to appear nosey. Of course it might have nothing to do with Abi but it's clear this was happening in the right place at the right time, so I thought you should know. It's probably worth calling the police."

It wasn't just the police she called. Miles took the first and said he'd make a couple of enquiries (to whom he didn't specify), then he'd drive over; and having tried once more unsuccessfully to reach Des, she had settled on Gavin. He arrived at the house within the hour. He had hoped the emotion of the moment would draw her closer to him and was slightly disappointed at her cool and distant greeting at the door, a welcome echoed by Milo who offered a growl before walking off to his bed.

"I understand it's very worrying. You shouldn't jump to conclusions. I expect it will all work out fine over the next couple of days," he had said. His words were meant to be reassuring but didn't do much for her confidence. He had been prepared to stay to support her once the police arrived, but having introduced himself and explained why he was there, she signalled she wanted him to leave.

It was the same two uniformed officers who had attended to investigate the intruder at the house and that experience seemed to have coloured their judgement. She endured their rather flat-footed questioning – had they had a row, what was she wearing, did she have her purse, could she think of anywhere she might have gone? They had dolefully noted the particulars, asked for a photograph of Abi and said they would make further enquiries.

The older one, a sergeant, made the point that, statistically, it was not uncommon for young people just to take off without any warning and she should try not to worry. In the meantime, he would inform the Met and take a look on local traffic cameras to try and trace the black van. The steady stream of visitors concluded with the arrival of Miles and that was when the emotion of the moment caught up with her as she hugged and cried in her son's arms. Miles said he had been to Abi's place to speak to her flatmates. He too had drawn a blank. No, she was fine and had no reason to disappear, especially as she had an audition the following week. They took Milo for an evening walk, ate pizza from the freezer and shared a bottle of wine to dull the pain. Tomorrow was a new day and might bring better news.

*

Williams and Moore may have sounded like a firm of old-fashioned Savile Row tailors but were 'Winston' Bannan's best agents in Germany. Neither knew quite how their boss had picked up his nickname, but somehow it seemed to suit his demeanour as an archetypal patriot. The man and woman were highly experienced observers used to trailing subjects of interest in an unobtrusive way. They had the misfortune to be in the wrong place at the wrong time. Normally based in Berlin, they had gone to Hamburg, documenting meetings the leaders of an Albanian people-trafficking gang, domiciled in Kent, were having with local contacts. Having completed their handover to colleagues at the BND, German intelligence service, they were expecting to take a flight back to London but had then had a new instruction to hire a camper van and go to Denmark. Williams did the hiring and driving, Moore studied the brief on her encrypted phone.

"So, it's windsurfing and sandsailing on the beach this weekend for us," she announced cheerily.

"That will be nice," her colleague said sardonically. "I had tickets for the Emirates tomorrow."

"Oh, we'll have more fun than that."

"What could be more fun than the match and a few beers at Finsbury Park?" Williams lamented.

"I was expecting to go and see my mum and dad in St Neots," Chemmy Moore announced. "Still, a bit of sun and sea air will be a real bonus."

"Who are we looking out for?"

"A nuclear physicist called Desmond Kelly. Winston wants to know what he's doing this weekend. Thinks he might be going native."

"What does 'going native' in Denmark look like? Stripping off and running down the beach?"

"Apparently, he's going up there on his own, but no one knows why. None of his family are involved and he doesn't appear to have any love interest. Maybe he's a secret twitcher."

"So?"

"So that's what we're being sent to find out."

"And why are we in this thing?"

"Because there is nowhere to stay in this place, and if you don't have a log cabin you'll be sleeping under the stars."

"Sounds romantic."

"Only if you are there with the right person. Besides, I am told it gets windy, so you will need some shelter and most people who go up there go in one of these."

“Well, that’s OK – I’m sure ‘Winnie’ will agree having a case of beer in the back will complete our cover. As we’re short of surf boards and sand yachts, I assume we are twitching, too.”

“Our essential equipment will be binoculars and a laptop to record sightings of the lesser spotted Kelly,” Chemmy announced.

“In the meantime, I have ten questions to ask you about birdwatching. I want to see how much you can learn before we arrive, but first let’s see where our target is. The last time I tracked his phone he was about an hour ahead, so I guess he must already be enjoying the sea air.”

Moore was right. Kelly had just arrived at Havneby, the main village on the island, and checked into the local ‘Kro’, an inn with rooms. He dropped his bags and sat on the bed, taking in the view from his window, the sea straight ahead. Just beyond was a detached, single-level women’s dress shop and esplanade; to the left, a parts warehouse operated by a wind farm company and to the right assorted bungalows nestling in sand dunes. It was not as he had expected. The vista was that of a modest working harbour with some small fishing boats, a little car ferry plying the short route to the German island of Sylt and light engineering services, not the holiday beach of sunny days and ice creams. And yet he had come to meet Nils, the friendly fellow from the YouTube video who was going to help him to plan his death. It all seemed a bit surreal. His visit to Rømø was private; he was not intending to leave an electronic trail of his movements and dealings. He had arranged to meet Nils in the little bar downstairs at 7pm so before then he would go for a walk and explore the locality. The wind had got up since his arrival and he was pleased to have a coat to insulate him as he walked. Coming out of the Kro he had chosen to turn right, then right again to a modern low-level complex of holiday flats above a range of shops and a small general foodstore geared towards serving the interests of the nautical industry. Of course, most of these shops were in the business of selling sports and leisure wear, surf boards and windsurfing paraphernalia. Yet from what he could see of his surroundings there really wasn't anywhere to be seen wearing or using it. Walking away from the block of holiday lets, a major car park emerged from the dunes with a tourist information block off to the right and a couple of cosy but pretty utilitarian restaurants to the left. Again, what was odd was that at this time, there were only one or two cars to be seen but no people. Walking in the direction of the sea, the car park gave way to a residential road of small summer houses on the right, before becoming a pathway climbing up an incline on the side of a bund to the esplanade once more. Surely there was more to this place than he could see. He remembered looking at the island online and seeing a huge expanse of beach, but wherever it was it was clearly out of sight from his present position.

It was time to wander back to the Kro, this time along the coastal path. This experience was becoming stranger by the minute. Looking inland into the sedge-topped dunes his attention was caught by a sudden movement. He stopped to look again to see not just one, but four brown hares bouncing around in the scrub, oblivious to him and probably anyone else who might have been passing. The experience was heightening his sense of solitude. To his relief the atmosphere changed once he got inside the inn. It was now a little after six in the evening and guests were starting to arrive for dinner and already the adjoining bar was getting busy. He ordered a bottle of the local brew, made at the back of the inn and flavoured with samphire, apparently collected from the mythical beach. If that seemed like an odd flavour for a beer it was – but it certainly wasn't unpleasant. He pulled his travel guide out of his jacket pocket to finally ascertain where this wonderful beach was, as so far, he had failed to spot it. All these impressions were contributing to a strange excitement as he anticipated meeting his contact. He was quite pleased he had finished the beer before his meeting started. He had to admit he was now starting to feel more relaxed. So relaxed he had stopped looking at the clock and answered a couple of pieces of 'fan mail' on LinkedIn. Had he done so, he would have seen Nils was nearly twenty minutes late, but apart from their planned discussion, he had some time to kill as well.

Of course, when Nils arrived, Des recognised him straightaway. Kelly himself must have been equally conspicuous as Nils spotted him directly.

"Mr Kelly, I presume? I am Nils Westergaard. A pleasure to meet you and welcome to our little community. I hope you didn't have too much trouble finding us, and I am pleased to see you are already starting to enjoy our beer, here in one of the most historical places in our village. In 1644, the Danish King Christian IV was aboard his flagship, the *Trefoldigheden* (Trinity in English) in the List Deep, a sea channel five kilometres to the south of here and defeated a Dutch-Swedish fleet offshore. Further skirmishes ensued, resulting in the King being wounded, losing an eye. Those on board thought he had died and ordered the flag to be lowered. Seaman Gram from Ballum on the mainland, just across the water from Havneby, disobeyed the order. The Danes fought on and won. The King summoned the brave seaman and offered to grant him a wish. Seaman Gram asked for the sole right to run a ferry service 'in perpetuity' from Ballum to this island. Christian IV granted the strange request; permission to build an inn and the Royal Privilege to sell alcohol followed. So I have a tradition to uphold. Brewing is one of my businesses that I run when I am not out catching fish or helping my family to cook what I catch at my restaurant over there."

He gestured in the general direction of the back wall.

"Making a living in this part of the world is hard; you need to have a number of complementary skills and trades."

"I have made a plan for your stay. The programme is contained in this folder. Don't worry about getting to the right places at the right time. I will be taking you personally to each appointment. By the time we are finished you should understand what is involved in our service and be able to know whether it is right for you. You can read it later. For now, we will eat in the Kro's restaurant next door. Tonight, I will tell you a little bit more about me and this place and why I think you will decide this is right for you. Please."

They took their beers through to the restaurant. Nils didn't need to speak to any of the staff. They clearly knew he had his regular table.

"We will have a traditional Danish supper of five fish courses, rye bread, beer and aquavit. The fish you will have is cured and smoked in our own smokehouse. Yes, it is mine also, so I can tell you it's excellent quality and a great way to introduce our local cuisine."

The evening started well with the first course of wild brown trout washed down with a glass of neat caraway-flavoured *snaps*.

"*Skal!* I must commend you, Mr Kelly, for your curiosity. I wasn't sure what to expect when I placed the original advertisement in the British magazine. It was a risk. I am pleased to say you and five others have taken up the invitation to come here. You are the first, so we are very keen to make sure we answer all of your questions, but firstly one from me. Why are you interested in what we do?"

His guest unburdened himself.

"I have advanced prostate cancer which has spread elsewhere. My medication is becoming less effective. I am living with increasing pain. I am scared. I can only deal with the fear by taking control to manage my death on my terms. I have contemplated suicide, but even under these circumstances, taking my own life seems an unnatural act and would require bravery that I am not sure I possess. You can help me find the courage and commitment I need to reach a satisfactory, early conclusion."

"Your wishes and circumstances are more common than you might imagine. I am sorry to hear of your predicament and I hope my team will be able to help. We should begin by explaining the point of coming here as opposed to, say, going to Switzerland. It is not to suggest Rømø is better than central Europe but we have something special that no one else has. It's not about our little island but the sea which surrounds it. Not the North Sea, but what we call the Wadden Sea. This sea is characterised by its shallowness, which delivers a great change in the landscape as the tide runs back and forth. In fact, in some places, the water level can vary by up to two metres in normal weather conditions. During a winter storm flood, it can rise by up to three or four metres , which is also why we have built sea defences along the coast to limit the number of flooded fields, villages and roads. Behind these lies marshland, which has a unique appearance with its bare and flat surface. It has developed naturally from material that has been supplied over many thousands of years by the tide bringing organic matter and clay along the coast. This clay and soil are incredibly fertile for both plants and animals. In fact, today you will find many herbs and plants that only grow in the marsh and the Wadden Sea area.

"Interesting though all this is, the real value of this location is the shifting sands. Here, you can almost recreate the near biblical experience of walking on water. There are routes where you can paddle with just your ankles beneath the surface, perhaps for up to three kilometres from the shore in certain directions, but suddenly the sand collapses and sucks you down. This can be a very unforgiving place. These routes are constantly changing and sometimes with extreme results. My brother makes a good living running a dredger. He has to work every day to keep a deeper water channel open for the Sylt car ferry. If he stops working, the ferry must stop, usually within forty-eight hours. Nearly fifty years ago we were not the most southerly island in Denmark. There was another, Jordsand. Over the preceding years it got smaller and smaller until the last residents had to leave. Now it is barely a sandbank. Have no doubt these waters are dangerous, even for me. Without warning you can be pulled into a quicksand which few can escape. Further, for those suffering this fate, there is no trace, bodies disappear into the sand and are never recovered. It is this experience that has informed our thinking of assisted suicide.

Even if we complete all the preparation stages, come the day of your departure we cannot guarantee success. Your demise is down to fate and natural phenomena. But when it works, which is most of the time, there is no doubt if you are planning to finish your days, a death here is quick, complete and untraceable, without the need for any prejudicial medicines."

Kelly was starting to adjust to the topic of conversation. Westergaard sounded so matter of fact, down to earth, as though he was selling a ticket for a fairground ride. His host read his expression.

"Please, don't misunderstand me, Mr Kelly. I fully recognise the sensitivities of this business. But that is exactly what it is – just a business. Not much different to some landowners in your own country operating burials for people seeking non-religious humanist services, only we encourage fate to give a helping hand. You're a paying customer; it is down to you to decide whether you want to buy our service. My view, and that of my colleagues you will meet during your visit, is that death is part of life, not a subject to be swept under the carpet but properly planned for, if not celebrated. Here, as much as nature allows, you are in control of the process; our job is to meet our responsibilities efficiently."

"Have you helped many people on this journey?"

"Maybe twenty or more. Quite a few start the process but drop out before the conclusion. Not everyone is strong enough to confront the challenges of preparation. Like any business our charges are sufficient to ensure we make a profit but again, the services we offer are not and will not be a mass market activity. For me, you are already understanding I have to make a living on this little island tucked away in the middle of nowhere, so I have many jobs and several different hats, as do the other few people who have their home, year-round, here."

"You talk about the challenges of preparation. What do you mean?"

"We will get to the detail on all that tomorrow, but we have to ensure all our customers have the right mindset. This requires a lot from the individual as well as from us, as the organisers. The steps we have developed I think are unique and based on the suggestions in many cases of previous customers. As you can imagine, that must be reconciled with legal requirements also, so like most other things in life, there is some paperwork we need to do to safeguard you and also us. But rest assured, as far as I can tell, we haven't had any complaints."

It was a well-timed remark designed to lighten the mood. They both laughed.

"Anyway for now, enough about me. You know I am a fisherman, restaurant owner, brewer, owner of holiday homes, and yes, unofficially an undertaker. But you?"

"I am a scientist, working in the energy sector."

"Wind? We have that here."

Kelly made his own light-hearted remark.

"Ask me after dinner."

They laughed some more. He was warming to his host.

"No, nuclear energy. I understand many consider it dangerous, but the science has moved on. It's much more efficient and sustainable than it used to be."

"That sounds interesting – we care passionately about nature here in Denmark. Will your work make us cleaner and safer?"

"As I said, I am a scientist – I do research and make discoveries. Others decide how these tools should be used."

"I detect you are not happy with these 'others' as you call them."

"As scientists we have a thirst for discovery and most seek that knowledge for the betterment of humankind. Unfortunately, our sponsors – the people who pay us – bring their own agendas to the table and apply our expertise for outcomes which, shall we say, are not for the benefit of all. In my career I have seen this on many occasions, and it tires me.

"Now, I am old. I have this critical physical diagnosis. There is a new generation that has to solve these puzzles – we will all be the poorer if they don't."

"Do you have children?"

"Two, one of each, but grown up and moved away."

"And your wife?"

"What about her?"

"Does she know what you are contemplating?"

"No. We share a house and a dog but that's about it. She has her life, I have mine. I suspect her life is a bit more interesting…"

"Because…?"

"Let's say she has a much fuller social life than me."

"How do you feel about that?"

"What do you expect me to say? Pissed off is the term that springs to mind. I'm pretty sure she won't miss me, when I've gone – anymore than she's missing me right now."

*

At that moment, Des would have been proved wrong.

Although she was relieved to have Miles to keep her company, she missed the opportunity to confide in her husband. Whatever his perceived feelings, he probably understood her as much as anyone else after thirty years of marriage. She still had a reluctance to share her innermost worries with her son. She knew she was in a state of confusion and anxiety and her thoughts of missing Des were at best contrary to her actions when he was around. Privately, she knew she lived a double life and certainly didn't want Des to know about her social failings, as she thought of them, and yet she badly wanted to speak to him. God knows she tried to call him. He must have had the five messages she had left on his mobile by now. She knew he had gone to Berlin, but having checked with the Adlon they had no forwarding address. She vaguely remembered him saying he was going to take a short break after the conference before returning home, but she had not been listening. Try as she might, she could not recall what he had said. He would not be back for a couple of days.

So far, she was getting through this with the help of Miles doing the cooking and walking the dog, Des's best single malt whisky and a pack of sleeping pills. Left to her own devices, she had no desire to leave her bedroom, let alone the house. She was starting to feel the outside world was encroaching on her and the bedroom door was her last line of defence.

FIVE

"MUM, ARE YOU OK?" Miles called through her door. She had to respond or else he would come in.

"Yes darling, I'm getting up."

"The police are here. They want to talk to you."

She looked at her watch. It was after ten in the morning.

Last time she had checked, it was just after ten the previous evening.

God, she thought, *I feel rough*, and thought better of looking at herself in the mirror.

"Can you put some coffee on? I`m just going to take a quick shower."

Dressed and freshened up, with a minimum amount of makeup to avoid scaring the dog, she emerged from her first-floor sanctuary. Downstairs in the lounge, her son was seated with two men, one bespectacled in a well-worn crumpled blue suit, the other, probably ten years younger, in cords and a black leather bomber jacket.

Miles started the introductions.

"This is Detective Chief Inspector…"

"Willoughby," he of the crumpled suit intervened.

"This is my Sergeant – Abraham, New Scotland Yard. I'm sorry to arrive unannounced. The case of your daughter's disappearance has been referred to us. I don't know if you are aware, but instances of suspected abduction are always passed to the Met for investigation."

"Abduction? You think she has been kidnapped?" Miles had articulated his mother's thoughts.

"We don't know for sure, but it is fair to say that there appears to be no other explanation for recent events. This is not a high-crime area, the perpetrators appear to have come from elsewhere, there is no sign of her on her journey to a local shop which she never arrived at, an eyewitness who claims to have witnessed a minor disturbance at the bottom of the road and an attempted break-in at your home a couple of weeks earlier. It is clear to us that someone has either an interest in this property or the people who live here. You will not have been targeted by accident. Thames Valley have made their initial report. We think we identified a vehicle of interest on the A34 close to the M4 junction and expect to have some news on that shortly, so this investigation is escalating. We have tried contacting your husband through work and understand he's been away in Germany for the past few days. He has a message to contact us, but in the meantime if you talk to him, please let him know we would like a chat sooner rather than later. I understand he is not due to be back at work until next Monday?"

"That's right." Sue nodded and smiled hesitatingly.

"I want to build up a picture of the circumstances leading up to your daughter's disappearance. I've already got members of my team talking to her flatmates in West Acton and it's been good to have had a word with her brother here, just now, but there are a couple of things I wanted to hear from you, Mrs Kelly. Firstly, I understand Abigail was staying with you during your husband's absence on business and that she did so to reassure you of your safety following this attempted break-in – that's right?"

Sue nodded.

"And Abigail herself was OK, not stressed or worried about anything?"

"Not as far as I'm aware. She's an actress so she is always dealing with the uncertainty of getting work – advertisements, TV, film, you know. When she's not working, she earns some money working behind the bar in a pub."

"The Dryborough Arms? Yes, we're looking into that."

"In fact, I know she was supposed to be doing an audition for some new chocolate commercial this week which she definitely would not want to miss."

"We saw the picture of her you gave to the Thames Valley guys. She's very attractive. What about boyfriends?"

"She was always popular with the boys but she kept that part of her life to herself. In fact, we were talking the other night and the subject came up and she said there was no one serious."

"And you would agree, Mr Kelly?"

"Absolutely – I think as her brother I would be less likely to know than Mum."

"And turning to the attempted break-in a couple of weeks back. This is the first time you have had this type of trouble since you've lived here?"

"Yes, we've been here well over ten years."

"Mmm. I don't need to go through all that now. I've read the reports and seen the pictures of the footprint. One thing though – your dog."

"Yes, we have a Rottweiler – he's in the kitchen. Do you want to see him?"

"No, no," Abraham intervened for the first time, "that will not be necessary."

"The incident report states that your dog was temporarily incapacitated, because of the attack. The vet's report claimed it to be some type of tranquilliser dart. But there is no other reference to it. Do you know where it went?"

"No. I think it was recovered by my husband, but what he did with it, I don't know. He is normally very precise and tidy. I expect he threw it away."

"Why would he do that?"

"Mum said that was what she thought. It's not the same thing as saying that was what he did. She doesn't know."

"I understand, thank you, Mr Kelly. We will discuss that further when we catch up with your father."

"Finally, for now, Mrs Kelly, have you had any strange phone calls or other form of communication about your daughter?"

"What do you mean?"

"In the case of an abduction it is normal for the victim's nearest and dearest to be contacted with a ransom demand. Have you heard from anyone?"

"No, I'm not aware we have heard from anybody."

"Thank you. That will be all for now. In cases like this it is normal procedure to appoint a liaison officer, who is experienced in offering support at this difficult time. I hope you can agree to put her up for a few days. She will make sure you're kept informed with the progress of our investigations and will be able to help you if you receive any communications or demands from the kidnappers. I trust this is OK and we will be in touch shortly with details. In the meantime, if there are any developments, you have my card."

The two men headed for the door, preceded by Miles to let them out. Sue's reaction to the police had changed. Earlier she had complained that she thought they were not taking matters seriously enough. Now she was worried they were too interested in what was happening.

That could only mean one thing. Her fears for her daughter were justified.

*

Most FSB operatives would have been envious of Gennady

Arbutsev's position. Chief Investigator in Baltiysk, almost a closed community with virtually no crime but with the freedom to drink in local bars and clubs on expenses in the name of safeguarding state security. Nearly all the people who he was responsible for policing were either in the military or serving their interests, chiefly prostitutes, bar owners or government administrators, which meant most already obeyed the law. The exceptions were generous in their favours to avoid his attention. It was fair to say he really didn't have to do that much to justify his salary, which was the same as he would have earned in Petersburg or Pskov, where he would have had to do a lot more to earn a crust. He didn't like the fact that this Ponomariev business was unresolved and had stirred the interest of his bosses in Moscow. That he had a relatively easy life had registered with them and they were interpreting his apparent lack of daily action as a sign of incompetence. After all, how could a high-profile state servant disappear, in a relatively small, high-security zone? He was in pole position to become head of blame in this scenario. The calls from Moscow were now a daily occurrence, so it was becoming increasingly apparent that he needed a credible narrative. His enquiries were starting to pick up some misdemeanours which in normal times would have been ignored. However, times were not normal now and he needed credible answers. He had only two facts, neither of which appeared connected to his immediate problem; some Pole on a day trip from Gdansk travelling on a false passport, in and out of Kaliningrad in a day, and then the matter of the physically unattractive maritime commissar (with a BO problem) who somehow had managed to bed the most eligible single woman in the town. Doubtless there were stories there that he needed to know more about, but no answer to the matter of Ponomariev. No obvious criminal link, no stash of cash in his house or in his bank account, no personal conflicts with colleagues, an exemplary track record of engineering for the Defence Ministry and, most importantly, no body. That last bit was the key. Without a body the FSB would assume he had absconded, and that scenario was politically unacceptable. A body, regardless of the circumstances, would draw a line under this unsatisfactory state of affairs. Finding a body in a place where drunkenness and drug-taking were rife would not be a problem. He had a backlog of around a dozen with a broadly similar age profile stored in the morgue awaiting identification. If necessary, one could be presented as being Ponomariev. He could authorise the identification through a false DNA test and then arrange an immediate cremation on health grounds, all before any more goons arrived from Moscow to fuck him over. This had to be his best reserve position and he arranged for a crime scene recorder to go back to School Street and find some material. As for so many, pornography was always part of the story somewhere, and for now, he had exclusive access to the missing man's laptop. His first check had revealed absolutely nothing of interest so adding some incriminating files would be easy. His man would become an unfortunate victim of melancholy. Living alone, his illegal personal sexual interests, alcohol, drugs and illicit contacts would justify his suicide in the estuary.

Job done. There were arrangements to be made without further delay. It was only a short time after planning his strategy that he got his daily call from Nikitin.

"What's happening?"

Arbutsev recapped on the Pole – enquiries were ongoing in Gdansk – and there appeared to be no irregularities with ship movements out of the port at the time, but also a body had been discovered in the estuary which, he thought, dated from the time of Ponomariev's recorded disappearance.

"Have you seen it yet? We need a positive identification."

"No sir, not as I speak, but I will go over there after our call, and take a look. If it all ties up, I will process the paperwork accordingly."

"Not only will you do that, but I expect you to call me immediately. I have a few people looking over my shoulder to see what we do with this. It is more important than ever that we get this right and closed down."

"I understand. I should be able to update you later today."

Was this his boss's tacit approval for his plan? That was the way he would choose to interpret it.

*

It was the first time that Dr Jakeman Roberts had had the opportunity to visit the new US London embassy in Nine Elms, south of the river. The building – a distinctive concrete and glass crystalline cube, with a semi-circular pond on one side and surrounded by extensive public green spaces, was open to the public in parts, but his appointment was with a division of the United States Commercial Service on the seventh floor. This little piece of America was off limits to all but those on official business.

Roberts had one of his quarterly meetings. As a rule, these would be relatively informal affairs over lunch somewhere in the West End, and he had been surprised that his contact, Chuck Barnes from the Nuclear Regulatory Commission, had called him into the office. Maybe the president had been complaining about the scale of diplomatic expenses claims in London. The security procedure for accessing the building and then getting to the seventh-floor reception had taken the better part of two hours, involving three stages of electronic scanning and physical searches. One of the first steps was the confiscation of his mobile, plus any other electronic gadgetry he might possess, from laptops to wristwatch-style fitness monitors.

His first reaction on meeting Barnes had been to ask why the appointment had been switched to the embassy. After all, the US government owned several properties in London arguably better suited to a clandestine rendezvous. The surroundings and the atmosphere seemed very formal – he felt relieved that he was wearing a jacket and tie, by chance.

He guessed an explanation would be offered at the start of the meeting and thought it wise not to anticipate what was about to unfold.

"Jake, great to see you. How's the family, how's Oxford? I keep meaning to have a weekend up your way. I have always wanted to see Blenheim Palace, it has so many connections with home."

Roberts was now realising the greeting was not for his benefit. If Blenheim was so great, he could have got there months ago. He was also pretty sure that Barnes wouldn't be looking him up if he was driving through the city. No, this relationship was purely professional.

"I called you in today because we have a special guest staying here for a couple of days. We've been talking business and your name came up in the discussion, so I thought I'd take the opportunity to make some introductions.

"Dr Jakeman Roberts of the Lauriston Foundation, Oxford University, meet Mr Robert Kleiner from the Department of Homeland Security."

A tall thin man with greying hair and clipped moustache, in a regulation black suit and red tie, turned from the window where he had been admiring the view looking towards the Houses of Parliament.

"Hi Jake – call me Bob. Isn't London wonderful? When you look at that view you understand why we do what we do and why it is all worth it."

As a scientist Roberts was used to short, precise communication. This was not it. He didn't know what Kleiner meant but didn't want to appear rude.

He nodded and offered a weak smile.

Barnes got the conversation going.

"Don't worry, Jake, I know this venue is different from our usual surroundings, but we have arranged coffee and rolls, nonetheless. Come and sit down."

He gestured to a small meeting table at the side of the office desk.

"Let's get straight to it. We're getting really interested in your work with Desmond Kelly on the diamond battery project." Kleiner stared right through him.

"I know you are a scientist and probably don't get the commercial applications of your work, but it seems our contacts in the oil business back home are getting a bit jumpy. I had a long call a couple of days ago with Hector Birnbaum from Maximum Power, who just got back from seeing a presentation Kelly did in Berlin. Man is he *pissed*! They have a feeling, and hear rumours, that you guys are about to make a breakthrough that will totally change the global energy market and could put significant numbers of US jobs and investment at risk. Max Power stock could be junk in hours! The president thinks about economic issues almost above everything (other than the forthcoming elections) and has instructed us to get a grip of what's going on. If you guys are making this happen, we either want to stop it or own it. Control is everything. So, tell us, Jake, what's happening and how do we get involved?"

"Well… Bob, I have been keeping Chuck up to date with how work on the project has been going so I guess you already have the big picture. It is true that the past six months have been particularly important. Dr Kelly seems to have found a process to extract high levels of electrical energy from sections of encased spent nuclear fuel rods, which is a first. But the problem is, as I understand it, he has only managed to do it in laboratory conditions and, even then, I have no idea how he is managing to regulate the levels of charge he is achieving."

"Dammit man! What do you mean, you don't know? That's why you're there! You are his number two, you should fuckin' well know – everything."

"I know most of it, but not all. Not that piece which, as you say, makes the work commercially relevant. About six months ago, he reorganised the duties of the research team, leaving some of the most sensitive parts of the project with him personally. Knowing him as I do, he hates writing up the reports on the tests and these documents. Even in normal times tests aren't usually registered on our system until six to nine months later. So I would say the information you want, if it exists, will only be known to Dr Kelly personally right now. As for the rumours, I guess that is just what they are – rumours. Kelly speaks at several international conferences on this topic and has taken a diamond brick to demonstrate its safety, but the vital science is always left out. If you look at the testing schedule of the project, although I personally have elements to contribute, even I don't get a look in when he's planning the assessments."

"OK Roberts, let's be clear – we are on the same team. The risks to us if other people get hold of this knowledge first are major. I've got Birnbaum, one of the president's golfing buddies, breathing down my neck, threatening to send his Girl Friday over here with a bunch of lawsuits which will blow the Lauriston out of the water. We put you in there to ensure this technology failed. But the reality is it looks like it's you who is failing because this thing seems to be getting traction. I have news for you, the days of your quarterly updates in cosy London restaurants have passed. We need to review your work for us and get this on a proper project footing. I want answers and you have to get them. Just in case you didn't realise it, you are in a competition. The world is waking up to Kelly and everybody wants a piece of the action. Did you know your boss has a big friend in Moscow and they had dinner together in Berlin last week? Doesn't look good. I am having my opposite number in MI6 talk to Kelly's boss about this. We think there may be others interested as well, but as you say, that might be just rumour. Anyway, forget the rest of these clowns, go and get on it, get a result and we can all go home happy."

"So, when you say get a result, you mean either get the full story or ensure the project is recorded as a failure?"

"That's right. The watchword here is control. This is a massive global market. We are the biggest players, and we don't want anyone else playing our game unless we are sure to win."

"How do I contact you?"

"It will be through Chuck as always, only the communication is gonna be a bit more regular from now on, so you had better get out there and make a plan before your open-ended sabbatical from Stanford runs out."

The meeting had been short. Kleiner's purpose had been to make a point. He wasn't going to weaken the effect through further qualification.

"That's what I like – a short, focused meeting," Chuck intervened. "You're welcome to stay for the sandwiches, Jake, I think they are pastrami rolls."

"It's OK, Chuck. I've heard what I needed to hear. Guess I'd better get going. I don't think I have time to lose."

He nodded to Kleiner before heading for the elevator.

He had understood Kleiner's message but hadn't cared for his approach. He realised he was now being forced to spy on his colleagues, who he had the highest personal regard for. And for what? Time would tell. If he couldn't get the information required, he would have to trash his boss's work. These were both actions he would have done anything to avoid.

Weren't the Brits allies of the Americans? That was a matter of debate and clearly not the case when it came to business.

*

Williams and Moore stopped at the old grocery shop on the outskirts of Havneby. Williams knew his weekend was likely to be longer than expected, especially in the company of Chemmy Moore. Better get the beers in. Bread, milk, coffee, butter, sausage, cheese and fruit. If he wasn't going to be getting much sleep, he was determined to ensure he stayed well fed.

Moore waited in the camper van while Williams did the shopping. When he returned she was studying the tracker.

"What's happening?"

"Nothing much."

"There's a surprise."

"He has had the phone off ever since we started checking."

"Because we are checking? Sounds like paradise to me."

"It doesn't help us much."

"Doesn't make a lot of difference as far as I can tell."

"At least we would have known if he was receiving calls."

"That's not our brief. We need to find out who he is meeting in this godforsaken place."

"Where is he now?"

"Looks like he hasn't moved from the village inn in the centre."

"We'd better go and at least do an eyeball tonight to keep Winston happy."

Williams nodded, fired the camper into life and headed for the central car park.

As they approached, they saw a separate car park for the inn and easily identified the registration of Kelly's hired Fiat.

"We'll park up round the corner, and I'll go in to do the ID. Do me a favour, Chemmy, put the kettle on. I'll be wanting a coffee when I get back."

His colleague gave him a withering look. They had arrived at dusk and the few streetlamps along the esplanade were lit. Williams zipped up his jacket and walked towards the inn. The restaurant appeared to have been built in a giant glass conservatory to the left as he approached, offering clear sightlines to any approaching visitor. Spotting his target was relatively easy. He had a head and shoulders portrait on his phone to aid identification but, as the restaurant was less than half-full, comparison with other diners was made at a glance. Kelly sat next to one of the main windows, deep in conversation with another man with a ruddy complexion and red and black checked shirt. He had no idea who he was but at the least he needed to get a picture so he could get London to run a trace. The main entrance gave way to a narrow hallway with a small, unmanned reception post, where the visitor's book was the centrepiece with the room key rack on the wall next to it. There were two doors, left and right. Left certainly led to the restaurant, but he wasn't sure about the right. Next to the reception post was a narrow steep stairwell which he presumed led to the guests' bedrooms. The visitor's book was open, showing the details of the day's arrivals. Clearly no need for security here, he thought, and there was the name of 'Desmond Kelly, Oxfordshire, UK'. Priceless too was the fact that the proprietor had neatly written the room number against the name.

Taking advantage of the moment when no one else was there, he took a picture of the open page and climbed the stair. Apparently, Kelly was in Room 4, front-facing, looking out on the car park where the Fiat was and beyond to the sea. The geography of the building told him the room window was the third to the right as you would see if standing outside the front door. At this stage, entering the room was not necessary but a cursory examination of the door lock told him it would be quick and easy if required. He had no brief to wreck the place in pursuit of his target anyway. He moved back to the landing to descend the stairs but had to wait, as someone was coming up. His heart was banging in his chest, but he didn't know why. After all, he had never met Kelly, so there would be no cause for alarm. Anyway, being based in Germany he was adept at looking like a German tourist and spoke with a guttural twang reminiscent of people from the eastern state of Brandenburg. Fortunately for him, he found himself waiting for a Danish mother carrying her young son up to bed. They exchanged smiles as they passed. His final task was to look behind the door to the right of the reception and to his personal delight it was a bar. The part of a slightly confused German tourist suited Williams well. With a respectable girth, Hawaiian shirt, denim shorts and open-toed Birkenstocks he fitted the bill. With no one in the reception area, he walked into the restaurant, where he was quickly met by one of the waiting staff. Looking deliberately confused and still staring at his phone he asked for directions to

'Langdalsvej', a road name he had observed at random when he stopped for groceries.

"Can you tell me how to get to the campsite there?" he asked.

The waitress looked as if she didn`t know and went to ask a colleague, taking sufficient time for Williams to get the picture he came for. Another few minutes of affable confusion followed before he left, but not before a brief visit to the bar. Who goes drinking in Rømø? He wanted a closer look at the clientele. That was his excuse. It was the local brew he really wanted to sample. This was still a puzzle. Granted, the bar was not full, but its occupants didn't look like the kind of people a venerable English professor would associate with. There were a couple of leather-jacketed bikers, an extended family devouring snacks and locked in animated conversation, and three boiler-suited workers from the local ferry line, presumably enjoying a bit of down time before going home. What he had seen so far, didn't add up.

Why was Kelly here on his own and who was the guy he was having dinner with?

Returning to the camper, he was met with a frosty acknowledgement.

"You took your time."

"I think I did pretty well. I eyeballed the target, picked up an image of some bloke he's having dinner with and identified the position of his room."

"And by the smell of it, found time for a beer, too."

"Yes, well, put that down to curiosity, I needed to get the atmosphere of this place. This all seems pretty low-key to me. Where's that coffee we talked about?"

"I've had it, thanks. Fix your own. I've set up my bunk so I will leave you to send the report back to Winston."

Williams knew his colleague of old. In the years they had worked together they had found a way to get along without winding each other up. They spent quite a lot of their work time on shared projects and colleagues just assumed as a result that they must be an item. Chemmy was not a beauty but, to the uninitiated, looked as though she could still be up for a bit of 'the other' under the right circumstances. There were some who would have regarded a weekend trapped in the confines of a camper van in the middle of nowhere as a great opportunity for a bit of hanky-panky but it wasn't on either of their minds. They had been called to this job on overtime, at the last minute, when both had alternative plans. What they were being asked to do must be important, even if they didn't understand the reason. Being professional they needed to focus on the task in hand and the need to ensure that their cover story was credible.

Chemmy disappeared into the back. Williams filed his report on his phone from behind the steering wheel before stepping outside for a cigarette.

*

"My darling Galina, it's been so long."

Colonel Dimitri Nikitin of the FSB was an urbane operator and well versed in the type of etiquette that women of a certain age appreciated. In fact, it was said that his personal qualities, and not his brain, had been responsible for his rapid rise through the ranks to his now comfortable administrative role, overseeing FSB operations in Western Europe; a promotion from doing the same job in the Eastern European theatre. Apart from his success in recruiting a network of agents in the newly democratic Baltic states and Poland, he had managed to sleep with the wives of his previous three bosses and handled it so well that each had rewarded him for service beyond the call of duty. Coupled with his own practical experience of derring-do, including the theft of evidence from the Hague implicating the Russian state in the downing of the Malaysian airliner over Ukraine and the kidnapping and subsequent imprisonment of the head of Estonian intelligence in a cross-border heist, Nikitin's star was still on the rise. He was a similar age to Rustanova and, as both were members of the elite, their paths had crossed from time to time. Nikitin had an ego and a personal confidence (regarded as arrogance by some) which made him believe he could bed any woman he chose, yet, although there was a time in St Petersburg when Rustanova was in his romantic cross hairs, he had not pursued the interest. Maybe because, alongside his vanity, he was also something of a coward.

Rustanova's husband was his fear. He was a hero of the state, a people's man, the archetypal Russian fighting man, a veteran of secret proxy skirmishes in Georgia, Syria and, most recently, Venezuela. His loyalty and bravery had won him the personal admiration of the president, and his special and secret role as chief military strategist for the Russian Federation gave him influence way out of the league of the pedestrian foot soldiers of the FSB. No, Ruslan Rustanovitch was a man of personal force and action who frequently used the tools of fists and automatic weapons. FSB colleagues in the main utilised the softer tools of misinformation, *compromat*, poisonings and unfortunate 'accidents' to achieve their aims. Nikitin shuddered to think of the implications of getting it on with Rustanova and was more than happy to keep his distance. Privately he was apprehensive about this encounter. Firstly, because Rustanova had requested it, and secondly, the location, Dzumbus, a smart but public restaurant south-east of the centre of Moscow, on an evening. He started to be concerned when, having accepted her invitation, she changed the venue only an hour before, citing problems accommodating a late request from her housekeeper for a couple of days' leave. The new venue was a good twenty minutes closer to her home which Nikitin knew to be correct. He had also been put off by her informal response to his greeting. While he had approached her to kiss her hand, she had given him a hug, her hands exploring his back and abdomen for any attached listening devices.

"It's good to see you, Dimitri, and that you continue to prosper following the balls-up in Salisbury. I rest easy in my bed knowing that you and your people are safeguarding our western borders. Oh, and Ruslan asked to be remembered to you."

"Absolutely – please return the compliment. We are indebted to the President's Office for their enthusiastic support. Working against Western interests is a constant challenge, but I must admit we are being helped by the generally confused political climate in Europe and their problems with Washington. We have cause to be optimistic about the future, I believe."

They ordered dinner and Nikitin insisted on champagne to mark the occasion.

"To you, Madame Rustanova, and to the work of the Academy of Sciences. It is only through scientific excellence that we can expect to keep ahead of the revisionist forces who plot against our success."

What was he talking about? This was the same party bullshit that led to the collapse of the Soviet Union. But she smiled and clinked her glass with his.

"Dimitri, I am delighted you accepted this invitation. I need your advice."

Nikitin couldn't help but puff out his chest at the perceived compliment; one of the nation's leading scientists was asking *him* for advice. He frowned to show his recognition of the gravity of her request.

"I think you know that if there is anything in my power, I would always be glad to help."

"Well, on this occasion there might be."

"I have a friend, a very dear friend, who is a British scientist, although not political in any way, who has made a very exciting discovery; a safe means of generating high-voltage electrical currents from spent nuclear fuel rods. Without getting too technical, this is a game changer for sustainable power generation. It will kill off the global oil industry, create almost limitless carbon-free power and help clean up spent nuclear deposits all over the world – even perhaps convert them into a tradeable commodity."

"Do we know all the technical details?"

"No – only some. My friend is the world authority on this technology. His discoveries are so new they have yet to be fully documented. His innovation is likely to be applied first in the military context, powering tanks, trucks, ships, submarines and missiles – not even the British establishment fully understand what he has achieved to date. But there is a problem. He is dying from prostate cancer, which he says is incurable; I don't believe it. From my own experience, I know we, too, are world leaders in cancer treatments.

"I want us to bring him to Moscow to find a cure. If we can fix him, we can get his expertise and use it before the British, Americans or anyone else can. This is a very big deal. If we can get control of this market, it will give us unparalleled influence in the world, greater than a victory in any armed conflict."

"So, what are you asking for?"

"I want you to sanction the collection of this man from a European location and bring him here."

"You mean a snatch, like we did in Estonia?"

"No, not like that. I believe I can persuade him to come voluntarily. What I need you to do is supply the means."

"Where from?"

"Probably Denmark, maybe Germany."

"When?"

"That is for you to decide, but clearly the sooner the better."

"How do you think this will play out politically?"

"Very well for us. Not many on my friend's own side understand the significance of what he has achieved. If he disappears, they won't realise what they have lost and, because this guy is one of their back-room boffins, there is no public loss to be acknowledged, so this is a real chance for us. We have only to keep him alive long enough to get his secrets committed as a matter of record."

"Yes, but he's not a traitor – he won't tell us willingly. We will need to apply some personal physical discomfort."

"Torture is a waste of time. He is already on morphine and will have a high pain threshold. If you went that route, he could give us any old crap and we wouldn't be any the wiser. No, we will only succeed through persuasion, gently extracting his knowledge as we help him to recover. I know he respects me as a professional and a friend. I will get him to tell us what we need, and he will be grateful to us for saving his life."

"Who is he?"

"His name is Professor Dr Desmond Kelly. He is based at the Lauriston Foundation at Oxford University."

Nikitin jotted down the details in a black pocket notebook, similar to the type used by the British police in the 1980s.

"Lauriston Foundation, you say? Don't they do secret stuff for the British government? The name seems familiar. I will need to give this some thought. I have to be careful. I have just had a near miss in Kaliningrad when one of the military propulsion engineers at the naval base in Baltiysk went missing. For a few days, I thought he had absconded. If he had, that would have been a major setback for me, but thankfully my lead investigator dragged his body out of the Pregolya last week. I didn't fancy having to answer for that one, so at least my nose is clean for this if I can put it together. You say your friend is willing to come. Have you offered him the opportunity?"

"Not in so many words."

"How will you do it?"

"I have a business reason to be in London next month. If this is a possibility, I can see him then."

"OK. Give me a week and I'll call you. In the meantime, I suggest we keep this strictly to ourselves. No colleagues, family members or anyone. Can we agree on that?"

"Of course, Dimitri. From now on, only we shall discuss this. I am interested in getting this right. If we do, it will be seen as a huge personal victory for you and a fantastic success for the country, worth many millions of dollars. Gazda, Rosatomic and

Russoil will be instructed to offer you directorships, I am sure. Even Ruslan will respect your achievement."

The mention of that name made Nikitin blanch. It was a challenge. She was saying her husband thought he was just another pen pusher on the make and that she had, in all likelihood, already discussed the idea with him. He would need to come up with a really good excuse for not supporting her plan.

"Yes, I get that. I hope you can be as persuasive with your British friend as you have been with me," he concluded.

They parted shortly after, with Nikitin already thinking how he could go about securing the authorisation he needed.

SIX

SIR GAVIN HAD A lot on his mind, and one way or another, Desmond Kelly featured in a lot of his thoughts. He had spoken with Sue Kelly on the phone the previous evening and caught up on the situation with Abigail and the involvement of New Scotland Yard.

He knew it would just be a matter of time before he had a knock on the door from the Met and he would need to have a briefing call with Bannan before then. News that it had been decided to position a liaison officer at the Kellys' home meant that he would have to limit his natural inclination to 'pop round'. Even if there wasn't a police officer present, her son might be hanging around so his opportunity for intimate discourse would be lost. He still smarted at Bannan's comments, words to the effect that he was not the only one, and had it in mind to have it out and find out who else she was sharing her favours with. All that would have to wait, not only for Des's return but a suitable time when he could go to see her undisturbed.

There was no doubt that Des Kelly's absence was an inconvenience right now; whether he was there or not he seemed to be front and centre of most of his conversations, and this particular day was no different.

This was the day he would interview Jake Roberts as part of Kelly's 360-degree peer review. It would be an opportunity to better understand Des's day-to-day behaviour and the potential risk he presented to the Lauriston's future operations.

It wasn't just Sir Gavin who was preparing for this encounter. This would be Roberts's first move on what he considered to be the patriotic Kleiner agenda of his home country.

The meeting in Sir Gavin's office was formal by Lauriston standards. Roberts entered Sir Gavin's seventh-floor lair and had dressed for the occasion in a grey suit and tie to impress any passing onlookers.

"Jake – good to see you. We are both so busy these days, we don't often get the chance to meet, so we need to make the most of it when the opportunity arises. Coffee?"

Sir Gavin's pleasure at playing with his personal coffee machine was well known.

"Cappuccino or ristretto?"

"Cappuccino is fine, thanks."

"Have a seat. So you've been with us for nearly eighteen months now. Doesn't time fly? Are you missing your friends at Stanford?"

"Only a little. The work I'm doing with Dr Des is way more interesting than the stuff my colleagues are into right now, and then at the weekends I can get away to see some great countryside and history. How you can have so much culture on a small island blows my mind."

"And it's all going well, is it?"

"I think so. My test series is on track, but perhaps we still have a little way to go on the analysis."

"Isn't that unusual?"

"Not really. Sometimes, it is easier to do analysis straight after testing when you have all the details to hand, but when you do that, you can lose some objectivity, I think."

"Does Des provide warning when he expects analytical processes to be undertaken?"

"He gives me a free hand to interpret the data as I see fit, but is a bit of a monster, though, if he thinks the categorisations and assumptions are wrong. And it can be tough. Part of the time I'm having to anticipate what he is doing, when in reality I don`t always know."

"Explain...?"

"Well, quite often he will take process outcomes and vary the control test parameters without me knowing. That runs the risk of throwing all our projections out of sequence with the result that we could lose several days or weeks of work."

"Has that happened often?"

"Not that regularly, but it has happened twice in the past six months."

"And how much work did we lose?"

"It wasn't work, so much as time; we had to recalibrate our equipment."

"So how much time?"

"Probably a couple of weeks, maybe three?"

"That's not good."

"These things happen to most of us at one time or another. It's really difficult to suggest that time was lost because that assumes we always make consistent progress, which we don't."

"But?" Sir Gavin looked quizzically at Roberts.

"My personal opinion would be that I'd like to see Dr Kelly getting back to his old ways. He always used to work so collaboratively. Now he sets a lot of individual testing regimes which make it really difficult to co-ordinate our efforts as a team."

"When did he change?"

"Probably about six months ago. I thought he'd lost his mojo. He always was a bright, happy-go-lucky kind of guy, but then he started to become self-centred and introverted. I always thought I had a good overview of HCCVD, but I'm not sure anymore."

"So, from your point of view, his technical leadership is good but personal communication needs development."

"In summary, yes, sir. You got it, and as his deputy that's one area I can really help him out with if he'd let me and there is a real chance for that. I told him at our last one-to-one that Stanford had asked us over to do a seminar, which I was keen to do. He seemed pretty laid-back about it, even when I told him some of the biggest science fund managers in the US would be there. Next thing I know, he's off to Berlin to present our plans to an audience of competitors. I just don't get it."

"I've made a note of that. And finally, how are the members of your research group?"

"Yeah, they're all good, thanks. My deputy, Werner Liebelt, was a good find from Dresden University. Very thorough. Because we work so closely, he is getting pretty smart at anticipating the next stages of the project. I'd recommend him highly."

"Good. I'll leave it there for now, as I want to make sure I have recorded our discussion fully. My impression is that you have become a valued member of the HCCVD team in a relatively short time. Well done and thanks from me. Please remember, as far as I'm concerned, my door is always open to you."

"Thanks, Sir Gavin. That's a real responsibility and a great personal compliment. I will keep you updated on my work as and when appropriate."

Roberts didn't wait to be shown the door; he had made his point and decided to quit while he was ahead.

*

Aldo de Leonibus had stayed longer in Berlin before returning to Sofia. Like Des Kelly, he was involved in a linked trip, but his journey was a bit more leisurely. Leaving the Adlon, he had taken the very pleasant stroll across the central Tiergarten parklands to the distinctive, modern metallic barrel-shaped construction that was the Embassy of Saudi Arabia. The informal meeting had been arranged following an approach at the International Sustainable

Energy Forum. Aldo had been seated next to the Embassy's Commercial Attaché, Mohammed bin Shararni, who seemed to have taken quite an interest in Des Kelly's presentation and was full of questions. Apart from quizzing Aldo about his work in Bulgaria, he seemed intent on understanding Kelly's work on HCCVD. The Italian had been happy to talk about the general principles but was at pains to tell the diplomat that the details were not known to him personally and that he should approach the Lauriston Foundation in the UK if he wanted to know more. But the Saudi seemed undaunted and not particularly interested in the science. His attention was all on the implications for the future roll-out and the global hydrocarbons industry. It was some forty-eight hours since they had met but the Saudis had been busy with their own research into de Leonibus and Kelly. They knew they were long-standing colleagues and of their shared interest in nuclear safety. It was a topic Aldo was passionate about, especially as he was aware of their plans to build two nuclear reactors, so for him the prospect of an impromptu cup of tea was to be welcomed.

"I very much appreciated your thoughtful comments when we met at the conference," his host began. "I was impressed by the quality of the presentations, as well as the audience. Of course, the topic is important of itself, but you may know we have close links with Maximum Power Corporation of the US and, as they were sponsoring it, we thought we needed to show our support."

"Yes, I, too, thought the programme was good and having the German Chancellor putting in an appearance made the point that this gathering was internationally important."

"We are striving for excellence in our nuclear affairs," bin Shararni continued. "We need the extra power capacity that our oil and solar activities cannot deliver for our growing population, but we also don't want the resulting waste on our territory.

"If we had come to the IAEA table sooner, we might have been able to do a deal with the UK for them to take it for long-term storage, but I think we are too late for that, so we must consider what to do with it now. If I understood Dr Kelly correctly, he is offering the prospect of unlimited battery power from spent rods that will prevent the need for long-term high-security storage, which we are very much interested in. What do you think the implications of Dr Kelly's work could be?"

"If he can reproduce his work at scale, it will drastically cut demand for oil and the burning of fossil fuels and offer the prospect of cleaning up and reducing contamination across the world. If he can do all that with his technology, he will not be short of people wanting to own that knowledge. You could say he has the potential to change the world economy, or perhaps more accurately, the country which develops it first will have that power. It's quite a scary thought that a friend of mine with whom I had dinner the night before this conference is responsible for this."

"Why do you say that?"

"He is a humble family man, not rich. He lives in an ordinary house near the River Thames in England. I don't think he is in this for the power or prestige. He is idealistic. I think he is doing it because he thinks it is a good thing for the world."

Bin Shararni smiled.

"Really, Professor de Leonibus? A man of your experience in cleaning up the nuclear mess the Russians left behind in Bulgaria cannot seriously believe that. He must want the recognition for the work or money, or both."

"You'd be surprised. In all the time I have known him, money has never been his interest, he genuinely loves his subject."

"How do you expect his work to be developed commercially?"

"I have no idea, but it will require international regulation, so I suppose the IAEA will get involved. This is all so new that they, too, will have to change their operating practices. But at this stage it all comes down to Desmond Kelly. He must document his research and he's going to need someone as smart as he is to fully lay out the commercial application."

"You, perhaps?"

"I don't think so; it's not my speciality, but I am sure I will know of the person he chooses."

"I very much appreciate your taking the time to visit the embassy before you leave Berlin. I have enjoyed our discussion and I am sure it will form the base of an ongoing dialogue in my country. I must say you would be welcome to visit the Kingdom to review our application of nuclear power-generating technologies. We are trying to adopt best practice and learn from the experience of others. We are ambitious and see the opportunity to become leaders in the field in the years ahead."

"I am sure I could help you in an advisory capacity. Knowing how to respond to Dr Kelly's work could be important for your economy."

"I agree. Thank you, Professor. I will write to you in Bulgaria in due course."

Returning to the Adlon, de Leonibus reflected on the discussion. It seemed a bit odd.

He had only agreed to attend as a means of completing the casual conversation that had been left open in the conference hall.

He thought it could be worthwhile and a means of perhaps getting some new knowledge on the Saudi energy development programme before it was officially published by the IAEA.

On that score, it had been a waste of time.

In fact, he felt as though he was himself being pumped, for information he didn't have about Des Kelly's work. But there was another way of looking at it.

He had secured an invitation to Riyadh and potentially some lucrative consultancy work.

*

Westergaard collected Kelly from the Kro at eleven the following morning. He left his car, a white Toyota pick-up, at the far side of the car park, closest to the harbour. It was a bright and breezy day, common weather on Rømø for the time of year and yet the sea looked calm. As he walked in, he didn't notice a woman with a pair of binoculars nearby, looking out to sea, and certainly didn't see her crouch down to tie her shoelace on the far side of this vehicle. Placing the small tracker took less than a minute and she walked on along the esplanade. Westergaard's guest commented on the absence of waves.

"You really need to be in a big storm here to see real breakers. I am going to give you a short orientation tour, which will include our famous beach. There you will see the nearest thing we have to proper waves."

"You look as though you've had a busy morning already," Kelly sympathised.

"Yes, this is true. But because of our evening together last night, I needed to get my son-in-law to take the boat out earlier to do my fishing run, so at least I got a couple of unexpected hours' rest," he laughed.

"Where do you live?"

"I have a farmstead on the edge of a wood, about five kilometres from here, where I keep some pigs and chickens. I am the main provider of fresh eggs and supply the local farmers' co-operative with pork, which comes back to me as frankfurters for hot dogs, which I sell to travellers waiting for the ferry to Sylt. As you can see, we try not to miss a good business opportunity when we see it. So, fish, eggs, meat, beer, holiday homes, nature trails and convenience foods, from hot dogs to the fish and chip restaurant – we do it all here."

"So I am part of a new business?"

"Yes, but as I said yesterday, perhaps not so new. You will be our twenty-first customer. We now have a better understanding of what we can offer, but we are learning all the time and, as I was saying, although we have to make a profit, this is a specialised activity. I liken it to the wedding business. These days, young couples have many ways of getting married under the law, irrespective of their culture or religious background. My view is that death is going a similar way. It is not such a taboo subject, at least not here in Denmark. Enough care is offered by the state and communities for the start of life. Death has traditionally been seen as the poor relation, with the only concern about the future of personal possessions and assets. I find my customers have very particular ideas about how they would choose to leave this life and want to be empowered to be responsible and take their own decisions."

While the discussion ensued, Westergaard had driven through a small network of domestic roads, past a sports hall and several rows of small single-storey wooden houses, each with their own patio and car parking space. Kelly took a break from the central subject of discussion.

"Are all of these holiday lets full?"

"At this time of year they are. These houses are the closest to the beach. The beach itself is rated in the top three, in terms of size, in Europe. People come here not so much to swim but to enjoy the wind sports; windsurfing, sand sailing, even paragliding. I own the two at the far end on the left here, near the copse of trees."

Kelly had expected the collection of houses to give way to a sea view but was, instead, treated to what looked like an arable field of potatoes.

"We are not quite there yet. This land is owned by another farmer friend of mine."

"It looks as if he is sitting on a pot of gold for the future."

"I don't think so. The Danish government is committed to protecting the environment here, so I don't think he will be getting rich with new development. The authorities won't even let tourists camp on this strip as they are worried about litter and fire risk. You'll understand why in just a minute."

His pick-up traversed another bund marked by a line of fir trees and, for the first time, Kelly saw the huge expanse of beach he had seen in the publicity photos online.

"Impressive, isn't it? You can understand why it is such a draw

– how all of us who live here depend on the visitors we have in the summer months."

The straight road finished and changed into a slipway to the beach itself, either side of a bank of sand dunes.

"You will recall this is the place I recorded the sales film you saw on YouTube," he said.

Westergaard kept driving.

"You can see how firm the sand is here. It will take another ten minutes to drive to the water's edge. Over there on the horizon is the German island of Sylt and the village of List. List is one of the most expensive pieces of real estate in the whole of Germany – they'd be over here if they were allowed to buy!"

He drove back the way he'd come, returning to the main theme of the conversation.

"Did you get a chance to look through that folder I left you with last night?"

"Yes, thank you."

"If we are to do this, preparation is key. I tend to think of it a bit like a court case where you are the defendant and God, or whatever higher force you believe in, is both the judge and the jury. You are seeking to deny the precious gift of life you were given all those years ago. You are seeking the power to give it back and you need to make the case. Doing so will be emotionally difficult as well as being administratively complex. You have to be capable of seeing the process through. I have had at least six who either couldn't or wouldn't complete the preparation. I do not regard this as a failure, because in these cases the people have found their own inner peace to continue their life's journey. This is not necessarily about you needing to be honest with me, but with yourself. In summary, if you are going to follow this process and reach your 'conclusion', you will have to visit us on three separate occasions. The trips must be separated by a minimum of four weeks' reflection time. This is not wasted but an important element of coming to terms with your situation.

"Each visit will consist of the same elements. You will meet with a psychotherapist, a faith expert and an *advocaat*, a lawyer. The first will conduct a review of your mental health to confirm that in their opinion you are of sound mind. The second happens to be a priest who is also a local conservationist; he will explore your personal motivations. And the third will ensure that your estate is properly distributed in accordance with your wishes and all necessary certifications and registrations are concluded efficiently.

"Each will conduct a series of tests and produce a report which is strictly confidential during your lifetime but could be shared with the authorities upon your death, in order to demonstrate that we have acted in line with your wishes, as we have our own business standards to maintain."

"So, these three visits take place after this one?"

"Absolutely. You are here to find out what we do and how we do it. You may leave here and conclude this is not right for you. That is fine. There is no obligation to continue. If you return, we start the process for real. At that point we would have a contract to govern our relationship."

"So, I would be literally signing my death warrant?"

"I don't think it is that. The contract means you have prepaid for the preparation process. That means you will pay for the service up front, regardless of whether you use it or not. You are free to abandon our relationship at any stage up to the physical point of departure – you just forfeit the money, which compensates us for our effort on your behalf.

"In the meantime, you can be sure that everything we discuss is private, and keep in mind the purpose is to make absolutely sure that what we are offering is right for you. Only you can take the decision. Our job is to help you collect the evidence and provide the reassurance you need to go ahead."

Kelly had to admit he remained impressed with his host's matter-of-fact delivery. He made it all sound so mundane, so ordinary. He wished he had a pocket version of Westergaard that he could take home, to address the shock and distress he knew some of his family and friends would feel.

"Where now?"

"Part of your experience must be to become an honorary citizen of Rømø and do things the locals do. As we are driving by the dock, we will pick up a couple of beers and hot dogs from my stand and go on to meet Marisa Kjaer, my resident psychotherapist. She teaches at the University of Southern Denmark."

His host was certainly keen on squeezing every last drop of commercial benefit from Kelly's visit.

Kelly's island tour was presenting challenges for Williams and Moore, who had started to follow Westergaard but gave up when they got to the beach, not least because at this stage of the trail they risked being noticed. They parked up next to two other motorhomes.

*

"Have we got any more on his Danish pal?" Williams enquired of his partner, who was studying her phone intently. She shared the screen.

"Winston drew a blank but has asked his mates in Copenhagen to see if they have some background. We got lucky with his licence plate record, however. The guy's called Westergaard, Nils Westergaard – the address puts him on what looks like a small farm back up the road towards the causeway, just there on Rislumvej. I'm running a check to see whether he has any company directorships. Think it could be slow work. Tell you what, seeing as we've lost them and it's sunny *and* we're on a beach, I fancy a short walk along the headland and I'm going to take the binoculars. You never know what you might get to see!"

Williams was forced to agree. Moore had leapt out of the camper van and was headed for the coastal path that followed the dunes. Williams watched her departing back and scrambled to lock the vehicle before following her. Overnight she had swapped jeans for shorts and briefly for the first time he stopped seeing her as just a work colleague and realised she was an attractive woman. He caught up with her on the far side of the slipway as she joined the path.

"Where are you going?"

"I want to see where the path leads; we may need to use this as a short cut back to the village… and besides, we might spot some wildlife along the way. I've heard there is a family of rare brown hares living it up somewhere in these parts. As we are supposed to be nature lovers, I will need to get a picture, so our story stacks up."

"I thought it was birds we were after."

"Funnily enough, they count as nature too, so if you see any get snapping. That way you have something to do tonight, identifying what you saw."

"Any news on Westergaard?"

"He went back to the harbour, and I think he's still there. Maybe he's waiting for the ferry?"

"No, he's been there too long for that. He must have business down there. I'll go back and take the camper round. It's possible one of us will get to see what's going on."

It was early afternoon, and the harbour was busy, partly with a queue of cars waiting for the next crossing to Sylt on the left, but to the right was a small group of local men, maybe a dozen by Williams' estimation, on the quay next to a stacked collection of lobster pots at the side of three small fishing smacks. The men seemed in active discussion, with hot dogs and beers in hand from the nearby kiosk, and on the periphery of the group he saw Kelly and Westergaard, deep in conversation with another man – judging by his appearance one of the local crewmen. Williams went into tourist mode, appearing to take a couple of general shots of the little harbour, then quickly turning to focus on Westergaard, Kelly and the other. That picture would be sent to London for identification. The scene seemed innocent enough, but it was up to London to judge its significance. On the edge of his vision he picked up Chemmy coming towards him. Playing to the gallery, she called to him in German before giving him a very public hug.

"Don't read anything into that," she muttered. "I'm just putting on a show just in case someone's watching."

Williams stood back to stare at her in delighted surprise.

"You did well to get here in just under fifteen minutes. See anything of interest?"

"Apart from the colony of brown hares, no. Just dunes, sea and marsh. What's the target been doing?"

"Just having a beer, a dog and a chat. Fancied one myself. What do you say? I'll buy and maybe we will get to catch some of their conversation."

"Before we do, London has come through with info on Westergaard. Apparently, he's a bit of an entrepreneur with a few directorships, most of which are pretty boring."

"Such as?"

"He has a fishing business, owns a fish restaurant, brews beer, has holiday lets, does meat processing, guided tours, but there is one that looks promising… Terminal Personal Conveyancing. There's not much to find. It turned over three-quarters of a million Danish kronor last year, registered office at Esbjerg, the main port on the west coast of Denmark, another couple of hours north of here. Tax is up to date, but four other directors, Mette Westergaard – probably the wife – a Marisa Kjaer, Maurice Glistrup, and Henning Triore, who is the company secretary. Kjaer has a profile linked to the University of Southern Denmark. Apparently, she's a shrink."

"Addresses?"

"All Rømø, with the exception of Triore, who is Copenhagen."

"Anything else?"

"Just their equity – each has twenty per cent.

"So, time for house calls?"

"Not yet, we're not here long enough, but useful perhaps to follow up on the addresses and send the pics back to base – they won't get much from Google Earth."

At that moment, Westergaard and Kelly laughed with the third unidentified person and walked away to the pick-up.

"Whoops! Looks like they're off on their travels, so no victuals for us yet – come on, let's see where the next stop will be."

Car surveillance on Rømø was relatively easy. With one road out of Havneby there was no chance of not being in the right place, but maintaining a distance to avoid recognition was harder. In that sense the least conspicuous vehicle to use was the camper. On Rømø, these were the most common form of transport.

They had driven north for about five kilometres to the village of Kongsmark and took a left towards Lakolk. The road was now less a highway, more a narrow access road into a thicket of pine trees and sedge. More small low wooden summerhouses peeked out on either side, placing some order on the relatively untamed environment. Here, it was easy for a vehicle, even one the size of a camper, to disappear, but the narrowness of the road meant casual parking without causing an obstruction was out of the question.

The watchers agreed to split up once more; Williams to take the camper back to the main road, Moore to continue, this time on a bicycle that had been locked on the back of their vehicle.

Setting off on her two-wheeled transport, she reflected this was one of her more enjoyable assignments, even if it had involved weekend working. There was an atmosphere of real peace, helped by the fact this place was set back from the coast and the island's trademark wind. Pedalling forward she was able to enjoy the almost laser-sharp shafts of sunlight creating pools on the ground, illuminating the way ahead, with mayflies cavorting in groups at intervals, enjoying the additional warmth they created. There was the odd car on the move, but it was clear bikes were the main transport in this locality if people chose not to walk. Apart from the vague indistinct lowered tones of conversations of householders coming from individual properties, the real noise was coming from the cacophony of bird song, so many different calls she couldn't identify them immediately, but neither could she stop to investigate them at this stage. She had a white pick-up to find and that required all her powers of observation. One of the other pleasures of Rømø, from a professional standpoint, was that most roads, especially side roads, were straight. As she came to minor junctions the sightlines left and right were good. It was the fourth junction she encountered which proved significant. She could see what looked like the back of a white pick-up sticking out of a driveway on the right. As she passed, she was able to make a positive identification, not only of the vehicle, but of Westergaard, Kelly and an auburn-haired woman in dungarees having a conversation. Whatever they were talking about appeared to be in earnest. They had no interest in anything in the background. Chemmy dismounted and appeared to be looking at a problem with her rear tyre. From her lowered position she was able to get the picture of the three. Was this *the* Marisa Kjaer, a fellow director of Terminal Personal Conveyancing? She cycled back to the junction and stopped again to check her phone. Yes, this was Kjaer's address. What was her connection? There were no apparent physical clues. She headed back to the main road where Williams was waiting.

They paused and waited together for the return of Westergaard's pick-up, confident in the belief that he, too, would have to retrace his route back to the main road, passing their position.

Two hours later, Williams decided to check the tracker. The pick-up had not moved.

"I thought you said they were just chatting outside and that they weren't going to be long?"

"That's what it looked like."

"Well, I think you had better saddle up and go and take another look."

Sure enough, when she checked, the Toyota pick-up had not

moved, but there was no sign of activity at the house. Chemmy decided to approach directly, ready to play the lost German tourist if required.

Firstly, she was able to confirm she had the right address. The name 'Kjaer' had been written on the post box outside. She rang the doorbell, and again, but nobody replied. Secondly, having waited a few minutes, she decided to return to the camper on her bike.

"He's given us the slip," she told Williams. "He could be anywhere now."

"True, but we know he won't have gone far; all we have to do is wait at the Kro. It seems to me he's not doing anything sinister. He's not running drugs or anything. I think we have got Winston all he needs for now. I suggest we take some time out and catch him later. So, if we're tourists what is there to do here?"

"Enjoy the nature?"

"I see there's a nudist beach we could try?"

"I think I have already seen enough of your physique on this trip. Besides, where will you keep your mobile? I'm not sure you will have a big enough hiding place. No, let's do some more birdwatching. Did you know over 280 different species can be found on Rømø as well as huge flocks of migratory birds?"

Williams dodged the question.

"Or see if we can hire a tennis court, go and have a hot dog and beer down at the harbour? We could check out the ferry times to Sylt. I quite fancy taking the long route back to Hamburg. Any word back from London?"

"Not yet, but they said they were on it. Let's not forget we are on station until Kelly leaves and the chances are we'll need to get to get back to base soon after. Tell you what, let's do both. I want to go and get some pics of oystercatchers and lapwings then we'll go down to the harbour, get that hot dog and talk to some of the locals, and by the time we've done that Kelly might have reappeared."

Williams was resigned to the fact that if he wasn't going

birdwatching, reading was the only hobby on offer for passing the time. Surveillance jobs were just so dull. As his mind idled, he had wondered if Chemmy had fancied finding a quiet clearing in the nearby pine woods for a quick fuck. After all, he had observed, she was perhaps a bit better-looking than he had first thought and maybe she could be persuaded to go up to the nudist beach to find her precious oystercatchers?

He stopped himself pursuing the thought, which, he recognised, was itself a sign of boredom.

"So where to?"

"We can leave the camper here in the central park and walk up over there, to a seat on the coastal path. It's about ten minutes away and from there you can look out on the mudflats."

Williams climbed out of the camper. It was pointless to argue.

Chemmy Moore had really got into the birdwatching business, which wasn't such a surprise as it utilised her professional skills as an observer in a recreational setting. She kept records, took pictures and provided a commentary for others, who didn't appreciate the finer points of the hobby. Time had moved on – it was now late afternoon. According to her phone, there was still no movement from the pick-up, which Chemmy reported to Williams.

"That means we need to get back to the Kro – now. He must be there."

Williams' faith was not proven by the evidence. Kelly was not there, neither was the Fiat.

"*Fuck*. Do a trace on his mobile. He must be close by."

Chemmy took the instruction, sharing Williams's nervousness.

"He's left Rømø. I have him now on the A7 near Flensburg."

"But he's booked to stay here tonight and go back tomorrow. Has he taken any calls?"

"He had the phone on briefly two and a half hours ago."

"Who has he called?"

"As far as I can tell, only his message service. His call lasted about four minutes, then he switched it off again."

"Shit, we've got to get after him. Let's see if we can catch up with him before we must break the news to Winston. We should have enough diesel to get us back across the border."

*

Bannan was less than impressed with Moore's message when it came in. She had been late with the news. What had she and Williams been up to? He would speak to them directly when they were back on station. For now, he had to assimilate what they had learned from Kelly's German and Danish adventures. Firstly, Kelly had dinner with a high-profile Russian government official in Berlin and subsequently made the acquaintance of a rather obscure Danish businessman and at least one other from a company that specialised in 'lifestyle experiences'. It wasn't much to go on. There were too many loose ends. His referral to the Danish authorities had drawn a blank, and there wasn't much to glean about Rustanova, that he didn't know already. He assumed the reason for Kelly's abrupt departure was that he had got the messages about the trouble at home and there was another question. The disappearance of the daughter, no ransom demand and a suspect vehicle with false plates. There was still a lot of digging to do on this.

The first thought was to interview Kelly himself, but it would need to be done in the right context. He would get Laidlaw to do that initially, brief him on the latest and request feedback once Kelly had returned to Oxford. Next, he would reach out to Willoughby to understand how far the Met's enquiries had progressed. Thirdly, he would conduct his own enquiries into Mr Westergaard and his Danish friends and finally he would look more closely into Rustanova's recently submitted visa application ahead of her planned visit to the UK at the end of the month.

Laidlaw seemed well informed on the situation, acknowledging he had been in touch with Sue Kelly and the police, and clear there had to be changes in the way Des was running the HCCVD project.

"My general impression is that in recent months the quality of his communication has slipped. I will be setting down new administrative arrangements to safeguard the work. I am promoting his assistant, Dr Jakeman Roberts, to be joint head of the HCCVD team. Kelly will be obliged to be more collaborative, but it will also send the right signals to prospective funding partners in the US whose help we are going to need in the future."

"I also want one of my own seconded into the team," Bannan announced. "He's no scientist but pretty smart. I think you should design a new administrative role for a document controller. I will have a CV prepared and sent over to you – he's a Welsh chap called Ifor Williams. I will have him make contact with your office next week, but his background should not be shared with anyone on the team, not Kelly, not Roberts – no one."

Willoughby would be a tougher nut to crack. There was a natural ambivalence between the secret services and the Met in particular, their fundamental relationship undermined by the issue of accountability or, in Bannan's case, the perceived lack of it. The strains were there at the beginning. Bannan was an untitled senior officer in MI6 and there was not an equivalent role in the Met, meaning his request for co-operation had to be made via the Commissioner, who in turn needed to instruct Willoughby to engage. In order to understand the status of the police case, he had to see Willoughby face to face, so a meeting at Barton Street was hastily arranged. For this encounter, Bannan would use another identity, Winston Carter-Jones of the Ministry of Defence.

Willoughby was experienced enough to understand the situation he was in. He had worked out from contacts with the Lauriston that Kelly was involved in state-sensitive research and that would be a factor likely to play out in his investigations. Maybe this Carter-Jones would shed some the light of some of his own knowledge that may have a bearing on the Kelly girl's disappearance. He would be obliged to share what he knew, but relieved that in reality, he didn't know that much.

SEVEN

"WHY ARE YOU TREATING this as an abduction, Detective Chief Inspector?"

"Whatever happened, this was a very quick, clean operation. In my experience, foul play tends to be messy in one way or another and there is usually a forensic trail to follow."

"But not in this case."

"No. So far we have one not altogether reliable eyewitness who observed some sort of disturbance to the side of a van near the Kellys' home at the time. Around fifteen minutes after we think the incident took place, an ANPR camera at the M4 junction picked up a van matching the witness's description turning onto the London carriageway. That vehicle had false plates. We are still checking other camera positions to determine whether the van got as far as London or went elsewhere. Not only is the family angle worrying us, but the fact is she is a relatively attractive young woman who might be a target for other criminal actions. I am expecting a ransom demand to be made and have positioned a support officer at the Kellys' home to report any incidents that may occur. The only other suspicious thing we have is from a couple of weeks earlier when the Kellys reported an attempted break-in."

"Yes, well never mind that. What else are you investigating?"

"We are unpacking her life story, mapping flatmates, friends, work stuff – the usual, but nothing to bite on yet. I'm also talking to some of our contacts in the underworld who specialise in this sort of operation, trying to identify anyone who has been a bit busier than normal in the past week. There are a couple of Albanian gangs who've got form on this. Finally, I understand Dr Kelly himself will be home from a European business trip tomorrow. I will be there to welcome him back. And you, Mr Carter-Jones? What was Dr Kelly working on that makes him of interest to you?"

"I think you already understand as much as I can tell you. But you will be pleased to know I don't propose to involve myself in your enquiries more than necessary, Detective Chief Inspector. Here is my card. Please keep me informed, so that I don't have cause to think I'm not being kept in the picture."

"I agree with your sentiments entirely, Mr Carter-Jones. This is *my* card. Upon reflection, if you think you may be able to assist us, I would be pleased to hear from you."

Willoughby had exhausted his reserves of diplomacy and knew it was time to depart. There was no doubt the situation was becoming ever more complicated.

*

His next step was the debrief of Williams and Moore, who were summoned to the more austere surroundings of the office south of the river.

Bannan's frustration regarding their surveillance activities had dissipated, especially as he had crafted some new duties that would give them the chance to redeem themselves in his eyes; but before then there was the inevitable inquest.

"Let me get this right, you are briefed to travel to a small island with a total population of 700 people and one hotel, to monitor a target for two days, and you lost him after a day and a half. What happened?"

The two operatives exchanged glances.

Williams went first.

"We don't know. We tracked him to a holiday cottage in a wood, where he seemed to be settling in for a chat with Westergaard and a woman, we believe to be Kjaer. We had a tracker on Westergaard's car and could trace the signal on Kelly's silent mobile. The immediate location was compromised for viewing and so we withdrew a short distance to avoid attracting attention. As it was clear Kelly was dependent on Westergaard in the locality we concentrated on the vehicle tracker, which did not move for over three hours."

Chemmy Moore spoke up.

"That's when I went round to check and found the house where they had been was deserted, even though Westergaard's car remained. That was when we checked on Kelly and found he was en route for Germany."

"We didn't miss him on Rømø," added Williams.

"If he had gone back to the hotel, we would have seen him. He left in a hurry, settled his bill remotely by phone and I assume Westergaard cleared his room."

Bannan looked at them almost mockingly for a moment before replying.

"You two are some of my best people. This wasn't your finest hour. I half wonder if the sleepy atmosphere of the place got to you. No matter. There is nothing to be gained by going over it again. The pictures and the positive ID on Westergaard and Kjaer were useful but I've got nothing yet on Glistrup or Triore. The Danish authorities reckon they're all clean, regular folks but I think there must be something going on there to attract a big hitter like Kelly. We're going to keep going on this. So this is what we're going to do. Ifor, you are going to join Kelly's research team at the Lauriston Foundation. They have a vacancy for a document controller and I'm delighted to tell you you've got the job. You will have sight of all project documentation which you will register and store. In a few weeks you will be an expert on Kelly and HCCVD. Your other job will be to watch him closely – who he interacts with. We need to get a clearer idea of his network of associates and how he engages with them. You have a new background which you will be tested on here at the end of the week and next Monday you will move to Oxford. A flat is being arranged for you and you will remain embedded until further notice. Usual communication disciplines will apply.

"Chemmy, you are going undercover, too, as Carrie Moore, divorcee of Otto Moore, a recently deceased German industrialist, living in Duhnen, near Cuxhaven. You have inherited some experimental gas drilling rights in the North Sea, south-east of Helgoland, and need expert advice about what to do with them. Documents have been prepared to support your story and an estate on the north German coast has been transferred into your name. Details are in the file. Again, learn it before you go. Your flight to Copenhagen will leave on Saturday morning. You have been recommended to consult with Henning Triore, a lawyer trained by Shell Nigeria who used to manage the Jutland Gas Field for Flogaz, the Danish energy co-operative based in Esbjerg. The connection is his late father, a Nigerian who married his mother (Danish). Triore moved back to Copenhagen after his death. Triore has his own small legal practice, which he runs alongside this Terminal Personal Conveyancing 'lifestyle' business with Westergaard. We will worry about Kjaer and Glistrup later, but on paper Triore looks as if he is the brains behind this operation, as he is the only city figure involved. You need to find out what he does for this TPC company and how they are involved with Kelly. We must understand how much of a security risk Kelly is."

Once Williams and Moore had left, Bannan ordered tea and turned his attention to Dr Galina Rustanova. He recalled he had met her once at some event or other on the social circuit in Washington DC, when she had been on secondment in San Francisco. He remembered forming a good impression of her at the time, thinking she would take the opportunity to defect once she had a taste of the Californian lifestyle. He had been wrong. Despite some not-so-subtle efforts on the part of the US administration, she had elected to return to Moscow and had been rewarded for her loyalty by promotion in the Russian Academy of Sciences. This woman was no party *apparatchik* but a serious scientist with a global reputation. He wasn't surprised she was acquainted with Kelly but reports of their intimate dinner in Berlin suggested more. Both were married with family commitments, so the prospect of illicit sex could not be a driver, but were they really spending an evening discussing nuclear physics? He doubted it. But at least he thought it more than a coincidence that she intended coming to London relatively soon after their meeting in Berlin, and to Chatham House in St James Square, of all places, to speak at a seminar on the benefits of international scientific collaboration. She used the London embassy as her address during the visit and had not expressed a wish to travel outside the capital. It was going to be a straightforward recommendation for approval to the Foreign Office. Looking at his screen of queried visa applications submitted by the FCO he hesitated over the green authorisation icon, opting for the yellow 'subject to' and typed 'observation'. In such cases, these duties were passed to the diplomatic protection team at Special Branch, but on this occassion, he made a mental note to offer one of his own people for this task. The event itself would certainly go in his diary and he would be a member of the audience. He wanted a closer look at Ms Rustanova.

*

No amount of willing himself to get home made Des Kelly's journey any quicker. He was naturally cautious about making calls on his mobile, for good reason, and despite the seriousness of the message he received, had not been tempted to make a call in advance.

He arrived more or less twenty-four hours ahead of his original schedule and was surprised to be greeted by WPC Wendy Graham, the police support officer. It seemed odd to find the person opening his front door was a stranger to him, introducing herself before letting him in, but these were far from normal circumstances.

"Your wife is upstairs having a lie down and your son is busy in the paddock."

"Thank you. Any news?"

She shook her head.

"I know Detective Chief Inspector Willoughby is keen to talk to you and is coming here this evening. He may be able to tell you more."

Kelly dropped his shoulder bag in the hallway and went upstairs to see Sue.

"Thank God you're back. I've been so worried. Tell them whatever they want to know and they'll release her – I know it."

"How do you know? Have the kidnappers been in touch? Why haven't you told the police?"

"No, no. I didn't mean that… no one has called. I am just trying to understand what they want with her. We're not fabulously rich, so it can't be money. I can only think it is something to do with you and your bloody work. In which case, just tell them what they want to know, and we can get on with our lives."

"We can't do anything until someone makes contact with us, so we'll have to sit tight and wait. I'm sure if there is anything that needs doing, the police will deal with it. Besides, Abigail was always the practical one out of our children. Even if she's in difficulty, she is resourceful. I have no doubt she'll get through this."

"Easy for you to say, it has been forty-eight hours now and still no word. She could have been killed… or worse and we'd be none the wiser."

"We'll have to ask the police their advice, but if she was going to be killed they would have done it by now and we'd have known about it. Have you spoken to Miles?"

"Oh he's so like you – acts like he's not really bothered."

Des understood how upset Sue was and realised nothing he could say would improve her mood. She just had to draw some comfort from the knowledge that he was back, and if there was any unpleasant stuff to do with the police, he would do it, while she rang her sister.

There was more tension downstairs. Milo had not yet got used to PC Wendy being around. He had grudgingly accepted her presence but watched her at a distance from the kitchen to ensure she wasn't going to get comfortable.

"I'm not sure your dog likes me much but I'm trying to stay out of his way."

"He's had a couple of rough weeks, firstly getting a dart in the neck and then me going away. I'm sure he will warm up after a while."

"Your son seems to have kept him busy today. They went on a long walk earlier, so he must be tired… your dog, I mean."

The joke lifted the mood just as Miles came into the house.

"Hi, Dad, good to see you. Are you OK?"

"Yes, fine. Mum and Wendy here have brought me up to date and it seems DCI Willoughby is coming by later on."

"I checked with her flatmates to see if they knew anything but they're as surprised as the rest of us. Now you're home, do you want me to leave you to it?"

"It's up to you. I thought your lot worked off laptops these days?"

"Only those who get a bonus, depending on the amount of unpaid tax they bring in. But I'm all right because they allocated a new machine to me six months back. Besides, my boss said I could have some compassionate leave."

"You decide. I'm sure your mum will be pleased if you stay."

Willoughby turned up at the Kellys' a little after 7pm. Wendy Graham answered the door and showed him into the front room where Des was waiting, whisky in hand. Mother and son were absent.

He offered his guest a drink out of politeness, realising it would be declined.

WPC Graham stayed in the background by the door.

"Dr Kelly, it's good to meet you at last. I wish it was under happier circumstances, but I guess if it was, we would be unlikely to be meeting at all. We are still at the early stages of our investigation. I regret that means we are still actively gathering information rather than sharing it, so there is not much I can tell you for now, except that we are becoming increasingly confident that this is an abduction and not a murder investigation. These cases are complicated by their nature and normally have at their root some failed relationship, perhaps between a worker and a subordinate, a disagreement about a business venture or family dispute. In this context is there anything that springs to mind as a source of conflict between you or others?"

"No. Not that I'm aware."

"No significant debts or problems with neighbours?"

Des shook his head.

"Can you tell me a little about your job?" Willoughby moved on, mentally ticking off issues on a shopping list of topics.

"I am an energy scientist at the Lauriston Foundation in Oxford, leading a research project looking to make better, more intensive use of existing nuclear technology in industrial batteries."

"Can you say more?"

"Not really. It's complicated and because my work is commissioned by the government much of the key details are covered by the Official Secrets Act."

"And yet I understand you gave a seminar about it last week in Berlin?"

"Yes, that is true, but only top line stuff of interest to the general science community and nothing that would constitute an official secret."

"So, am I right in assuming you are an inventor?"

"Of sorts, yes. You only become an inventor when you can prove your product works and that is what I am doing now."

"If you are successful, who will benefit?"

"It could be very big. Potentially the world will benefit from a new source of sustainable energy. But I am not a commercial man. I am a scientist – it is for others to look at my work and decide how best to use it."

"Will there be losers?"

"Inevitably. But again, hard for me to predict. I would imagine the most significant effect will be to cut demand for fossil fuels, but that will only happen if the market price is right. I suppose in that scenario there are many thousands of losers – businesses, investors, maybe governments. But I can't believe it is a major factor here – very few people outside the scientific community know the nature of the work I'm doing."

"But if I understand you, that scientific community is international?"

"Yes of course."

"So, there could be colleagues who are directly connected to some of those interests you describe?"

"Yes, but I don't think it likely that they would get involved in this sort of behaviour."

"You may be right, but we need to check it out. Did you spend time with any of these conference delegates outside the formal business sessions?"

"Only one or two. Some are personal friends."

"Such as?"

"Well, there was a woman from South America, some executive with Maximum Power Corporation from the US, someone else from the IAEA – an Italian, a director in the Russian Academy of Sciences who has recently been on secondment in San Francisco, there were some people from the Japanese government and more besides. I have the conference delegate pack here. Out of 500 or so people, I probably interacted with a third of them."

"It would be good if you could let me have that, for sure. Was there anyone there from Turkey?"

"It's interesting you say that. I would have expected to see someone from there, but in the end I didn't see anyone."

"Have you heard the name Hayet Suker?"

"Suker? No, should I?"

"He's a Turkish-born arms trader and restauranteur who lives in north London. Dabbles from time to time in plutonium but not in significant quantities. He's been chatting to some associates about acquiring spent components from nuclear power stations. He is predictable in as much as he would not be chatting about the subject unless he has a client in mind. Am I right in assuming you deal in that type of merchandise as well?"

"Yes, but not in commercial quantities."

"You may not think your use of materials is commercial, but for a man like Suker, it is an opportunity for profit. Where does your material come from?"

"As far as I'm aware, Cumbria, UK."

"Anywhere else?"

"I wouldn't know."

"Is it impossible to consider that some of the material you take from Cumbria could have originated outside the UK?"

"It is possible, but unlikely; I don't select the material we get. All we do is specify quantities, grades and timings. Even then we rarely get what we want when we want it. But what has any of this got to do with Abigail?"

"For all we know, nothing. But we have to look into all possibilities."

"Why are you interested in this chap, Suker?"

"He happens to be one of those people we were already keeping an eye on before your daughter's case came up. We thought there was the prospect of an interface. A vehicle of interest has been seen close to a number of his premises. It is nothing more than a line of enquiry. Thank you for your help, Dr Kelly. I am pleased we had this conversation. Am I right in assuming you don't have other plans for overseas travel?"

"Not for the moment."

"Good. If that changes, please let me know. I will be in touch."

*

Kelly had a strange feeling about returning home. The atmosphere was different and it wasn't just the strain caused by Abi's disappearance. Sue seemed to have a support network laid on, particularly with Miles and WPC Graham. His own existence felt very separate, detached. He had seen enough in Denmark to want to follow Westergaard's process, especially when the Dane had explained first and foremost that it was about clearing his mind and focusing on tidying up his life before his departure. He would be expected back on Rømø in eight weeks' time, when the serious work of preparation would begin. There was clearly nothing he could do regarding his daughter, and he had to respect the view of the police that he would be contacted when her kidnappers were ready. His best short-term move was to redouble his efforts and push on with HCCVD. That meant getting back into the routine which he had stuck to for the past two years. His arrival at the Lauriston was as predictable as it was welcome. The normal cheery exchange of greetings with security and reception staff took place before he took the lift to the office. He was normally one of the first in, and so could sit in his glass cocoon and watch most colleagues arrive as he got stuck into the predictable stack of emails, most of which he considered to be dull and others he thought irrelevant to his interest. Even though he knew he should be methodical and work forwards from the oldest, he settled on the reverse, which took him straight to the most recent, from 21.57 the night before, from Gavin Laidlaw.

"Welcome back! I hope your trip was successful and that you're

OK. Can you get to my office for ten in the morning? It's been a busy time here while you were away and I want to get you properly briefed asap. G."

Des guessed it was likely to be more bad news but even if it was, it was better to face it out.

He duly presented himself at Laidlaw's office at five to ten.

Predictably his boss was fiddling around with his coffee machine.

Des smiled.

"A cappuccino would be great, thanks."

Coffees to hand, both sat on the not very comfortable sofa, offering views of his TV, (mercifully switched off) and the panoramic seventh-floor view of suburban Oxford through the slatted blind.

"And how was Berlin?"

This was calculated to set him at ease.

"Fine. Most of the usual people were there. The Chancellor attended the opening dinner and the sponsors, Maximum Power, were all over it like a rash."

"What came out of it, from our point of view?"

"There is no doubt that we are seen as market leaders, and we are not short of eminent people wanting to visit, some of whom have money to invest. I will copy the correspondence as I receive it."

"And the couple of days' break?"

"Good as far as it went. I got a call about some family business halfway through the second day, so I changed my flight and left early. But I intend to go back and finish what I started."

The comment missed Sir Gavin. He took it to mean something much lighter, as though he had started a painting in an art class, and Des noted his discomfort.

"Before we get into the detail, I should tell you that I am aware of your problems at home. Scotland Yard contacted me, and I tried to reach you while you were away, but found your phone was switched off. Having checked with the Adlon in Berlin and subsequently with Sue, I had no other way of making contact."

"Naturally – I was on leave, so part of the pleasure of taking time off was to stop being a slave to the mobile."

"Quite. So firstly, is there any help you need? The resources of the Lauriston are fully available to support you."

"No. I'm fine and so is the family. The situation with Abi is, as you say, with the police."

"How's your wife?"

"As well as can be expected. She seems to have a good support network around her. I understand she had a few visits from well-wishers while I was away."

Sir Gavin cleared his throat.

"Indeed. But nonetheless you must be under a lot of strain."

"HCCVD is a stressful project – doubly so given the financial uncertainties. I'm not feeling it any more than normal."

"Yes, but we... *I*, am concerned. We are approaching our five-year review and so much depends on you. If you are not at a hundred per cent neither will we be when we get in front of the minister. I need you to slow down your research and put your effort into preparing for the next round of government funding."

"I'm not sure that is such a great idea, Gavin; you know there are a lot of talented people chasing our tail right now. It's critical we stay ahead."

"I would agree with you and, following on from your 360-review, I am convinced we need to make some adjustments to the project, which is why I called you in so soon."

"Adjustments? Such as?"

"There is no doubt that you have a brilliant mind, and at the moment you are an irreplaceable asset to us. On that basis we have a duty to protect you, because by so doing we safeguard the future integrity of the project. Despite your widely acknowledged professional excellence, there are one or two areas of your performance as team leader that require attention. As your line manager, I cannot ignore these matters."

Des was quiet. His full attention was on Sir Gavin's words.

"On most assessments of your work you are at the higher end of the top quartile, and for that you must be congratulated. Well done! But there are other points that are less positive. And it is at least consistent that these matters relate to your people skills. Members of your team tell me they are often frustrated by your lack of effective communication and project management demands which do not allow much scope for feedback and dialogue.

"Whereas you are considered effective at issuing instruction you don't help your subordinates' personal development needs by analysing their work with them. Although they understand their immediate tasks and objectives, they don't have a clear view about how these incremental contributions fit into the big picture. The result damages morale, leads to delays and in some cases, errors. I have prepared a short dossier on the topic which I think you should go away and read before we discuss it further. At this time, it is imperative that the HCCVD team is strong and consolidated – especially while it is under government scrutiny. So there are a couple of staff issues which will come into effect immediately. Firstly, we are promoting Jake to become joint project lead with you. You will be able to retain and extend the work you are best at – the scientific propositions. Jake will take some of the necessary crap off your shoulders by assuming a higher management responsibility. Both of you will have a prime obligation to share all your knowledge of the project with each other as well as me. As a threesome, we will have a better grip on the essentials and will be able to ensure our case for funding is sustainable. Jake will be given the news at lunchtime today, and I want you to be present when I tell him. In order to do this effectively, Jake will lose some of his personal research duties, which his assistant Werner Liebelt will take on, and I'm bringing a new member to the team, Ifor Williams, to extend our capability some more. I've sent you details on Williams today and I understand he will report to us here in two days' time. Looking slightly further ahead, I also have the prospect of bringing in another world class research brain, from Russia, who I believe can ensure we dominate this innovative field of technology."

Sir Gavin's last comment really drew Kelly's attention.

"Russia? How come we're working with them?"

"Well, as you can imagine, it's all rather hush-hush for now and only the two of us will be aware of it within the Institute. There are still some administrative steps which our friends in government are dealing with so I hope there will be more to tell next week.

"All you need to know for the moment is that, thanks to you, we can afford to be optimistic about the future and our world-leading position in this technology."

*

Kelly and Sir Gavin met with Jake Roberts a couple of hours later.

Roberts understood the action he had initiated had worked, but kept a poker face as Sir Gavin outlined his vision for the future.

"These changes will come into effect immediately," Sir Gavin concluded.

Roberts permitted himself a smile.

"Yes, *sir*. I think I can bring new momentum to the project and that will include bringing some new investors to the table."

"OK Jake, you had better go away and draw up a plan. Remember, the clock is ticking on all this. You need to come back to us by the end of the week. Des, have you anything to add?"

Kelly shook his head. He had read the situation clearly.

"Good. Now let's make sure our new team approach works. The three of us will talk on Friday." Sir Gavin closed the conversation.

Kelly and Roberts left together and shared the lift back to their respective desks in silence. As they approached their destinations, Roberts said awkwardly: "Des, I just wanted to say, no hard feelings." He had cracked in the silence, almost admitting his part in forcing the changes.

"I've heard of your difficulties at home and I can help you get through this. Trust me."

"I am sure you'll bring a new perspective to the work, so let's see what you can come up with on Friday. The restructure will change nothing without a plan."

It was not said out of malice but out of fatigue.

Sir Gavin had positioned himself as friend as well as line manager. What had he said to Roberts about Abigail? Whatever it was, it was too much. Reality was difficult. Work offered a way of keeping his problems in perspective. If he could leave his problems at home in order to do his job, what was Sir Gavin doing bringing his private business into the office, and who else was he sharing Kelly's situation with?

Sir Gavin's assertion that Kelly remained at the centre of the team was going to be tested, and privately he knew that no amount of reorganisation would affect the fortunes of the project unless he chose to share all that he knew. He was far from convinced that was a good idea given the circumstances. Recent events in Berlin, Rømø, Oxford and his home had only focused his motivation to continue his association with Westergaard. Back at his desk, his first action was to book a return flight to Hamburg and email his new Danish friend.

*

Nikitin stared out of his first-floor office window at the front of the yellow-bricked neo-baroque building that served as the FSB headquarters off Lubyanka Square in the Meshchansky district of Moscow. From here he had a personal view of all the people coming in and out of the building. Most of these were civil servants; the more questionable types tended to use the tradesmen's entrance around the back. The majority were, of course, just random nondescript sorts, mostly young, suited executives, who would not have looked out of place on Fifth Avenue in New York, or ample, florid-faced women who had clearly grown up on a diet of borscht, dumplings and vodka. But the view was a perk. From his window he could see the main one-way thoroughfare heading away to the north-east suburbs from the Kremlin, but also the approaching cars of the elite through the semi-private, partially closed Kuznetsky Most Street.

Being forewarned meant being forearmed against any unexpected visitors, an occupational hazard in his line of work, so he regarded his regular gazes as an important and legitimate aspect of fieldwork. The Western European department was one of the most active in the organisation and arguably the most prestigious. Intelligence victories in this theatre were generally recognised by the President's Office as being more valuable than elsewhere because of the relative quality of the counter-intelligence services in Britain, France and Germany in particular.

And then there was the politics of the Baltic. Although relatively small, the president had always considered operations in this region to be of the highest strategic importance to the state, and there was a general acceptance that the loss of Estonia, Latvia and Lithuania to democratic forces had been a blow to national prestige from which the country had not yet recovered. That had been tough on those running the government machine in the enclave of Kaliningrad. This small strategic outpost in the west sandwiched between the European Union members of Lithuania and Poland was the focus of a disproportionate amount of military and intelligence activity. Consequently, it hosted four large strategic airbases, the third-largest naval dockyard, with submarine servicing, and the latest ground-to-air nuclear missile batteries. Those considered fortunate to work in the territory were either some of the best brains or hardest workers in the quasi-military apparatus – certainly the most scrutinised and often the best rewarded. Despite his varied intelligence assignments across the continent, it was always the news from Kaliningrad that seemed to attract more interest amongst his bosses on the State Committee for Foreign Intelligence. Maybe it was because they considered it the one place in the whole continent where the FSB had effective control. It was almost as though they regarded it as a separate, (albeit friendly) entity, a bit like Belarus. As a result, operations in Kaliningrad were normally geared to ensuring their own people didn't step out of line, as opposed to actively harvesting competitor intelligence or instigating 'black' operations.

So the prospect of running an offensive initiative from Kaliningrad would attract attention and he would need to cultivate some allies on the committee before tabling the plan. His ability to succeed, he reasoned, would depend on the quality and prestige of the prize. He reflected on his dinner conversation with Rustanova from the previous night. At the time he hadn't been able to put his finger on why he was familiar with the Lauriston Foundation but now in the cold light of day he remembered. Yes, he knew that the Lauriston managed several research programmes for the British government, some with military applications, but he had forgotten he had a sleeper agent there, who they had managed to place three years ago. Putting a man there had always been something of a punt for the future, as the FSB had no control over the projects he would get to work on, but he had always had the sense that it would come in useful one day. Maybe now was the time. He went to his computer to check the record. The name escaped him but he'd do a geographical search of southern England to see what he had available. Interestingly, all his intelligence assets seemed to be in London, but there was one, paid a retainer, in Oxford and conveniently working at the Lauriston. That was why the name had been familiar. Details were thin, however, because the agent had not been activated and there was a question on the file to the effect that if they hadn't had cause to use him in three years, maybe he was surplus to requirements. It was amazing, even in Moscow, the power of the accountants to influence operational decisions. He decided to take a look into his personal background. Name: Werner Liebelt, German citizen, ex Dresden University Engineering Department. Captain, German Democratic Republic Army, 4th Mechanised Division. Doctorate in Applied Mechanical Engineering, Humbolt, Airbus Hamburg, Airbus UK Senior Engineering Partner and now Lauriston Foundation Energy Research Unit. What exactly was he doing? This is where the trail went cold. He had been allocated a code name, 'Lutz', and a six-digit reference login. He could use this as a means of putting him on standby. God, it seemed no one had bothered him for years. Nikitin guessed the surest way of making contact would be to stop his annual retainer, paid to a shop in Oxford city centre through Western Union. That would be sure to produce a reaction, but he could not be certain he would be disciplined enough to remember the protocols for contact. It was clear he would have to make the first move through the FSB station manager in London. Using the secure line, he told London to activate Lutz, find out what he was doing and what he knew about a scientist called Kelly, Doctor Desmond Kelly.

*

Aldo de Leonibus had come to like Bulgaria, as a result of his year-long contract. He could understand why so many of his countrymen found a home from home here. The relaxed pace of life, good weather and even the food was quite to his liking, even if the locals seemed more likely to use English as a second language and not his native Italian. He had found a 'live-in' girlfriend, Iveta, a statuesque woman with dark, shoulder-length hair, a former beautician building her reputation as a politician, and had a two-hour daily commute out of town in his light blue Fiat 124 Spider soft top, three times a week. But that was where the good news stopped. Arriving at the Kozluduy 6 reactor complex on the banks of the Danube was a stressful experience. Failing Russian-built hardware, crumbling concrete mouldings, unscheduled discharges from waste storage ponds, inefficient management and a casual attitude to safety (if you can't see it, it won't hurt you) combined to make working life a trial. He had been parachuted in by the European Nuclear Safety Regulators Group to ensure the chaotic power plant was shut down. He had to guarantee it had been secured to internationally acceptable standards and his insistence on rigorous inspection and certification procedures had not won favour with the locals – not least as one in three had been employed at the plant. Many were losing their livelihoods as a result.

Trying to explain the importance of security disciplines to Bulgarian officials in the locality was hard work, like herding cats. Why was such a high level of protection needed for a redundant plant? He knew in his heart that it was only a matter of time before a significant accident or, worse still, a serious theft by organised crime gangs occurred. His personal reputation would be on the line and so he was focused on making his own tactical withdrawal before serious trouble occurred. Whether or not he would be able to effect it with his glamorous girlfriend remained to be seen. He knew she was only with him because he was a figure of influence in the country and she would benefit from being seen out in public with him. But as he approached the more senior part of middle age he was not complaining. He was getting plenty and she seemed satisfied, so it was an equitable trade.

The options out of Bulgaria were more limited than he had expected. The reserve position was a senior teaching post at the University of Bologna but he still had the itch of ambition which needed the occasional scratch. It was his encounter with the Saudis that was starting to make him fidget. That was a big deal, and he was surprised that few of his peers seemed to know much about it. Reflecting on the meeting, he was starting quite objectively to conclude that his dialogue at the embassy had been no accident. Was he being headhunted? Now he stood the chance of finding out. He had taken a call from his contact, Mohammed bin Shararni, who said he was passing through Sofia on his way to Riyadh and invited him to dinner at his suite in the Grand Hotel in the city centre. He was initially surprised that a meeting would be taking place in a public place on what was such a sensitive issue, but that was not a problem for him. It was clear that his host had a plan. Fortunately, the suggested date would fit in with his office duties for the European Nuclear Safety Regulators Group in Sofia, which meant he could avoid a mad dash road trip back from Kozluduy, so this was going to be an appointment that would be easy to keep.

Arrival at the Grand was a smooth operation. The concierge took his car (and gave him a ticket). This was probably the only place in town where such an arrangement was possible without engaging with the police. Once Aldo had made the clerk at the ornate reception desk aware of his identity, a butler appeared to escort him to a private dining room where his host was waiting.

EIGHT

"**PROFESSOR DE LEONIBUS, IT** is a pleasure to meet you again. I'm so pleased that you were able to accept my invitation. I have a full schedule once I get back to Riyadh so the opportunity to talk further is appreciated and justifies my stopover here."

A traditional dinner of *Drob Sarna* with chopped lamb, topped with a savoury egg custard known as *zalivka*, followed, with inconsequential conversation, mostly about members of the diplomat's extended family that he had not seen for months.

Aldo had to wait for tea to get to business.

"I should begin this part of our conversation with some news about me. Next month, I will be moving back to Riyadh permanently to run a new state-owned energy company aimed at offering sustainable alternatives to oil. Although gas, crude and solar are our key businesses, as alternative sources of energy generation become available we have taken the strategic decision to ensure the Kingdom protects its sovereign interests. That means we will aggressively pursue opportunities in the latest clean nuclear sectors, and we are particularly keen to take an influential position in the emerging HCCVD technology, both in adopting and controlling licensing in overseas markets.

"As you can imagine, this is both a sizeable risk and a sign of confidence in the science we discussed at the conference in Germany. In order to be successful, we need an insider, someone who really understands what is happening and can lead and train our own homegrown talent. You won't be surprised to hear that our meeting in Berlin was no casual acquaintance. We have identified you as the person best placed to lead our work. Our discussion in Berlin only confirmed our decision previously taken by the Crown Prince.

"Professor de Leonibus, we want to you to come to Riyadh as our expert adviser. We will double your renumeration and provide a five-year rolling contract which should address all your personal requirements. We will provide you with the resources to hire the best expertise in the international market. Further, the Kingdom will write to your bosses at the European Nuclear Safety Regulators Group confirming that we regard your role as being strategically important, and that we will be applying for associate membership of the organisation. Just think of it, you could return to Bulgaria to buy their entire stock of spent nuclear fuel rods. You will be a hero here as well as in Saudi Arabia. If you are as ambitious as we are, you will understand the value of time and the importance of proceeding without delay."

Aldo knew this to be a powerful offer. In that moment, he understood that he would not have greater influence over the country's national energy strategy than he presently had. Although the salary and benefits would be personally advantageous, he was in the act of being bought. Once the transaction was done, he would be locked in, in terms of policy and actions – a reputational trophy kept in a gilded cage.

"You pay me a great personal compliment, Mr bin Shararni. Your researches would have revealed that although I am knowledgeable about the theory of HCCVD, I do not consider myself to be an expert. My colleague and friend, Professor Doctor Desmond Kelly in the UK, knows more about its application than anyone. You will remember seeing him in one of the seminars in Berlin. For my part, I would need to defer to his expertise on some issues."

"Yes, Professor de Leonibus, that may be true. But no one understands better the questions that need to be asked and the likely answers that may follow, than you. Your expertise, analysis and connections with Professor Doctor Kelly and others will give us the knowledge we need."

"There is much to consider, and I would need the opportunity to study your energy strategy to better understand how my work would contribute to realising your national objectives, before making a decision. May I respectfully suggest we agree that I will visit you in Riyadh and you can show me your plans in more detail? I will have some time available at the end of the month."

"You know how to contact me. Once you have confirmed your availability, I will have you flown to us from wherever you happen to be."

Already Aldo felt that he was being treated like a can of beans in a supermarket and that bin Shararni had already picked him off the shelf. It was time to go to the checkout.

*

Chemmy Moore arrived in Copenhagen a day later than originally planned. She had no idea how long she would have to stay but had come prepared for the week. Understanding her brief, passing the knowledge stress test at headquarters with forty-eight hours' preparation and getting her new identity documentation had delayed her departure. She had decided to travel via Hamburg to ensure that anyone checking airline passenger lists would easily be able to follow her trail and story.

As Mrs Carrie Moore, resident of Cuxhaven, holder of a German passport and the widow of the late Otto Moore, her cover was complete. With a 'pocket money' account with Commerzbank in Hamburg and a platinum American Express card, she had access to at least five times her annual salary in euros (thanks to an inter-departmental government loan) and the confidence to match. Her part was to play a beautiful, lonely and sad woman wondering what to do with her new-found freedoms and investments. She would be wary of financial advisers but would recall the name of one in particular which her husband had mentioned – Henning Triore. It had taken a few weeks to track him down but having seen his experience on his website she knew he would be best placed to help her. Tactically she had chosen not to book an appointment with him in advance online, but to arrive by chance at his office to make an appointment in person, before easing her staged anxieties with some retail therapy. She knew that her chances of successfully getting to her target would be increased if he saw her in person at the outset, especially as research had shown he was a bachelor with a track record of squiring eligible women. This was an assignment she would enjoy. A chance (for once) to play a high-profile glamorous role, not the anonymous downbeat surveillance duties she would normally get.

Getting into the spirit of Carrie Moore, she would imagine what such an heiress would be doing and act accordingly. Her first move had started in the transit lounge at Hamburg airport, calling the hotel and ordering a chauffeur to pick her up on arrival at Kastrup, followed by an appointment with a masseur that evening and at a hair salon first thing in the morning. Another reason for her delayed departure from London had been because the wardrobe had to be right. It was a little-known fact that MI6 used the services of two West End theatre dressers, experienced in supplying appropriate clothes at short notice. Carrie Moore was travelling with two evening dresses, three day wear business outfits and five pairs of designer shoes. Who said she couldn't enjoy her work? This was better than birdwatching in Rømø from the back of a camper van.

Her white Mercedes limousine was standing by as arranged, with a uniformed driver waiting with a name card, which he quickly cast aside before helping her with her hand luggage.

"Good afternoon, Mrs Moore. I hope you had a good flight. The car is just outside the arrivals hall. Please follow me."

Deferential, understated. She could definitely get to like this.

Arrival at the Nimb hotel in the city's famous Tivoli Gardens was not disappointing either. Originally built in 1909 as an Arabian fantasy castle by the pleasure gardens' Danish head architect, the flamboyant exterior in Italian marble stucco was an imposing sight. The interior, featuring solid Dinnessen wooden floors and Oland granite, gave its entrance a simple clean quality feel with a warm welcoming Scandinavian designer influence.

Dusk was descending and the evening – cool and dry – cosmetically hid the prospect of rain, promised by the growing cloud cover. Multi-coloured lantern lights of the Gardens were switched on, puncturing the growing gloom, attracting visitors to the numerous and diverse restaurants clustered under the park's trees and its permanent funfair, complete with big wheel and roller coaster. The atmosphere was created by the sound of chatter, laughter and occasional distant screams from the funfair, together with the gentle tones of jazz music, although she was unable to see exactly where it was coming from. The view was a feast for the eyes, but Carrie (as she now was) had simpler tastes.

Tonight was about 'R&R' and preparing in detail for the day to come.

*

Triore's office was about a twenty-minute taxi ride away, on the second floor of a red brick mews building above a stationery shop, close to the Stock Exchange and the Nikolaj Art Gallery. She timed her entrance to be at exactly 10.50 in the morning, gambling on the fact that, in all likelihood, her target would be finishing a meeting before going on to the next. Although there was a lift, she chose to climb the stairs, using all her observation skills to better understand his surroundings, in order to help build a picture of the man. The area was A-list and in all probability had rents to match. The camel-coloured walls were adorned with framed modern art posters acquired from across the road. The floors and stairs wooden. What was it with the Danes and wooden floors? Perhaps the noise of her heels on the stairs was a useful informal warning to those in his office that a visitor was approaching. Outside the office there was a modest Perspex plaque, simply inscribed 'Henning Triore, Advocaat'.

The door was ajar and she walked in. If the noise of her steps had served as an early warning system, nobody in this office had been paying attention. Her first sight was of a desk strategically positioned to block any unwelcome visitor getting access to the open plan area behind. It was simply furnished with three workstations occupied by as many studious-looking young women staring at their screens earnestly, as a customer would doing their online grocery shopping. To the right, a glass partition subdivided into two rooms, with both hogging the available window space. One was clearly a meeting room (empty at that moment), the other a glass box occupied by her target, Triore, leaning forward as he spoke rapidly on his mobile. Despite being engaged on the call, Triore looked up and registered the office's new guest. He nodded and offered a vague smile. Their communication was interrupted by the woman closest to the door (behind the biggest desk) eyeing her up before asking, "Yes, can I help you?"

It was almost as though they were already in a conversation and Moore's attention had lapsed.

She had already noted that the visitor wasn't a local, hence the English language from the outset.

"Hello. I am a visitor in Copenhagen and would like to make an appointment with Mr Triore."

"What's it about?"

"I have documentation relating to claims to speculative hydrocarbon drilling rights in the southern North Sea. I have been recommended to talk to Mr Triore."

The receptionist's interest waned.

"May I have your name?"

"Mrs Carrie Moore."

"Address?"

"Here is my card – my office address is in Hamburg. But as I am in Copenhagen for a few days I suggest you use the mobile number."

"Mr Triore has a scale of charges for consultations."

Carrie looked directly at the receptionist and wondered whether she had noted her designer outfit. Maybe, given this upmarket neighbourhood, all women dressed this way.

"I am more interested in the quality of his advice," she replied.

"Mr Triore will not be available for a consultation until 16.00. Is that OK? Do you want to leave any documents for him to review in the meantime?"

"I think not. I really want to discuss the matter with him in the first instance."

"Right, shall we look forward to seeing you later?"

Carrie took the opportunity of looking beyond the receptionist into Triore's office, making a point of establishing eye contact once more.

"Yes, thank you. I will see you then."

The receptionist offered her an obligatory smile and returned to her screen, Carrie to the staircase. Roll on 16.00.

Her initial objective had been achieved.

*

Roberts understood that he had a week, in effect some five working days, to present his plan for the revamping of the HCCVD project. He knew he had the support of Sir Gavin but, owing to the 'standoffish' relationship with Des Kelly, the critical support he would need from that quarter could not be assumed. Yet he felt in control of the situation. He had got to know Werner well and knew he would be loyal, and then there was this new guy, Ifor Williams – he shouldn't have any pre-determined allegiances to anyone. Communication would be his mantra and his mission would be to ensure that three of his immediate colleagues were documenting each and every instruction from Des Kelly, not with the purpose of challenging his authority, but of making sure that an appropriate record was maintained. Part of his plan was also about bringing new funding partners to the table whose resources would enable the pace of the project to be accelerated.

With this in mind, he was confident about getting Maximum Power Corporation to the table. They certainly had the resources to turn the project into a significant commercial concern. Roberts knew the stakes were high, and not just for him personally. To get his changes through he needed to prepare the ground and sell his ideas in an informal setting.

Knowing Des's fondness for a pint of real ale, he didn't have to be too imaginative to come up with the right location for broaching this sensitive topic and the Woodstock Arms was an obvious choice.

Jake had worked hard to get this right. Reserving a table in a corner by a window at the furthest point from the bar had been the first move. Together with Kelly – Liebelt and Williams.

Pint in hand, Roberts took the initiative.

"Guys – we are the management team for HCCVD. Our work will shape the development of the project and ensure that the Lauriston remains the leading research institute on this topic globally. We wouldn't even be in this game it wasn't for the extraordinary efforts of Des, so our focus must be to support him better so that he can get a grip of the scientific challenges ahead and take care of his family. As a management unit our decisions will ensure the other 200 technicians we are responsible for will not only keep their jobs but have careers in this new industry.

"What I am talking about is not the direction of our work but the management processes we should follow. If we continue to be so reliant on Des, then we all become vulnerable. God knows what we would do now if he was to get run over by a bus."

Des raised an eyebrow and sipped his beer.

Roberts continued, "So I don't want to be responsible for introducing a load of bullshit procedures. I would rather we adopt a set of principles to work to. The key one is that nobody on the team works on any practical component testing alone. The test leader will allocate at least one person to document the procedure and once recorded the test leader must review it, authorise it and submit it to you, Ifor, for cataloguing and sharing with us as a management group. I envisage the four of us meeting for a day each month to review all the previous month's activity. We will also have time to discuss any other business of relevance, for example, our shared effort to secure new project funding. Des, are you OK with this?"

"We can give it a try and see how it works. Provided we could make adjustments, based on our practical experience, I will support it. I think, Jake, there will be another heading for our new management team meetings. That is 'forthcoming prospects' where I will set out our future project deliverables."

"Werner? Ifor?"

The others nodded in agreement.

"That's great – so we can present a united approach to Sir Gavin in the morning? That's worth a couple of pints on me, I think. Same again?"

Jakeman Roberts' approach had worked well so far, and he felt he was fulfilling the expectations Sir Gavin had of him. Privately, he had hoped for a one-to-one with Sir Gavin ahead of the team meeting but his offer had been declined, the boss realising that it could be misinterpreted in the present circumstances.

Laidlaw was indeed happy with Roberts's plans and the group broke up early, having covered all outstanding matters. It was at this point that he decided to break the news.

"By the way, team, I have just been advised of a pretty important development which I wanted to share with you. Within the next two weeks a fifth member of the SMT will be appointed, who will report on a day-to-day basis to Des, with a dotted line to me. Professor Doctor Boris Ponomariev, late of the Russian Academy of Sciences and recently working on specialist military propulsion systems in Kaliningrad, is joining us on a permanent basis. He has decided to leave Russia for good and has been through an exhaustive process of assimilation before his British citizenship could be confirmed. He is a major asset for us and, together with Des, we have genuine cause to be excited about our prospects. His departure has yet to be realised by the Russian authorities and will be a major loss of face for them and a real security risk to us. I have been personally involved in planning to ensure he is safeguarded. Amongst other measures he is being given a new identity – Guntis Karins – and a fellowship of the University of Riga, Latvia. It is in all our interests that the Russians believe him to be dead, as the likelihood of them pursuing him here is high. May I remind you all that your work here requires compliance with the Official Secrets Act. Under no circumstances is there to be any reference to his true identity outside of this group, no internet searches and no social discussion relating to him personally or where he will be living. Outside the monthly team discussion your contact with him must be pre-authorised by Des. Is that clear?"

There was little doubt the group had been taken by surprise and even Des had not been aware of his intended role of chaperone. Leaving Sir Gavin's office there was an immediate temptation to talk about it but with their boss's words ringing in their ears, each thought better of it. It was Des who changed the subject, talking to Ifor.

"This must all be coming as a bit of a shock to you?"

The Welshman shrugged his shoulders.

"Not really. I was the chief scientific document control officer at Imperial, and that job had its moments, for sure. Once we get into the way of working together, I'm sure we can pick up the pace all round, especially with the new guy, Guntis, on board."

News of the new addition created uncertainties for Jake. Firstly, this man was obviously pretty senior to be inserted into the team. Secondly, Sir Gavin was undermining his new collegiate approach by designating Des as his line manager. Thirdly, what did this say about his own relationship with Sir Gavin, which was clearly not as special as he had been led to believe.

*

Aldo de Leonibus had a lot on his mind following the previous night's dinner at the Grand Hotel in Sofia. There was little doubt this was a career-defining moment and ideally timed, with some five years to go until his retirement. This deal would take care of all his personal concerns – he could take Iveta, give her regular flights home to see her family, work three days a week, have extended downtime in Arezzo and take global leadership for the most significant scientific development in his professional career. But it wasn't all good news.

To begin with, he would have to live like a prisoner in one of those claustrophobic secured estates for foreigners, eat out of a token supermarket, limited to a diet of basic products that no mature Italian would want to keep in their cupboard, and with limited supplies of alcohol-free lager to drink; the prospect of drinking quality wine was non-existent. Strangely, these frustrations of daily life would not be deal-breakers in his mind, but the freedom to operate as an independent international expert in his field could be.

This idea that he would be able to make policy and take actions without referral to a state official of some description was troubling. He could see situations emerging where his chosen course of action could be overruled. Reputationally it could be disastrous. There was little point in starting a job like this only to fall out with his new employers months later.

Yet he was torn, driven to escape from the present professional backwater that was Bulgaria, and to step out of the shadow of some of his peers like Des Kelly.

He had undertaken to fly to Riyadh at the end of the month to look before making a final decision. Frustratingly, he also realised that under the circumstances, he would need the support of a handful of other global experts, including Des, to educate him on some of the technological intricacies with which he was not familiar. His initial conclusion – there was another trip he had to make before going to Saudi.

That was to the UK to catch up with Des Kelly.

*

Carrie had used the hours prior to meeting with Triore well, having toured the Nikolaj Gallery and had an open sandwich at the nearby Maven wine bar. She arrived ten minutes early and was shown into the glass-enclosed meeting room. She thought being positioned next to Triore's office she would get to eavesdrop on his business of the moment, but he wasn't there.

"Don't worry, madam. He knows you are coming. He is very precise and punctual, so he will be here in just a minute."

The girl receptionist, whom she had met earlier, laid on the charm now she was aware Carrie was a client. Either that, or she wasn't a morning person.

As predicted, Triore arrived with a minute to spare and with no sense of apology. Tall, athletically built, with a smart shirt which looked as if it had been sprayed onto his torso, this was a man who looked every inch an urbanite – clean-cut French designer suit, English brogues and a relaxed demeanour.

"Mrs Moore? A pleasure to meet you. Please be seated. My assistant is bringing coffee and almond cake. It's a Danish tradition. Is this your first time in Copenhagen?"

"No, but it is a while since I was last here. Much has changed."

"For the better, I hope. Speaking as a Dane of colour, this is still one of the most civilised cities to live in Europe, I think."

"You are probably right. Hamburg definitely has a rough edge to it these days."

Coffee and cake arrived.

"How can I help?"

"I am recently widowed. My late husband, Otto, was a commodities investor and trader, who I lost to a heart attack. Before he passed away, he told me he had acquired hydrocarbon exploration rights in the North Sea, within a 20-kilometre radius of Helgoland, the island off Germany's north-west coast, and they were potentially valuable and a key part of his estate. Although he didn't explain why, he mentioned your name, in particular, as the person best placed to advise what to do with them. When you are a woman in my position, you tend to be vulnerable and prey to unscrupulous financial advisers. He thought you were trustworthy. Unfortunately, he passed away before he could tell me where to find you, so for the last few weeks I have been trying to trace you."

Triore studied her face as if considering whether her trust could be reciprocated. He didn't take long to decide.

"Forgive me, I don't remember him, but that may have been because he operated through a nominee company, which is not unusual. We probably had dealings when I was working on the Jutland Gas Field for Flogaz, in Esbjerg. At that time, I was negotiating rights on the neighbouring sector off Rømø, close to the German jurisdiction."

"I think you are right – he did say he thought you lived there and that was how I found you here."

"Well, your efforts have been rewarded, Mrs Moore. I can definitely help you with this. Have you got the certificates?"

"No, I can be absent-minded and didn't want to risk losing them on my travels – but what I do have are the certificate serial numbers."

Carrie leafed through a notebook she had theatrically pulled from her handbag, offering it to him for inspection. He scribbled the codes down on his jotter, double-checking each in turn.

"I can tell you now that the sequencing of the numbers is consistent, so it shouldn't take me long to run the necessary checks with the North Sea Maritime Management Organisation. How long are you here? I expect to have news within forty-eight hours."

"In which case, I think you have given me a good excuse to stay." She gave him her best, but slightly sad, smile. Was he getting her vibe?

Triore stood up and proffered his hand.

"Excellent. Shall we say we will meet on Wednesday afternoon at 16.00?"

She got up to shake hands, gently squeezing his fingers a little longer than necessary, and fixed him with a warm look.

"I will look forward to it."

She left his office and started down the stairs. Before she got to the bottom of the first flight, she heard him calling after her.

"Mrs Moore, please wait, you forgot to take your notebook."

It took seconds for him to catch up with her.

"How silly of me. I told you I can be a bit absent-minded. I have so many things to think about these days."

He smiled, glanced down the stairs and back at her face.

"Er… look, if you're on your own here, perhaps I can take you to dinner and show you around the city. It looks so different at night."

She smiled. "I know. I am staying in the Tivoli Gardens."

"There's much more to see here than Tivoli. I'd be happy to show you a couple of great places that only the locals know."

Carrie could already feel the electricity he generated.

"Why not? Pick me up at the Nimb at eight o'clock?"

He nodded, smiled and stood on the landing watching her descent.

*

Hector Birnbaum stared out of his penthouse window on the East Side, looking towards Central Park, gripping his mobile and twisting his wrist to check the time.

"Chuck. Hector here. I didn't realise you were still in London. Glad I didn't call you later. Can you really run the NRC from there? With me five hours behind it looks like a great opportunity for you to go into the fortune-telling business. Tell me, will I have a great day today? Will I get good news? I'm hoping to make my fortune."

He chuckled to himself.

"You're sure spending a lotta time with those Limeys these days. I can understand that. I saw Bob Kleiner, the homeland security guy, in Washington last week, and he's brought me up to date about your boy, Roberts. Do you think he'll cut it?"

"Hi, Hector, I think he's got the message. I hear he's gotten a promotion to be joint head of the HCCVD project at the Lauriston Foundation in Oxford, along with Kelly. I think we may have got him wrong. He's certainly shown a bit of spunk in recent days dealing with Kelly's boss, Laidlaw. Word has it he's become Sir Gavin's best buddy and the two of them are running a scam to get around Kelly."

"Really?"

"Sure, it's really smart. Roberts has chosen to hide in plain sight. He's building in mechanisms to force Kelly into sharing information, and I, in turn, am forcing him into converting that knowledge into reports for me and getting the bits I don't get looked at by Stanford. That way you can be sure we're getting this situation under control."

"It's good to hear you think progress is being made. I think we must really keep the pressure on. I've told Kleiner the hard facts about the market implications from both the commodity and stock perspectives. You know, I really think he didn't get it first time around and now I think he is ready to talk to the president. He'll certainly want to avoid another hike in the unemployment numbers."

"Maybe that's not a good idea right now, Hector. You know what the president's like. He might like to tell it to the UK prime minister and the media, but the chances are he won't either understand or remember the key points. My sense of this is we should wait for more news out of Oxford first. I wanna be able to talk about solutions not problems. If we can engineer an opportunity for him, I think he'll decide to butt out and let us run the fuckin' show the way we want to."

"Can Kelly be bought?"

"I have asked the same question. I'm not sure we know. Roberts seems to think he's got family troubles at home, but that's probably bullshit. I got troubles at home and so have most people, even if they don't care to admit it. What I do know is the prime minister here would welcome major US investment in the project so if we are able to walk in and underwrite the Lauriston for the next five years, we can either mount a full takeover or sink the thing.

"Last time I spoke to Roberts he seemed to think Kelly was more bothered about the reputation of the Lauriston than anything else. I bet he must be pissed off with his boss, who looks like he'd sell his mamma if the price was right."

"There is nothing wrong with having a commercial attitude. He must know he needs big money if he's gonna keep the Lauriston ahead of the game. How do we help Roberts in the meantime?"

"I understand he has already flagged Maximum Power Corporation's interest in the project to Sir Gavin and maybe one or two others as well. Think it would be good to send someone over officially to talk about it. I don't want anyone to think that we are not prepared to be upfront about this."

"Who have you got in mind?"

"Kelly shared a dinner table with your head of special projects, Eve Grainger, in Berlin. If she turned up in Oxford at least she'd be a familiar face. She seemed to think they got on well. If anyone can get him to come round to our way of thinking, she can."

"And if she can't?"

"We'll have to tell him the facts of life. But be clear, if we do that, there'll be consequences not just for us but the whole world order. America will not be held hostage by some mad professor from England. No, you gotta be from China, Iran or North Korea to be able to do that."

"I'm gonna talk with Eve. She's due in New York tomorrow. I'll send her over to shake things up a bit next week – that should help Roberts to get some momentum into this."

Birnbaum closed the phone. He only ever spoke with people he knew so he never bothered with greetings like 'hello' or 'goodbye'. He relied on his callers instantly recognising his Texan drawl and knowing that, if he was on the line, the call was important.

*

Carrie hailed a taxi and headed back towards Tivoli. If she had a handler with her she would have been told her job was done for the day, but she was on her own and living as the character she was playing. Besides, for all she knew, Triore or someone else could be watching. As a professional watcher herself, she knew the signs to look for, but perhaps the relative ease of her achievements to date was lulling her into a false sense of security. Her alter ego would not be returning to her hotel for a quiet dinner and evening in front of the TV but would be making plans to enjoy the best evening's entertainment that the cosmopolitan city could offer. Tonight this was not about a visit to the ballet, classical concert or the opera, even though all three were on offer a short walk from her hotel. This was something altogether more basic. Her host was really fit, and she intended to take full advantage.

In real life, she was divorced, but had the benefit of no children to think about. She considered herself to be average-looking in all respects. Good, but not exceptional size 12 figure – tits, bum and legs all looked respectable, but privately not utilised as often as she might like.

All in all, she was perfect for her normal job, where she regularly needed to blend into the background and avoid personal attention. Although she would not have described herself as inexperienced, the prospect of a close encounter with a *man of colour* would be a first. Was it true what they said? She planned to find out. Oh God, what would her friends say? Worse still, what might Winston think? Well, what they didn't know wouldn't hurt them.

The modest pampering she had undergone, new makeup and wardrobe, topped off with a clearly expensive hairstyle created at the Nimb, had changed her appearance and even excited her a little. She not only looked more attractive but felt a new confidence, a newly rediscovered sexiness that had been dormant for some years. In this moment she saw an opportunity to enjoy a rare perk that went with the job. She would go out socially, playing the part of a character and enjoy it for what it was worth. Reality would bite soon enough. But 'now' wasn't about that for her assumed character, this was about playing a part.

Chemmy might have been in jeans and a T-shirt, crashed out on a sofa in her cluttered lounge with a cuppa, listening to some 90s music mix on her phone and certainly would not be comfortable in the present luxurious surroundings. But for Carrie, this was normality. Normality meant a long soak in the bath, selecting her newly acquired lilac lingerie, taking time to get her makeup and her lashes just right, selecting her scent of choice and then slipping into the sheer black silk gown, whose creases had dropped out as a result of hanging in the wardrobe, before testing her new heels. That was a tall order to complete in just over two hours but her anticipation of her evening motivated her to take care of the details.

Her preparation in the bath was almost embarrassing. She was imagining what was ahead and wanted to get in touch with her femininity. Soaping herself slowly with a warm sponge was just the start. Touching herself, as she imagined her dinner partner might do later, came next as she concentrated on recognising the warning signs of arousal within her own body, all contributing to her growing sense of anticipation.

What was she doing? Chemmy would have called her incorrigible, feckless even, but this seemed right for Carrie, and fuck it; who cared?

Her preparation was immaculate and undertaken like a military operation. The lingerie was like nothing she had worn before, comfortable, supportive and a guaranteed spectacle when revealed, the black dress more demure but suggestive in all the right ways. Her final checks, involving a pout and a selfie to remember her completed image before it got ruffled, were completed ten minutes behind schedule. Grabbing her clutch bag and shawl she headed to the reception where Henning Triore, soberly attired in classic blazer, open-necked shirt and grey flannels, was waiting. She was right again on the timing. He needed to be kept waiting to get the full benefit of her grand entrance.

The power of her appearance had the desired effect and not just on her dinner host but on the twenty of so others in the lobby at that moment. She was the star. All that was missing was the red carpet and the film premiere to attend.

"I'm so sorry to have kept you waiting," she gushed, "I almost forgot the time," kissing him lightly on the cheek. He smelt good.

"Don't worry. I'm normally chasing the clock myself. May I say—"

He didn't get the chance to complete the sentence.

"May *I* say," she interrupted, "how grateful I am that you have been able to take some time with me this evening. I might have spent the coming hours wandering through the gardens watching everyone else enjoying themselves."

He smiled.

"I hope you are hungry. I have a driver parked outside ready to take us to a special place for dinner. Please…"

She put her arm in his as he walked out to the street and opened the door of the blue Audi saloon.

"The restaurant we are visiting is tucked away just north of the city docks. It's a real gem and we Copenhageners like to keep it to ourselves. It is a working fisherman's jetty, so you won't find anything fresher in the capital."

"What about back in Esbjerg?"

"Well, that's a little different. Those born and bred here cannot imagine there is anything better anywhere in Denmark and they regard us Jutlanders as a bit backward anyway, so if I dared to say something was better on the west coast, they'd just dismiss it. But providing the fish is fresh, it doesn't matter where it has come from."

Carrie needed no convincing of the authenticity of the venue when they arrived. That unmistakeable marine smell, combined with a wisp of woodsmoke, gave the setting a rustic feel to complement the dimming view of the Kattegat and the twinkling lights on the horizon from the Swedish coast.

They were ushered to a quiet table near the front window, which perhaps during the day would offer a great view of the ferries and merchant ships entering and departing the port. At night the glass was covered with expensive wooden shutters which retained the warmth but cut the reflection and glare. Classic recordings of Ella Fitzgerald and Nina Simone added to the moment, alongside the general buzz of fellow diners and theatrical shouting from the kitchen.

The food looked good too, but the company made it special.

NINE

WITH ORDERING OUT OF the way, it was time to continue their conversation, started in his office.

"Tell me, Mr Triore—"

"Henning, please. How did someone like me end up here?"

Her makeup failed to hide her embarrassment.

"I'm sorry, I didn't mean to suggest…"

He laughed.

"Don't worry – most of my conversations start like this. I am a lawyer, so explaining myself is second nature. The short version is that I had a Nigerian father and a Danish mother. I was born in Lagos and educated at a boarding school in Odense, before going on to university here in Copenhagen to read law. In the holidays I would go back to Nigeria to be with Mum and Dad. My dad helped me to get my first job in the administration department in Shell Nigeria, but it was a dangerous time, with a lot of localised terrorism taking place. Although he had retired, my father got caught up in some trouble and was killed. My mum decided it was time for us to move back to Denmark and I had to give up my job to support her. As a result, and through some of the connections I had made, a role came up at Flogaz, in Esbjerg, which was ideal for me, managing legal documentation for exploration rights in the Danish sector of the North Sea."

"Why did you move on?"

"I guess I outgrew the job. The Danish sector is only so big and Flogaz had secured all the drilling rights it needed. I could have stayed on in some administrative backroom role, but I was still young enough to have a bit of ambition. Setting up as a legal specialist here was a logical thing to do, as I work as a subcontractor to many international firms and can control the volume and the quality of the projects I take on."

"Do you miss Esbjerg?"

"In a strange way, yes. Business is obviously better here. The Danish west coast, though, is a special place for most citizens and many people here in Copenhagen have summer houses out in the dunes, as I do. The real difference is that I am only able at best to spend six weeks at a time in Jutland, instead of living there. When I first started, I used to take my mother with me, but she is too old to travel now. I still go to have some downtime and catch up with some of my friends. My summer home is on Rømø – the nearest island of Denmark to Germany and close to one of the German hydrocarbon sectors your late husband had gas options on."

"And girlfriends?"

"What girlfriends? And no, before you ask, I'm not gay. Just haven't found someone who I want to hook up with… at least, not here."

"So there is someone?"

"*Was* someone – an engineer who I worked with at Shell. I thought she'd come to Denmark with me but she took a job with Maximum Power in South America, so that was that."

"What's next for Henning Triore?"

"I'm not really sure. Can any of us see the future? Being a Dane of colour, who speaks four languages, is a bit different, so maybe something new will come to the fore. In the meantime, I know I need to diversify and get a new legal specialism to sit alongside my exploration rights business. I think I have found the right thing, but it's early days."

"What's that?"

"Well it might sound mad, but I've become a partner in a new euthanasia business…"

"What?"

"Strange as it may seem, I am running a service to assist people who have expressed a wish to die. But probably this is not the time or the place to talk about it."

"But you can't stop there, I'm interested. What do you do?"

"Essentially, I act as an attorney for dead people who have complicated business affairs which require ongoing management beyond the normal terms of a will. These people who decide to die have many and varied reasons for doing so, but all leave very specific instructions to be implemented after they have gone. It means I get involved in a wide variety of businesses well beyond the scope of the energy market."

"Is it legal?"

Triore laughed.

"What a question to ask a lawyer! I guess it's a grey area. The answer is both 'yes' and 'no', depending on who you ask and their interpretation of the law. It's not written in statute here, like it is in, say, Sweden or the Netherlands, so I suppose there is an argument that would say it is illegal. But there again, providing your interventions do not in themselves directly cause the death of another person, it can't be viewed as second degree murder, which is the alternative. What is clear is that for whatever reason more and more people are seeking a managed end to life and my company is clearing a pathway for that to happen, not just for Danish people, but for those from elsewhere where the law is more draconian. Anyway enough of this. You certainly ask a lot of questions for a casual date!"

"Casual date? Is that what you think this is?"

"I'm sorry, I couldn't find the right description."

"Listening to you, with my recent experience, I might be more than a casual date, more a business opportunity."

"I am so sorry, that was insensitive of me. Life must be tough for you right now."

"I was with Otto for eight years, so I have had three lives already – before, during and post.

"I was born in Germany to British parents who served in the military. Went to college in Hamburg and stayed there when my parents retired and returned to England. I got a job working as a secretary to Otto and ended up marrying him. We had a good life while it lasted – big house in Cuxhaven, parties, fast cars, travelled a lot, kept horses, went sailing. Even nearly had a child but ended up miscarrying and then…"

"Then?"

"He gets pneumonia, then a heart attack and suddenly my new life begins. I am plunged into darkness and sadness. You know, as his secretary, I am still amazed by how much of his work I didn't know about and so I find myself doing trips like this to find out about his business dealings and another life I knew nothing about. I know he loved me, but I am coming to realise he cannot have trusted me."

Triore sensed her upset, reached out and put his hand on hers.

"It may not be so bad. He probably had his reasons."

"Based on some of the people I have met since his death nine months ago, most are bastards of one description or another and are focused on ripping me off. God, now you understand why I'm so lonely. Maybe I should be hiring your euthanasia business."

It was her turn to laugh, not out of humour, but of irony.

"You ask me why I am asking so many questions for a casual date. I think you know the reason why. If I am going to sleep with you, I want to know the man behind the dick. It's time we left, don't you think?"

Had Chemmy been watching she would have been amazed and appalled at Carrie's behaviour. This was looking increasingly dangerous.

Triore had been taken by surprise and slightly alarmed by Carrie's new directness; despite her understandable sadness, he had noted a steely side to her character.

"My place or the hotel?"

"Yours, and quickly."

In her heart she was nervous but knew she was past the point of no return. Triore's flat had only been ten minutes away and they sat in silence in the car as they approached. Both knew what was coming and were prepared in their different ways.

For Triore, this was nothing more than a routine fuck of a wealthy client with the objective of making her infatuated with him, thus offering lucrative repeat business. For her it was a life lesson in lust. It was not an emotion she'd understood or given much time to in the past and probably wouldn't in the future. But right now, nothing was more important – least of all Winston and his conspiracy theories.

Entering his place, her normal observational antennae were switched off. Her heart was pounding and she was aware of her growing wetness.

He pulled her into his room, sensing her need and becoming aroused by the ease with which her dress deserted her body. The prized lingerie only lasted long enough for him to escape from his clothes and his solid phallus to nuzzle against her belly. Seeing it for the first time, her show of confidence evaporated as she wondered how she could accommodate him, and he began the systematic exploration of her intimate recesses.

"Don't worry, it will be OK," he whispered and so it was, time and time again, until both had no more to give and collapsed, exhausted, in each other's arms under the quilt.

She had blacked out, but stirred when her cheek was stroked. Next thing she knew, he was looking down at her, fully clothed and ready for the day.

"Hi baby, I've got to run – got a conference call in an hour. There's some coffee in the kitchen. Stay as long as you want. Just drop the latch when you go. There's a subway station on the next block that takes you straight to Tivoli. I'll see you at the office tomorrow at four."

He kissed her on the top of the head, and she vaguely remembered seeing his departing back with a jacket over his shoulder, followed by the slamming of the door.

It had been a mad few hours. She had had premeditated sex with a potential target of interest which, although she had enjoyed it, had not provided any extra information as a result. Carrie was only just coming to terms with her situation, but Chemmy was already weighing up the opportunities that were presenting themselves.

She had made use of the shower and the spare pair of clean knickers in her bag before reassembling her clothes as best she could. Despite playing with her hair, she still looked more like Chemmy and less like Carrie than she wished. The Chemmy in her started to take in her surroundings. There was a small balcony beyond the French window in the lounge. Stepping outside to take in the view it was on the third floor of what looked like a warehouse conversion near the docks. She really couldn`t remember how they had got into the lift, but still...

She had found the coffee, neatly arranged next to a cup, and hugged it while looking around the interior. Nothing out of the ordinary here. Wall-mounted TV, blue and white themed décor, a framed map of the North Sea, sparse functional designer furniture, glass dining table, wooden chairs, a metal pillar and what looked like an expensive patterned woollen rug. Not much in the way of art but most wall space was devoted to books, unsurprisingly. Everything from a weighty volume on *International Trust Laws* and HLA Hart's seminal work, *The Concept of Law* to Harper Lee's *To Kill a Mockingbird* even Dickens' *Bleak House* – naturally. Well, he was a lawyer...

Returning to the scene of the crime (for in the moment, that was what it felt like), the bedroom was similarly spartan. A white room with now-soiled blue bedlinen. What had she expected? A leopard skin on the wall? The only pictures here were a big landscape image of a flock of birds taking off at dusk (facing the bed) and a picture of a religious icon on the opposite wall over the bed. How odd. She hadn't thought Henning to be a man of faith. Either that, or perhaps he recognised in Carrie that preaching would not get him very far.

She was about to leave the room when, out of the corner of her eye she noticed the edge of a laptop protruding from underneath where she had been lying. Was this the break she had been looking for? Chemmy had been employed for her tech skills, so wouldn't have to refer to anyone else to work out how to get into this, with the added luxury of time on her hands.

It took a couple of hours to bypass the security and access the files. The computer's defences had been adequate but not complex for the initiated to deal with. Most of the stuff on there was of no interest and in large measure had borne out what he himself had told her; but then she came across documents relating to Terminal Personal Conveyancing and stumbled on a comprehensive series of records of customers and their confidential histories. According to these, Triore's euthanasia business had over 300 clients, all making regular payments for services rendered. It was not clear how many of these were alive or at what stage of potential termination they were, although it was obvious this was a significant cash-generating trade. But the real thing that caught her eye was the small group of British-sounding names (no more than half a dozen) and one in particular, Dr Desmond Kelly.

Opening his files she found correspondence, an invoice and receipt. Kelly had become a client. Interestingly there was also an impersonally written background dossier which had clearly been researched by an individual with little insight into the man. Biographical details, professional relationships, bank records, published papers as well as some press clippings sourced from specialist magazines such as *New Scientist* as well as newspapers including *The Guardian, Daily Telegraph* and *Washington Post*. What was particularly interesting was that all this information had been recorded within the past month. It was evident Triore was thorough about his record-keeping and careful about who he intended to do business with. She took copies of all material relevant to the Kelly case, and transferred them onto a memory stick. Before she logged off, she saw a file marked 'Prospects' – what she found there was a list of enquiries not yet registered as clients. At first sight she estimated about 300 names, sourced by country, with around a quarter from the UK. Although most meant nothing to her, among them were a couple of retired sports people, three actors, and half a dozen politicians. Wow! If she was an investigative journalist, this would be gold. This time she took a picture of the list, secure in the knowledge that 'Six' would bin it, if it was not relevant to their ongoing enquiry.

The laptop was closed, wiped down and returned to its original position under the bed. Time to go but… oh no, she took fright at the sight of herself in the mirror on the back of the bedroom door. Without makeup, she was reminded she looked as rough as she felt. She found a rubber band in her bag to tie her tousled brown hair back and then realised that she would be embarrassed travelling on a train, looking as though she'd been dragged through a hedge backwards. OK; if a relaxed casual look was the order of the day, she would at least borrow one of Triore's sweaters to cover her up a bit. A suitable beige crewneck was found in a nearby chest of drawers. Despite being a few sizes too big it sort of looked right, hanging off her breasts in a laid-back way. Certainly nobody on the suburban commuter train to Tivoli gave her a second look. Copenhageners were clearly sophisticated, used to this type of situation.

It was with a real sense of relief that she got back to her room at the Nimb, leaning back on her closed bedroom door before throwing her few possessions on the couch. Room service delivered a sandwich and a tall glass of juice to accompany her morning-after pill. She crashed out on the bed, feeling the aches from her lower abdomen.

The rest of the day was cancelled except for a zip file which would be sent to Winston that evening. She knew he would be ordering her home so she would make sure she was out of touch until the morning.

It was amazing the difference a day made. Rested, bathed, made up, fresh outfit, this was the return of Carrie in business mode. Arriving at Triore's office in the afternoon, she found it empty save for the man himself – shirt-sleeved, sitting at his desk. He stood and gestured to her to come in. He noted her bewilderment.

"Today is staff shopping day – they get an extra half-day per month to take a late lunch, go shopping or do whatever personal bonding they want. It's a special perk available exclusively for my people and is great for morale."

Carrie hadn't noticed the benefit to her because of her experience as a customer.

"I hope you don't mind," she began, "I borrowed one of your sweaters yesterday. I realised I didn't have many clothes with me."

He smiled.

"Thank you… and even some of the items you were wearing got left behind."

He offered her a plain manilla envelope. For a split second, she looked surprised until she looked inside and saw the lilac briefs she had been wearing.

"Pity not to have the set," he said with a grin.

She asked, "Is this a formal or informal meeting?"

"Well, I hope we have done the informal part."

He was still standing up at the side of his desk. From where she was standing, it was impossible not to imagine him as she had seen him less than forty-eight hours ago. Her eyes were drawn to his crotch and that 'thing' which seemed to have a life of its own and whose absence seemed to have left a yawning void inside her.

God, I hope he doesn't start that again, she thought, knowing that if he did, she would in all probability be powerless to resist.

"Please..."

They sat on opposite sides of his desk, providing the separation and formality the moment required.

"So, Carrie... Mrs Moore, I have good news. Your late husband's North Sea exploration options are worth in the region of fifty million euros and, if activated, could become worth significantly more. Congratulations. I would be honoured if you would retain my services, in the event that you decide to either sell on or exercise these rights. I am sure I can help you make a success of these investments. My terms are competitive and good value at three per cent of gross transactions. I expect you are not surprised to know this and at this stage I intend only to levy a nominal diligence charge for the research. I will email my account later today. Can we work together? What do you say?"

"Henning, right now, every day is a learning experience, and I am sure my life is in a transitory phase. At the moment I don't know what I will do. I am fortunate that I have money and am free of responsibilities, so I will reflect on what you have said. Regardless of where I am in the world, you have the means to contact me and I, you. So for now, we will go our separate ways, but I am sure we will keep in touch."

"Where will you go?"

"I have a friend in New York who I've not seen for a while, so maybe I will go there for a few weeks... then, who knows?"

She got up to go. Turning away, she hesitated and almost as an afterthought returned and kissed him on the cheek.

"Thank you," she said. "I'm glad we met. It's true the song Danny Kaye sang in the Hans Christian Andersen movie, *Wonderful Copenhagen*. Copenhagen is wonderful – more wonderful than I remembered."

*

Time was passing slowly at the Kelly residence in the Thames Valley. Miles had returned to work but was commuting from his parents' house. WPC Wendy Graham was becoming closer to Sue Kelly and providing the emotional support that her increasingly absent family could not. The strain originally shown by Sue had spread, not only across the male family members but to their friends and acquaintances in the surrounding community. Des was continuing to spend long hours at the Lauriston or over at the labs in Harwell. The absence and subsequent silence of any communication regarding Abi had sent a cloud of depression over the community. The local church held a special prayer meeting. The pub had started a collection for a missing persons charity. A poster of Abi had been displayed on the church notice board and village store. It was clear people wanted to help, but no one was sure what to do. Willoughby was making it his business to get better known in the locality and kept a weekly appointment to call in for a cup of tea just to chat through different aspects of Abi's personality in the hope that something, anything, might spark a thought that would ignite a new line of enquiry. He had changed gear a bit, moving from sharing any scrap of information that came his way to saying very little, even when prompted. His early predictions, about a kidnapper getting in touch with extravagant demands to be negotiated down, had not been realised, and there was an uneasy realisation that behind this apparent lack of energy was the sense that he was investigating a murder. WPC Wendy was herself supplying surreptitious reports to Scotland Yard on her observations on the Kellys as individuals, their marriage and the various local people who interacted with them. A distinct pattern of behaviour was emerging. Des Kelly seemed to take every opportunity to stay at work but was seen as something of a local celebrity in an understated sense. An important ambassador for the village doing work of national importance, but nobody knew quite what, except that one or two remembered that a few years ago he had been interviewed on TV's *Newsnight* about a controversial new power station that was going to be built by the Chinese in the West Country. Most agreed he seemed to be a bit of a loner, with a life detached from that of his wife, and they were rarely seen in the same place at the same time. If they both happened to be in the house they tended not to be in the same room and opportunities for conversation were limited to meal times. The locals had not seen either of their children until relatively recently, so there were few contemporary anecdotes to glean about their private life. Talking of private life, there was always a local wag, prepared to speculate about Sue's 'active', 'carefree' lifestyle and her 'friendly' disposition, but that was it.

WPC Wendy had integrated well into their domestic scene, helping out with household chores, accompanying Sue to the gym, the church choir, bridge, the shops, walking Milo, as well as doing her own office work via a laptop. She would come and go, but she was there for a reason – to observe the Kellys over time, as Willoughby seemed sure they were in some way implicated in their daughter's disappearance. One thing that had caught the WPC's eye in the past few days had been an unexpected visit from Sir Gavin Laidlaw, Kelly's boss, at an unusual time, mid-afternoon, when Des would not be expected to be at home. She had answered the door to him and he seemed surprised to see her there, almost assuming the company of a police officer at the house would not occur until after dark. He had come in for a cup of tea, as he 'happened to be passing', but it was clear the conversation felt stilted and somehow false – a type of discussion more easily conducted on the phone than face to face. But that was purely her impression. Another had been the almost daily evening ritual of Miles returning home and asking her what progress was being made and her stock reply, "Enquiries are ongoing." Miles seemed to spend more time tinkering in the paddock with his motorbike or down at the Dog & Duck.

The latter was becoming a regular part of his new routine, a place to relax before returning to the slightly crazy world of the family home, but the frustrations of his parents were taking a toll on him, with the result that he wanted a friendly non-judgmental ear to hear his thoughts. That ear was provided by landlord Bryan, someone who, Miles knew, was trusted by the family. Of course the pub was getting busy by the time Miles would arrive, but when the Kelly boy said he wanted a private chat, Bryan showed him into the small snug bar around the back.

"Pint? Still no word then?"

"No – it's weird, as if she's just disappeared without trace, and the cops either don't know anything, or aren't telling. It may be a big enough deal to get Scotland Yard out here, but I don't know what difference they are making, other than making us have a lodger. What a job she has! Just seems to be trailing around after Mum."

"I'm sure they have a plan."

"You haven't met them yet. You know they were much more open at the beginning? Told us they had identified a suspicious van and some Turkish dude called Suker who was a person of interest but nothing more. You know what I think? They went round his house, asked whether he had been involved and when he said no, shrugged their shoulders and walked off."

"Why did they think this Turkish bloke was involved?"

"Apparently, according to their DCI, this guy is a bit of a shady wheeler dealer, does all sorts of trades to make a buck. I got bored the other night and did an internet search on him. Found out he is a ball sponsor at Tottenham, owns the chain of Topkapi Nights restaurants including that really big kebab shop up Green Lanes, and fundraises for Islamic Relief. So he's establishment. They aren't going to touch him."

"Have they linked this suspicious van to him?"

"Not in so many words, but the inference was clear. There is a connection, it`s been seen close to a couple of his shops on a number of occasions."

"And nothing since?"

"No. They won't even talk about it. But I spoke to someone at work about it the other day and they called me back yesterday, saying that the authorities know of this guy for employing a lot of his so-called brothers as waiters direct from Turkey. He was laughing about it, saying when immigration officials rang Suker up to check why he was not employing local labour, he told them his business was running an authentic Turkish restaurant chain and needed people with special skills from the home country. Special skills? To cut a doner kebab?

"This guy Suker is a twister all right and knows how to play the game. They can't touch him; he's the kind of guy who does his business without the law getting involved. Anyway, what the hell – time for me to go home and cheer up my mum."

"What about your dad?"

"God knows. He seems to have gone further into his shell as a result of all this. Sure, he'll be back soon and will be sitting with the whisky bottle staring at the CCTV and listening to that bloody awful Wagner on his headset."

"Don't be too hard on him, lad. Like you, he's probably just trying to get through this."

"I know I'm being a bit mean, but I'm just pissed off. I had a life before all this crap – even a girlfriend – but it's all on hold now. Thanks for the chat – I'll see you tomorrow."

Bryan watched him depart, washed his empty glass and reflected on their conversation.

*

Miles was in a better mood the following night, probably because he got back an hour earlier.

Beer bought, he had intended to sit in the lounge and read the evening paper, but Bryan called him to come into the snug again for another conversation.

The room was empty. The landlord shut the door behind them.

"Listen lad, our discussion last night got me thinking. Your poor mother! With your dad away she must be going nuts! Maybe I can help. You tell me this Suker bloke at the Topkapi Nights is involved in Abi's disappearance and that the police don't seem to be doing anything about it because of the person he is, right?"

Miles nodded blankly.

"And you also said you think this guy is untouchable and operates above the law?"

Miles nodded again.

"So you need a way of getting some reaction out of him to help Abi? Well, I was thinking about this last night and I had an idea. You may not know this, but I have been a landlord for over twenty years and used to run a pub in north London. Not like this – it was a bit basic – but we made money because it was around the corner from Highbury. Whether I liked it or not, I had to become a Gooner and got to know many of the supporters' groups. Like most football clubs, most of the fans are just ordinary Joes who want their Saturday afternoons at the match and their celebratory beers after. Well, there was a section of my customers who liked a bit more than a beer on a Saturday night and liked some entertainment, especially when Arsenal had matches against Spurs or West Ham. They used to organise fights for the hell of it, venturing into each other's territory like a military operation and kicking the shit out of any of the unsuspecting opposition they came across. These lads regarded arrest as an occupational hazard. If they got nicked they would be bound over by the local magistrates and kicked out again. It was like a badge of honour and although the club would always distance themselves from their actions they were never penalised because they never got convicted."

"So?"

"I still know a couple of these guys. True, they're all a bit older, but now they've nurtured a new generation in the same traditions. I can ring them up and get them to turn over one of Suker's kebab restaurants. If Suker is the man you say he is, he won't want the police involved in sorting it out. He will want his own justice, and you can say he can have it, if he hands over your sister."

"Can you really make that happen?"

"It's a phone call away."

"Bloody do it. At least that way we can smoke him out and get something moving."

"I'll see what I can do and let you know."

Living from day to day was an existence Miles was getting used to.

With conversations like this, his mood was improving even more.

Bryan called a couple of days later.

"I wasn't sure if you were coming by the Dog tonight, but just in case you weren't, I thought we'd meet for a drink in the Grapes off the High Road in Tottenham at six on Monday night. You might meet some of the boys. Thought we could have a quick beer and a chat in 'enemy territory' before going around the corner to Topkapi Nights for the floor show. Best if you come on the Tube. I'll have a car, so I'll give you a lift home afterwards. What do you say? Are you up for it?"

"No worries."

"Dress smart but casual. Trainers. No boots. We're just going to deliver the message and enjoy the spectacle. My mates will take care of the rest. Keep smiling and I'll see you soon."

Who would have thought it? Mild-mannered Bryan from the Dog was in reality a retired north London yob below the veneer of respectability.

Miles had no idea what would be involved in this plan, but at least he was doing something positive to break the energy-sapping inertia that seemed to be affecting those around him. Even stranger, listening to Bryan, it sounded as though he was relishing the prospect of the confrontation. He certainly gave the impression of being the man with the plan.

Given this new arrangement, Miles decided to stay clear of

the Dog & Duck in the meantime. He certainly didn't want to provide any early clues about the action being contemplated, or his own role in it.

When the day came, he left for work with a slightly dry mouth, anticipating the event to come. Sitting on the train into Paddington he rehearsed what he would say to this Suker guy, imagining him sprawled on the floor in front of him.

He was searching for the sort of line that might come out of a Clint Eastwood movie. Perhaps something like, "You think you're having a bad day? It's about to get a whole lot worse."

He wanted to be able to say it with some menace, so he started to practice curling his lip and watching his reflection in the glass of the carriage window. Work certainly dragged that day, with the minutes reluctantly transforming into hours. Fortunately the Victoria Line to Seven Sisters was a relatively fast journey and so he arrived at the Grapes ahead of schedule. He had a beer while he waited and used the time to look for a suitable picture of Abi on his phone. He made sure he had it to hand. He would need it when the time came to jog Mr Suker's memory.

"All right, boy?"

The shout took him by surprise. He looked up to see Bryan approaching.

"I was going to get you a beer but seeing as you had already bought it, thought I'd just get one for me!" He laughed. "What's up now?"

"Just looking for a picture to show of Abi. I feel sure I'm going to need it."

"I think you will. He will know, of course, without the picture, but the act of showing it will make him understand why we have all gone to so much trouble. I have spoken to my people. Suker's office is in the back of the restaurant and his personalised Roller is there too. The action will start just after seven and we will give them an hour to get warmed up. I'll get a call when they are ready and then we'll just walk in."

"Are you sure we'll get away with this?"

"You know what they say about omelettes and eggs? Whatever happens you are drawing attention to a personal crisis and inviting those involved to propose a solution. Relax – it will soon be over and if it helps your sister, your family will thank you."

"Thank *you* more like. I don't know these... what are they? Rent-a-mob? Thugs?"

"I think they would like to be known as 'practitioners of informal combat' or 'destructors' – sounds a bit more sporty, recreational, don't you think? They are not here for money but for the fun of it. We won't witness the game, just the aftermath."

Time moved on in the same slow way it seemed to have done all day. A few more beers boosted Miles's confidence, so he was fired up when the call came through on his mentor's phone.

Bryan's light and breezy manner changed at this point. He gripped him by the arm.

"Time to move. Remember, do as I told you. I will run the conversation inside. You only speak when I tell you and you leave exactly when I do. Clear?"

Miles just nodded, realising he was out of his depth, but still wondering what had happened to convert this mild-mannered rural pub landlord into this dark, menacing character.

They strode out of the pub, turned left into the High Road and saw the entrance to Topkapi Nights about fifty yards away. In this situation timing was everything. The neighbouring shops had closed for the day, their frontages replaced with steel-slatted shutters. It was the early evening twilight zone between the day businesses packing up and the few night businesses opening. Apart from traffic on the road, there were no pedestrians around at that moment. At a distance, there appeared to be little wrong at Topkapi Nights. The window had not been smashed, itself a difficult job, assuming it to be plate glass, and the door was wedged open. A casual observer would have seen two ordinary blokes just walking by, but one of them looked in through the open door and was immediately pushed out of the way by two athletic figures in jeans, grey hoodies and sunglasses, who sprinted up the road.

"Hey! Stop!" the figure shouted, but that was the end of the protestations. He moved inside, followed by his companion.

What greeted them was a sight of chaos, devastation, overturned tables and chairs, smashed cabinets, crockery, wine bottles, shisha pipes and glasses, white paint thrown at the walls and a simple word sketched in spray paint on the front of the bar: Abi. On the floor, in amongst the breakages, the sound of moaning and the crunch of their shoes grinding the fragments into the carpet. The smell, a strange mix of paint and spilt red wine. One, two, three, four, five bodies in white but in two cases, bloodstained, uniformed jackets lying prostrate in various states of collapse, their Tommy Cooper-style *fez* hats distributed to the corners of the room. What was even more bizarre was the sound of Turkish dance music playing on the restaurant's tannoy, as if encouraging the fallen to stand up and party.

"Oh my God, are you all right?" Bryan had knelt down next to the nearest body.

"Yes, we are OK, thanks."

The response had come from behind the bar. A balding, rotund figure, with an impressive, waxed moustache and four ostentatious, heavy gold signet rings, stood up slowly. The man's patterned shirt and tie provided camouflage, covering what looked like a good half-bottle of red wine that had been emptied on it. Under his muscular arm he clutched what looked like his most important possession, the cash till, and he exuded an air of triumph, like the expression a rugby player would have as a result of scoring a try.

"Can I call an ambulance and get the police?" Bryan enquired.

"No, no, we are a little shaken, but we can manage."

Bryan continued, "It looks as if a couple of your guys have been cut. You should get them checked out."

"Yes – they used kitchen knives to defend the restaurant. It was a stupid thing to do. They could have been seriously hurt. I will get them patched up."

"Are you sure you don`t want the police?"

"Police? No – absolutely. This is north London. Unfortunately, this sort of thing happens from time to time. We just have to deal with it, but I am afraid we will be closed for a while while we get this cleaned up. If you go to Wood Green there is another Topkapi Nights there, next to the Tube station. I can call and book you a table. It will be on the house.

"Don't worry, we can sort ourselves out. The offer stands. If you go there tell them to call me, my name is Mr Suker, Mr Hayet Suker. I own this place and the other Topkapi Nights."

While his staff were dusting themselves off and helping each other, Bryan and Miles moved closer to the bar.

"Do you believe in coincidences, Mr Suker?" Bryan began.

"What do you mean?"

"Terrible though this situation is, it is remarkable this has happened at the branch you use as an office. These thugs who have vandalised your restaurant don't seem to have bothered causing a trail of destruction elsewhere. It is almost as though they targeted your business to send you a message."

The Turk looked momentarily confused.

"They have sprayed the letters A, B, and I on the front of the bar. Maybe it means something?"

"Probably they are writing a shit message in English but didn't get time to finish it."

"Maybe – but maybe they did. Maybe the letters stand for something or the name of a person.

"I have to tell you, Mr Suker, I met my wife on the top of a Number 16 bus some twenty years ago. That was a chance meeting that changed my life. Maybe this is also an important moment.

"My mate here has a sister called Abi. Show Mr Suker her picture, lad. Good-looking, isn't she? I wonder if all this is one of life's coincidences. You get your restaurant trashed, we happened to be passing and my mate here is very worried looking for his sister Abi, who has disappeared. He is trying to get on with his life, walks in here with me to help you and sees her name is sprayed on the front of your bar. Strange that, isn't it? Take another look at her picture, Mr Suker. She's the sort of girl you'd remember meeting if you were lucky enough. Because I believe in coincidence, there is a bit of me that wonders whether *just by chance* you may have come across her. Personally, I wouldn't be surprised. My friend here has told me she likes a kebab, once in a while."

"I do not understand. I do not know her. She doesn't work in my restaurants."

"But I think you know her. Think hard, Mr Suker. After all, it would be great if something positive came out of this sorry situation. Tell you what, I can see you have your hands full cleaning up this mess. Please think about our conversation. It would be a disaster if this was to happen again at one or more of your other restaurants. People would start to think you had something to hide. If, on reflection, you think of something that will help, call me on this number."

He left a piece of paper ripped from a notebook on the bar.

"Thank you. By the way, my name is Bryan. If you talk to this girl, Abi, you can tell her you met her brother."

"Are you threatening me? In Turkey, we don't like being threatened."

"Mr Suker, it is my sincere wish we never meet again. All I am saying is that if I do not hear from you, I may make it my business to renew our acquaintance once more. That might not be a pleasant experience for either of us. For now, if you are sure we can't help, we'll be on our way."

Bryan walked confidently out of the door, to the relative calm of the street, Miles a couple of paces behind.

TEN

AS THE DAYS PASSED, Des Kelly felt that he was becoming ever more detached, not only from his family but his work colleagues. The matter of Abi's disappearance had inevitably tainted life at home, in so far as that was possible, given the indifference of his wife and the preoccupations of his son. He realised that in this domestic crisis the expected strength of the family bond was just not there. They were just three individuals ploughing their own wavy furrows through the situation. Not talking, sharing feelings, drawing strength from each other. This had really been shown since the arrival of WPC Graham, who, apart from her official duties, was acting as a sort of unofficial facilitator and communications link between the three of them, much as Des's late mother had done in a past life. The scary part of the present situation was that there was no sense of how or when it would end. Of course, the immediate end would see the departure of WPC Graham, and Miles too, but what of Sue and his own prospects? Given his longer-term plans, in a strange way he saw opportunity for his wife. Unencumbered with family responsibility and with her own independent resources and friends, he could imagine her relishing the freedom it would offer. When you live with someone for as long as he had lived with her, he knew her personality and personal strengths and weaknesses. Indeed, she was fortunate for a woman of her years. She was still reasonably attractive and kept herself well preserved. But her personality had changed, maybe too subtly for him to notice on a daily basis, but nonetheless the person of today was markedly different from the person with whom he had fallen in love and raised a family. He recalled how they had met at a drug-fuelled university party as undergraduates, where they had shared a love for sixties rock music, art and hiking. Back then he had fancied himself as a bit of a guitarist in the mould of Hank Marvin, and to his mind, she could sing like Petula Clark. Unlike so many romances of the era, he had been surprised when the relationship survived their college years and getting married had never really seemed like a big deal. Neither of them wanted a big fuss. They found a compliant vicar in Buckinghamshire to tie the knot with just a dozen or so friends and family. She never had a desire for a career beyond family and maybe that was the problem. The family grew up. Despite her particularly close relationship with Miles, which seemed to have continued long after he had moved out, a void had developed. Des's career had to take priority and that meant long days when he was absent from the family home. His relative success allowed her to live comfortably and that, too, had been part of the problem. As Des well understood, necessity is the true mother of invention, and for Sue, necessity and therefore purpose, had disappeared. Her focus was about filling time, not pursuing an objective where the application of time was an ingredient. A major complication had come with her insistence a couple of years back that they occupy separate bedrooms. It had started quite by chance, with Des getting home late one night from a professional engagement, slipping into the spare room to avoid disturbing her. It was like a spark to tinderwood, facilitating a fundamental change in their relationship, which as far as he was concerned, had not recovered.

His domestic issues were not his only concern. For many years, he had been quietly developing his own scientific brief on behalf of the Lauriston, but since Sir Gavin's arrival three years ago, his work had been subject to greater scrutiny and management interference. His boss had always defended his regular interventions on the basis of cost, but Des was far from convinced that was the true reason. Kelly's work was reaching a point of maturity when commercial applications were becoming clearer and so the intellectual property rights were steadily rising, to a point where the book value of his work had tripled in the last year alone. Kelly was far from convinced Sir Gavin wanted to retain ownership of the work, and it might suit him to offload it at a premium that would fund other potentially lucrative initiatives in other high-growth sectors. All this stuff about lack of communication was bullshit in his mind, but he saw why Jake was pushing it. After all, he hadn't had to try too hard to earn his recent promotion, just brown-nose Sir Gavin a bit. No. Jake was a good enough scientist – a jobbing journeyman whose implementation skills were excellent – but he lacked the brilliance that came with the interpretation and analysis of data. Privately he thought Gavin knew it too, otherwise in this new senior team culture, why was he given personal responsibility for this Russian chap? He hadn't really got the energy to waste on conjecture. All he knew was his personal motivation and the love of his own area of research was being tested as never before. His vocation was morphing into just a job at the most crucial point, when he was about to realise his lifetime's ambition. Well, he would be damned if he had the final prize snatched from him before he crossed the finish line. Strangely it was the thought of that finish line that made him look forward to his next visit to Rømø and his second encounter with Westergaard and his colleagues.

Willoughby had not been impressed to hear of his impending weekend trip, but as Kelly had observed, there had been little reason to stay at home. There had been no news about Abi in the weeks that had passed since her disappearance. Even if something happened during his absence, this trip would be relatively brief, so he wouldn't miss out on formulating a response with the Met.

WPC Wendy and Miles would be there to keep an eye on Sue. Besides, he wouldn't have time to go back to Rømø for another month, because he saw from his diary that he had two visits to host, one of which would be pleasurable – his friend Aldo, and one which would be tiresome – Eve Grainger from Maximum Power Corporation. And then, there was the matter of the Russian, Ponomariev. He would be expected to focus on getting him integrated into the project but had no real information yet regarding the man's capabilities, therefore no sense of knowing how long that might take. His first formal meeting with him would follow in the coming week. In the meantime, he had provided Willoughby with the address of the Kro, although in all honesty he had no certainty of staying there. He had made no reference to the purpose of the visit, only to say he needed some downtime to think through some complex issues at work, and he found walking in the local environment conducive to positive thought. Knowing the setup as he did, he knew that if someone was looking for him, they would be redirected accordingly. He would travel out to Hamburg and back via Billund. The journey time would give him adequate time to prepare.

Sue had greeted news of his imminent departure with her customary indifference. Her diary was made up for the next few days and her own support network was in place, so the presence of Des made no difference to her, other than encouraging her to plan an extra outing which she would make unaccompanied.

Circumstances worked out well for Sue. Within hours of Des departing for Germany, WPC Wendy announced she needed to go home to get a change of clothes and she would be back in the late afternoon. As she was leaving, Miles arrived, bursting to tell his mother of his adventures in north London with Bryan. Given Wendy's absence, Miles told her all about the visit to the Topkapi Nights and what he thought had come out of it.

"I can't believe we got away with it," he told his mother.

"It was like something out of a gangland movie – I didn't

realise Bryan knew such people. It was as though he had his own crime syndicate. He was transformed – quietly impressive with just a twist of menace. It certainly put the shits up Suker. He didn't admit to anything, of course, but we got him worried. I think he knows what's happened and he's going to crack. This was something Willoughby should have done a while ago. I think we're going to find our own way to get Abi back."

His mother responded, "Darling, you are so brave, you should have talked to me or your father before doing this. I shudder to think what might have happened if it had gone wrong."

"Well, it didn't and I'm going to take real pleasure in telling Dad Abi is safe very shortly. Then we'll see what excuses the police offer. Anyway, I'm going back over to the paddock to fit a new headlight on my motorbike. I'll pop in to check things are OK later."

"Better wait until after five. Then we can go and take Milo for a run."

"OK, Mum. See you then."

For the first time in God knows how long, Sue had the house to herself. Even Milo looked chilled in his basket in the kitchen. She fixed herself a coffee and reached for the phone.

"Bryan? It's Sue. Yes, Miles has just told me. I didn't know about your connections in London. It's really thoughtful of you to try to help. Miles seems to be optimistic something may happen... yes. Well, I don't know how you are fixed today, but Des has set off to do something in Germany, my police minder is taking a break and Miles is pulling his motorbike apart in the paddock, so I'm a free agent for a few hours. I thought you could make me a cup of tea or something? Sure, give me an hour..."

For Bryan, the call was payment enough and reward for his endeavour. Like Miles, he had surprised himself with the 'hard man' approach he had taken almost out of the blue. Until he had spoken to Miles last week, it would never have entered his head to try to pull such a stunt. But he had decided to do it, in part to relive his former life and catch up with some old acquaintances. These days, few knew him in London so he could be whoever he wanted to be, without fear or favour. The exercise had even given him a bit of an adrenaline rush. In years to come, he would have a good story about this which he could relate across the bar, especially after Abi was back with her family. As a divorcee, he had long been an admirer of Sue's and, although he was loath to admit it, he had heard talk about her free-living ways in the bar from time to time. But here was the prospect in very clear terms that he would soon benefit from her favours. He had just closed the bar after lunchtime opening. It was time to take a shower and use some of that cologne that had collected dust at the back of his bathroom cabinet and prepare for her visit.

He was not disappointed, either. Opening the back door when the bell rang, he saw Sue standing there; slim figure, made up, hair tied back, jeans, blouse and jacket. The epitome of smart but casual in his eyes. But the blouse was what the outfit was all about, casually open to the third button, the contents barely restrained by her bra and the silk which covered it.

"Bryan, how wonderful to see you, and looking so well." She kissed him on the cheek and walked past him into his private lounge.

"I can't thank you enough for helping us to find Abi. We're terribly grateful."

"Well, I'm not sure we have yet," Bryan could have kicked himself for spoiling the moment.

"Oh, but you will. Miles is very confident. He tells me you can be very persuasive in an understated way. Perhaps you can convince me I should stay for a while?"

She took his hand and held it to her chest.

*

Dimitri Nikitin was not the sort of person to be shocked easily, but the latest intelligence report from London was certainly out of the ordinary and testing his inner calm. Intelligence gathering in the UK had become more challenging in recent years, owing to the British government weeding out what they considered to be non-essential diplomats, and those who remained requiring special authorisation to travel outside London.

Activating his sleeper in Oxford had not been as straightforward as he had hoped; and had initially been reliant on the Russian wife of a British insurance magnate taking a day trip for lunch among the 'dreaming spires' with Lutz to establish the link. Although Nikitin had not yet heard directly from Lutz, the courier filed a report that was, at best, unexpected. The news on the main subject, Dr Desmond Kelly, was thin, but of more interest was the fact that Lutz had told her that a new senior scientist was joining the HCCVD team at the Lauriston who was believed to be Boris Ponomariev, who had apparently absconded from Kaliningrad. Instinctively Nikitin banged back a coded reply to London station: "Confirmation required, preferably visual."

Forget this 'Kelly'; if the report from London was correct, this was serious.

He immediately checked Arbutsev's reports on the confirmation of Ponomariev's drowned remains. He reread them again before reaching for the phone.

"Get me Arbutsev in Kaliningrad *now*."

While he was waiting, he was calculating the ramifications of the situation. As of that moment, the file on Ponomariev had been closed and the news of his demise communicated at the highest level. If he had managed to defect, the policy was clear. He would need to be found, recovered, and removed, or liquidated – their favoured term. He had been in the presence of the senior advisor of the President's Office once before when bad news was imparted. He understood the fear that could be created through silence at such a gathering. It didn't bear thinking about. Before then, he would need to instigate punitive actions down the chain of command. Arbutsev would need to explain who had helped him to reach the false conclusion and would have to deal with them, before he himself acted against his man in the enclave.

"*Fucking hell* – this is a mess. I must come up with a response before more people get to know about it," he told himself.

The immediate option would be to claim Ponomariev had been sent to the West under some sort of elaborate undercover brief to obtain information vital to state security. The emphatic communication of his demise was key to ensuring his real purpose was not discovered. What would that be? There wasn't much going on in the UK that represented a threat to Russia that he wasn't already aware of. And why would that happen? If he had sent Ponomariev to infiltrate the HCCVD research team at the Lauriston, why would he have activated Lutz? No, that wouldn't wash. The alternative would be to sacrifice Arbutsev and propose remedial action. That would involve snatching Ponomariev back with the bonus of sweeping up this Dr Kelly at the same time. After all, if the rumour was to be believed, there would be every chance that the two of them would be in the same place at the same time. There was, of course, another option. Just send a hit squad to Oxford to kill Ponomariev. He could consult his library of casual murder scenarios to pick one, but there was no doubt the ease of either polonium poisoning or planting novichok contamination were regarded as effective tools, with the added value of creating wider panic amongst the public and reminding the renegade community in the UK they were still within Moscow's reach. Keeping faith with the President's Office and the committee had to remain his focus. He would need to pursue a multi-disciplinary path. If he became sure Ponomariev was alive, he would be dealt with. If he could arrange the Kelly snatch as well, that would win him friends in high places – Ruslan Rustanovitch in particular. No, there was still everything to play for and he could still grab a victory out of the jaws of defeat. His new clarity of thought had emerged just in time for him to receive the requested call from Arbutsev.

"Morning, Colonel."

"I thought you would appreciate a little early warning from me. I am picking up good information to suggest Ponomariev is alive and somehow has got to England. Of course, this may prove to be bullshit, but there is a chance, a good chance, it is correct. That being the case, there are implications for you, as the investigating officer, which could impact on your career or potentially worse. I suggest you look at your file, in particular your DNA matching evidence, and consider if you want to revise it. If you do, I think you will be obliged to reopen the case and take proceedings against those whose testimonies could be judged to be false."

"Yes sir, but—"

"No buts – I had the clear impression you had this matter under control and it was closed down. It now looks as if my faith in you was unjustified. I will find a suitable way to express my disappointment if you find yourself unable to provide new information."

Arbutsev held the phone to check the line had gone dead and then kicked it across his office.

Fuck! With all the usual crap intelligence reports he was expected to read, he had this seemingly impossible case to clear up. He thought he had done what Nikitin had told him to do – find the quickest, most plausible way of closing the case. He had a body of approximately the right height and physical attributes of Pomomariev, admittedly his face lacked the square jaw, which was a consistent feature of his pictures, but near as dammit, it was a match. Yes, the DNA was different, but a minor adjustment of the recorded sequencing was all that had been required to make the tragic story believable. He had even tidied up after himself. Once the documentation had been completed and authorised, he had arranged for the School Street house to be deep-cleaned and the body cremated. Information regarding the abandoned Polish-made tent and the coincidental day visit of the Pole, Zanowsky, dismissed as casual smuggling, an everyday occurrence between Kaliningrad and Gdansk despite border checks. The only other interest had been the late departure of the fishing boat B474 with the skipper, Igor Poliarkin. Not much to look at there, either. He had a criminal record for low-level smuggling of cigarettes, but who didn't? And then there was that lazy bastard, the commissar, Moscovoi; in Arbutsev's book, the man most likely to be involved in any wrong doing. Apparently, he was the reason the B474 had set sail ninety minutes late because he had got carried away, fucking a tourist guide. It all looked perfectly plausible, so what else was there to discover?

He would start over and that meant a more forceful discussion with Moscovoi.

He found him sitting in the sun at the kiosk on the quay, next to the fishing boats.

"How come an old dog like you gets off with a voluptuous woman like Lyudmilla?" Arbutsev was already focusing on the pieces of the story that didn't add up.

The commissar stared into the middle distance, hoping that if ignored, Arbutsev would go away. When he saw it wasn't working, he fixed him with a disdainful stare.

"I've got a big dick. Want to see the evidence?" He stood and put his hand on his belt.

"Now come on, I am sure a woman like that is a bit more demanding…"

"So why don't you ask her?"

"I intend to, but for now I'm happy to work with your answers."

"Sometimes, when it's quiet down here, I go up to the tourist office and sit round the back. I got to know her. I could see she was lonely. I offered her the hand of friendship and then… well, she decided she wanted more."

"So, you are in a relationship?"

"I wouldn't say that, exactly. I happened to be in the right place at the right time – you're a man of the world."

"So Lyudmilla was the reason why Poliarkin went to sea late that night?"

"Ask him."

"But he couldn't sail without you because your name was on the manifest which you delivered to the harbourmaster's office three hours earlier."

"That is the process."

"What would have happened if you just got carried away with your lady friend and forgot the time?"

"I didn't – I was just a little behind schedule. But if I had Poliarkin would have had to stay in port."

"It was a rough night out at sea, wasn't it?"

"As I remember, there was a squally sea, but it eased off on the way back."

"Which was what time?"

"Around four in the morning."

"What did you do when you got back?"

"The usual. Helped to unload the boxes of fish, had some breakfast, went home to bed… for some sleep."

"OK, we'll leave it there for now. Commissar Moscovoi, let me tell you why I am good at my job. I have a built-in bullshit detector which flashes in my head when I listen to someone like you. Have no doubt I will be making further enquiries and if I don't like what I hear you can be sure I will be back."

"If you're looking for Poliarkin he's flushing out the hold, third one along."

Not only was Arbutsev going to speak to Poliarkin but two of his investigators were already searching his flat.

The investigator walked further along the quay to where the boats were moored.

"Skipper Igor Poliarkin? Chief Investigator Gennady Arbutsev, FSB. Hope you don't mind me coming aboard to look around? A couple of my people just want to do a couple of DNA checks in the wheelhouse and down below. You must forgive me; my team is a little overworked and I'm playing catch-up. A prominent citizen has absconded, and I am investigating whether he might have had help."

"Absconded?"

"Gone missing is a better description. He may have moved away without notifying the authorities or he may be dead. I just need to establish the facts. I'm here because his disappearance seems to coincide with one of your Baltic trips about four weeks ago, when Commissar Moscovoi was late boarding."

"Oh yes. I remember."

"Was his lateness out of the ordinary?"

"I suppose it was. He is normally punctual."

"How did he seem?"

Igor frowned. "I'm not sure I remember that far back. Nothing springs to mind."

"Can you remember what the weather was like?"

"Funnily enough I can – it was a pretty shitty night. A couple of the lads puked as I recall. It's an occupational hazard, although we always say it's lucky for us as it serves as extra bait. The cod normally start following us on those occasions."

"The harbourmaster's log from that night shows a radar position off your designated route that took you to within thirty miles of Swedish Gotland."

"Yes, our system is a bit old-fashioned, and I think it got a little sea spray inside because of the rough weather. Fortunately Baltiysk Control alerted us to change direction or else we might have been arrested by the Swedes for spying. We are always being warned to look out for their naval patrols, and we certainly didn't want to share our catch with them. We were a bit behind the other two boats that were out that night, but we caught up with them and returned in convoy."

As Poliarkin spoke, Arbutsev's phone lit up with a text.

"It must be a good living you make as a fisherman these days. How do you get paid?"

"Cash or bank draft depending on how much we land. Most of it goes to the central market in Kaliningrad, then on to Moscow, St Petersburg or Pskov, so a lot of the time we sell to agents in account. But hey, if we come across a customer who will pay a higher price, we'll do it."

"Roubles or euros?"

"US dollars, whatever – if the price is right, I don't care."

"Based on the half million we have just found in your flat, euros seem to be your favourite. Shouldn't that be kept in a bank and declared?"

Poliarkin's face fell.

"I get it, this is a tax bust, OK? So I've not declared it yet, but I will go to the revenue office on my next day off and sort it out. I had expected such an eventuality. The notes and seals are marked with smart water so if you have had your dabs on it and helped yourself, I'll know and some of my friends won't care if you are FSB or GRU, they'll want your balls."

"Where did it come from?"

"Some is fishing, I do a bit of import/export with Poland like a lot of us do. I normally send vodka out and bring second-hand or hot cars back. I don't get involved in the ordering of black-market cars; I just process the orders. If you bust me for that, you'll have to arrest at least half the town."

"Least you're not doing drugs. I'd have to nail you for that if I found any. For now, we have only taken some pictures and dusted the containers down. We might need it as evidence and we have left it where you hid it. I wouldn't advise breaking it up. I am interested in what happened to the guy who used to live on the corner of School Street, a stone's throw from here. Tall, thin, fair-haired, thick-set jaw, called Ponomariev. You must have seen him around."

Poliarkin shrugged.

"Probably did, but I don't think he made an impression on me."

"Heard of a guy called Zanowsky?"

"Yeah – I meet him occasionally, normally in Kaliningrad, sometimes here. He brings me the deals. Mainly cars but sometimes other things – TVs, fridges, you know."

"He is travelling on a false identity. Did you know? If we pick him up, he will be charged. You can warn him."

"Sure, but I think you are more likely to find him before I do."

"Just be careful, Poliarkin. Stick to fishing. I have enough on you to stop you going to sea for a long time if I decide to get difficult. Talk to your crew. If they know anything you'd be well advised to call me."

His next stop was back across the estuary at the tourist information office. Lyudmilla had her standard bored expression, which didn't send a positive signal to the prospective tourist looking to part with their cash.

"I'm Arbutsev."

"I know who you are and what you do. I've seen you around."

"Good – that's got the pleasantries out of the way. I am here about Moscovoi."

She stared at the ceiling.

"God, it only happened the once – I just want to forget it."

"How come a good-looking woman like you picked up with a slob like him?"

"Can't you guess?"

"Roubles or euros?"

She snorted and started rearranging some leaflets on the counter.

"What I want to know is how long he was with you."

"Too long. I don't know, I can't remember. It was dark when he came. Dark when I sat on him and dark when he left. It was good. I was able to imagine I was with someone else. Now if you will excuse me, I`m busy."

"If you think of anything else I should know, please call. After all, you wouldn't want me to guess what really happened, would you?"

He turned and headed out of the door, back to his office.

It was time to face the music. He called Nikitin.

"In the process of investigating this matter further I have

discovered several smuggling scams but nothing new that relates to your interest. Residences and boats were searched and swabs taken. I am sorry, sir. I propose to update the file to record the error in the DNA matching. The mortuary assistant involved in the testing has been dismissed. As the senior investigating officer, I understand the extent of my responsibilities and offer my resignation with immediate effect."

*

Driving across the causeway from Jutland to Rømø was a therapeutic experience. The long straight elevated highway was interspersed with laybys but promised the driver no deviations along the way. The journey allowed him to clear his mind of the stresses of work and home and to refocus on his personal project managing his demise. Unlike organising his own funeral, something many terminally ill people tended to do, Kelly had no interest in ceremony; he was a process man, whose wish was to leave his affairs in order for the next generation. Perversely, he drew some comfort from this situation because it was the one element of his life over which he had control. The driver's view of the road combined with the wide-open overcast sky illustrated his life well – a blurred mix of shades of grey broken by the occasional red of the distance markers on the parallel pathway. Next to the laybys were descriptive signs telling the visitor what wading birds they would be likely to see on the mudflats on either side. He had meant to stop to take it all in, but realised he lacked binoculars or the time. This trip would be shorter than the last and he had an appointment to keep. Fortunately, the clock was on his side, but there was no margin for error. He would go straight to Havneby to check in at the Kro, (around fifteen minutes from his present location) and then off to complete the second stage of the preparation process, the meeting with Dr Kjaer, around an hour from now.

Leaving Havneby he checked the address on the satnav. Although there weren't too many roads on Rømø, finding the house, which he vaguely remembered was in a wood, might not be so easy, especially this time without Westergaard to drive him there. He would catch up with the fisherman in the bar later when he would be able to report on the day's events. Bolstered by finding the family name on the letterbox at the end of the drive, Kelly made his way to the front door. It was with a feeling of trepidation, which reminded him of how he had felt reporting for his O level exams way back when. He was about to be tested, about what he couldn't imagine and therefore could not be prepared. He was immediately put off his guard as when he reached for the bell the door was thrown open.

"Dr Kelly, welcome back to Rømø! I have coffee and cake ready in my front room. Do come through. Please..."

"Call me Des."

"And you must call me Marisa."

She gestured him towards an armchair with a view through partially opened French windows to the forest behind. A gentle breeze created a calming atmosphere, even though it was cloudy overhead. She took the armchair opposite him, picking up a pen and A4 scribble pad from a nearby coffee table.

Marisa Kjaer was a typical Danish woman, late thirties (so he guessed), auburn hair, arranged in two ponytails, and dressed in floral dungarees, with gold earrings, fashion watch, no wedding ring.

Instantly he liked her and knew exactly why – her smile. Broad, revealing a perfect set of white teeth that would have won her a part in an Arm & Hammer commercial.

"Have you travelled up from Hamburg today?" she enquired.

"Yes, I arrived about an hour ago."

"And back to England tomorrow?"

"Pressure of work, I'm afraid."

"I quite understand. I was pleased Nils was able to introduce us, albeit briefly, on your last visit. He has subsequently told me more about you, that you are coming to terms with a life-changing physical diagnosis and this information I will use to shape our discussion today. I am a consultant psychotherapist specialising in mental health diagnostics at the local university here. Has he told you much about what we are going to do?"

"Not really, other than what you told me when we were introduced last time; that you are going to interview me and write a report on my mental health, which will then be assessed to confirm that I am of sound mind and can proceed with my plans."

"Yes, that is basically it. I will interview you so don't be surprised if I ask you some strange or personal questions. You might feel unsettled. I have to try to understand what makes you tick. We need to make a record which demonstrates that you fully understand what is happening and have prepared yourself for the process. I should say, you are welcome to view the record when it is complete but not to alter the contents, as that will be my professional opinion and necessary in the event of any subsequent legal action by your relatives. Do you understand and are you happy to proceed?"

"Yes."

"Good. How are you feeling?"

"All right – pleased to be here. I started to feel more relaxed when I drove over the causeway. I only seem to feel a bit under the weather when I get tired."

"Mentally or physically?"

"Probably both – doesn't one feed off the other?"

"Tell me about the mental tiredness you feel."

"What can I say? It is driven by uncertainty. I could die this afternoon, next week or not perhaps for a couple of years. I am not only coming to terms with my imminent mortality but the sense of mission I feel to complete my life's journey. I now understand that I have been socialised into fitting into other people's agendas and expectations for too long. I need to find some personal calm and must recognise the possibility of doing that in another life. That is what makes me tired."

"What makes you happy?"

"I don't know, I've never really thought about it. Good food, wine, a book, music, walking... I have even taken to corresponding online occasionally with a female colleague I barely know, because I am discovering a new personality. That is stimulating and, in its way, a source of happiness."

"Sex? Do you like it?"

Kelly blushed.

"Er..."

She shrugged. "You're a good-looking guy for a man of your age – why wouldn't you? Personally, I like it, it's very healthy."

"Well, it's been a long time."

"Don't worry, it's not a proposition, just a test of attitude. When you last had sex do you remember the experience? As you said, you've not been too well lately. Does talk of it leave you cold?"

"I'm not used to having an intimate conversation with someone I don't know..."

She finished his sentence with a slight smile, "... especially a woman. And yet you say you have opened this dialogue with a female colleague?"

"Yes, but not in *that* way. It's semi-anonymous. We know each other's names but that's it. We talk from time to time about a scientific world we both understand. I have no expectations and have no idea why she keeps in touch. Maybe for her I am a mentor. In a low moment, I told her I have been diagnosed as being critically ill and that our dialogue makes me feel better. Yes, I am OK for the moment, but it is this reality that is driving me to take control so that I can manage my forthcoming demise in a way that suits me."

"What is that way?"

"I want to increase the possibility of dying naturally by grappling with fate. Tipping the odds against survival in a situation to find peace, preserve my thoughts, hopes, fears, achievements, and to perhaps shape a new future for my family members – without enduring excessive pain."

"Very laudable and a tall order. Are you a vain man, just trying to export responsibility to somebody else for arranging your own death?"

"I don't think so, but I am a scientist. I like order, control, tidiness, fulfilment – qualities of what you might think of as mindfulness. I do not fully understand it but I have read some books on the topic by Brantley and Jon Kabat-Zinn. Kabat-Zinn's work referencing mindfulness to waves and their relationship to the unpredictable winds of stress made sense to me when I first came here. If it wasn't for mindfulness I doubt whether I would be here now. Completing my story, tying up loose ends, and resolving ambiguities are my aims now. I am coming to terms with my mortality, pain and am learning to be brave. I hope to leave a mark on the future, but that isn't vanity, merely making my own contribution to destiny coherent."

"I take from that you have low self-esteem?"

"Probably. I am self-critical, I judge myself by my own successes, which is always frustrating in a scientific environment because every time you achieve an outcome a new horizon of investigation opens. You never get to the end of the road."

"Are you emotional?"

"If you mean do I feel hurt, angry, anxious – yes – all the time, and I know it results in poor personal behaviours. I am more sensitive to threats, less tolerant of people, family and work colleagues."

"So, you suffer from Ivings' *Malevolent Parrot* syndrome, whereby you carry an imaginary parrot, a bully, on your shoulder?"

"Yes, I do."

"And you don't think you can put that parrot in a cage and cover it with a towel?"

Kelly laughed for the first time. To him, the imagery was absurd. He thought they were having a life and death discussion – so far it seemed to have focused on sex, the weather and a parrot.

"I'm not sure I follow."

"You don't think you can offer yourself compassionate thoughts as a means of making sense of your problems?"

"No. To me, compassion is love. As a young man I knew love. I loved a woman who I knew could never be mine. I settled on a lesser love, more a marriage of convenience, as a means of blocking out the pain. My marriage produced two children, which showed me a different facet of love which has sustained me through my middle years until now. That, too, largely disappeared as they took on their own independent lives. My wife treats me with indifference, and has found alternative physical comfort, thinking I don't know her, or care about her anymore. I have tried talking and failed."

He deliberately decided not to mention his fears for Abi.

"Do you really want an assisted dying service? Seems a bit excessive when perhaps marriage guidance would be better."

"No. I am in a box, personally and professionally. Time is now limited and there is no other way out. My marriage is effectively gone. I wonder if I am too old to invest in an alternative relationship, but time will tell. My work is the same. For years, my area of expertise was ignored, ridiculed. Now there is some mad competition to strip my knowledge and sell it to the highest bidder. You may not understand this, Marisa, but scientists rarely work for sectional commercial gain but for the broad-based good of society. My work should be carried forward and shared internationally, helping to improve our climate and provide limitless energy for all. Instead, individual countries and corporations are competing to control it and use it as a tool to benefit their own sectional interests. That, more than anything else, is my parrot. It has a poisoned bite and will attack me if I try to put it in a cage. My destiny is to find inner calm, complete my journey and the bird will have to come with me."

*

"Cheers, *Skal!*"

Westergaard clinked glasses with Kelly in the bar at the Kro, sampling one of his latest brews.

"Good, eh? This is the bit of my work I enjoy the most. It is a pity I don't have enough time for tasting," he laughed.

"You certainly made an impression on Marisa today, Des. She was quite taken with you, in particular, your focus and motivation under such personal stress. Her report will be copied to you next week but I can tell you it meets all the assessment criteria Danish government inspectors would require. So we can celebrate – you are now halfway to completing your preparation. Am I right in assuming you still want to move forward?"

"Of course, I made up my mind to follow this through at the beginning. We have come too far to stop now."

"I will get you booked in with Maurice Glistrup next. He is an interesting guy. He is our local pastor and deals in the faith aspects of our work. I think you'll get on with him well. He is a very human, right-thinking person, which is probably why he has a second job as the Rømø conservation ranger at the Wadden Sea National Park. He will explain the theological support we offer at Terminal and how you can prepare for your time in the water. Do remember, these meetings are spread out for a reason. When you go home and reflect on the experience, you may change your mind. When do you think you'll be able to come?"

"I'm planning on being back eight weeks from now."

"I'm sure it will be fine. I'll email you tomorrow with confirmation and the invoice for the next part of the process."

ELEVEN

FORTY-EIGHT HOURS LATER AND Rømø seemed a world away to Des. Dr Roberts's new way of working was still bedding in, but it was already clear that the additional reporting procedures in the team were slowing up the research effort. He knew there was no point in making the case to Sir Gavin, as it would just be dismissed as negative thinking, and in any case would be judged way too early an intervention to be considered objective. Notwithstanding the new communications and documentation arrangements, Des was also constrained by the impending visits of Aldo de Leonibus and Eve Grainger. Both were much more than social calls, requiring tours of the Lauriston and Harwell as well as formal peer assimilation and project validation assessments.

It was always a pleasure for Des to meet Aldo. Although their meeting had a formal element, theirs was an old friendship forged over many years which provided a social dimension to their dialogue. The timing was good as far as Des was concerned. Despite the relative success of his second Rømø trip, the news from home had been less so. Still nothing on Abi, except Miles seemed to think some Turkish kebab seller in north London was key to the investigation. It was true he vaguely remembered Willoughby talking about it but that was a while ago and there had been nothing since. Curiously, Sue had been in a better frame of mind. He had put that down to a game of bridge and a choir rehearsal in the church hall. Trying to make sense of the upheaval in home life was difficult. Strangely he was getting used to Miles becoming a fixture once more, having previously moved out six years earlier, and even WPC Wendy seemed to have an unusual ability to become anonymous, considering she had almost become their unofficial lodger. The stress of the return to work was influenced by his need to put together an induction for the Russian – Latvian or whatever he was – Guntis Karins, over the coming week. That in itself should not have been difficult but it was trickier to tell from the CV he had been sent what grasp of the technology the man actually had. What's more, it would in all likelihood take him several months of personal observation to know. That was the real reason why Sir Gavin had made Des the mentor; it was just another load he had to bear, an obstacle to be overcome.

But for now the attention had to be on Aldo. Sir Gavin had not been aware that this visit had been a personal request from the guest and had assumed it was a periodic inspection for the IAEA, a reputationally important opportunity for the Lauriston.

Sir Gavin instructed that Professor de Leonibus was to be regarded as a VIP guest and was to be given access to all research data. Kelly had smiled when he had read Sir Gavin's emailed instruction. Aldo was, of course, very good and an undoubted expert in his field, but HCCVD was new and there was no way he could get value from accessing the project's data as he would have difficulty interpreting it. Still, he would help him through and leave Sir Gavin to follow up to secure the updated international valedictory.

He saw the value in being able to have a private dinner with his friend and share his personal worries with one of the few people he knew he could trust.

It didn't quite work out in the way Des expected.

The tours, networking lunch and the laboratory inspections had gone like clockwork. Now in the evening of the visit the two men were able to talk as friends, over dinner at an exclusive restaurant on the banks of the Thames.

"This hastily arranged trip has worked out well, Aldo. I don't often have the excuse to enjoy dinner in one of the best French restaurants in southern England. The food here even by our international standards is sublime. I don't know why they bother with menus. It is often better to get the *maître d'hôte* to serve up whatever is on the go. All the selections seem to go well with any of the thirty or so clarets on the wine list. I'm feeling lucky tonight so I'm going for number twenty-one, which should go well with the duck and artichoke."

"Desmond, I am most grateful to you for accommodating me at such short notice. Your work here is truly amazing. When I leave you, I will be reflecting on the implications of all I have seen and heard. I wondered whether your government sponsors fully understand the capability of HCCVD?"

"I think they do to an extent, but not from a scientific perspective. For them, this is just a big revenue earner for the country and in due course I am sure they will sell out to the highest bidder."

"That seems a shame."

"It is, but I've been in this game too long now not to understand the way it is going. I won't be surprised if we end up losing our leadership position in this field in the next five years. Anyway, that is a subject for another day. I know when you asked to come here, that you wanted to speak with me privately. Well, here we are. You didn't have to go through all the formalities at the Lauriston for this. You could have called me. It would never be a problem."

"You are most kind. I visit you at a strange time. You may know that my assignment in Bulgaria will be ending over the next year and then in all likelihood I would be returning to Bologna to lecture at the university. Surprisingly, from a personal point of view I have found Bulgaria to be very agreeable. I met Iveta, for a start, and generally the weather is to my liking. The assignment has been frustrating, however. There have been all sorts of lapses in containment and security procedures and to me it is a miracle there have not been any fatalities. Bulgaria may be beautiful but professionally it is a backwater and I am not yet ready to retire. Unexpectedly, when we were in Berlin a few months ago, at your conference seminar, I met a representative of the Saudi government. I subsequently learned that they had been monitoring my work and they have offered me the job of running their state-aided HCCVD project. I know what you are thinking; how can this be when I have not been working directly in this field in the way you have? I told them so and they said they understood that, but they still wanted me – I guess because of my networks in the international energy futures business. The Saudis are worried about your work, Desmond. They have concluded that if you continue at the speed you are going you will cause a crisis in the global hydrocarbons market, their core business. They would like to see your work slowing down and are pursuing diplomatic efforts to this end with the British government. In the event they are unsuccessful, the Crown Prince has decided *at whatever cost* the Saudis must get global control of the technology and they are offering me a five-year contract and all the resources I can ask for, to achieve that result."

"That is fantastic, my friend – that's quite an offer. I am sure you don't need a reference from me. What are you going to do?"

"I don't know yet. Personally, it's is an attractive offer. It is everything I could have expected and potentially a great way to top off my career…"

"But?"

"It is a gilded cage. In some ways I have authority. In other ways, I have none. I will front up their work on HCCVD internationally but will have to submit my policy papers, development proposals and staff hires for approval to the Crown Prince."

"Is that so surprising if he is picking up the bill?"

"It's not about money but reputation. I could be totally compromised if I am taking forward a course of action that he chooses to withdraw support for or change without notice or prior agreement with me. Potentially I will become a professional hostage at risk of public humiliation amongst my peers."

"I think your peers will be more understanding than you imagine. I suffer from much the same type of risk as you, or perhaps the pressure on me is more institutionalised, less personal."

"There is something else. I also have some gaps in my knowledge of HCCVD."

"So do we all. That is the point of innovation."

"But you know more than me."

"I spend all of my time on researching it so that, too, is inevitable. Don't worry, Aldo; as a friend, you can always talk to me, especially if you need a second opinion or technical guidance. I will help you all I can, so long as I'm still involved."

"Have you made alternative plans?"

"None of us can ever be sure about our prospects. It is possible something could happen to me during the life of your commission. Then you'd be out there on your own or having to buy in support from wherever you could find it."

"You are a true friend, Desmond. I am travelling to Riyadh in two weeks to meet them all and talk through their plans. You have given me the confidence to accept if I feel comfortable with their assurances. Now, you mentioned you had some news you wished to share with me?"

Had circumstances been different, Kelly might have discussed something of the disappearance of Abi, his own health problems, Maximum Power, Rustanova, or even the impending arrival of the Latvian, but in all cases, he judged the time wasn't right.

He would just live in the moment, enjoying his dinner with convivial company and make small talk about their shared passions of football and opera.

*

Chemmy Moore had risen in Bannan's estimation.

She had done a pretty good job in Copenhagen and certainly filled in a lot of the blanks about Terminal and its operations.

"I get the impression you were getting to like your alter ego," he told her as he looked out of his seventh-floor office window across the water in the direction of Millbank and the Houses of Parliament.

"It was fun having an expense account and the feeling I was worth over fifty million euros even for an hour or a day or whatever. It was also a change to have a more active assignment. Being a watcher can be a little boring at times, even on the Danish coast."

"True. But it's a pity you are clearly so good at it. Now at least you can say you have another string to your bow.

"I don't think I want to know how you went about accessing your target's personal computer but I must compliment you on opening up his files. We are still reviewing the contents. Seems Westergaard and his colleagues are in a high-growth business – amoral possibly, but legit. Kelly has paid them forty thousand euros so far. I still want to know more about his clients and how Kelly got involved in the first place. My one frustration was that you didn't get details of their customers in other countries. We would have been delighted if we knew anything about their operations in Russia, for example, but maybe there will be another time."

"Maybe," Chemmy repeated, almost in a whisper.

Bannan continued, "According to his email traffic he's due to meet another of Westergaard's associates, Ranger Maurice Glistrup, at the end of next month. Apparently, he is the warden of the Wadden Sea National Park, but clearly is involved in other matters. Better go and dig up as much as you can on him. Make sure we know what he's about before Kelly gets there. Oh, and by the way, I want you to keep a special look out for Kelly next week. I think he will have a particular reason to be in London on a bit of private business on Wednesday. I'll tip you the wink when he's on the move and you can pick up his trail."

"Is Ifor coming with me?"

"No, he's got his hands full on a separate but related exercise. He won't be back until we've put the Kelly business to bed."

With Chemmy gone, Bannan returned to his computer and the incomplete Terminal customer list. No names were standing out. Surely Kelly wasn't seriously contemplating assisted suicide? His medical records showed he had a routine health check six months ago but there was nothing there to link him to Denmark. No record of depression to trigger his employer's interest. No record of any health insurance claims. The bank showed he was freely financing his own demise. What was the story here? It was too early to brief Sir Gavin to intervene. He made a note to check for any news on his behaviour with Williams. Next week, he noted, Rustanova was in London at the Chatham House seminar which he would also attend in a private capacity. He would be paying close attention and with Chemmy shadowing his subject he expected to learn more. As part of his preparation he made a note to check what progress Willoughby was making with his enquiries. He was missing a trick somewhere.

*

They were now a month into the new life of the HCCVD team at the Lauriston and Des Kelly had prepared the induction to welcome the newest member of the senior team. Although amongst his immediate colleagues the true identity of Guntis Karins was known, it was agreed it would never be publicly referred to in any context – formal or informal.

Sir Gavin had been relishing this moment. Karins was undoubtedly a major asset and the fact that he had been secured for the Lauriston was his personal achievement, or that was the impression he wanted to give.

With the key players all shoehorned into his glass bubble office on the seventh floor, the new man faced his first big test, understanding what coffee he would prefer to have from his boss's state of the art machine. He went for a cappuccino. An Americano, the main alternative, seemed somehow inappropriate.

"Professor Karins, it is my pleasure to introduce you to the Lauriston's HCCVD senior management team," he began expansively. "We are delighted you have chosen Oxford as the place to develop your career. I think we can rightly claim this team and our work here is world class and you will be able to contribute to a project that will have profound consequences for how we all live and relate to our environment. We have a total learning culture where all our people, regardless of seniority, have their efforts embedded in the project, and rewarded as a consequence. You can expect to have an influential role in our plans. As we go forward you will spend time with each member of the SMT although your main relationship is with Dr Desmond Kelly, who operates at the cutting edge of our research activities, at a level which frankly I am struggling to keep up with. As we have already discussed, Guntis, I know your own specialism of micro ambient propulsion technologies has involved limited appraisal of HCCVD, but with Des's help we can show you how it can be taken to a whole new level."

"Thank you, Sir Gavin. My new friends, thank you for your welcome. It is an absolute pleasure to be here in Oxford, a beautiful and tolerant place where I am feeling instantly at home. I am very excited to be working with you and your teams and plan to give my all to developing a new science that will benefit mankind and help the environment. Life for me in the old country was much harder because all our work was first dedicated to the achievement of political objectives. A culture of threat and duress permeated everything we did. Our achievements were limited to finding more efficient ways of punishing the enemies of the state. It is instantly pleasing to be working in an environment free of politics.

This alone creates the best conditions for innovation. Already my thanks must go to you, Dr Kelly. While I have been confined to my temporary home, the opportunity to read your reports has been most stimulating and will allow us the prospect of developing a quality dialogue. I spent some of my early formative years at the Russian Academy of Sciences studying the energy co-efficient of nuclear rods with Professor Galina Rustanova, whose work you are probably familiar with. So, although I am an ethnic Russian and you English, we already have a common language."

Des was taken by surprise at this but kept a poker face.

"It's really great to have you on board," Jake Roberts intervened. "The work here is difficult, uncertain and expensive and we are constantly trying to secure funds for the next phases of the project. We will be keen to showcase your role and contribution to our investors."

"And as a boy I learned Russian in school in Germany, so when you get tired of speaking English, I will be happy to help with a bit of translation."

It was the first time Liebelt had contributed to the conversation.

"That is useful to know, Werner," the Latvian replied. "I am sure I will be testing the limits of my English vocabulary."

"This feels like a historic moment," Liebelt continued. "When I joined the Lauriston, I had my picture taken with my colleagues and you, Sir Gavin. I still have it on my wall at home. Now we have established a new senior management team we should have a picture to mark the start of working together. My phone will do a delayed time image so if I set it up and we can all squeeze in either side of you, Sir Gavin, we will have a great picture for the office."

The German had sensed the momentary bemusement in the room to get his way.

Karins then turned to Williams, now conspicuous as the only one who had not spoken, as if inviting him to say something.

The Welshman looked slightly uncomfortable.

"I'm not sure you'll want to have much to do with me. I

deal with most of the boring stuff, ensuring our documentation is prepared, cross-checked, certified and catalogued. It's the hard wiring of a project like this. I will have expectations of you which I will talk through when we have more time together."

Karins smiled and nodded.

"Well, gentlemen, time to get back to work. Des will be looking after you, Guntis, but remember my door is always open."

"Thank you, Sir Gavin. I still have some liaison work to finish for my sponsors in London and then they are helping me to find more permanent accommodation in the locality, so I will be in and out of the office in coming weeks."

"Just keep Des in touch with your movements, Guntis, and Des, can you pop back in to see me later on, say about four-thirty?"

Sir Gavin diverted his attention to his computer screen, indicating the meeting and the welcome was now over.

*

It proved to be a nondescript day, taken up with getting Karins registered on the Lauriston's electronic systems and helping him to order the necessary equipment for his office next door to Des. It was ironic that it tended to be the simplest things which seemed to take the most time to organise. Karins had been collected mid-afternoon by a useful-looking suited civil servant from the MoD, clearly his nominated minder, who had taken him away somewhere for some purpose Des was not concerned with. Sir Gavin's friends at the ministry had been thoughtful enough to at least issue him with a mobile, so Des had the means of making contact if necessary.

Des duly arrived back at Sir Gavin's office at the appointed hour.

"Well what do you think?" his boss enquired.

"He's certainly polite, but it's going to take a bit of time for us to assess his knowledge and potential. His induction programme will start next week and involve low-level engagement and participation with the secondary research teams. I will spend time with him to monitor his progress and mentor where appropriate."

"Good – one way or another we have a lot riding on Dr Karins."

"How do you mean?"

"Firstly, it is a real compliment to the work of the team that he was offered to us in the first place, so we want to do everything possible to get him integrated into our work. It probably means the government are keen to fund us in the next budget round. Secondly, given his background, we will be able to diversify the HCCVD product offer which will attract new project sponsors."

"Diversify?"

"Karins' skills are in military applications – in particular, ships, submarines and missiles. He has brought us invaluable intelligence, especially about Russia's efforts to develop safe nuclear powered conventional missiles. If he can design and adapt the heavy-duty diamond brick battery then there is big money for us, not least from the US defense department."

"So, the prime outcome for our work will be military hardware not civilian applications."

"It's fact of life, Des, that is where the money is. Karins must develop the military portfolio as a priority because that is the route into the scalable commercial stuff."

"Does Karins realise that? He wasn't speaking that way earlier."

"He's going to work it out for himself. It was his decision to get out of Russia. We have helped him and given him a route to a better life. This is the price he has to pay."

The comment made an impact on Des. He had understood exactly what Guntis had meant. He was about to find out that although he had changed sides the rules of the game were the same.

And that was why, in his heart of hearts, Des knew he needed to get out.

*

There was still much to do before then. In the car on the way home, he started to think about his next big meeting in forty-eight hours with Maximum Power Corporation. He would be hosting Eve Grainger, Birnbaum's head of special projects and all-round personal assistant. He knew Grainger by reputation to be clever, intuitive, in some ways smarter than her boss and the word in the office (as shared by Jake Roberts) was that she was on a mission to buy out the Lauriston. Roberts was probably right. It was being left to Kelly and Roberts to manage the visit to Oxford and Harwell, but it was interesting to note that Sir Gavin would not be there. This all felt as though it had been carefully choreographed. Who would have thought it? Laidlaw was not around when the Lauriston's biggest suitor was in town. It made no sense, other than the fact that he probably wanted to meet her in London to talk turkey where he could feel in a more comfortable negotiating environment. Also the visit to Oxford would be on a day that Karins was out of the office. Maybe he was reading too much into it.

He knew he was right to be cautious when she arrived at the Institute the following morning to be received by Jake. A casual look at the visitor's security log later in the day had shown she was in the building an hour earlier than expected, and Roberts appeared not to have arrived at his desk at that hour, before bringing their guest into his office.

"Dr Kelly, good to meet you again."

"Doesn't time fly? It seems as though it was only last week that we were together in Berlin."

"For me slightly longer I'm afraid. I've been in Asia and back to the States in the meantime. I must admit I'm looking forward to cooling my heels in a couple of weeks with the family so I can get my body clock reset."

This lady was a power dresser of the first order, and she looked ready for battle. True to form her heels were indeed red (the same shade as her lipstick) and perfectly co-ordinated with a black two-piece business suit with scarlet braid, and black pearl necklace and earrings. She gave the impression that her reference to family was not necessarily limited to her nearest and dearest.

"I must thank you for going to so much trouble to accommodate me today. As I said to Gavin over dinner last night, your arrangements for my visit appear most thorough. I am particularly looking forward to viewing some of your tests at first hand."

So this was a fix.

"I cannot take credit for that, I'm afraid. Jake is the man who has our communications and administration under control. I am more the nuts and bolts department. I hope you will recognise me later when I see you at Harwell, as I will have changed into one of our yellow laboratory safety suits and be talking to you from behind a face visor."

He smiled to himself. Visitors' face visors were green; together with the yellow safety suit and her present red attire she would look like a confused traffic light. He didn't envy Jake telling her she would not be allowed in the lab with her large Vuitton handbag. Instinctively, Kelly took a leaf out of Sir Gavin's 'Meet and Greet' manual.

"Coffee?"

"No thanks, I managed a good breakfast at the Randolph and Jakeman here topped me up on arrival. I understand that you are busy, and you will have realised that this is not a social call. I think it important that, thanks largely to the efforts of Dr Roberts, Maximum Power is interested in collaborating with the Lauriston. Hector sent me here on a personal mission – to sound you out, and to understand what your attitude is to working with us."

"Wow, this is a bit unexpected," he lied.

"I suppose my first question is why are you interested in talking to me about it? I assume you discussed it with Gavin last night?"

"Only in broad terms," Jake interrupted.

So I wasn't invited to the party last night, thought Des. *This looks like a very efficient stitch-up all right.*

"Well, as Jake will have told you, I am a humble man of science. I spend money in pursuit of knowledge. I leave it to Gavin and Jake to worry about how we attract the investment we need. Besides, HCCVD is not a new concept to Maximum Power. You already have your own research programme."

"That is the point, Dr Kelly... Des, we do, and we have thrown a considerable resource behind it, but we are still too far behind you in terms of outcomes."

"But you know a lot of our recent achievements are still on test, so even we aren't fully sure we've cracked the performance issues yet."

"The word in the market suggests you're being very modest and that you have solved the biggest technical barrier, of focusing and extracting commercial levels of electrical charge. We have the unparalleled production capability for the diamond brick but cannot get a wattage much more than a lightbulb out of it right now. You seem to have a way of using high-performing conductors which no one else has managed to replicate."

"It's very generous of you to say that. I cannot comment because I am bound by confidentiality clauses with our present funding partner, the UK government."

"I think we can say that in terms of the development of the technology we are probably the thought leaders, so the Maximum Power interest may just be about underwriting the IP – intellectual property," added Roberts, desperate to avoid Kelly's effort to kill the discussion.

Grainger continued, "Jake is right, Des. Working with Maximum Power will instantly release millions of dollars of new investment for your work. Just our association will triple the value of the intellectual property and put some serious points on the share price on Wall Street."

"How would a deal work?"

"How would you want it to work? We can stay separate and have an exclusivity agreement or take a minority stock holding or buy you out altogether. There are regulatory aspects to all three routes, but your government seems ready to talk, as does Sir Gavin."

"So, again, if this is such a good idea, why isn't this just happening? I still don't really understand what it has to do with me."

Grainger gave Kelly a withering look as if telling a child to behave.

"Des, it is clear to us, as it must be to you and your colleagues, that you personally are the embodiment of the IP of the HCCVD project. For one thing, Maximum Power would be unlikely to proceed to form a financial relationship with the Lauriston without your personal participation and commitment. You should be clear, few corporations could offer you the package of personal and professional benefits we can. You will be a millionaire in your own right and have the lifestyle. You will have all the resources you need internationally, in terms of supporting professional expertise, test partners and financial muscle to commercialise your technology and deliver what we know you want most."

"And what do you think that is?"

"To give the world access to unlimited power and address global climate change in a way that makes a difference."

"That's a very noble objective. I didn't hear Hector Birnbaum saying too much about that, in his speech in Berlin a few weeks ago. Is Maximum Power changing into an international environment charity?"

"I understand you are sceptical, Des, but there are two things you need to bear in mind. Firstly, as a US corporation in the energy business with internationally traded public stock we need to be seen to be making meaningful responses to the demands of our shareholders. Right now, there is one issue that people from

Tulsa to Tokyo are getting to understand – climate change. As one of the leading hydrocarbon traders in the world we need to have policies to counter the environmental lobby. Secondly, what we are proposing will have a major impact on the world and the way we all live our lives. This is not just the window dressing of corporate social responsibility. It will mean a fundamental realignment of our investment strategy. We can only make a sensible return for our shareholders if we can control the global market. Control is more than owning the new technology, it is about managing down demand for hydrocarbons while building the new energy market. No national government can achieve this on its own. It will take a multi-national with financial muscle and strength of purpose to get commercial momentum going across the world. Are you seriously suggesting working with Maximum Power is a bad idea? Sir Gavin and Jakeman didn't need that long to think about it."

"If this bright new world which you imagine is going to come about, and we or I am going to help you make it happen, our role must be guaranteed, not just in what we do, but your undertakings must be enshrined tightly in contract. I would want to know how Maximum Power could deliver on that. After all, what would stop you getting control and killing off the project altogether, especially when you have so many jobs around the world dependent on your present operations?"

"I have no idea what would satisfy you, Des, on this, but as a sign of good faith I will take that back to H in New York and talk it through with him. Do I have your commitment in principle?"

"If you know me to be a man of principle you would understand my answer for now is no. For me to change my mind would require a fully worked out proposition. If you are confident and serious, there is nothing we have discussed that should prevent us talking again in the future – but I would seriously advise you not to bring this proposal back unless you have worked the detail. Listening to you now, there are a lot of gaps you need to be able to fill."

While this impromptu discourse had been taking place, Jake Roberts had become increasingly nervous. He fidgeted as Kelly and Grainger played conversational tennis. He had done everything he could to move the Lauriston close to a deal with Maximum Power as Kleiner had asked. He could only hope that Des would reflect and come round to his way of thinking.

He said breezily, "Well, Des, this took an unexpected amount of time. I need to get Ms Grainger up to the presentation suite to review our corporate plan. By the time we've done that, got a bite to eat and driven over to Harwell, I think we will be around forty-five minutes behind our original schedule."

"That suits me, Jake. I need to ensure that our two test rigs are operational so I will need at least an hour before I can be ready with a demonstration. We'll try not to make you too late, Ms Grainger. I assume you are away to London tonight?"

"Yes, that's right. I have a ticket for the ballet tonight and I have to call in at our embassy first thing then I'm off back to New York."

"OK. As you have come all the way out to see us in Oxford, we'll put on a bit of a show before you leave. See you later."

Jake followed her out towards the lift.

*

Des found he tended to do his best thinking when driving. It was a half-hour trip down to the labs at Harwell, just outside Didcot, beyond the Marcham Road which he would take on his journey home. Today's musical score in the car was Shostakovich's 'Chamber Symphony', suitably sombre to match his mood. What on earth was going on? He was in effect being offered a 'name your price' deal by one of the biggest players in the global energy business, an outfit which tended to ignore many national governments, bending over backwards for him personally. What were they scared of? Did they know something he didn't? If this was all so good, why hadn't Sir Gavin done some sort of deal with them anyway? Knowing Gavin, he really wouldn't worry about Des's feelings if that was the only barrier between him and a result. Maybe Maximum Power had said the whole thing was dependent on him. If that was true, it wouldn't just be Sir Gavin and Jake pressuring him to get on board. At the back of his mind remained an important factor. He was working for the good of mankind and the planet. His research should not be private and his outcomes could not just be bought. He wondered if the conversation would have gone differently had Karins been around.

Sometimes the simplest demonstrations were the best. Grainger was given a full tour of the lab to see the energy monitors which were still performing well after eighteen months of constant use. He was right, in her lab gear she looked like a walking traffic light in search of a zebra crossing. Des had explained that the achievement of conducting the heavy volt charge, which so many considered so revolutionary, was not the most important innovation – managing the charge at a consistent level was the reason for their success. That would be the most important factor when the product was ready to move into commercial production. In a strange way Kelly quite enjoyed these presentations. It was clear to him that despite her obvious intellect, Eve Grainger might know about corporate deals but did not understand the basic technology, and would not be able to analyse the test results that had emerged. Provided she was unable to take photographs he didn't worry about showing her what amounted to confidential test reports. The reports were basically crap, but her earnest expression reassured him that her interest was as cosmetic as her face. She was clearly operating under orders and provided she had a story to take home it would be all right. His final move had been to offer to give her a lift to the station to catch the train back to London. Only as he was dropping her off did he tell her that the car he was using was powered by a diamond brick. She expressed a mix of nervousness and enthusiasm which was exactly the impression he wanted to leave her with. He wished he could be a fly on the wall in Hector 'H' Birnbaum's suite in New York. But there again, Birnbaum didn't strike him as a man who would willingly entertain flies.

Of course, a key element of Des's responsibilities was to ensure Karins was settling into his new life in England. It seemed as though his government minders had thought of most things. He had a chauffeur-cum-guard, who was constantly in the background and spoke Russian. He was living in a safe house somewhere in commuting distance of Oxford and seemed to have struck up a personal relationship with a professor at St Anthony's College, who in turn seemed to be plugging him in to the vibrant social network of the local expatriate community. Whoever was watching over his induction understood the importance of getting him settled early before plundering his mind for the secrets of his former employers. Looking in from the outside, this looked like a dirty business but he guessed the potential rewards justified the means and by the look of it, his new colleague seemed happy enough. The induction, Kelly judged, had so far gone well. He had been impressed with Karins' understanding of the conceptual approach to HCCVD and his analytical test results were bordering on the exceptional. It looked as if Sir Gavin might be right. Karins could be the man with the necessary capability to aspire to a leadership role at the Lauriston. The timing was potentially good, too, especially as Des had already set his own career direction of travel. Des's strategy was twin track; not only about understanding the professional capability of the man but learning more about his personality. What made him tick. At first it had seemed Karins had settled on a standard script he would recite when he met new casual acquaintances. He played his part well. Kelly had heard the same lines now on countless occasions and had observed he had not deviated either in the basic account or the language he used to describe it. But Kelly's intention was to get under his skin, and he would only be able to do that as their relationship as colleagues developed.

Part of the process was to see him from time to time in social situations. Roberts had continued with his plan, of informal team meetings down the pub on a monthly basis, and Karins so far had attended only one of these gatherings, at which he had seemed ill at ease, not sure of the behaviour expected of him, probably wondering whether this was itself a test.

Des had taken a different approach, inviting him to dinner at his house with Sue and Miles. The invitation had been well received, especially as Karins' government minder was able to enjoy the company of WPC Wendy while the Kelly family provided the entertainment at table. Karins was the perfect guest, smartly attired in a navy polo, fawn trousers with evidently new brown brogues and armed with flowers for Sue and a jeroboam of Veuve Cliquot for his boss.

"Thank you for inviting me to your home. Please… let's get this party started!"

It had been the right call to bring someone new into the Kelly household who was entirely unconnected with the domestic crisis its occupants had all been sharing. Just for a couple of hours there was an opportunity for them all to live in the moment and enjoy some new company. Three litres of good champagne, a traditional British roast and *Stan Getz's Greatest Hits* contributed to the lively atmosphere.

The occasion succeeded in getting Karins to open up about his former life beyond his official script.

"In Russia, if you are a professional you hope to be able to get a job in Kaliningrad. It is a better paid, more relaxed way of living than I had previously experienced in Petersburg or Moscow. Provided you are careful and live the way the authorities expect you can enjoy many privileges. I was well paid by local standards. I had a nice office and technical equipment. I loved my home by the sea and in some ways it is the thing I miss most. The house was owned by the state, and it was only rented to me because of the job I did. The food was good, you could buy all the consumer goods you wanted, if you had the money. The health services are excellent and if you are a straight guy, then the social life is pretty good too, provided you play the game and kick back. Being in a managerial role in Kaliningrad makes you fat. You are not paid to think, just to do as you're told. You have to accept you will live on a diet of bullshit which pumps up your body with hot air, sucking the oxygen out of your lungs. It is dictated by the authorities and you cannot conduct your life in an open and honest way, without state interference. I am a gay man and have known it for over five years and when my employers found out as a result of an anonymous tip-off, my life changed. I was followed, harassed. My friends got arrested for petty crimes or beaten up by unidentifiable groups of thugs. Two of my junior managers in the naval munitions centre were appointed to supervisory roles above me. My private life and personal relationships had to be conducted in secrecy through a series of hastily arranged house meetings that could be initiated before those spying on me had time to report to their bosses. The final straw was when my last steady boyfriend, a battery commander in the Missile Defence Forces, was knifed in an apparently random attack at a burger bar. Was it just fate? Well, if the police had attempted a proper investigation, it might have been possible to reach that conclusion. But they just shrugged their shoulders and dismissed it as an unfortunate mugging that had gone wrong. I complained to the State Prosecutor's office, who would only say that if the police did not think the circumstances merited an enquiry, there was nothing they could do. That was the thing that made me realise I had to leave."

Listening to Karins' emotionally charged outburst, Des was struck by how he reminded him of his younger self. The Russian spoke with passion and anger – qualities Des used to have as a Cambridge undergraduate, but which years of battling with British officialdom in the scientific research community had worn away. There was a brightness, idealism and vitality about him which Des recognised from his days as a student activist, and which was still present in the personality of his missing daughter. In fact, looking at the scene around the table, Des had the uneasy feeling this felt like a closed family group, not a family gathering with a guest.

TWELVE

TUESDAYS WERE ALWAYS BUSY for Bryan at the Dog & Duck. For starters he had to make sure the cellar was tidy, with empty barrels ready outside for the draymen to collect, and that the ramp was ready to receive his weekly supply of beer. Given his years of experience in the licensed trade, he had perfected a method of managing the intake quickly and with the minimum effort, but it would still take the better part of a couple of hours from start to finish. Checking the stock level was a key part of the proceedings, involving ticking off all the items he received, so when the mobile rang, he answered it in a slightly distracted, absent-minded way.

"Hello, is that Mr Bryan? This is Hayet Suker."

In a split-second Bryan altered his voice and adopted a more authoritative tone.

"Yes. This is Bryan."

"Mr Bryan, I think I may have some news regarding your recent enquiry, but I cannot speak on the phone. Meet me at four this afternoon, in the car park at Trinity Buoy Wharf. You know it?"

"Yes, I know it."

"Come alone. No friends or police. Give me the registration of your car. I will be watching. If you mess about, I will not make contact."

Bryan did as he was told, and the phone went dead. There was no intel on the caller ID either; the details were withheld.

"'Ere Bry, can you just sign off the delivery docket? You're not the only one with a lot on. We've got another six calls ahead of us and I've got a bad back."

The moans of the grumbling delivery driver brought his attention back to the here and now.

He scribbled one of those imaginary signatures with his finger on the tablet computer placed before him on the bar and the boiler-suited brewery man departed.

In half a minute, Suker had succeeded in distracting Bryan from the day job. Getting the beer into the cellar was the easy bit – getting bottled up would take longer and this day the lunch-time bar staff would need to take care of it.

He was starting to get that adrenaline rush and heart flutter he had experienced when he was last in Islington and he had to admit this short walk on the 'wild side' was like a strangely exciting hobby, a chance for him to live the dream as some sort of north London 'Don'.

The real buzz would come from sharing the news and when it came to that, there was only one person he could tell – Miles.

As he had hoped, Miles treated the news like a lottery win with a childlike enthusiasm to match his own.

"What time are we going?"

"*We* are not going. He said just me and him and if I try to change the rules there will be no meeting at all. I will drive there after I've got lunch service started. That will give me plenty of time to get to the rendezvous."

"Have you ever been there before?"

"Along time ago when I had the pub in Highbury. It was just a shitty quay by the Thames with a load of containers and a sandwich van. If you'd gone down there a few years back, you would not have known of its history as the workshop of all marker buoys in the Thames estuary. It's still the site of the only working lighthouse in London – been there since the eighteen sixties. Now it's gone posh. Got things like art studios and flats built out of the old containers. Even the sandwich van got replaced with an American-style diner."

"Will you be OK?"

"What's there to worry about? We`re in a public place in London in the middle of the afternoon. It's just me and an oily Mediterranean sort. I'm not bothered. Besides, if we get some news on Abi then we can have a bit of a party later on and show those plods they're not the only ones who can play detectives."

He could imagine the stories he would be able to tell over the bar and how his own reputation as a fixer would benefit as a result. What he was really focusing on, however, was breaking the good news about Abi to her mother. Although she would inevitably get to hear later on from Miles, he was confident he would be able to make time tomorrow for her to express her appreciation in her own special way.

He couldn't wait to set off, even making sure that he dressed the part. Doc boots, jeans, black bomber jacket, Ray-Bans. Had he been married, his partner would have told him to grow up and act his age, but hey, he was living in the 'zone'. His look didn't quite co-ordinate with his sky-blue Volvo XC60 but nevertheless it made him feel up for it. His journey into town was aided by coming in during the quiet hour, before the Thames Valley commuters jammed up the Westway, and the progression east towards Canary Wharf and East India was smooth, with most of the traffic coming the other way.

The approach took him down Orchard Place towards the landmark of the red lightship then right towards the lighthouse itself, the diner and the Jubilee Pier. It was a sunny and breezy afternoon down by the water as he searched for a parking place, which he eventually found, looking across the river towards the Millennium Dome. The place had certainly been spruced up since his time in London and yet it was quieter than he had expected.

As far as he could tell there was some private meeting taking place in the conference area which in his mind explained the number of cars and absence of people at that moment. Now what? He hadn't thought this through. He had his mobile, but didn't have a number to call, to say he had arrived. Neither had anyone tried to call him. He fiddled around with the phone, checking his other apps for messages. Nothing. *Fuck!* Suker had told him he would be contacted once he arrived. He had planned to keep the voice recorder on his phone on in his pocket in the hope Suker would just give him the information he wanted. But it was four o'clock now and no sign of anyone. He threw his phone into the glove compartment below the dashboard and opened the door to stand outside the car, in the hope that Suker would clearly recognise him and approach. After all, he assumed the Turk already knew he had arrived, having been given his registration number on the phone earlier.

Despite his caution, he had not been aware of Suker's approach from behind.

"Please get back to the driver's seat, Mr Bryan. Do not look around. I will sit in the back of your car, behind you. After all, it is not in either of our interests to make a fuss."

For reasons Bryan could not understand, he did as he was told instinctively. There was a kind of assertiveness in the Turk's voice which suggested non-compliance could have unfortunate consequences. There was no point in starting a meeting where he sought co-operation by refusing a simple request.

Inside the car, Bryan pulled down the vanity screen allowing him to see Suker`s face in the mirror.

"Thank you for meeting me this afternoon, Mr Bryan. I don't propose to take up too much of your time, or my own for that matter. Let me begin with a few courtesies that I thought were missing from our last meeting. You clearly knew who I was, but you didn't tell me who you were. I like to know who I am dealing with before I do business. Also I thought your approach was rather disrespectful. You come looking for my help but get your friends to trash my restaurant first. Do you think that makes me want to do business with you? Well, I have to tell you it doesn't. It just pisses me off. I have to spend a considerable sum getting my restaurant open and giving my staff extra time off to recover. I have to spend money getting my friends in the police (and you should know I have many) to find out exactly who you are. And then I must work out how to respond to your invitation. This is the thing that has taken me the longest to work out. No matter. We are where we are. So perhaps you can tell me, how did you get to hear about me?"

"The police said they were investigating a van traced to your business."

"Who?"

"A guy called Abraham, Scotland Yard, told the missing girl`s brother".

"Thank you. That was just a circumstantial enquiry which I resolved within twenty-four hours of it being made. Didn't realise Scotland Yard were sharing their theories with members of the public before they had been investigated. Who trashed my restaurant? Think carefully, Mr Bryan. I'm sure you can guess that the hard object you can feel in your back has the ability to do you some personal damage."

Forget the padded extrusion; Bryan already felt a knot of anxiety in his stomach.

"The North End Ultras – Arsenal fans. They know of your Spurs connections."

"As I suspected. I have two of their faces on CCTV. I will find them and return the compliment. And so to you. You have caused me a problem, Mr Bryan Smyth with a letter 'y' of the Dog and Duck in Oxfordshire. I really have wondered what to do. Should I visit your business and trash it, as you did to mine? Perhaps I should burn it down and put you out of business or should I just kill you and close this unfortunate incident altogether? I should tell you I have sought advice from my client whose activities you have expressed an interest in. They are simple people, they think the latter. I, however, defended you. I recognise it took balls for you to do what you did and despite your method of operation I think you deserve some respect. So here's what I have decided. You came to me seeking information – you should have it. It is true a couple of my somewhat clumsy operatives did come to Oxfordshire to collect a Miss Abigail Kelly on behalf of my client. She was taken to order and exported by air within twenty-four hours to one of my Middle East associates. I cannot imagine why they specified her and she took some finding. Although I remember she was a pretty little thing, the terms of the deal were that she was to be delivered unharmed and… not tampered with. If anything bad had happened, I would not have been paid. As a father myself, I took this to heart and followed my client's wishes to the letter. She left the UK on a private plane from Biggin Hill within four hours of her collection. And that is it. There is no more to tell. I have received payment and not heard anymore. End of story. But not quite, there is you. Now you know the truth you can see it is a heavy burden and so it's time to close the book. Those who may mourn your departure will know there is no point in following in your footsteps. They will get nowhere. I wanted to meet you here so that you could take in this magnificent view of the river and the Dome. One day, when perhaps you meet your friends again in a better place, you can tell them how beautiful it looked in your last moment on earth. So that is it. I must go. I have a thirtieth birthday party in the restaurant tonight and you have an appointment with your maker. Goodbye and good luck, Mr Bryan Smyth with a 'y'. It has been a privilege to meet you."

There was a muted cough from the back of the car and the faint smell of cordite. Bryan's body slumped sideways.

Suker climbed out of the back seat and walked away.

*

It would have been too easy to have just sacked Arbutsev and put someone else in his place and maybe that was a judgement he would make in time. For now, it was difficult to see how this simple measure would resolve the issue; rather it would confirm the position that, he, Colonel Dimitri Nikitin, owned the problem that could prove to be his own hospital pass.

Instead he had opted to suspend his man in Kaliningrad pending further investigation. What investigation? Privately he knew Arbutsev to be old school, not brilliant but solid, methodical, loyal, *honest*. It was unlikely he had missed any material evidence but he knew he lacked imagination – the ability to link seemingly unrelated incidents to the bigger picture. The action he had taken was a stopgap, a signal to his bosses that he was on top of the situation and not prepared to tolerate failure. He had bought time, not a solution. Somehow, he needed to find a way to snatch a victory out of the impending jaws of defeat. He would need to employ all his tactical abilities to manage his way out of this situation.

His thoughts were interrupted by the alert of an encrypted message from Oxford, passed via London, from Lutz. It was a picture of Ponomariev with his other target, Dr Desmond Kelly. Nikitin could hardly believe his eyes – could he truly believe it? Two of his primary targets in one place. Maybe there was a God after all!

He hastily sent a message back asking for more information. Where was he living, was he working and what was he doing?

His research had revealed Kelly as a high-value asset but he could not be sure of his personal co-operation. That had been offered on his behalf by Madam Rustanova. He got the sense that there was more to her relationship with the Englishman than he knew. If he was to accede to her request he would need to investigate further. Also, what was the relationship between Ponomariev and Kelly? He would need to consult Lutz again, at length, once he had responded to his outstanding information request. Could he spin a situation where Kelly could bring Ponomariev to him and both could be brought to Moscow? That would be a victory indeed worthy of Ruslan Rustanovitch and ensure his own legacy in his department's Hall of Fame.

He called the Academy of Sciences and arranged to meet Galina Rustanova that afternoon.

*

It didn't take long for Bryan's body to be discovered. The security guard was inspecting the site before locking up for the night and was checking on the two cars left in the visitors' spaces on the river frontage. Given the angle of the shot it was surprising that the interior of the windscreen was not covered in blood, but the bullet had passed through him and the car dashboard. The body was clearly visible through the side window and was slumped over the front passenger seat. The police arrived ten minutes later, a PNC check on the car leading to Willoughby being advised within the hour.

Miles had already sensed something was amiss. He had made two unsuccessful attempts to call his friend but on each occasion the call went to voicemail. He had comforted himself by assuming the reason for the lack of response was because Bryan was driving home, armed with new information. His initiative in making the call paid dividends as the sound of the ringing phone drew the attention of the police officers examining the car. The check on his number made sure the trail to his door was easily set.

These days Willoughby's trips to the Thames Valley had been few and far between. All that changed now. He arrived at the Kelly residence later that afternoon, looking for Miles. The stilted and stiff body language contrasted with his measured tone. The case had crossed a rubicon – the police had a body – hard evidence, and a very short list about who could be responsible.

"Given the circumstances, I am amazed you and Mr Smyth

took the action you did without speaking to me or at least WPC Graham here. Police procedures require us to collect evidence before we act – that way we can secure convictions. We were in the process of investigating the Turkish connection before you took it into your heads to intervene and now there are serious consequences. I should warn you that your action in this matter could materially make you an accessory to a murder and potentially open to prosecution. That is, of course, assuming that some of Suker's friends don't decide to come looking for you, in the meantime. As a result, I require you to surrender your mobile and computer. You should not leave the village without getting express permission for doing so and further, please make sure WPC Graham is always made aware of your movements. I hope I have made myself clear. And you, Mrs Kelly, I assume, knew nothing about any of this? WPC Graham reported that you met Mr Smyth the other day…"

"It is true that I met Mr Smyth at the pub, but we didn't really talk much. Miles had told me that he had met up with him in London last week, and that they'd got caught up in a bit of trouble at a Turkish restaurant. I was grateful to Mr Smyth for getting Miles away. Running a pub, he is… *was*, good at defusing those kind of tense situations. I really didn't give it a lot more thought."

"And you, Mr Kelly? If I've got this right, you and Mr Smyth happen to turn up at the Topkapi Nights restaurant on the High Road in Tottenham early doors last Wednesday, just after some vandals had burst in and wrecked the place?"

"That's right, you could say it was bad timing. I remember two of these thugs pushed by us as we were walking past. That drew our attention and that is why we went in to help. We offered to call the police but the guy behind the bar, who we took to be the one in charge, was most insistent. He didn't want us to call the police."

"What did you do?"

"I'm sorry to say – nothing."

"So, you are saying you were not part of an attack on the restaurant?"

"Yes, and I am sure they have CCTV which will back me up. I felt uncomfortable straight away, but Bryan, Mr Smyth, started a conversation with the owner. I didn't catch it all, but I think it had something to do with football rivalries, you know the Gooners and Spurs. Bryan told me he used to run a pub near Highbury and the fans were always planning fights on each other's territories. According to him, it was a long-standing turf war which got worse if either team was enjoying a period of supremacy."

"Why did you go in the first place?"

"I'd been drinking regularly at the Dog since Abi went missing. Probably drinking more than I should but it was a break from being here that I needed. I admit I talked to Bryan about my situation. We regarded him as a friend of the family. They say landlords are a bit like priests in the confessional. You can say stuff and it goes no further. I don't really remember what I may have said, other than that it was probably too much. He had suggested we went out for a few beers and something to eat in his old manor, I think because he, too, fancied a break from his own personal worries."

"What worries?"

"Well, in the end he never got around to telling me, but I assumed he found life at the Dog difficult following his divorce and although I think he had a girlfriend, or maybe two. I got the impression he wasn't happy."

Sue Kelly looked unsettled at her son's account.

"So he said, 'I'll give you a lift to London, we'll have a few beers and whatever and I'll drive back'?"

"No, he was a landlord, he didn't need reminding about not driving when he'd been drinking. If we'd got pissed, we'd have been on the train home. The incident at the restaurant affected our mood. We just decided to drive back here, and I dropped a couple in the Dog before I came home."

"Dropped a couple?"

"Pints down my neck."

"OK and what about these thugs? You didn't know them, and you don't think Mr Smyth knew them either?"

"I certainly don't know anything about them, and I'm not sure Bryan did either. They didn't stop to make introductions."

"But given Mr Smyth's past history, he might have recognised them?"

"I suppose it is possible, but we'll never know."

"What were they wearing?"

"It's difficult to remember. It all happened so quickly."

"Black, white?"

"I assume white. They looked pretty athletic. They were in jeans, grey hoodies and sunglasses but that's all I can remember. I assume their CCTV will tell you more."

"I *assume* you are right. OK, that's it for now. If I need more, Sergeant Abraham will be in touch. I'll take your phone and computer with me. WPC Graham will sort out the receipt. Remember, from now on, you're grounded until I tell you otherwise."

*

Rustanova's next encounter with Nikitin took place in her office on the twentieth floor of the Russian Academy of Sciences block in Leninskiy Prospekt, Moscow. It was a spacious room but utilitarian, dominated by a meeting table with space for a dozen or so guests. Her personal desk housed her computer and keyboard, and three neat piles of papers, the height of a couple of coffee cups, precisely ordered in a system that only she understood. The room was painted a standard tint of blue, the same colour of that element of the national flag. The two bare walls were each dominated by a picture, one of her receiving her Hero of Russia medal from the president some four years ago, the other a family portrait with

Ruslan and their two children. In the corner next to the window, a pole with a Russian tricolour and in another, by the door, a hat stand with her coat and a spare pair of boots. Her domain felt like an oasis of permanence in an uncertain world, thanks largely to the presence of a bright green leather-leafed pot plant which sat in the third corner by the window. Quite what sustained it in this arid setting was in itself a scientific anomaly which most visitors were either too polite or distracted to comment on.

Russia retains a visibly hierarchical approach to public administration, so in general terms the higher a visitor had to climb in a block, the more senior the personnel they would be engaging with. Since arriving in her new domain, Rustanova had only requested one change – which was the replacement of a ventilation window with a solid pane, to prevent either a visitor using it as some high-level ash tray, or, as often the case in the security services, it being used to propel a problematic individual to a certain and unfortunate death on the street below.

Nikitin was an honoured guest, so Rustanova had told her secretary to prepare tea using her best high-patterned cups imported from Armenia.

They sat either side of the meeting table, Rustanova positioning herself with the beaming image of the president behind her.

"Thank you for finding time to see me at such short notice, Galina. I can assure you I have been active on your behalf and believe I have found a way of transferring your Dr Kelly to our jurisdiction. Of course, this is not just a matter of what is technically possible but depends on the co-operation of the subject. It is too big an undertaking for us to take on without having the certainty of success. It is with this in mind that I feel obliged to interview you today. I need to understand why Dr Kelly, your friend, wishes to come to us or why you think you can persuade him to make the transition."

"I have told you. He is dying. I think if they had the skills in the West to keep him alive, they would. I know he has had treatment which he has managed to shield from the authorities, but it is only extending his life by a few months. If we can give him extra years of quality life, he will be grateful and our reward will be access to the new HCCVD technology. I can persuade him that our medical services are better. That will make him come to us."

"Is that the only reason? I took you to say that you had known Dr Kelly for many years, even before your sabbatical in San Francisco. Is that correct?"

"Yes, it is."

"In fact, you met him ten years earlier, did you not? According to my records, in Vienna."

"That is true."

"Reading the report from the embassy at that time, there is a suggestion that you might have engaged in an impromptu dalliance with him."

"We did have a meeting of minds and yes, that was the start of a professional relationship."

"Professional, you say."

"Well, Dimitri, we were all young once…"

"And I notice a short time afterwards you took a career break?"

"Yes, you know I moved from Novosibirsk to Petersburg."

"Hmmm and found time to start a family. You and Ruslan both had children before you came together."

"I am sure your records are correct."

"You moved to Petersburg as a single parent?"

"No, I was pregnant when I came to Petersburg. My baby was born there."

"But you didn't keep him?"

"No, I did not. My career came first. He was adopted and went to a good family."

"You chose not to keep in touch?"

"Yes and I regret it – to this day. But it was right for me at the time and subsequently right for him too. He had a stable upbringing."

"You followed his career?"

"Yes, from a distance. He was a bright boy."

"And eventually came here to the Academy of Sciences."

"I helped make it happen and taught him alongside hundreds of other able students."

"Who was his father?"

"I think you are being impertinent. It is not necessary for you to know."

"Perhaps it is, Galina, especially if the father was Dr Desmond Kelly."

"I am not prepared to discuss this further. All this happened when I was very young and before my present family life started. I have told you my reasoning for going ahead with this action. I have discussed it fully with Ruslan, who is completely supportive."

The reference was supposed to put Nikitin back in his place but failed.

"Do you remember the name of the family who took your child in?"

"Of course I do. It was Ponomariev. They christened him Boris. When he graduated from the Academy, he joined the navy research unit in Petersburg and then I lost track of him."

"Seems you have a habit of doing that, Galina. I have reason to believe that the father of your first child is Dr Desmond Kelly, and today he is Boris Ponomariev, until recently Chief Engineer in the missile propulsion unit at the Navy's base at Baltiysk, but now defected to England and working with his father at a research facility at Oxford University. Your son is a traitor, Galina, and a suspected homosexual. Irrespective of the interests of Dr Kelly, we want him back to face justice. Given the circumstances, it is clear to me that one way or another, you have created the problem that you are expecting me to solve. So, this is what I propose; that you make contact with Dr Kelly, and plan to meet him, together with Ponomariev, somewhere at four weeks' notice. I don't mind where, but it will be easier if it is outside the UK. Let me know and I will make the necessary arrangements. Do this well, help me to make the pick-up and nobody else needs to know about your sordid past. Your exemplary reputation and career, as well as that of your husband, will remain unblemished."

"He will have you for this."

"As a stand-off, I'd rather be in my chair than yours. Do remember my trade is about lies and deception. In the end, no one will care about who is right and wrong in this situation. I have a whole government department behind me. Who have you got? This will be decided by the one who can shout loudest and longest. I realise I have outstayed my welcome for now, Galina. Thanks for the tea. I look forward to hearing from you soon."

Nikitin smiled to himself as he left her office.

He had taken a wild guess about the situation and had hit the spot. His route to a winning position was now clear.

*

Grainger had instructions to return to New York as soon as she had briefed Barnes at the London embassy. Arriving in Manhattan from La Guardia, her driver took her straight to the 'Power Tower', as it was known, on Fifth Avenue and East 97th Street. She took the elevator straight to the president's suite.

"So, what to do, Eve? If I understand you properly, we're ready to roll on HCCVD and the Lauriston."

Hector 'H' Birnbaum's direct New York influenced style was often confused, by those who didn't know him, with his being abrupt or just bad-mannered. He would just think of it as being focused. Fixing his head of special projects with a laser-like stare, powerful enough to reach well beyond her seat, he was about to be unimpressed with her reply.

"In some ways we are and in other ways we're not. Sir Gavin Laidlaw is supportive of a takeover, but we need to see him selling the deal to the British government. There are a lot of issues to weigh up for them; competition policy and national security concerns are high up the list. I'd be surprised on either count if their government could just push this through – and as for Kelly, he's playing hard ball." The predicted explosion came next.

"Fuck Kelly – we can't have one guy screwing up what's in our national interest. I think it's time to throw a grenade into the works and let's see what or who falls out. I wanna make history – put a billion dollars on the table and leave the door open to more if you think that can make a difference. There's no point in hiding our intentions and, by the way, run a global search around other HCCVD experts not on the Lauriston payroll. How has Kelly got himself in a position to hold the whole world to ransom? We are the fuckin' US of A – this is our game and we're not about to lose it. Don't just brief Barnes in London about what we're doing, tell him to get active. He should be talking to the British government now to unblock the process. I'll get hold of Kleiner and put the squeeze on the White House. We need to reel this thing in before some other fucker gets in on the act. What's all this about a Russian?"

"Roberts told me they've got hold of some Russian guy at the Lauriston – said it was all hush, hush, but he'd get some more info and brief us when he could."

"What? Who? Why? Implications? Eve, baby, tell me you're on top of this. We're about to make a billion dollar bet. I get the feeling you're sitting on a volcano with an itchy backside and it's making me twitchy on your behalf. If they are bringing some Russian into this, why don't we know about it and why didn't we get him first? That's another thing I'll pick up with Kleiner."

"As you say, sir, events are moving quickly on this. Roberts didn't think there was anything here that affected the fundamentals."

"I am not running a global corporation on the hearsay of some Stanford geek. Get this nailed and put me in the picture. This is your absolute priority."

*

News of Bryan's demise seemed to spread like wildfire, but no one was sure quite how. The problem got even worse when the news was carried on the next day's local bulletins on radio and TV. The reports contained no information about the circumstances and their impact was exacerbated by the arrival of a TV crew in the village, asking people what they thought about the situation and what they knew about their local publican. The responses were truly predictable, ranging from "it's terrible – that sort of thing doesn't happen to anyone who lives round here" to "it's a poor do that the brewery hasn't sent someone to get our pub open". There were also one or two who came out of their houses to see if they could get their faces on TV. The crew themselves went looking for the proprietor of the village shop, Mrs Harris, who predictably added a sinister edge to the story. "We've never had any trouble before. Bryan was a salt of the earth type, but I think he's had his fair share of personal problems. I've thought there have been some funny goings on round here recently, and I think they're all connected."

Miles had the distinct impression that, since the death, communication with the Scotland Yard team had all but ceased. WPC Graham had only provided very general non-committal answers like "enquiries are ongoing" or "we'll have to wait and see". Sergeant Abraham came a few days later, saying in effect that there would be no news until after the inquest, but they had been successful in collecting new evidence that he was confident would lead them to a conviction, although there was still no news on Abi. The general disturbance the incident had caused in the valley had been largely missed by Des, who was cocooned in the day-to-day world of his work. He had been preoccupied by the insistence of Sir Gavin that one of his test rigs be moved to a military setting at Aldermaston. He was as shocked as anyone about the apparent murder of Bryan, and more so, as he knew from Miles that he had died trying to obtain information about his daughter's whereabouts. He was trying not to admit it, but his worries were driven by the thought that if someone was losing their life by enquiring after Abi, then she must be in serious trouble. As a father it was galling to realise that, apart from getting angry, which might have the effect of making him feel better, there was precious little he could do. The police had assured him that if she had been kidnapped, a ransom demand would follow and at least then he could do something. But nothing had happened. Nothing, that is, until Bryan got murdered. Sometimes doing nothing was hard to do, but Des knew that in his situation, there were no easy options.

Keeping the driveway gate closed had been helpful in keeping the small knot of press people, who had set up a makeshift encampment in the road outside, at bay. He had lost count of the number of pictures taken of him leaving and returning home. He never took much notice of the papers at the best of times and seemed singularly unaffected by the media interest. Although he would need to come to terms with the long-term consequences of the situation, he doubted whether others – neighbours, friends – would really give a damn, unless their own privacy was infringed. As a result, a scientific mind was helpful in managing to deal with the pressures of the moment. In his head Des lived his life in compartments, rooms which allowed him to open and close doors as he saw fit. The advantage was that when he opened a door, he would think afresh about the challenges inside. When he closed the door, he shut them out. The approach was basically sound. The real problems would occur when he entered a void – when all his mind's room doors were closed. These were the times he felt uncertain, depressed and not in control of his destiny. Superficial thoughts were not really part of his makeup. Every situation required some form of analysis. Yet this void he experienced was a black blob, not even a cloud. It had no means of definition or articulation and so offered no rational understanding. The efforts he made to banish the blob were getting more difficult to marshal. He had touched on it in his dialogue with Kjaer, but pride or a sense of vulnerability prevented him acknowledging the extent of the problem. This was intensely private and personal. Bigger than the bad-tempered parrot they had discussed.

The opportunity to see Galina once again was one of the few occurrences that helped him out of this disabling state of mind, and on this day, the prospect of joining the audience to hear her speak at Chatham House and then to have her company all to himself at dinner was definitely something to look forward to.

*

He arrived at St James' Square less than half an hour before the seminar was due to start, thanks to his train into Paddington having been delayed and the length of the queue for taxis.

The room was half-full by the time he arrived. Judging by appearances, the number of bespectacled people, corduroy jackets and bright young things engrossed in their phone Twitter accounts, it was an eclectic mix of academics, policy wonks, journalists, and parliamentary researchers. These were clearly people who had time on their hands. As the clock moved closer to the start time, a more interesting group of well-heeled sharp-suited professional types, most likely representatives of international conglomerates or diplomats, and one or two military personnel joined the throng. This event was to be a full house. On the appointed hour, a line of panellists walked in single file onto the dais and took their seats. Galina was second in line, behind some Indian military man and followed by a Japanese professor of peace studies and an American who Kelly had heard of – Chuck Barnes of the RSA. Kelly could only imagine the negotiations which had gone on, not only to get these four speakers together but to agree their order of appearance. Galina had clearly done her homework. She sparkled like a jewel in a spotlight against a background of dull conventional-looking grey men, the sort which seemed to be the same the world over. As befits a representative of her country she wore a scarlet two-piece with a high collar and black braid, almost making her look like a toy soldier. The casual observer would have their vision interrupted should they be looking anywhere else.

Her message was as confident as her look, talking about the importance of scientific research being one of the core pillars for international co-operation. Space exploration had been a great example of how the Europeans and Americans had worked together for the good of mankind and increasingly there were other examples, such as food and drugs research, where more scientific collaboration was taking place. Then there was the political message about how the world of science had to come together to fight the revisionist forces of individualism and greed. The West was failing future generations by not engaging with Russia on issues of climate change and nuclear proliferation. Russia was looking for signs from the West that dialogue was being sought, and if these signals were forthcoming she predicted the base of commercial research would fundamentally change from weapons development to technologies geared to fighting disease, hunger and protecting the sanctity of life. So far so good.

Then the questions came. This was the only point at which Galina had looked less assured. When she was invited to comment on some of the more leading challenges coming from the press pack, he noted her darting a look to a suited figure in the front row, as if reciting lines she had been fed hours before. It was probably only noticeable to those who knew her and didn't detract from what had, otherwise, been a faultless performance. Almost on cue, she had taken the opportunity to attack the economic imperialism of Western energy companies, such as Maximum Power, who were actively blocking research in renewables, to hold onto their dominance in the oil market and the comment had been well received. It was almost as if the audience had conveniently overlooked the state of the Russian economy and its over-reliance on exports of gas and crude. A kinder person may have interpreted her remarks as signalling Russia knew of its present susceptibilities and was embarking on an ambitious programme of reform, but clearly there was little evidence to support that view.

The event closed and the audience started to drift away towards the back of the room, where an obligatory glass of tepid wine and a canapé was on offer as an excuse to charge non-members an eye-watering fee for attending. A residue of press people looking for interviews gathered at the front. Galina had clearly performed well as she was temporarily surrounded by a phalanx of smiling rotund balding men in ill-fitting suits and another equally large woman who appeared to be some sort of media manager organising the hacks into some sort of priority. Half a dozen rows in front of Kelly at the far end, a suited figure with black hair was tapping into his phone at pace. Probably a journo chasing a deadline, he thought. Away to his right, by the exit door, another woman was just hanging around, as if loitering to get a personal word with one of the presenters.

THIRTEEN

ONE OF THE ASPECTS of the present scene which engaged him most was the response of the American, Barnes, to the proceedings. He seemed disappointed that Galina was proving to be the centre of attention. Perversely, Kelly noticed him trying to get close to Galina, listening to her comments then chipping in with his own contribution, clearly trying to share the limelight.

In the rapidly emptying room, Kelly was becoming more conspicuous. Galina was a class act. She had scanned the room early in the proceedings and registered his presence, and they had agreed to leave the building together once her business was concluded. He caught her eye and nodded his head, indicating that he would wait outside. Almost imperceptibly, she returned the gesture in acknowledgement; reeling off her government's views on the regulation of the nuclear industry to an expectant reporter who seemed to be hanging on her every word.

As he walked towards the door, behind him came the sound of raised voices. He stopped and looked back at the small scrum on the platform. Chuck Barnes had clearly run out of patience playing second fiddle to the media.

"Ms Rustanova is entitled to her view, but in the States, we don't read the situation like that. If the Russians came to the table in an open and honest way, then the collaboration she talks about could happen. I can't see any signs from Moscow that there is a serious interest in doing that." The comment was the spark for a little unseemly pushing and shoving between officials surrounding the two main speakers while the journalist involved did his bit for international *détente,* calling to Mr Barnes that he would be happy to record an interview with him after he had finished the discussion with her.

Kelly continued his route, sharing a smile with the loitering woman standing in the doorway.

He waited a further fifteen minutes before Rustanova emerged into the lobby. Her circle of officials appeared to have been reduced to just two, and they were locked in a flow of Russian he could not follow. Again she had seen him and he stood back, knowing she would come over when her business was concluded. And when she did, he knew the wait had been worthwhile. She kissed him on the cheek.

"Well, hello Des. I am so sorry to have kept you waiting. When the government sends us on these trips there is so much to do. I don't think they are bothered about what I say in my presentation to the room, but they care strongly about the media side. I gave quite a long interview to *Izvestia* on the flight over and have done *Reuters, Bloomberg* and the *Financial Times* just now, so I think I have earned my dinner and no, I am not required to spend time doing small talk with members of the audience. I think my new American friend will be better than me at that. Oh, and I should have told you that I have changed my plans here in London. I was staying at the embassy tonight but have checked myself into the Park Lane Hotel instead."

She saw the surprise on Des's face.

"Don't worry about it, I will tell you over dinner. Shall we take a taxi? Where are you taking me?"

The loitering woman decided to take a taxi after they left.

*

Shepherd Market was the answer. A small square surrounded by bijou restaurants strategically sandwiched between the back of Park Lane and Curzon Street in Mayfair.

"I like this little corner of London, especially when there is so much choice, all within a few paces," said Des. "But it still has a bit of a reputation."

"For what?"

"A place for illicit lovers and high-class sex. It is surrounded by a network of anonymous-looking mews flats, occupied in the main by prostitutes and frequented by 'high net worths', looking for good times without complications. All of life is around here. Smart hotels, casinos, art house cinemas, members-only night clubs, good food, beautiful people, lots of cash, no questions."

"Does that include you?"

"Maybe once. But not now. I am of an age where I don't need to play games. I am the person I am. A flawed character certainly but old enough to appreciate the memories of past adventures more than the prospect of what is to come."

They settled into a French restaurant and a small table in the window, looking out onto the small, cobbled square frequented by drinkers from a nearby pub enjoying an al fresco tipple.

They ordered chateaubriand and an overpriced bottle of claret.

"So tell me about your change of plan. Why aren't you staying at the embassy?"

"Because we must talk, and whatever time I got to the embassy I would have to spend another two hours debriefing on today, so my reports will be back in Moscow before my return. I will go and do what needs to be done first thing in the morning. Tonight is my time. I have a different plan. I have also checked that there is an hourly train from here back to Oxford through the night, so that we can continue until we have had enough of talking."

"You sound as though you have already decided what we should discuss."

"That is what I like about you, Des. We are the same. I too am the person I am. I too am too old to play games. You are right, of course. It was convenient that I had a natural opportunity to come to London otherwise I'm not sure how we would have managed this dialogue."

"Perhaps on a Zoom call?"

"Absolutely not. I think we have to be together face-to-face for this. Anyway, firstly, how are you?"

It was with a sense of relief that Kelly unburdened himself, telling Galina of all that had happened since they were last together, including his private fears about Abigail's disappearance. He was confident of a sympathetic and confidential ear.

"As you can see, I find myself being systematically disassembled by my peers, to weaken my influence, and sold off to the highest bidder. Against this background I am worrying about my family, which seems to be crumbling, and the uncertainty about just how much longer I will be able to work. But strangely the time in Denmark is helping me to plan for the future."

"To be honest, ever since you told me your news, I have had trouble thinking about anything else. Back home, I have used my contacts to discuss potential treatments for your condition. The responses I have received are encouraging but are inevitably general, as no doctor will commit themselves without undertaking a personal examination. I was right in my basic view that there are still options available which can manage your condition, perhaps adding another ten years to your life. I told you before, whatever anyone's view of Russia is, the state takes genuine pride in its leading-edge medical technology and at the top level does not share its expertise or research internationally. In short, we can help you if you let us. We can give you treatment which is not available in the West. Care which has only previously been available to senior figures in the government machine. I can ensure you get that help if you come to us. Further, we will ensure that you have a luxury house in the woods near Moscow, a senior position at the Academy working alongside me, and all the funding you would need to continue your research. In time, once the transfer has been made, you would also be at liberty to bring immediate members of your family over to be with you. Apart from my own commitment, my husband is a senior influencer in the military, with the highest levels of access. He, too, will use his power to ensure that you are properly looked after."

"So, all I need to do is to buy an air ticket to Moscow?"

"Under the circumstances, as we both know, although you could buy the ticket, I expect you would be prevented from joining the flight. The more complicated element will be arranging your transfer and again I have consulted with my government colleagues, who can help. All they have asked is that they know where you will be at the time you are ready to make the move. It was also pointed out to me that organising this from outside the UK would be easier as our people are less tightly managed in other places, especially continental Europe. Des, you and I are first and foremost scientists, not politicians. We work for the good of mankind, not sectional political interests. That is why it makes sense for you to be based in Moscow. From a professional point of view, it is the only place where you can be free of commercial pressures and focus exclusively on your work. What is on offer is in effect another ten years of quality of life. You don't have the luxury of time anymore. Say you'll do it and together we can change the future."

"I understand what you're saying, but whatever the advantage to me, my motivation will not be understood by my friends, colleagues, family or country."

"This is life, Des. It's not a zero-sum gain. People will get hurt. It is even more important in that scenario that you clearly understand why you are doing it."

She paused like an actor delivering her lines, adding emphasis to her words.

"There is also something else you should know."

"Yes?"

"In all the years I have known you, there is only one thing about the past I have not shared with you. It goes back to the beginning of our story – Vienna."

Her eyes now locked with his and he thought he detected them starting to water.

"The night we spent back then was incredibly important to me," she began. "My mother always told me to save myself for the man I would want to spend my life with. Yet I met you out of the blue and we just went to bed. I really didn't need to think about it that much – it was just the right thing to do. To be honest, I didn't think about it that much afterwards. It was only a month later, when I was back home, that I discovered I was pregnant. I knew you were the father. But you and I had met by chance. We had come together by chance. We lived in different worlds. It was impossible for me to consider that we could ever have a life together. My career was starting as well. The timing of all this was wrong. My mother told me to get rid of it. She told me many Russian girls had the same problems and the doctors would just do it without asking questions. That was what I was ready to do, right up until the day I was due at the clinic. I couldn't go through with it. I decided to have the baby and arranged for the boy to be adopted before I could form the feelings of motherhood. I severed all connections and lost myself in my work. A few years later I met my husband, Ruslan. He had been married before and although he had children from his first wife, we started a family in the conventional way. At last, my personal and professional life came into balance. But the past kept me as a prisoner. I had known about who had fostered my… *our*, child. They were a good couple living in Petersburg. His foster father was an engineer at a steel works, his foster mother, a kindergarten teacher. He had a stable upbringing and education. I admit I followed his progress from afar but even I had a surprise when I found that after high school and university he had applied to be a student at the Academy. His grades were exemplary, so I could hardly ignore his application. My job was also to tutor the best and he fitted the bill. If I had rejected his case, questions would have been asked. I coached him through his doctorate. His achievement saw him joining the navy as an apprentice in the Experimental Propulsion Unit. At this point, I considered my job done and felt absolved of my responsibilities. At no time did he know of our special bond and still doesn't, to this day."

"So why tell me now?"

"For several reasons. When investigating how I could help you I stumbled on some information that for me changes everything. My story is no longer a secret and if it is shared, I haven't fully come to terms with the implications. Our child took the name of Boris Ponomariev. He achieved a high-level classified role with the navy in Kaliningrad, becoming the base's principal research engineer. I think you may know the rest."

Des made the connection in his head and remembered the strange feeling of a family bond from the Russian's recent visit to his home. His instinct seemed to have been correct.

"Are you sure?"

"Completely. The authorities have an informant in Oxford, with either direct or close access to your people at the Lauriston. They know he is with you. The price of all I have shared with you is dependent on bringing him back with you when you come."

"And then what, are they just going to take him back and pretend the whole thing never happened?"

Galina did not answer.

"What happens if I decide not to come or he refuses to come with me?"

"They're not worried about you. For them, your fate is sealed but for Boris they will send a liquidation unit to eliminate him, just like they did with Litvinenko and tried to do with Skripal."

"Where do you fit into this?"

"I bring the two of you back and life for me carries on as normal. I can make Boris's rehabilitation my personal responsibility. I travel the world as a roving ambassador of the Academy. If I don't then my story gets told, I lose my job and career for mothering a traitor, Boris is killed, my husband's reputation as a military hero gets trashed and God knows what awaits our children."

"But if I come with Boris there is still no chance of us becoming a family, especially when you have commitments elsewhere."

"That is true, but we would see each other regularly and I will help you to build a life there, and your work would generate new social as well as professional contacts."

"Can Ruslan help?"

"Short of killing the one person in the FSB who knows about this, no."

"Is that an option?"

"Not for a decorated military hero."

"And you're sure Boris himself knows nothing of this?"

"Yes. As his tutor I think he retained a distant respect for me, but he loves his adopted elderly foster parents who have moved to Rostov. If all this fails, the FSB will leak the story to ensure that any bond you may have with him is undermined. In their view that will be worthwhile because at the very least it will prevent you from forming a working relationship."

Their conversation died at that point. The shock Kelly felt was palpable. All he had done was to pursue his career to the best of his ability and now innocents were getting hurt.

"What do you expect me to do?"

"I cannot make up your mind for you, Des. My bosses want your knowledge on HCCVD, but they also want to stop our son's expertise benefitting the West. Their attitude to Boris goes against everything I always believed my country stood for. But now my life is being held hostage by a shit-faced civil servant who plans to exploit my situation for his personal benefit."

"You know I can't just give you an answer on this."

"You don't have to. The FSB people who I must notify say they need four weeks' notice to organise your transfer. So all you need to do is to give a location and a date, then just assume it will happen. Perhaps you can plan a business trip outside the UK and tell your colleagues about it? The FSB mole can do the job for you. He will tell us when and where the collection can be made. You won't have to announce it to me. No one has given me any deadlines, but I guess they will need to know within the month."

It was getting late. Des paid the bill and they walked arm in arm down the narrow alleyway from the market square to Piccadilly.

When they arrived at the main thoroughfare, she turned and hugged him.

"You are welcome to come in for a nightcap."

It had been some time since he had held a woman close – in fact, the last time must have been at their dinner in Berlin. Somehow, her touch seemed more important now, her perfume intoxicating.

"No, Galina. I think we have enough problems to solve without adding to the list. It is right for now we go our separate ways."

"Remember to let me know."

"I will."

He watched her turn right and walk in the direction of Hyde Park Corner towards the hotel. She didn't look back.

*

From her position in a gaggle of revellers in Shepherd Market, Chemmy Moore had a grandstand view of Kelly's dinner engagement with Rustanova and was free to take pictures of the proceedings on her phone. Although it was impossible from her position to pick up the detail of the conversation, she was struck by their animated expressions. To the casual observer this did not look like a business meeting or even a light-hearted social engagement, but seemed much deeper, intense, emotional. If this was a normal couple contemplating a divorce, the scene would have been understandable, but between professional colleagues from other countries? There was more to this than met the eye. As she watched the pair leave their table, Moore's police training kicked into action. She watched them walk slowly across the square, arm in arm. Once their backs were to the restaurant, she hurried in, announcing to the first surprised waiter that she thought she'd left her mobile on the table where she had been sitting. Without hesitating, she squeezed through the crowded restaurant to their table in the window, which had not yet been cleared. Almost comically looking for the phone, she grabbed the wine glass with lipstick on it, slipping it into a polythene bag. She kept her movement going with the sleight of hand, distracting anyone watching from her actions, like a magician doing a card trick. Full of apology, she left the already busy restaurant staff in her wake as she spilled back out onto the street and set off past the King's Arms, down White Horse Street towards Piccadilly, to catch up with her target.

She witnessed their parting and shadowed Kelly back to Paddington.

The next morning, she took her trophy from the night before into the office, presenting it with the same theatrical aplomb that she had demonstrated at her targets' dinner table.

"So this is all you have to show from your night out in Mayfair?" Bannan smiled.

"I had to work quite hard for this one," Chemmy countered, recognising the lightness of her boss's mood.

"Thought you'd like to see the evidence before I sent it for DNA testing."

"Why do you want to do that?"

"Just an ex-copper's hunch. Kelly and Rustanova seemed to be having a heavy conversation last night. It didn't look like a lot of fun."

"We picked up a burner-to-burner picture of the Lauriston's HCCVD team sent from Oxford to London, a couple of days back. We're still looking into it, but the receiving phone was close to the UK offices of Gazda. At the time it was sent, Kelly was in Aldermaston, so it doesn't suggest he is personally involved in spying, so maybe we should assume that if this wasn't a social call, she was delivering some sort of message from Moscow. Do you think they are having an affair?"

"Not really. I didn't get the sense that there was much passion involved. Possibly that's just the Russian way."

"Funny you should say that. While we were at Chatham House, I noticed her making eye contact with him almost as much as with her embassy minders. It was as though she had two agendas going on. She's certainly smart enough to cope with that, but she looked to be under pressure. In fact, in that way, I thought the ineptitude of Chuck Barnes seemed to help her out. If the Americans had fielded someone half-competent, she might have experienced a meltdown. So Chemmy, what is the theory you're trying to prove?"

"It might seem a bit wild, but if you look closely at Rustanova's face and compare it to Ponomariev's, there's a likeness there. I'm going to put both faces through the biometric imaging computer and I think I will get a probable resemblance. If I can compare her DNA to Ponomariev's, then possibly we could make a case for them being blood relatives."

"You really think Rustanova could be Ponomariev's mother?"

"Why not? For me, it's a woman thing. She has a distinctive, almost Slavic, square jaw. The only other person I have seen recently with a look like that is our friend from Kaliningrad. If I am right, it opens a whole new vista on the case, and we might be able to guess what they were talking about."

*

Willoughby was making progress of a sort. Although he seemed no nearer to locating the whereabouts of Abigail Kelly, dead or alive, his original theory about the involvement of the London-based Turkish criminal fraternity and Hayet Suker was bearing fruit. He wouldn't care to admit it, but often, in his experience, seasoned criminals were identified because of personal mistakes or complacency, and not the outcome of serious sleuthing. That was certainly borne out in the case of Bryan Smyth. Despite Willoughby still having some doubts about the motivation for Smyth's actions in engaging with the Turk in the first place, evidence of the criminal act was proving to be little more than an administrative exercise. Ballistics had recovered the bullet from his car, which had been fired through the driver's seat and had somehow lodged in the sump, causing more of a fuel leak from the car engine than the amount of blood that escaped from Smyth's body. The weapon itself had been easily found by divers, the notorious Thames mud not having had sufficient time to conceal it. CCTV at Trinity Buoy Wharf had picked up a small thickset figure, dressed in a raincoat and wearing a trilby, crossing the car park, meeting Smyth and getting into the back of his vehicle. It showed the same figure getting out a short time later, throwing something into the river and walking away. There was no sign of the motor which delivered and collected him.

And then there was the phone.

Smyth's mobile had been found in the glove box and had recorded the conversation between Smyth and Suker, which confirmed the Turk's actions, and also his involvement in the kidnapping of Abigail.

From the recordings and subsequent interviews, it was clear that Suker had acted instinctively and was motivated by what he had regarded as a lack of personal respect. For him, the death of Smyth was a matter of honour, and sent as a signal to some of his business rivals that in such matters, he would not delegate responsibility to others. The action was irrational and motivated by rage and apparent loss of face, hence his carelessness.

Willoughby knew he would nail him, that he would get a life

sentence. He would continue to run his business behind bars and with good behaviour could be out on parole in eight years. But that was far from the end of the story. Willoughby still had his mission to trace Abigail Kelly. He had yet to find out who had ordered the kidnapping, how much and by what method Suker had been paid and where the plane that had left Biggin Hill had gone. This was now the focus of his interest. Flight plans had shown the Jetstream had arrived from Austria, refuelled and had flown on to Cyprus. But for the moment, that was where the trail went cold.

The other interesting thing about Smyth's phone was that it contained details of other texts and voice messages he had obtained in recent weeks, including exchanges with Miles's mother. The development would necessitate another trip to the Thames Valley – perhaps at a time when he could be sure Des would not be there.

*

Aldo de Leonibus and his girlfriend, Iveta, were collected at Sofia Airport, flown to Riyadh and transferred to a suite at the Kempinski Tower on the King Fahad Road. Acclimatising to the oppressive heat of the city would be a test if this was to become their new home. Both were grateful of the respite from the sticky, airless environment of the street where the naturally arid conditions combined with the concentrated emissions from the high-octane cars which crammed the freeway. It had been a long day and the novelty of travelling by private jet had long since worn off. Iveta had stripped off and stayed in the cold shower, freshening up, as Aldo stared at his programme of meetings for the coming day. It was true to say the visit was something of a gamble; his list of engagements included several with members of the Royal Family, but precisely who they were (at least half a dozen appeared to be crown princes) and how they would relate to his prospective job was far from clear. No doubt all would be revealed in the morning. He was grateful for having the benefit of being escorted throughout by a familiar face – Mohammed bin Shararni, and the Saudi authorities had laid on a cultural tour for Iveta while he would be locked in meetings and a plant tour. An early night would see them ready for their official initiation into life in the Kingdom.

Their host arrived to collect them at eight; he had brought along one of his wives. Iveta thought it impolite to enquire how many he had but, judging by the confidence of the dusky-eyed *hijab*-wearing woman who greeted her, she was one of the most senior in the pecking order, if not the pre-eminent. Two cars were outside the hotel. The first would take Iveta to the King Abdul Aziz Historical Centre, not the 'historic centre' as such but located in the former compound of the Murabha' Palace. That would come later when she would tour the Masmak Fort and the Central Mosque in the Dira district, before being taken to visit a junior school and technical college for girls, where, in her capacity as an MP she would open a new sports hall.

Aldo's day looked more mundane by comparison, starting at the Ministry of Foreign Affairs, a break for lunch, then on to the Ministry of Energy and the site of a new industrial city being built some thirty kilometres south-east of the capital.

The day involved meeting ministers and senior officials. The morning was dedicated to the Kingdom's global strategic interest in HCCVD technologies as a net contributor to its energy portfolio, the afternoon to the parameters of the job he would have as executive director for HCCVD policy & implementation. It was not unusual for the state to hire foreign expertise in emerging markets where locally generated knowledge was not available, but a clear element of his role was to bring the national capability in the field to internationally competitive standards. As a result, bin Shararni would become his pupil, guide and 'critical friend'. De Leonibus would have ninety days to develop a five-year plan to develop HCCVD capability and establish a new industry based on the manufacture and application of the diamond brick technology. He appreciated taking a break from the bland but cool blocks of government meeting rooms in the middle of the day and was grateful for the opportunity of visiting a local restaurant, the Najd Village in the Al Mazar district, which had been closed to the public to accommodate de Leonibus and the accompanying phalanx of hosts and associates.

"Most visitors regard the Kingdom as a relatively modern state without heritage or distinctive culture. We are always keen to show honoured guests the true face and hospitality of our nation. The local Najd tradition provides an excellent introduction to the personality of the Saudi people," bin Shararni announced on their way into the rustic ornately decorated villa in the Arabic style. This was a new experience for the well-travelled de Leonibus, joining his hosts in a cavernous room, cloistered onto a shaded garden, sitting in a circle on the floor on highly decorated hand-sewn mats and cushions under an oak beam and reed ceiling, a gentle breeze provided by tastefully obscured electric fans. Saudi army musicians performed *Samri*, a traditional folkloric music and dance native to Najd, involving singing poetry while a drum was played and two rows of men, seated on their knees, swayed and clapped to the rhythm. The occasion provided an oasis of calm in an otherwise intense series of exchanges with his prospective employers.

Lunch was a traditional Sofra platter made up of classic local dishes such as *kabsahs*, *badyas*, and *goursans*, the meat – mutton, chicken and camel – a very different cuisine to either Bulgaria or Italy. "The Najd Highlands is the name of the area around Riyadh. Its borders extend from the mountains of Hayel to the north to the Empty Quarter to the south, and from the desert of Nafud to the east to the Hijaz Mountains to the west. It has been a fertile land rich with pastures, wild birds and animals such as ostriches, deer and rabbits, and with many oases and palm farms. It was also home to a number of Arab tribes and many of our old poets wrote about Najd which has a special place in the hearts of Saudis," his host explained.

Despite his years of international experience, Saudi Arabia felt like a world apart. Behind the hospitality was a steeliness which he had not experienced before. It reminded him of bin Shararni's confidence at their dinner in Sofia. There was an assumption already that he had been bought and would just do what they wanted. It was strange for him not to see any women around, even at a distance, as he moved around the capital. Where were they? Also, he didn't see anyone who he took to be Saudi, doing any sort of menial task out on the streets. They all seemed to be from the Indian sub-continent – a point he commented on to his host.

He replied, "Much of our practices are sourced in our conservative interpretation of the Sunni muslim faith – *wahhabism* – which requires men, women and foreigners to live their lives separately, even if they need to spend time working together. I think I am typical of most Saudi men. My family time at home is private and I have a live-in couple from India to take care of all the domestic tasks. When you come to live here you will be accommodated in a separate compound for foreigners where you can live your life in line with your own beliefs and standards without affecting local people. It seems strange, but we find it works well for our guests, coupled with the generous time allowances we make for people to return to their native countries. I have no doubt you and your lady will feel at home in our expatriate community. I will show you your apartment tomorrow."

The day continued with further meetings at the energy department and then on to the site of Riyadh's newest industrial park a half-hour drive into the desert. Stopping their Mercedes four-wheeled drive, bin Shararni unfurled a huge blueprint and pointed at the empty horizon.

"This is the place that will be home to you for at least half the working week. We are planning on building about twenty of these industrial camps every year in the present five-year cycle. This one is important as we plan it to be powered sustainably by solar and your HCCVD technology. We have not yet got as far as agreeing to import spent nuclear rods but will provide for you out of our own national supply from our two operational nuclear facilities. Show us we can run this commercially and we will build it into a world-beating industry. Our finance and your knowhow are a powerful combination, my friend." It was the first time he had used such a greeting. Was this the signal that he had passed his interview?

By the end of the afternoon, Aldo was relieved to get back to the hotel and to hear of Iveta's day. Both had found the experience exhausting but neither was sure if it was because of the oppressive weather or the oppressive company.

The hotel lobby was one of the few places where Aldo and Iveta could enjoy a drink, so they went to admire the view and the twinkling lights of the conurbation and share their adventures. In the same way that he had not seen women, Iveta had only seen men from the back of her darkened glass limousine but shared what she took to be one of the strangest incidents in her day. At the school, she had met a British girl called Abigail and had been surprised that she seemed to be living independently of any immediate family.

"It was strange. I suppose we were introduced because there were not any other white European women there and she was wearing a hijab. I took her to be a student teacher, but just as I was going to ask how she came to be here, she was ushered away for what I was told was an urgent assignment. I can't explain, but it just seemed wrong. I know if I had a daughter that age, even if she had an adventurous spirit, I don't think I would be happy about her being here."

"What sort of social life does she get?"

"God knows – but staring out into the mountains every night doesn't seem like a healthy pastime to me."

The next day was about the domestic agenda, how they would live and their accommodation. Their ever-jovial host and Aldo's prospective right-hand man arrived at eight to take them to their guest compound in the Uum Salim district in the west of the city, a well-heeled gated community consisting of a network of low-level villas and apartments.

"So here we are – everything you can imagine on your doorstep – pool, gymnasium, beauty parlour, coffee bar, supermarket which sells beer and wine, tennis court. You will have a valet to take care of your laundry and cook your meals; a spacious lounge with satellite TV so that you can watch your favourite shows from Italy. I have seen that Italian detective, *Montalbano*. He is very big here. Your neighbours are British, French and German, no Bulgarians as far as I'm aware, plus I am told the social life of the diplomatic community is very good."

The place allocated to them looked wonderful and Iveta was sure it would benefit from some of those ornaments and knick-knacks that would make the house a home. They were about to leave, when Iveta spotted the British girl she had met the day before, reading a book by the pool, now not wearing a head covering.

"Abigail? Hi – it's Iveta, we met yesterday."

They were both taken aback by her reaction.

She jumped up, dropping her book, and ran over to them.

"Please help me, I am being held here against my will. Please take a message back to my parents. This is their number. Tell them I need help."

Bewildered, Aldo asked, "What is your name?"

"Abigail Kelly, I live in London."

"I don't believe it! Is your father called Desmond, and does he work in Oxford?"

Abigail looked equally surprised.

"Yes, yes. How did you know?"

"We are acquainted. What are you doing here?"

"I don't know; I have been kidnapped. I can stay here in the complex but am not allowed out. They have guards on the exits, and I'm not allowed a mobile."

Just at that moment, bin Shararni approached them, with another man in blazer and dark glasses, having just locked up their apartment.

Aldo heard him say something in Arabic, before he firmly ushered them away from the girl and added his standard spray-on smile.

"So, Mr & Mrs de Leonibus, I hope you think everything is in order. I will drop you back at the hotel. They will arrange a transfer to the airport in the morning. One of our jets will be ready to fly you to Sofia at ten o'clock. Your contracts, visa application and other necessary documentation will be issued to you by courier from our embassy at the end of the week. If you have any other concerns, please call me on any of the numbers you already have. I will be pleased to answer any subsequent questions. I am really looking forward to welcoming you to Riyadh and working with you as an esteemed colleague."

While he had been talking, they had been steered outside the compound to his waiting car.

"Just one question for now, Mohammed – the girl, who is she?"

"Oh, she is just here temporarily. Her father is finishing a contract for the government in Jeddah before coming to collect her. We are just looking after her until he gets back. She is helping out at a local school, giving English lessons, which is how your lady met her yesterday. Don't worry, she won't be here by the time you move in. You can be sure of a peaceful environment and look forward to a happy time with us."

FOURTEEN

WILLIAMS WAS FED UP. Having to locate an out of the way phone shop where someone would have bought a pay-as-you-go set in the last couple of days without wanting to be seen was not that straightforward. Somehow, he had to fit this instruction around being seen to be fulfilling his commitment as document controller on the HCCVD project at the Lauriston. He had used some of his office time to draw up a shortlist of likely places to go, which were, in the main, 'corner shop' type places, not the big supermarkets. These tended to specialise in 'no questions asked' transactions and seemed to correspond with the type of electronic cash transfer services favoured by expatriate workers wanting to send wages home to far-flung parts of the globe. It was a challenge as he had to try to visit locations that were close to the Lauriston and had handled cash sales in the last forty-eight hours, then cross-reference that against a list of new numbers logged onto the 4G network. By his reckoning he had a list of fifty-four places to check out. He also needed to carry pictures of four of his colleagues to assist in identifying the customer. This was one of those gumshoe jobs that were the hallmark of 'Six' operatives – far from the James Bond stereotype. Fortunately most of the stores he was targeting were open to ten at night so his searches filled the time he might have otherwise spent chilling over a beer in his local, going for a run or indulging his interest in carpentry. Looking back, he thought he would have done his nut if he had needed to visit all of them, but number nineteen on his list, the Chopra General Store in Headington Road, proved to be the one, on his fourth night of asking.

Not only had the shop's namesake positively identified the customer, but the cautious retailer had also taken the additional precaution of writing down the serial number of the phone and SIM card he sold.

"I am always doing this. It is not unusual for the police to come round making enquiries about these things. In my line of work, we cannot be too careful, even when the customer looks respectable."

"And you're sure it was the guy with the bushy beard in the picture?"

"I tell you he wasn't one of my regulars. He dressed smart and spoke with a funny accent. I think he was foreign but I'd know him again anywhere. Do you want to buy one while you are here? I have one just the same – very good price for cash to you, as you're a gentleman."

Williams bought one and used it to take a photograph of Mr Chopra holding Liebelt's picture outside his shop. It wouldn't count as evidence, but he thought Bannan would appreciate the gesture.

He was right. Williams had indeed come up with an important part of the picture. He also had to give credit to Chemmy, whose hunch about Rustanova and Ponomariev was supported by the evidence. Sir Gavin had warned him that a buy-out proposition for the Lauriston was expected from Maximum Power in the next couple of weeks, but he hadn't yet had the opportunity to think through the implications for the present situation. It was now more important than ever that he was ahead of the game on the information front, and so he had sent a message to Willoughby inviting him to Barton Street for coffee in the persona of 'Winston Carter-Jones' of the Ministry of Defence. He knew in advance that this would not be an easy discussion with the plod committed to picking up every scrap of information he might inadvertently divulge, as he had no intention of sharing the full nature of his discoveries with Scotland Yard at this point.

"Detective Chief Inspector – thank you for taking time out to come and see me. I just really wanted to know how you were getting on. You know we tend to take an interest in cases that may affect our assets and are keen to help where we can."

"We are always happy to take on board offers of help, especially now. The key points from the investigation are these. Firstly, we still hold the view that Abigail Kelly is alive and have reason to believe she might well be held outside the UK, but are still pursuing lines of enquiry about that. We are especially keen to understand the motivation of a would-be kidnapper as at the present time there has been no contact with a ransom demand. Secondly, you will have heard on the news about the murder of the Oxfordshire landlord, Bryan Smyth, at Trinity Buoy Wharf. We have harvested some strong evidence to link this to the Kelly situation and have made an arrest."

"What is the link to Kelly?"

"For reasons we have not been able to fully establish yet, it seems Smyth hatched a plan with Abigail's brother to press a Turkish restaurant owner to share knowledge of her kidnapping."

"How come?"

"We had a witness in the Kellys' home village, who saw the abduction and was able to describe the assailants' vehicle. We linked the description to a van with false plates picked up on an ANPR camera at the junction of the A34 & M4 about that time and discovered the true registration was held by a Turkish restaurant owner. It was the only bit of investigative detail that I shared with the Kelly family in private, and unfortunately it seems that her brother, rather prematurely, decided to act on it. Quite how Smyth became involved is not clear, but it ended up costing him his life."

"So does this kebab chap know anything useful?"

"It's too early to be sure. The story seems to be that he, the accused, seems to think Smyth organised a gang of local hooligans to trash his restaurant to get him to talk about Abigail but despite his story, trying to make that stick is not easy. This chap is a sponsor of Spurs and is a high-profile target for disillusioned Arsenal fans anyway. It doesn't look as though they would need to be persuaded to have a go. He says he was disrespected, and you know that's a big issue with those Mediterranean types..."

"But this Turk knows something?"

"Certainly, although it is clear that he was not personally involved. I think that when it sinks in that he's lined up for an extended stay in chokey, he might have a bit more to say, but I'll let you know."

"How can I help you?"

"I wanted to know how well networked you were in Cyprus. With a military base on their territory, I guessed you ministry people would have some connections over and above the 'copper-to-copper' dialogue. There is a flight plan for a Jetstream which flew in and out of Biggin Hill the evening Abigail was taken. We think there is a possibility she was on the flight. But although we know it landed over there at Larnaca, it flew on again somewhere else. We've tried the normal channels and been blanked at every turn. We've sent out a missing persons notice via Interpol to support our case, but nobody's biting."

"Leave it with me, Detective Chief Inspector. I will look into it."

*

Bannan decided he liked Willoughby. The policeman was inherently honest and had told him what he wanted to know without having to be interrogated more closely. Slowly but surely the picture was starting to come into focus. But there were some more theories to test.

If Kelly himself was not involved in espionage and was indeed the father of Ponomariev, why was he still talking with Rustanova? After all, she had her own family back in Russia. Perhaps it was possible they were just professional associates. Bannan had found a reference to them sitting together on the judging committee of the International Andromeda Prize for Science for the past three years. He wondered perhaps if Kelly knew he had fathered Ponomariev or indeed, if the Russian was aware of his true parentage. Further, Bannan clearly understood the reaction of the Russian state when it became known that Ponomariev had defected. Traitors would be traced and killed. Maybe his mother had sent a warning – certainly someone in Moscow would now know where to go looking.

*

Iveta wanted to talk though her impressions of their short trip to Saudi on the flight back to Bulgaria, but had noted her partner's finger on his lips and contented herself with a lime and soda and a copy of the latest edition of *Vogue*. Aldo's mind was racing. He had too much to think about to engage in any reading or relaxed conversation – for work or pleasure. He was on the horns of a dilemma. In many ways the trip had lived up to expectations – status, accommodation, transport, renumeration, resourcing. But he was not sure if the role had any power. In fact, the only power he might have is that of influence by, in effect, presenting the views of the global energy community in the Kingdom. Would Iveta put up with the semi-detached relationship that the move would necessitate, split between Sofia and Riyadh, and how would she adjust to the clear demotion in personal status when she visited the Kingdom? The hard choice would be to either accept the generous terms, which would see him financially secure for the rest of his days or return to his present unpredictable and relatively low-key professional existence in Bulgaria, with all its familiar frustrations. From the Saudi perspective, his hosts had already convinced themselves that his decision was made and he really didn't like their brusque attitude which regarded him as just another commodity. But the thing that dominated his mind was his twenty-second encounter with the British girl. It was just an amazing coincidence that he should know her father, even though he could not recall meeting any of Des's family in the past. The circumstances told him that this was not some premeditated introduction. In fact, bin Shararni, normally smooth and urbane, had looked momentarily disturbed and anxious to move them on. The girl had told them she was there under duress and yet she was sitting next to a swimming pool reading a book in the sunshine. It seemed ridiculous that he, a peer of Desmond Kelly's, was once more going to be obliged to consult with him before he would be free to make his own decision.

All the papers promised by bin Shararni arrived on time. In all respects they were as expected. He felt sure that the flexibility of his contract would allow him to work between Riyadh and Sofia, which would accommodate Iveta's requirements as well as his own. And for all that, he was still preoccupied by the brief and unexpected meeting with the British girl by the compound swimming pool. It was all too much of a coincidence – the daughter of a friend, 'held prisoner' (the girl's words) by his new prospective employers. The casual dismissal of her presence by bin Shararni and the role of his security man in moving her away; it didn't add up.

Rather than seeing his future as establishing a commercial and diplomatic first for an emerging world power, he had the feeling he was being initiated into an international crime syndicate. He may have got entirely the wrong idea, but he had to get to the truth before signing up.

He took bin Shararni up on his 'call me anytime' offer.

"Have you got a start date?" It was the Saudi's first question.

"Not yet, Mohammed, just a couple of minor issues."

"I am sorry, Aldo, I thought I had included everything."

"Yes, you did. That is all OK, but I am concerned about that British girl I met at the foreigners' residential compound. You see, by an extraordinary coincidence, I know her father. He is a friend of mine. Is she being detained for some reason and does her family know?"

There was a silence at the end of the line.

"I'm not sure I would call it detention. She is on a sabbatical, teaching English in a local secondary school, the one your lady visited. I hope you agree that she looked well and was enjoying the sunshine she doesn't get in England."

"She told me that she was being held prisoner. I assume that to mean she cannot go home if she wanted to. Has she committed a crime?"

"No – we have just had some delays processing her visa and exit papers."

"I am glad you have not had the same difficulties with mine. To be clear, Mohammed, this position causes me personal embarrassment. I would like you to arrange her release and transfer to the United Kingdom before I sign your contract. I expect to speak to her father soon and to tell him about this situation. He needs to be reassured that it is being resolved."

There was another pause on the line.

"The British girl is an insurance policy."

"For what?"

"To guarantee we get the technical co-operation we need to be successful on HCCVD."

"Isn't that my job?"

"You said yourself, that there were aspects of this technology you did not understand and that you would need to refer to other experts, from time to time. We note that the world expert is the girl's father."

"Are you suggesting that you anticipate holding her indefinitely, just in case your strategy doesn't work out?"

"We would expect you to get input from Dr Kelly into the plan you produce. Once created, we will agree it and, assuming you have secured Dr Kelly's contribution, she will be released safe and well."

"This is madness. I can just ask Dr Kelly – you don't have to engage in such action."

"We find it to be an effective method that has worked for us in the past."

"How did you find her? She didn't appear to have come willingly."

"We arranged her collection in the same way that we will arrange her repatriation."

"OK, Mohammed. I do not wish to be misunderstood. I will not sign the contracts until I am informed by her father that she is back home. I suggest you think about how to make this happen, as from a reputational point of view, your actions will not be understood in the wider world."

*

He had no idea where Des would be when he put in a call to him that evening from their flat in central Sofia. Predictably the call was not answered and went to voicemail.

"Des, it's Aldo. I've just got back from Saudi. Trip seemed to go well but need to talk to you urgently. I think I may have met your daughter, Abigail. Did you know she was there? Let me know."

Kelly had the message within the hour as he arrived at Heathrow. He returned the call from the departure lounge and heard Aldo's story with a mixture of relief and puzzlement. His professional life was once again taking a personal toll. He passed the news to Willoughby.

"This fits with our enquiries. We knew Suker was working for a Middle Eastern client but he hasn't yet told us who or why. There are others I must talk to, as this is moving beyond a criminal investigation to a diplomatic incident. Please make sure that I can reach you on your mobile and for now, don't discuss this with anyone – not even your immediate family."

*

Chemmy had a spring in her step as she walked out of the Havneby Kro. Fresh from her achievement in linking Rustanova to Kelly, she knew her star was on the rise at 'Six'. Her reward: a return trip to Rømø – this time in her own hired car and with the prospect of a comfortable bed for the night. Better still, this was a simple dress-down occasion allowing her to indulge her natural interest in ornithology. No need for makeup and posh frocks. Walking boots, jeans, T-shirts, camera and binoculars were the order of the day. There was, however, a new identity to take on – 'Gudrun Heintze', divorcee from Munster, booking a solo birdwatching experience run by the local tourist board, featuring local expert, Ranger Maurice Glistrup. To help her get into character she had made two important cosmetic changes, dyeing her hair black and arranging it in a single pigtail, and wearing gold-framed spectacles, complemented by gold stud earrings. Bannan would often joke about the trouble she went to to disguise her appearance and, whereas it was not always deemed necessary from a professional point of view, Chemmy would do it as part of her preparation for taking on a new identity, in the same way that an actor might before taking to the stage.

"You are in for a truly memorable birding experience, Ms Heintze," promised Glistrup as he walked her to his Hyundai people carrier. "Is this your first visit to Rømø?"

Glistrup was every inch a Viking. Big-boned, tied-back red hair and beard, fair skin, broad smile, good teeth. In his green Wadden Sea fleece, navy blue docker-style trousers and calf-length boots, he looked like a model ambassador for his employers.

"Yes, it is," she replied. "My sister visited a couple of years ago and spoke very highly of it. She said it is a really great place to come, relax and forget your troubles."

"She is right. You know, people say not much happens here, but for our nature, every season is packed with sights and adventure. Today I will be giving you a general tour of some of the best nature spots around the islands and marshes. I'm glad to see you are well-dressed, as you may get your feet wet before the day is out."

Their journey commenced, back up the main road to the causeway. After ten minutes he took a left turn into the car park of the local church.

"Please excuse me, I have some post to collect from the mailbox. If we had been here in the evening, I could have showed you our resident colony of long-eared bats, but maybe later."

He noted her surprise.

"I guess I should have told you, that apart from working for the National Park Authority, I am also the pastor here, and provide counselling services to those who ask for it. I am sure you have heard that making a living on Rømø is hard. Most people have more than one job. You could say it's logical for me to combine nature conservation with faith."

"So I understand. I was talking to one of the regulars in the bar at the Kro last night who said the same. There seems to be a bit of competition to see how many jobs a single person can have."

"I don't think there is much doubt about that. Westergaard, the fisherman down at Havneby, is the clear winner. He has a saying that nobody who visits Rømø leaves without spending money in one of his businesses. At last count I think he had about half a dozen. Personally I think his fish restaurant by the harbour is the best. No one I know understands where he gets the time."

"So, you're responsible for this church?"

"St Clement's, yes – but I can only do it with the help of an army of volunteers. This is a community resource, a meeting place we all share. Would you like to have a quick look?"

They started to walk towards the main porch.

"The oldest part was built sometime after 1250 and expanded four centuries later. Possibly in the latter half of the 15th century, the church tower was built in the Gothic style. The church was expanded in the 17th and 18th centuries and the interior includes several model ships. It is a regret that I have to keep it locked during the week unless I have a wedding or funeral booked, but I like to leave it open to guests at the weekend."

The whitewashed exterior in the Lutheran tradition was well-maintained, the surrounding graveyard manicured, with even some of the oldest tombstones surprisingly undecayed, a fact commented on by Chemmy.

"We have protection from the sea and the worst of the winds by the woods, and it is mainly the salt which decays the stones. If you look at the outside edge of the graveyard walls, you will see the damage caused over the years. If you had time to read the stones here, they give you a pocket history of our little island. The oldest we know of here is from about 1330 – rumoured to be an illegitimate son of Abel Valdemarsen, a former Duke of Schleswig, a local nobleman who we know to be one of the founding fathers. But as you go round you will find the remains of warriors, fishermen, sailors, farmers, boat builders, whalers – up to the Second World War. The Germans kept a major radar station here – long since dismantled – but many soldiers perished because of Allied bombing. These 'brothers in arms' are together in a separate place on the edge of the graveyard. Since then, just locals are buried here, including our most famous son, the former boss of Denmark's biggest shipping company. Last century, it looked as if the church would run out of money, so we had to get the pews inside sponsored by local families. As you go round you can still see their names etched on the arms."

"Would you allow people who were not locals to be buried here?"

"Well, it's a good question. We try to respect the wishes of the dying and so if there was a connection with Rømø, a strong faith and the relatives obtained the necessary licence, then I guess we would, but death goes in fashions. These days, I get more requests to provide blessings for people who disappear at sea."

"How do you mean?"

"Rømø is an increasingly popular tourist destination. Despite warnings, it's not unusual for people to disappear here. This island has marshes on the mainland side but shifting quicksands on the three sides of the Wadden Sea. People get seduced into paddling out in the shallows and sometimes get taken by surprise. That is often difficult for those left behind. The sands here take the bodies without leaving a trace. It's worse than drowning. If people die in a conventional water accident at least there is a body to grieve over."

"What do you do in such cases?"

"We normally take a boat out to the place they were last seen and conduct a short blessing. It's not ideal but at least it offers the families something and of course we earn fees, which help us to maintain our services for local people."

He paused.

"Well, I suppose I mean 'I' not 'we'. There is a market here for people who want to talk about their faith, find peace of mind and seek spiritual guidance; I don't need to advertise."

"Has this happened much recently?"

"Yes, about a dozen times a year. Personally, I draw comfort from telling the families that their loved one knew of the area and the risks and were probably more prepared than they might have thought."

"You mean some may have committed suicide?"

"It's a possibility. I would describe it as 'assisted dying' which is not illegal. Some people are very organised. They leave a paper trail explaining their actions. Secretly, I think the police are quite pleased about that. It helps them to manage statistics for unexplained deaths."

"Have you met any of these people?"

"Some. A few who have disappeared have been people of faith and the church here is often their last opportunity to make peace with their maker before they go. Those that come are often very private, but one or two take the opportunity to talk. They are quite a mixed bunch from all over the world, but generally wealthy. It proves a point – wealth cannot buy happiness. If I come across them, I always tell them life is a gift from God and only he should have the option of taking it away. Anyway, I am sure you have not come here to talk to the pastor, but as I'm dressed as the National Park Ranger, let's go and explore our nature."

The tour resumed, visiting bespoke hides on beaches, woodland and bog, some so well hidden in vegetation that Chemmy knew she would never have found them without her guide.

As well as a plethora of bird species, raptors and the brown hares she had seen on her last visit, Glistrup's programme involved sightings of otters, beavers, red squirrels, newts, and crabs. The Dane took his responsibilities seriously, explaining little-known facts about the flora and fauna as he went. Clearly an enthusiast for his subject, Chemmy found herself warming to him and felt she was getting an insight into his character – their sporadic conversations between sites ranged from the environment to politics, even to their shared interest in Country & Western music.

As the day was ending, Glistrup introduced her to the most dramatic sight.

"There is one final special place I wanted to show you before we finish. This is the thing you will remember most from the day. One of the most spectacular sights here at this time of year is called the Black Sun. You've heard of it? It's when hundreds of thousands of starlings dance the dance of survival in a gyrating cloud. Starlings used to be so common across the continent but their populations have declined in recent years, so we are very lucky they still come here in such numbers. The reed beds are a favourite nesting spot for them. The beating of millions of wings darken the dimming sky. It's the closest you'll get to a real-life (but less scary) re-enactment of Alfred Hitchcock's *The Birds* film. Just before dusk, hundreds of thousands of European starlings gather from all corners of the skies to perform an impressive twist-twirl ballet, with the flocks almost entirely eclipsing the sun as it sinks. These aerial acrobats are actually en route from Norway, Sweden and Finland to their breeding grounds in France, Britain, Belgium and the Netherlands. They gather like this for two reasons. First, safety in numbers: predators such as peregrine falcons find it hard to target one bird amid a spellbinding cloud of thousands. Second, to stay warm and exchange information, such as where the best mud flats for feeding are. It goes to show that if you know where to look, the best free shows are offered by nature."

The strange spectacle lasted for a half hour, Chemmy completely absorbed in the natural phenomenon, gasping, pointing, taking pictures. For her it was over too soon.

"That was wonderful. You speak with so much passion."

"Yes, Rømø is my life. I was born and raised in Tønder, the nearest little town on the mainland, and used to spend much of my time playing in the marsh lands so I am fortunate to have a job protecting this special place."

"Protecting?"

"We have problems sometimes with poachers, egg collectors and litter hooligans who leave their plastic wrappers around for the birds to eat. Picking it up sometimes is tricky as I have to avoid disturbing the nests. I am glad these are a minority, however. The majority of people come to share our peace and tranquillity, and, in some ways, they never leave."

*

When Glistrup met Kelly a few days later, he demonstrated his talents as a faith counsellor. Dressed in a safari suit and dog collar, they met at St Clement's and sat on neighbouring pews in the nave of the church. When he had first arrived Kelly had wondered if he was in the right place. The main door was shut, the car park empty, save for an old cream-coloured Beetle, but when he found the door opening easily at his touch he looked in, half wondering in the silence if he was interrupting some other consultation. Glistrup stood and beckoned him in.

"Mr Kelly, I presume? Welcome to my office! I am blessed to be able to use a corner of God's house when I am on his business," he said, employing his broad Viking grin.

Kelly walked in slightly apprehensively in these unfamiliar surroundings.

Both knew this to be a business meeting so there was none of the historical tourist preamble.

"Reverend Glistrup?"

"Maurice, please. It's good to meet at last – I have read the briefing notes from Nils and Marisa and so I feel I already know a little bit about you and your diagnosis. I'm not here today to discuss your motivation. I cannot understand your situation in detail, but I respect your wishes. I am here to overlay a spiritual dimension to your plans. As a result, I will either have inspired you to continue your journey with us towards your conclusion or signposted you to an alternative way of coming to terms with your situation. I, too, will be writing a report on our dialogue which will remain confidential, seen only by those in our Terminal network, but as you understand, this is part of our own insurance, assuming you decide to leave this world with our assistance.

"A good way to think of the situation you are facing is, like Nils suggested, to compare it to a court case, but with a twist. In most situations that would involve you coming into a courtroom, you would be mounting a defence against a prosecution counsel. Your effort would be based on proving your innocence. Here the role is reversed. You are the lead witness for the prosecution making a case before the judge, our Lord. Now the difficulty with this is, the Lord God is by his nature a forgiving God, who would much prefer to turn you away from sin through forgiveness instead of meting out punishment. So for him to find you guilty could be regarded as a failure on his part. He is also an all-knowing God, who will have followed your progress from childhood. There is nothing you can say about your life that he won't already know, so there is a real challenge to be objective in presenting your case. With me so far?"

Kelly nodded. "What then is the point of the Ten Commandments?"

"Well, that's a big discussion. I think of these as a set of guiding principles, not hard rules. I doubt whether anyone managed to live a life without falling foul of one or more of them at some time. Even the disciples were far from perfect. In fact it was their struggles which made them the role models they became. This is more a point about persistent offenders as opposed to more isolated transgressors. So is your proposed action to punish yourself or punish others?"

"Probably both."

"Why you?"

"Because as a scientist, I am not supposed to believe in God or heaven."

"But you do?"

"I believe in something, but I can't explain it. Heaven for me would be peace of mind. As a scientist I am here to help mankind and yet my work and discoveries are being highjacked by nations for nefarious purposes. It should be a source of professional pride but instead feels like a curse, which is making me regret making the discovery I have made in the first place. Faith had helped me to redress the balance, but not anymore."

"This is something to do with producing limitless energy and cleaning up old nuclear sites, right?"

"Yes, and I am being pursued, blackmailed, into using my knowledge either for the benefit of my own country's sectional interests because, as a citizen, they own me, or the United States, because they want to buy me, Russia, because they think they can heal my condition, or Saudi Arabia, because they are holding my daughter hostage to gain my compliance.

"This situation would not have developed without my discoveries and the only solution is for me to take my knowledge with me to another place or a new dimension or whatever it proves to be."

"If you go through with this, what do you think your legacy will be? What do you want to be remembered for?"

"My work is still at an experimental stage. If ultimately it proves not to have a commercial application, I doubt anyone will remember me outside my family. But if my hopes were realised, I will be known as someone who made a difference and contributed in a small way to the greater good of mankind and the planet. If my plan succeeds I won't be worrying about it and I am sure my colleagues will pick over the bones of what is left of my reputation."

"You admitted your proposed action would also punish others – who and why?"

"My boss, who is relentless in pursuit of profit and personal advancement at my expense. My wife, who likes the lifestyle my work has allowed her to enjoy while she conducts affairs with men, including my boss, that she thinks I know nothing about."

"Are there others you care for who you think would be adversely affected?"

"Yes. I have one or two friends, and my children, but I can only hope that when I have gone and they discover my story, they will understand."

"And if they don't?"

"People today lead complicated lives. When they die, those who mourn give eulogies, which are often difficult to compose. The reason is simple. Regardless of the relationships we have, nobody can completely know the life of another person. We all have inner torments, secrets we don't get to share."

"Very true. I can help you with that. I often find people contemplating the end of days don't want to leave with a heavy heart. For Terminal's customers, we offer a special service – a secrets vault. We give you a special book which you can use to record your innermost thoughts and secrets. We keep this in a locked vault under the altar here. There it stays for twenty years after your death. Then it is passed, still sealed, to your next of kin. This is not the same as a will. This has no legal status, it is just a means of passing on your thoughts to your family, for them to treasure as part of your life story. My experience from other clients suggests it really helps. I will give you a special book, which itself comes in a lockable box, for you to take away today. I know you are near the end of your counselling period with us and at your final visit, when you settle your legal documentation with Henning Triore, you can hand it to me personally for safe-keeping. And do remember, as a result of completing this task, you may decide you don't want to continue this process and find another way to manage your situation. That is OK. The alternative could be just as big a benefit as taking your situation to its conclusion. At Terminal we never forget it is our client who is in charge. You should also reflect that our approach, in itself, doesn't guarantee death. In some ways that is the point. Our service takes you before God for judgement. You will walk 'the walk of high risk' through the Wadden Sea. You may succumb to the sands, but there is a possibility you may not. That is not a failure of our system or yourself. That is the judgement of God, who may decide that, despite your burden of guilt and unhappiness, you must find an alternative way. You should also know that this is a one-off process. If you continue and survive it, you cannot take it again. The decision in every sense is final. That is God's will."

"What happens if I get across unscathed?"

"We can only support you to the sea border. If by chance you make it to Germany, that is the end of your relationship with Terminal. You will find the clause in your contract confirming this. We will have your passport and all of your documents by then, so in a legal sense, you will be dead anyway and in due course these will be returned to your next of kin. I wouldn't worry about that possibility too much. I cannot recall any of our customers surviving in the way you suggest and even if one or two have done, we certainly have not been made aware of it."

*

One of his private lines buzzed into life.

"Mr Carter-Jones? Willoughby here. There has been a development in the Kelly case, seems like the missing girl has turned up in a government compound in Saudi Arabia. Bit of a long story but the source is Dr Kelly himself. One of Kelly's international peers met her by chance in Riyadh last week and was told she was helping out in a local school while the authorities sorted out some visa wrangle. Apparently she told him she was being kept a prisoner but seemed well and unharmed. Anyway it will help me move the Suker file on a bit. Now things have got to this level I suppose her repatriation becomes a matter for government."

"How did she get there?"

"I think we can be sure she was abducted to order. It seems the Saudis have some big 'hush-hush' project that they wanted Kelly's co-operation with. Taking the girl was their way of securing his involvement."

"Why not just pay him?"

"Well, he has a reputation of being a bit of an idealist. He has a track record of turning down lucrative deals in the past."

"How did Kelly react?"

"Hard to say. I guess it is a mixture of relief and regret. I told him not to say anything about it until you guys had worked out what to do."

"We'll notify the relevant people in the FCO and make some

enquiries. Thanks for letting me know. I'll be in touch shortly."

*

As far as Bannan was concerned, Willoughby's news seemed to make sense of the whole mystery. Not just the Saudis but from what Sir Gavin had told him, the Americans were going to join a bidding war for Kelly's services. There was now enough circumstantial evidence that the Russians were coming to the table too, perhaps with a double agenda – to secure Kelly's services and eliminate Ponomariev. But this was an auction whose outcome did not depend on money; so what had the Russians got that would possibly tempt Kelly? Perhaps Rustanova had made their bid over dinner in Shepherd Market?

Coincidentally, a short time later Chuck Barnes from the Nuclear Regulatory Commission, based at the US embassy (and also the CIA station chief in London), called on the same number.

"Gerry, I thought you'd want early warning. Washington is gonna back Max Power's bid for the Lauriston for big bucks… really big bucks. Upwards of half a billion. It will put some pressure on the stock but the president's team are talking about underwriting it with emergency federal funds. They've got support on Capitol Hill. This is a financial nuclear bomb. You need to tell Downing Street they need to get out of the road with this. We don't need any regulatory crap. The future of the US oil industry and consequently about fifty thousand UK supply chain jobs are on the line."

Bannan reflected that the passionate outburst of the Texan was completely at odds with his recent lacklustre debate with Rustanova at Chatham House.

"Thanks for letting me know, Chuck. You know we Brits like the money but it makes us a little nervous. I can't see how we will keep the Westminster cabal out of this."

"I'm not interested in your sensibilities – just your actions. I don't want anyone in London to misunderstand our purpose. This thing has to be stopped, or controlled, now."

It was starting to turn into a busy afternoon for Bannan. Next in line for his attention were Chemmy Moore and Ifor Williams – it was rare these days to see them in the office at the same time.

"So Chemmy, Terminal looks clean?" She nodded.

"And Ifor, Liebelt is leaking to the Russians?" He nodded.

"And it seems Kelly is out of his depth at the centre of some international intrigue?"

Chemmy fidgeted.

"OK, not a good analogy with this Wadden Sea thing, granted. But you know what I mean? He doesn't appear to be confiding in anyone. How will this play out?"

Williams responded, "Kelly is always criticised in the Lauriston for his lack of documentation. Part of my job is spending time chasing him for reports. A lot of people think he's absent-minded, but observing him, I don't think he is. I've heard him say on several occasions that the secret of HCCVD is not the testing regime but the interpretation of the data. There is a clear lack of objective analysis in his reports, but not enough people have latched onto that yet. In short, he knows much more than anyone and he's not sharing. It is also clear he is an idealist, doesn't seem to get, or participate in, Roberts's discussions about finance. He's not interested, so he's not a target for bribery or corruption."

"Sex?"

"Again, I don't think it features. He's always polite in company but never *forward* with female colleagues, from what I hear."

"Is he patriotic?"

"I think so. He seems to have a strange loyalty to the Lauriston, but there's no love lost between him and Laidlaw. He is also sure that Roberts is just passing through. But he seems to have connected with Ponomariev – that relationship seems to be going from strength to strength."

"What about his health?"

"No one complains about the hours he puts in, but he has been looking increasingly drawn and tired. I did see him popping a couple of tablets in his coffee last week, but couldn't get close enough to find out more."

"Ifor, find out what tablets he's taking and who prescribed them, as there's nothing showing on his GP medical records. I'll ask Willoughby to get his woman who's staying with the family to look around for clues. Whatever it is, this could be influencing his state of mind. Do we put him on the watch list?"

"I'd say no. He's savvy and might pick up on it; that could cause him to react. He is a creature of routine. I'm pretty sure that, even without specific knowledge, I could locate him if I needed to."

"Even if he went back to Denmark?"

Chemmy spoke up.

"He has a reservation at the local inn in three weeks, so I think that means he'll be hooking up with Triore."

"Presumably that will be decision time, when he decides to take a gamble with Terminal."

"Do you want me back in Rømø to watch?"

"This Glistrup knows you, so you'll need to stay out of his way. You will have to be careful about Triore as well. Happy you're there if you can manage it. We'll reconvene next week when I've had the chance to think things through. I think we need to run another check on his bank records."

FIFTEEN

TIME WAS MOVING SLOWLY for Kelly. He was back at his desk in Oxford, having completed the next stage of his Terminal preparation in Denmark, and the weekly HCCVD team meeting was due. It felt as if he'd never been away. In the glass-walled second-floor meeting room, Sir Gavin sat at the head of the table, Jake Roberts, Werner Liebelt and Ifor Williams to his right, Des and 'Guntis' to his left.

Laidlaw revelled in the formality of the occasion, calling the meeting to order and asking Jake to go through the minutes of their last gathering and the dull formulaic agenda.

"Any other business?" Laidlaw looked at Kelly.

"Not as far as we're concerned, Gavin. You will know Guntis was called to London for government meetings, and I was out of the country for four days."

"But our outputs have not been delayed as a result?" he queried, staring over the top of his glasses.

"Not at all. We are on programme and preparing to take a prototype propulsion connector to Aldermaston to test operational velocity in hypersonic conditions. That is likely to dominate our work over the next three months anyway. It's also good that the military designers get to see how the HCCVD technology can work for them in missiles. Even better that Guntis will conduct the assessment of the experiment. If we can reach their threshold targets that will make their manufacturing partners place orders."

Laidlaw watched Kelly intently. Had the penny dropped? Was this the recognition he had been seeking that Kelly understood the commercial imperative?

"Excellent, Des. Just the news I think we needed. I can tell you that I have had word that Maximum Power Corporation intends to make an open offer for the Lauriston in coming weeks. When they do it will be at the top of my agenda. The offer will need shareholder approval and UK government clearance, but I hear it could be north of half a billion pounds. At that price I'm not sure anyone is going to stand in the way."

"Does that mean the Lauriston's operations will move to the United States?" asked Guntis.

Jake Roberts intervened.

"Possibly in part, but not completely. I think Max Power's ambitions relate to setting up a new defence company, probably under the Lauriston brand, and basing it closer to the US military, perhaps at Fort Bragg. It would be a great shop window for us."

"Surely it will be difficult to get UK government backing for that?" Des countered.

Laidlaw raised his eyebrows.

"It's early days, I think if the strike price is right, the deal will be done. Some people will be upset but let's be clear. Everyone will have forgotten about it in six months' time. Anything else?"

"Yes, one other thing from me," said Des.

"As some of you know, I have been going on a retreat in Denmark for several months now to further develop my own critical reasoning skills. I have found it very beneficial, so much so that I think this team would gain from some of the instruction I have had. I would like to suggest next month we all go to this place in Southern Denmark for a workshop day or conference. We can use the time to develop our policies, strategies and ways of working which will undoubtedly make us match fit if we get taken over, but anyway in the long run accelerate the pace of the project."

Had anyone other than Des suggested such an initiative, no one would have been surprised, but coming from the man at the centre of the project the assembled group were stunned into momentary silence.

Laidlaw made the response.

"Well Des, perhaps you can set out a short paper for me on this and we'll talk about it." He offered a faint non-committal smile.

As the meeting broke up, Liebelt muttered under his breath to Williams.

"He seems in an unusually good mood."

"Yes," the Welshman agreed, "I think he looks like a man who's had some good news."

*

Williams watched Kelly heading for the Gents as the others headed back to their workstations. He paused by a vending machine then followed him into the toilets. Kelly was drying his hands, having left a notepad, glasses, plastic water cup and a packet of tablets in a pile next to one of the basins. Momentarily he had his back to the door as Williams entered and stayed there just long enough for his colleague to observe the scene before turning to collect his things. He knew Williams had noticed the pack of tablets, which he immediately consigned to his trouser pocket.

"That's what gets me through the boss's team meetings – happy pills!"

Williams smiled and passed him heading to the urinals as Kelly left the room.

As he used the facilities, Williams used his photographic memory to recall the fleeting sight of the tablets and the brand name. What was it? Nilandracin… Nilandrone? Something like that. He fixed the thought in his head and resolved to check it out when he got back to his desk.

*

Willoughby was starting to feel a lot more positive about the Kelly case now that he had established the fate of Abigail. The sighting in Riyadh had been instrumental in the British embassy securing an acknowledgement from the Saudis that she was safe and well. There is no doubt the eminence of the witness, together with the fact that he was a national of a third-party country had helped secure the admission. On that score he had been grateful for the assistance of Carter-Jones who seemed to have galvanised the machinery of government efficiently on this occasion. Willoughby couldn't imagine how the matter would be resolved by the two governments, other than by the fact that her repatriation would just be a matter of time, and neither party would have the appetite for publicity on such a sensitive subject. Also, although Suker had not been directly responsible for the kidnapping, it wouldn't take long to identify his henchmen, and they, too, would be arrested and charged, assuming Suker had not already made them go to ground. There were just some niggles which had to be ironed out. There was still no plausible reason (as far as he could tell) for why Smyth had got involved in the first place, and he had been frustrated by the activity drawn from Smyth's mobile. Most calls were easily accounted for – friends, the brewery, staff, accountants and the like, and exchanges with Miles, but there were half a dozen calls with Sue Kelly in the period leading up to the encounter with Suker which puzzled him. What could they have talked about that in the normal course of events would have been shared through Miles? In a quieter moment, he had already had some ideas, but he had a duty to find out the facts. Besides, he wanted a word with WPC Wendy about Kelly's medication. It was funny but it always seemed the best time to get out to Oxfordshire was in the afternoons, if possible, ahead of the evening rush.

It usually meant arriving at the Kelly residence about six-thirty – along with the first wave of London commuter traffic. In some ways it would be convenient, as the Kellys never sat down to eat before eight, and Dr Kelly would not be home more than half an hour ahead of time. The setting of the kitchen while Mrs Kelly cooked and consumed a couple of glasses of Chardonnay would create the right atmosphere for a one-to-one chat. He was sure this night they would have plenty to talk about.

He had had the nod from Carter-Jones to tell Kelly about Abigail, but had imposed his own embargo, understanding that the news would create a frenzy with the media. The media circus would of course happen at some point, but better it occurred when Abigail was back in the UK and had the benefit of coaching from the FCO. For now, the objective was to provide the family with some comfort – the first stage of getting back to some sort of normality.

He was welcomed with a cup of tea, but first indicated his wish to talk to Sue on his own with WPC Wendy ensuring they weren't disturbed.

"As you know, Mrs Kelly, as part of our investigations we recovered Mr Smyth's mobile and had it analysed. It shows it sent and received seven calls between you and Mr Smyth in the period leading up to his murder. Can you tell me what these calls were about?"

"Bryan… Mr Smyth, was a family friend and from time to time I have needed to talk to someone openly about my feelings."

"Yes of course, but the timing of these calls is interesting. They seem to fit quite neatly around the incident at the Topkapi Nights restaurant and also the morning of his death. Can you tell me what you spoke about, exactly?"

"I'm not sure I can remember in detail."

"But you did know he was going to meet Mr Suker?"

"No, he told me he thought he had discovered some information relating to Abigail and that he would call me later – which of course he never did."

"You see, Mrs Kelly, in all of this strange story, the one piece of the puzzle I have trouble making sense of is Mr Smyth's involvement in your private family situation. If your husband had taken these actions, I could understand it."

"Well, he wasn't around."

"But nonetheless, WPC Graham tells me she was also unaware of the dialogue, which, bearing in mind you have been based at home throughout this period, suggests you may have gone to some trouble to hide your exchanges. She also logged you making two visits to the Dog & Duck outside normal licencing hours, and not as part of your own dog walking routine. On one level, I understand you had contact primarily through your son but on another, I don't understand your motivation."

"I wanted to impress on Mr Smyth the need not to put my son in danger and…"

"Yes?"

"Not to put himself in any danger on our behalf."

"Did you think that he would?"

"He told me about the unfortunate timing of his arrival at Topkapi Nights when all the damage was done."

"Did he tell you when you were in bed with him?"

"Pardon?"

"I put it to you, Mrs Kelly, that you seduced Mr Smyth to undertake this risky activity because you were frustrated with the speed of our enquiries and the seeming inaction of your husband. I am also aware there have been prior difficulties in your marriage, so here we had a perfect storm which created a series of unforeseen outcomes. Finally, I urge you to be honest with me, as I don't think you would want me to draw my own conclusions. After all, it could be argued that you were in some ways responsible for one crime, and possibly implicated in another."

"All right, I did have a brief relationship with Mr Smyth. But it wasn't premeditated; for me it was a way of relieving the stress of the situation. I cannot believe Mr Smyth took the actions he did in order to impress me."

"Well, it seems we will never know now, but the key thing is that you are sure you never encouraged him to threaten Mr Suker?"

"Very sure. I only became aware of his actions after he had taken them."

"Did you sleep with him after the attack on the Topkapi Nights?"

"Yes, I did."

"So, it was possible he saw this as a reward for services rendered?"

"I don't know; that wasn't what it was about for me. The sex was nothing more than a release from the strain of the situation – it wasn't planned."

"I will try not to make this more difficult than it needs to be. WPC Graham will take a statement for now..."

There was the sound of the front door opening. Milo barked his cautious welcome. Des Kelly came into the kitchen, accompanied by Miles.

"Just found our boy fiddling around with his bike outside the paddock. Looks like he needs feeding. What's for dinner? Oh, this looks a bit official. I hope everything is all right," he said.

"Yes, Dr Kelly. I thought you would be home about now. I've only just arrived. I have some good news. The Foreign Office have followed up on the tip-off we received and have located your daughter, Abigail, apparently fit and well in Riyadh, Saudi Arabia."

Willoughby didn't want to make things harder for family relationships, by explaining more about the tip-off. He wasn't sure whether the name of Aldo de Leonibus would mean anything to anyone other than Dr Kelly himself.

"It appears she was kidnapped to order as a means of

blackmailing you, Dr Kelly. It seems they wanted to hire you for a government project and thought the fact they were holding her might prove to be some sort of incentive for you. Personally, I find that surprising, but it seems this is often the way they choose to do business. The Turk who we have under arrest has admitted arranging her travel to the Middle East, but we still have some way to go to bring the final story to a conclusion. So as of today, we can wind down our enquiries here. WPC Graham can tie up the last pieces of documentation, then return to the day job and her own family. I'll keep in touch as the paperwork is completed."

"When will Abi get home?"

"I don't know yet. The details of the arrangement are presently being sorted out on a government to government basis. The Foreign Office will contact you directly – most likely tomorrow. I think they are arranging to have her transferred to the embassy and then there will be a chance to talk to her on a Zoom call. What I am instructed to say for now is that this good news must remain with family members only. The UK has some sensitive trade relationships with Saudi and so any embarrassment must be avoided. Negative publicity at the wrong time could delay the resolution of the matter. I'm sure you will understand. That rule won't just apply to you, but also to me. I have to arrange the paperwork on Suker in a particular way that avoids reference to Saudi, so we have a common purpose.

I will, of course, ensure you are kept informed."

The finality of the handshake with Willoughby was well received by his wife and son, but Des knew this was only the closure of a chapter in a longer story.

*

Bannan's methodical approach to the Kelly affair was bearing fruit. Bit by bit, the story was becoming clearer, although he did have to give his subject credit for covering his tracks. Willoughby had reported that the woman PC at his house had been unsuccessful in uncovering any stash of medication, but Williams's report of identifying a drug called Nilandrone had been useful. Upon investigation, it proved that it was licensed in the United States for the relief of symptoms of advanced prostate cancer and at the present time the only European licence for it was held in Switzerland. That had been enough to tell him there was no point in continuing to interrogate his UK health records. Whoever had prescribed his medication was not going to be accredited within the National Health Service. He would need to look elsewhere. The answer came from a single transaction, not from his current account but from a standard building society savings account, some five months previously. A payment for £46,837 to a company called Zenith Pharma Resources. Further investigation showed Zenith operated a private health retreat in Lausanne. An approach for information dispatched to the appropriate authorities had been rejected by Zenith under local confidentiality laws but had produced a copy invoice from their tax agency. Frustratingly the descriptor only referred to 'services rendered' and the initials 'GHW'. It was clear that he wasn't going to get the information he needed without resorting to a black op, which frankly, he didn't have time for. Williams had reported Kelly's latest plan to take the Lauriston's HCCVD leadership team over to Denmark for a residential business planning seminar. The news had only come in since the discovery of his daughter's whereabouts had been established. He had been even more surprised that Gavin Laidlaw had not only approved but agreed to take part. That, in itself, was unusual, as Bannan expected Des's regular foreign trips to provide Laidlaw with the excuse to visit Sue Kelly, just to check on her 'personal wellbeing'. What would he expect to learn anyway, other than the fact that Kelly was hiding terminal illness and, given what he already knew, for good reason?

All that was needed for that was evidence of the drugs themselves, a photographic task Williams could easily supply.

Why was Kelly pushing the Danish thing? As far as could be established there was no connection between Westergaard's Terminal business and this Zenith outfit. Was he planning some major announcement?

The shopping list for Williams to pull together was getting longer by the minute.

*

It took four days for Abigail's release to be confirmed. That was the time it took to agree the story about how she had arrived in the country to research a film about a plane crash in the desert and how her visa hadn't allowed her to travel outside the capital. She agreed to an account which stated that her abduction was part of a test stunt, and she hadn't realised the need to inform the police in advance before she went. The Met confirmed they had received an apology from her and the matter was now closed. Willoughby would be required to check that the evidence collected in the Smyth murder was consistent, citing that the dead man had underlying links with a criminal gang of football supporters who had attacked the Topkapi Nights and Suker's revenge had been out of proportion. Apart from being flown home on a government jet, she had received a bursary of £10 million towards the development of a screenplay for the plane crash movie script, or perhaps something different entirely, provided it promoted the Kingdom in a positive way. She would be welcome to visit Riyadh again in future. The UK government had approved a £5 billion order for new fighter aircraft and the Royal Navy would be deployed to escort Saudi oil ships passing through the Strait of Hormuz.

Her return was cause for celebration in the Kelly family, although tinged with obvious sadness, and the family held a party with her London friends and acting fraternity.

Des had been surprised at how liberated he felt at the turn of events. It is said truth is often stranger than fiction and that was the case in this instance, but despite his disparate family bonds, he felt free and able to focus on his own life journey once more. He had taken the unusual step of penning a personal letter of thanks to his friend, Aldo, for his help.

Having spent a few days recuperating with her parents, Abigail was ready to return to her life in London, which he was pleased about. Hope that Miles would now follow her lead was unfounded. He seemed to be looking for a reason to stay, aided by his mother's mollycoddling and 'dinner on demand' services.

Yet, this trajectory back to normality didn't feel quite right. There seemed to be an unspoken barrier between Des and Sue, which neither seemed to fully understand. It was almost as though they knew they were on parallel tracks but likely to veer off in different directions at any time. Privately Des wondered how things between them had got so bad. It was not because they didn't love each other, he thought, but they each seemed to have lost the ability to express it. Perhaps, had he been ten years younger, he might have had the motivation to try to resolve the situation, but it was now too late, and time was thieving his life chances. Being a creature of habit, his daily routine continued much as it had done in recent years. In the office Mondays, Thursdays and Fridays. In the lab at Harwell Tuesdays and Wednesdays. The difference being that given the pressures of the project, Wednesday was starting to become a recurring commitment to working at Aldermaston with his new Russian colleague.

Evenings fitted a pattern too. Eight o'clock dinner and washing up. Internet surfing and classical music to follow, plus a short walk with Milo and a nightcap before bed and another lonely night contemplating a very different future. No diversion at the Dog & Duck yet as a new landlord was awaited.

Was this all that was left in his life? What could he look forward to? Would adrenaline ever again rush through his veins?

*

Work on coupling a micro rod and conductor unit into a basic missile propulsion system had proceeded well and Ponomariev was already being credited for his contribution.

Kelly's plans suggested that if all the tests scheduled under laboratory conditions continued in line with performance targets, a prototype could be ready for live testing in around eighteen months. He had been less worried about the reliability of the technology, but more concerned about the bulk and weight of the prototype, which was close to aerodynamic tolerances. No such problem existed for the test rigs for vehicles and although adapting missile technology was the priority, Kelly was keeping back the real prospect of converting the existing commercial vehicle diamond battery unit to a tank in the next financial year. That at least would keep Sir Gavin happy and out of his hair. Laidlaw's interest seemed entirely focused on burnishing his personal reputation with No.10 and the government machine, emphasising the potential contribution the Lauriston stood to make to the UK defence industry, national security, and the economy as a whole. Although he couldn't be sure, he sensed that he would be keeping Eve Grainger closely informed of developments even though his Official Secrets Act registration should have prevented it. It was a classic example of why he felt he would be wise to keep his own counsel, whenever circumstances would allow.

As they started to work together, Kelly was becoming ever more confident of Ponomariev's contribution. They had started to create an effective bond, like father and son, like a sorcerer and his apprentice. Despite the occasional language hiccup, Kelly was beginning to anticipate Ponomariev's approach on key issues. He had been genuinely impressed by his all-round technical abilities and critical reasoning. His Russian colleague was still having to live a strange existence, being chauffeured to and from work locations by a close protection officer, unable to have any social life connected with the Lauriston after the end of the working day, unable to engage in casual conversations about how he spent his leisure time or where he was living.

In his quieter moments in the car, driving to and from the office, Des wished he could find the right words, the right occasion, to tell him of their personal connection, but knew it was out of the question. His overriding worry was that if he helped to get him back to Russia, as Galina hoped, how could she protect her son? Her assurances that all would be well seemed hollow. Russia was not a free society and although she had influence, there could be no guarantee Ponomariev would not be exposed as a traitor on his return, whatever the circumstances. Des wished she was there to reassure him.

The prospect of taking the HCCVD team to Denmark was a much more positive thought in his mind. He would contact Westergaard directly, so that he could set the date and make the necessary arrangements. He was strangely buoyed by the idea of staging the Lauriston event before he undertook his sea walk to oblivion. To his mind, it would offer a fitting conclusion to his professional career. He would also be due for his final phased meeting with Terminal, this time with the lawyer Henning Triore, at which he would hand over all his legal personal identity documentation.

The date for both activities was set some eight weeks ahead. Although in some ways it seemed a long time, in practice it wouldn't be. Professionally, he drafted out a work programme for the HCCVD team, interspersed with a few team-building activities ranging from sports such as archery, kayaking and orienteering to practical problem solving, from building a birdwatching hide on marshland from scavenged natural materials to preparing 'survival' food foraged from the local countryside. Each member of the team would act as a lead on a designated professional and recreational topic and have four weeks to submit their proposals to him for agreement.

Westergaard would provide all the logistical assistance

required and would manage the itinerary. His personal business would be kept entirely separate. He would arrive in Rømø ahead of his colleagues to finalise arrangements for the handover of his documentation and the sea walk.

When he came to present his plans to the leadership team, Des was pleasantly surprised by how positively his proposal had been received.

His two biggest critics, Laidlaw and Roberts, seemed to have suddenly become enthused about the idea. Des couldn't help thinking that the new corporate collaborative atmosphere had been driven by their recognition of his tacit co-operation with their military research stakeholders, who they both imagined would hold the key to the long-term funding challenges of the Lauriston as an independent institution. Kelly still retained his reservations about this approach to the future and its inevitable consequence, the plundering of the Lauriston's intellectual property by the Maximum Power Corporation. Since his meeting with the pastor, Glistrup, however, he had come to realise that this threat was not as unmanageable or uncontrollable as he first thought.

With the plans agreed, Laidlaw would decide which members of the Lauriston staff would be eligible to attend and he would pass the details to Westergaard.

On a personal level, the most complicated part of his preparation was the secrets book. Writing down his innermost thoughts to be preserved for a period after his passing was a challenge. Being a scientist, this was not just an issue of what information he wished to record and preserve, but also something to do with its prioritisation. He was aware of the criticism often made of him that, despite his professional brilliance, he seemed to have a natural aversion to documenting and analysing in anything like the detail that would constitute commercially valuable information. Now he had to reverse engineer his thoughts to get the detailed interpretation of his experiments down in the book, so that future generations might benefit from his vision and strategy.

That wasn't something to be handed on a plate to any sectional interest, not least Maximum Power Corporation.

News of the Lauriston residential programme was warmly received not only internally, itself a new departure for the institution and bigger than Kelly had originally envisaged, but became a talking point as colleagues waited to see who would be invited to go. Interested third parties in 'Six' and the FSB took note.

Both saw the occasion as playing to their own individual agendas.

When Williams informed Bannan of the plan he immediately interpreted it as some highlight in Kelly's activity – a sign that something was coming to a head – and somehow he and his team would need to be involved.

In Moscow, Nikitin was reading the situation in a similar way, having received his advice from agent Lutz. What better opportunity would he get to snatch Kelly and Ponomariev in a low-security environment close to Russia's sphere of influence?

*

Back at home, Miles was also in the business of grasping a new opportunity. It had been a week since Bryan Smyth's funeral, and there was a sense in the locality that it was time to move on. The Dog & Duck had been closed until further notice, creating a physical and social void in the heart of the community that even Mrs Harris at the general store could not fill.

Des had come home to dinner to find his son in celebratory mood.

"I would just like to announce a change of career," he said.

"The brewery has just appointed me manager of the Dog & Duck with immediate effect. I'm going to collect a set of keys in the morning with a mission to get it open as soon as possible. How about that?"

"But what about your civil service job in London?"

"I was fed up with that before I came back to help you and Mum. This job pays a good wage and comes complete with accommodation and managerial responsibility for half a dozen helpers. Besides, in a strange way I also think I owe Bryan to get the Dog going again. I'm sure it is what he would have wanted. It's much better that someone like me clears up his stuff rather than some man with a van who will just take what's left of his personal effects down to the local rubbish dump. There's a good crowd down there and I know I will soon settle in."

"Don't you think it's a wonderful idea, Des?" Sue was brimming with excitement. "Having our son working in the village will be great – we can see him every day. I said I will help him to tidy up Bryan's things in the flat. I know his brother said at the funeral that the family had taken out many of his more personal possessions so I think it will be OK for us to be there. You never know, I might even start a new business cooking lunches. I could come up with a simple menu from sandwiches to bangers and mash – maybe a couple of vegan alternatives!"

Des had not reacted in the way Sue had expected. Her comments were crafted to provoke a negative reaction, which she knew would motivate Miles more. She had anticipated him saying it was a mad idea, that he should follow his sister's lead and get back to London, his own career, flat and friends, at a convenient distance from the family home.

Instead, he smiled and offered his own muted, slightly distracted congratulations.

In the light of what was to come, Miles's initiative should be commended, he thought. It would be a fresh and positive interest for Sue and further relieve him of the burden of personal obligations.

He had a couple of items to put in the post that night, some emails to send, and would then take Milo for a walk.

This particular journey seemed special, his senses heightened to absorb the sights and sounds of the village and neighbouring properties settling down for the night. Lights on, curtains drawn and the reflected light of TV screens communicating a timeless sense of reassurance. Outside the raucous caw of rooks – the scavenging birds were heading for their nests. Their smaller brethren, including the myriad of smaller garden finches and tits, massing and squabbling in a couple of nearby shrubs, desperate to secure the most comfortable shelters for the coming twilight hours. Across the village green, the Dog & Duck – its usual welcoming illuminated façade dark in the growing shadow of the evening. The scene spoke of convention and conformity, it was safe, unchallenging and, to him, uninspiring.

It was the place of his past, not of his future.

Despite the circumstances of Bryan's friendships with other members of the family, Des would remember Bryan as a friend, the archetypal confessor, a man who you could say anything to and would be sure it would go no further – always assuming that you had his personal attention, when business was quiet in the snug bar. What on earth had Miles said to get him mixed up with this man, Suker? It had proved to be such an unnecessary business, which he now felt a strong sense of personal responsibility for. All that trouble for Abi – if only he had known that it was all down to him.

It was now time to consign these thoughts to the back of his mind. The family had a new future; his departure would underwrite their personal financial security for the rest of their days. The time to determine his own prospects was drawing near. He would face it alone, understanding that the choices were likely to be extreme – heaven or hell, but not anything in the middle.

*

Nikitin put in a call to Rustanova the day after hearing from agent Lutz.

"Galina, my dear, you will be pleased to know that I have

completed my preliminary enquiries regarding your request to recover and repatriate persons of interest to the motherland. I have identified an opportunity to conduct this activity at minimal risk and received authorisation from the State Security Committee and the President's Office to proceed. Given the circumstances as you explained them, I will be seeking your assurance that you can solicit the co-operation of the targets with our plans before the action is undertaken. I expect to be able to propose a date and location for the collection to be made within the next forty-eight hours. I should also make clear that the State Committee were particularly interested in the circumstances that resulted in the formulation of the proposal, and I have little doubt that their approval was in no small measure down to their respect for you. I am sure you will not need me to point out that this carries potential reputational risk for you personally. Assuming the mission is a success, you will be seen as a national icon, alongside the likes of Anna Kushchenko; if it fails… well, who knows? Maybe your career and prospects might not be so bright."

"Thank you, Dimitri. I trust your explanation of my personal situation was managed appropriately?"

"For now, yes. Your role as a tutor of Ponomariev is known and was an important consideration. Unfortunately, if we are not able to complete the mission as planned, I may not be able to prevent further details from being released."

Rustanova understood his coded language. If the mission went wrong, he would implicate her as a means of avoiding any personal blame. She would be his insurance policy.

After the call, Rustanova thought further about their exchange. If Des Kelly could be brought to Russia for medical treatment, that would be great. Why wouldn't he trade his technical knowledge, for the gift of perhaps, another twenty years of life? Finding him a suitable place to live to match his status wouldn't be a problem, and it was probable that he would be given a role at the Academy – something that would be in her gift.

But the position of her son Boris would not be as straightforward. He could carry the stigma of being a traitor, a factor that would weigh heavily against his successful repatriation. The worst-case scenario was that he would just be quietly, casually, killed – 'liquidated' in FSB-speak. The best: he would be ostracised from professional circles, omitted from engagements with his peers and subjugated to assignments of marginal value. The second scenario did at least offer the prospect of a manageable existence but was still fraught with uncertainty.

She considered how she would have approached the problem had she been in Nikitin's position. She would start a rumour that he had been sent to the UK on an espionage assignment and returned with valuable intelligence that would benefit Russian military procurement. There was no doubt, even in the circles which she mixed in, that most Russians loved and respected the concept of intrigue, and this would certainly be a story she could help to pitch and spin. This initiative was starting to achieve a political dimension with implications beyond her own ability to control.

She knew she needed to discuss how to proceed with Ruslan.

*

Nikitin had no such doubts. This was his type of game; whichever way the dice fell there would only be one winner. His next call was to Arbutsev in Kaliningrad.

"I have been reviewing the Ponomariev file and have noted a number of aspects in your investigation which are less than optimal. You seem to have made a good job of identifying a separate crime, smuggling, from the matter which you were charged with investigating in the first place. I am only interested in the informal trading activities of the locals if there is a link to the main subject of the case. So far, I haven't seen anything that associates local crime with the Ponomariev defection other than the possibility of the involvement of Zanowsky the Pole, and your presently unsupported claim that you had found his body has proved plainly untrue. Despite your personal wishes, you well know that FSB operatives do not have the option of resignation. As I could not accept your sloppy work, you were suspended and had your privileges withdrawn. Having said that, your failure on this case stands out as the exception rather than the rule and your track record suggests that you are unlikely to repeat your recent errors. I think it would be a shame for us to lose your knowledge at this time and so I want to propose a solution that will help you to re-establish your reputation and position."

Privately Arbutsev was irritated by the suggestion that he had made an error in reporting the body pulled out of the Pregolya and was convinced that he had followed an instruction from Nikitin to amend the DNA evidence. This was not the act of an incompetent, but Nikitin was his boss for the moment, and he had to accept his reading of the situation.

"I'm glad you see a way forward," he responded.

"We have traced Ponomariev and have identified a location and time where we know he will be present. I want you to arrange to pick him up. I am lifting your suspension as a result. It will be a clandestine snatch operation. I have reason to believe your targets will co-operate but if not, they will need to be subdued. The pick-up will be made from the west coast of Denmark in six weeks' time. I will confirm the details in the next forty-eight hours. Judging by the file, you seem to have had some issues with Poliarkin and Moscovoi. I think they must owe you some favours. We will offer a fresh start to all who take part, dropping ongoing criminal investigations as well as providing ample rewards for success. Take Poliarkin's fishing boat. I will sanction all the resources you need, but you must start to make plans now."

*

Bannan had decided that circumstantial evidence that Kelly was preparing some action at this Danish residential was now too great to ignore, but it was frustrating not to be able to anticipate what might happen. From all he had seen and heard he didn't get the sense that Kelly was naturally a traitor, planning some unexpected flit to Russia, but by the same token, neither could he dismiss it. Was Kelly hatching some elaborate plan to have an audience for a euthanasia attempt? Somehow, that idea didn't fit either. Whatever Kelly was, he was not a narcissist. Perhaps there really was no hidden agenda. It was difficult, given his trade, not to be a conspiracy theorist. It was perfectly possible that Kelly's trips to Rømø were just therapy and that he was recovering from some hidden form of mental breakdown, brought on by his cancer treatment. Bannan hadn't liked to see the formal part of the event's agenda supplied by Williams, which included presentations by Eve Grainger from Maximum Power and Professor Aldo de Leonibus from the European Nuclear Safety Regulators Group.

What next? Was Chuck Barnes going to put in an appearance? If that happened, he would understand that the US authorities had formally labelled Kelly as a security risk and would inevitably swamp the quiet rural community with their own assets. What he could be sure of was that whatever intel he was receiving, Liebelt was passing the same information elsewhere. All options were up for grabs. The solution was to maximise his available resources to monitor the situation with a capability to intervene where necessary. Chemmy Moore would have to intensify her surveillance of Kelly. Williams would be attending the residential anyway as part of the HCCVD team. He would request a Royal Navy SBS rapid action combat incident unit (RACI) to be on standby somewhere in the vicinity and for insurance, he would engage the services of two of his most reliable arms-length freelance contractors, the Zanowsky brothers of Gdansk, to assist as required. Given the sensitivities, he knew it might be useful for Winston Carter-Jones, his alter ego, to appear as a last-minute speaker. In this case, his flexible persona could represent the Competition Directorate of the UK government's Cabinet Office, to talk about policy considerations affecting the proposed acquisition of the Lauriston, but he didn't need to take a decision on that just now.

SIXTEEN

KELLY WAS FEELING THE pressure of working to a definitive timetable. He had just over a month to condense his expertise into the secrets book as well as collating all of his personal documentation. It was more challenging than he had expected, distilling the knowledge built up as a result of a career in research into the crammed pages of a little book. He worked with speed and precision, focusing on being ready to pass on his story to posterity. In the back of his mind was the question that, if the book were not seen for twenty years or more, would it still have commercial relevance, or would his musings be dismissed as some quaint, if misguided, ramblings of an aging boffin? On top of the day job, and his domestic duties, he was devoting up to three hours a night to the task, hampered in part by the challenge of writing all his work in longhand – surprisingly difficult after years of using computer keyboards. Anyone trying to follow up on his work would focus on computer drives, not on longhand notes of his analyses. His newfound purpose hadn't gone entirely unnoticed. After the first week, even Sue detected that he was unusually stressed.

"Gavin is working you too hard, darling. He has a team of bright people who must be capable of sharing the load. You must speak to him, or if you won't, perhaps I should?"

Des wasn't sure whether the remark was meant genuinely or asked deliberately to rile him.

"I am sure if Gavin could delegate to others he would, but unfortunately the stuff I need to write can only come from me. Don't worry, though, I am making good progress. I should have this finished in the next couple of weeks before I go back to Denmark."

"Well, I still think I should talk to him. Why don't I invite him over for dinner, next week?"

"I'm not sure that's such a good idea right now. I've got a lot on and so has Gavin. He needs to sort out all this political mess surrounding the potential sale of the Lauriston before we go to Denmark and the way things are, Gavin and I are spending enough time together during the day. Besides, I thought you were taking over the catering at the Dog & Duck?"

"Yes, that's true. I need to conduct my own experiments on you to plan out the menu! I'm not worried about mass producing individual servings of shepherd's pie, but I'm not too confident about my vegan alternatives. I will have to test them on you."

Despite their years of marriage there were still moments when Des would look at Sue and wonder if she was entirely serious. On this occasion there was no suggestion of humour in her demeanour.

Their limited exchanges highlighted another problem for Des that he was unsure how to resolve. What, if anything, should he say to the family about his departure? That was a real conundrum. Part of the reason Des had got to the point where he was, was because of the absence of family interaction. Before Abi's disappearance, Miles had not been around and he and Sue seemed to pass through the house at opposing hours. True, most of the time, Sue and Des slept under the same roof, but that was it. They were not a family in any conventional sense, doing things together, taking an interest in each other's work, sharing hobbies or interests. In recent stressful times, Abi had wanted the support of the family unit, but now the moment had passed, she was gone, back to her own personal support network of which he knew little. Miles was driven in a different way – by convenience. The family home and its occupants were there only to help to make his life easier. The concept of contributing something in return was not on his horizon unless it suited his purpose. No wonder his mother, of all people, had lectured him on the relationship side about being considerate of others' interests. Des thought it ironic that his son would soon swap a sterile office environment for running a pub, the ultimate service industry. No – the Kellys were not a strong family unit, merely two people, sometimes three, separately sharing the company of a dog, in a house far too big for their respective needs.

Miles and Abi were making their lives in their own ways. Des didn't feature, so they would not be hurt by his absence. Issues with Sue were more complicated.

He bitterly regretted the mess of his relationship with his wife. The fundamental problem was that he still loved her but she didn't love him anymore. Des was almost embarrassed to remember Marisa Kjaer's question about sex. He was struck by the direct and matter of fact way she had asked the question about his sex life and his embarrassment at not being able to answer. He had no idea if he had the ability to bed a woman at his stage of life and no desire to try and be seen to fail. Besides, he wasn't a robot; he wouldn't just have sex to satisfy an urge. It had to be part of a bigger relationship. There had been no bigger relationship than that with Sue and he had been wounded by the fact that she'd turned away, and doubly so that he knew his boss had intervened in his private life.

But all of that now was history. Things had gone too far for him or her to retrace their steps. The future (or what was left of it) was all that mattered now. He would write her a letter before he went to Denmark for the last time.

*

Arbutsev hadn't crossed the Pregolya from Baltiysk since his suspension, preferring to take the train into Kaliningrad with his wife, Tatiana, looking for a flat for their retirement. He had not been a natural country dweller, preferring the bustle, lights and sounds of the city. His location of choice was the so called 'Fishing Village', an exclusive district situated on the banks of the river between the Honeymoon Bridge and High Bridge. The locality had a cosmopolitan air by Kaliningrad standards, recreating a slice of the city's pre-war fishing quarter with a series of cafés, restaurants and hotels housed within old German-style architecture and a thirty-plus metre-high lighthouse. The picturesque setting made for a very pleasant afternoon stroll or a carefree coffee, and the lighthouse offered a great view out over the river and Kant Island. But the bohemian lifestyle came at a price, which was more than the value of his present utilitarian quarters next to the naval station on the coast. Perhaps just a few years ago the prospect of being able to move to such a neighbourhood would have been out of the question, but, given his boss's plans, Arbutsev saw a limited window that would make his personal ambition a reality. Technically his suspension could not be lifted until such time as the necessary certification from Moscow could be issued. He knew the process well and understood it would take three working days to take effect. Three days to remain an ordinary citizen, where if he or anyone else he sanctioned was suspected of committing a crime, their record would automatically be wiped clean on grounds of state security.

With the prospect of this imminent change of status looming and news of his temporary suspension not being widely known, his first action was to arrange a visit to the apartment of Igor Poliarkin. The timing would be good. He knew Poliarkin to be a late riser who would not yet have had the chance to set out for the fishing quay.

One of the more useful aspects of his training was perfecting the ability to knock on a door in a hard staccato 'tap' which saved him from having to shout his introduction and frighten the neighbours. At Poliarkin's door, it worked at the third attempt.

"Good morning, Igor. I thought you'd appreciate an update on my enquiries."

The fisherman opened his door wide and walked back into his flat, leaving Arbutsev to close the door.

"What now, Investigator? I have followed your instructions to the letter. There is nothing new to find, so please don't ransack my place again. I've just got it tidy."

"I think I may have some positive news for you."

"Oh yes?"

"I can see a way of bringing the state's interest in your... *casual* business activities to a close. I have been informed that your nation has an errand that it seems to think you might be well placed to assist with. Clearly you will be motivated by your patriotic duty, but nonetheless the government would show its gratitude by wiping your past criminal records and cancelling all present enquiries into your private activities. Think about it. It means you can hold on to your earnings, retain your fishing licences, maybe invest in a new boat or buy out a competitor – all with no questions asked."

"What is this errand?"

"We want you to pilot your boat the B474 on an extended fishing trip. Once you get to the destination you must wait a short time at my discretion before starting the return journey. We have a couple of VIPs we wish to repatriate without a lot of fuss."

"Why not just fly them back?"

"When did you last go on a plane? Too much paperwork – flight plans, passports and the like."

"What about a sub?"

"Out of the question. The sea at that point is too shallow, and a surface navy ship in that area would attract too much attention. Your way may be slower and less comfortable but is best for this type of operation. Think of that reward – having a clean slate is better than money. Lasts longer, too, provided you keep your nose clean. The alternative isn't great, Igor. One of the great qualities of the Russian criminal system is that we can take a relaxed approach to evidence. In your case, the burden of proof is set low, very low. When it comes to a prosecution I can fill in the blank spaces on the warrant however I like. The senior Oblast judge doesn't have an enquiring mind. Going to prison and losing your livelihood is not an attractive prospect."

"When do you want to go?"

"Not for a couple of weeks yet. Oh, and by the way, there is the matter of my commission for making the arrangements. We can sort that now before I go. I think two hundred and fifty thousand euros – fifty per cent of the cash behind your boiler – seems reasonable. I brought a bag with me to carry it in."

"Hold on – not all that money is mine."

"It's your choice. Those are my terms. If we manage this amicably, I might be able to assist you in other ways. For example, if you give me a list of those you think will be out of pocket as a result, I will have them arrested. I understand that would be socially difficult, but on balance it really does seem to offer the best deal to safeguard your future. For you, this is a genuine once in a lifetime opportunity. Do it right now, otherwise I will find assistance elsewhere and impound your cash anyway."

Arbutsev left the flat ten minutes later with the cash. He was feeling ill at ease. This was the most dishonest thing he'd done in his life, but he told himself it was OK, because he hadn't done it when he was a serving police officer and he would be rid of the cash in a couple of hours. Even if news of his action leaked, he and any others he took on the Danish mission would have their criminal records wiped. Besides, he had taken money from a thief so how could that be regarded as a crime? He drove directly to his lawyer's office, paying upfront for the property and legal fees. The transaction would be completed in the required time available before his investigator status would be renewed. Now he could be sure of securing a happy retirement in Kaliningrad, safe from the prospect of prosecution.

*

Sir Gavin was mulling over just how to manage the Maximum Power takeover of the Lauriston and called Chuck Barnes to discuss.

"Chuck, national security or not, there is just no way we can get this through the UK regulatory system without scrutiny. It's just too big a deal. Even the PM wouldn't fancy his chances with this right now and God knows what would happen if the news got into Parliament at the wrong time. We need to get smart and think about presenting this in a different way."

"What do you have in mind?"

"According to our lawyers, the best way will be for us to set up a fully incorporated arms-length entity in Delaware and then a programme of asset and resource transfers from here. It's a bit unwieldy but it gives a way of achieving the desired outcome by the back door without attracting too much attention."

"Shit, man, how long is that gonna take?"

"Two years? Maybe more. But if you present things the way they are now the whole deal could be fucked."

"Not sure Hector will buy that and if he doesn't there's not a cat in hell's chance of the president signing up for it either. As far as the commander in chief is concerned he won't like the idea of setting a new corporate rule on this type of thing because the senate will regard it as being anti-competitive and be on his back straightaway."

"If I was in your shoes, Chuck, I'd start the conversations now. Your people won't be pleased if you start talking after you've had a knock-back from London. There is another sweetener I can add to the mix that might make them decide to play ball."

"What's that, Gavin?"

"There is no reason why the Lauriston can't enter into an exclusivity agreement with Maximum Power, which would give you the option of sanctioning any or all intellectual property transfers to a third party. It doesn't buy you the intelligence but effectively puts the plug into stopping it being released."

"OK. We'll look at it, but I can tell you now, the first question I'll be asked is can such an agreement be used to control Kelly? As far as I can see, he's running rings around you and is mastering this whole agenda. You know how nobody Stateside finds that acceptable."

"If keeping Kelly under control is the real price of the deal, Chuck, we will… *I* will, guarantee it happens."

Sir Gavin wasn't sure it was a commitment he would be able to keep, but, somehow, he would have to find a way.

*

My Darling Sue,

By the time you receive this letter you will know I am not coming back and you will not see me again.

I must tell you that my present life, both professional and personal, has become a burden I am no longer able to bear. It may come as a shock to you that I have been diagnosed with terminal cancer and have been told I could die at any time in the next six months to perhaps two years or more. I am not in pain as I write but already find myself having to take more and more tablets to keep going. It has taken a while for me to come to terms with my situation and to accept that I must take control of my final pathway out of this world. I have chosen to work with a progressive euthanasia consultancy in Denmark which has helped me through the necessary process of preparation. Don't worry, where I'm going will not require funeral arrangements to be made. They will contact you in due course to explain the steps I have taken, in order to ensure the welfare and long-term financial security of you, Abigail and Miles, and I can be confident you can all go forward to live the rest of your lives in the way each of you would choose. In all my years as a scientist, the last two have been the most challenging, when they should have been the most rewarding and stimulating. Rather than doing the job I love, I have been subject to continual bullying and pressure to direct my work to the interests of sectional international defence interests and not for the good of mankind, which has always been my focus. The recent abduction of our dear Abigail was the final straw for me. How could these heartless people ever think they could have secured my collaboration through blackmail? This was so terribly wrong and reason enough for me to quit my work. I have been constantly badgered by Maximum Power to buy my technology so that they can control the world market and protect their international oil interests. The price of that deal could only have been to accelerate global warming to even more extreme levels. I don't wish to be held responsible for killing the planet, when every right-thinking person is trying to do the opposite. And then there is our own national interest. Does our country have any morals left? I am continually reminded that my expertise should be sold to benefit British business, and yet I am prevented from forming alliances that would promote the civilian use of the HCCVD technology before the knowledge has been approved for military uses. It is wrong. I am old and this is a battle that others in the Lauriston will have to wake up to in the years ahead. I have done as much as I can do to slow the application of my discoveries but I know in due course, others will follow my path and discover the secrets of free, safe limitless energy from spent nuclear waste. They will be the ones to be remembered and celebrated in the future. Not the likes of foot soldiers like me.

In my quieter moments I have wondered if I could have withstood the pressure of my professional life if we still had a viable relationship. I wonder if you ever reflect on some of the truly happy times we spent, bringing up the children when we used to share our hopes and fears for the future? We even had some laughs! Surely you remember? What happened to change that? I still don't understand except that, somewhere down the line, unwittingly, I said or did something to turn you against me. The past ten years I have felt you have treated me with indifference at best and on occasion with hostility and yet I have never understood why. Effectively banning me from our shared bedroom throughout that period, yet continuing to assume I was OK with it, is simply cruel. I have come to feel like a bee captured in an old glass honey pot. A prisoner trapped under constant observation attracted to the light, yet starved of air and food. Despite the brightness there is only one inevitable consequence. I cannot help but wonder what your personal motivation was to start an extra-marital relationship with Gavin Laidlaw behind my back. Were you naïve enough to think that I wouldn't find out? Although you picked times to see him when you knew I would be away, you forgot that I could monitor the front door security camera from my phone. Each time I saw him arrive I deliberately called him to see what he was up to. There was never an occasion when he answered me. When I met Gavin professionally, he was not always discreet, often imparting some small piece of tittle-tattle that he could never have known if it wasn't for you. It was humiliating. And despite all this, I stayed loyal to you, not because I am a hero, but because that is the type of person I am. In saying these things it is important for you to understand that I am not bitter – I am past all that now. But there is one personal secret that I have never shared with you, not by choice, but because I didn't know it myself. I have recently learned that I have a son from a relationship before we got together. The man himself doesn't know of this and I cannot imagine how he would react if he knew. He has been very successful in his life and this knowledge would doubtless open old wounds long since healed. I cannot help but share my regret. Regret of not knowing. Regret of not telling. Regret of not loving, but that moment has gone. You stand on the verge of achieving a personal ambition. I must assume you have been waiting for a long time – freedom and the money to enjoy it. My lawyer will be in touch to sort out the details shortly. I can only hope it lives up to your expectations. I have left my house keys in the usual place. Good luck! With all my love, Des.

This letter would not be given to Triore. It was too raw for that. He would post it when he departed for the airport.

*

Arbutsev's reappointment letter came through as expected and contained the information he had anticipated. He could leave the weighty administrative arrangements connected with moving house with his wife, while he got focused on the immediate priority of the Danish mission. Bringing that plan together was the guarantee of immunity from the prospect of future prosecution so it was vital he not only got it organised, but that he personally joined the crew tasked with delivering it.

For a trawler of the size of the B474 he would need a sizeable team. Between accommodating the number of people and the extra supplies of fuel it was just as well there were no plans to catch fish.

He called Igor Poliarkin and they arranged to meet on the fishing quay at Baltiyskya Kosa across the estuary from the naval base.

"If we are going to work together you're going to have to tell me what this is all about," demanded the skipper.

"If we are going to work together, first you and your bosun,

Anatoly, over there, must sign this. By doing so you will become temporary members of the FSB, accountable to the national government and answerable to me. That means you will not discuss any aspect of this assignment with anyone who is not designated for the mission. I shouldn't have to remind someone with your track record of the consequences of non-compliance."

"OK – so the past is behind us – agreed?"

"Sign here and you wipe the slate clean. No track record, prospect of investigation or prosecution."

"I hope you are right. Me and Anatoly are a team. Wait here while I get his signature. You know, those of us in the informal economy have long memories."

"If anyone you know demonstrates signs of having a long memory, I will have them arrested. We are going to Denmark to repatriate a confused Russian citizen called Ponomariev, who recently decided to defect, and a sick British man."

"I guess you think they won't come quietly?"

"I'm not so sure – the British man needs specialist treatment here which has already been sanctioned by my director in Moscow. As I understand it, the defector has been incentivised to return."

Poliarkin laughed. "So, you have told him that you won't send a hit squad overseas? You'll just kill him when we bring him home. Got to hand it to you, Arbutsev, you are clearly careful with the government's money."

"I don't know what will happen; that's up to others. We just have to collect him and… subdue him if necessary."

"Whereabouts are we headed?"

"To an island called Rømø in the far south-west, close to the frontier with Germany. I have estimated it will mean three days at sea. All you have to do is to get there, wait while the recovery team goes ashore, and bring everyone home again. You won't need to dock anywhere. The recovery team will land in an inflatable, which will be launched at the closest point outside Danish and German territorial waters. I will authorise the crew and give you forty-eight hours' notice of our departure. You had better consult the charts and tell me how much extra fuel you will need to carry. I can then get it ordered and you can keep fishing in the meantime until I tell you to stop. For the purposes of this mission, which I will lead, you will be my deputy. You will carry the minimum crew to operate the vessel; the rest will be tactical people who I will bring."

"It's quite a cruise you are organising. I presume you want to go through the Danish back door – down the Baltic, up the Great Belt, Kattegat, Skaggerak and North Sea?"

"I'm not interested in a geography lesson."

"You should be. Getting round Denmark means either Great Belt or Copenhagen channels. The latter is shorter, narrower, busier and surrounded by observation equipment."

Poliarkin's point was unnecessary detail to Arbutsev.

"You work out the route."

"You need to get your story in place," the skipper countered. "We could be intercepted by a Danish pilot. If we haven't a credible explanation for why we are in the area we could be impounded."

"Naval ships pass through from time to time on their way north to Murmansk from here and they don't appear to get bothered. We are just another vessel passing through."

"We will need a better story than that," Poliarkin persisted.

"What do you suggest?"

"We should say we're surveying fish stocks and migration routes for herring. They will know that is our main interest and will explain why we are cruising and not dropping our nets. Whichever way we go, we should return the other way. I don't wish to raise more questions than necessary."

Arbutsev made a mental note to fine-tune the proposition. In the meantime, he had more business back across the other side of the water at the *Ded Pivko* bar in Baltiysk.

It was as though time had stood still when he arrived. The scene was almost the same as when he was last there a few weeks before. Smoky atmosphere, pool tables occupied by a dozen or so young off-duty sailors making the most of the opportunity to do some serious drinking, a few women, most of whom wore too much makeup and had seen better days, looking for a quick bit of business, and a couple of old-timers sitting in a corner with glasses of beer, reliving their days at sea. Propping up the bar, alone, was the man he had come to find.

"Bit early for you to be starting in here, isn't it, Moscovoi? Surely you aren't scheduled to be going out until tonight?"

The commissar gave Arbutsev a cursory look before returning his gaze to his beer.

"I need to prepare. I have my routine. Besides, in my book, any time is a good time for a beer. What do you want anyway, Arbutsev? I told you everything I know last time."

"It is true you were more than helpful, *tovarich.* I discovered how you traded a night with a very expensive lady in return for falsifying port records and taking an unscheduled and unrecorded night off, meaning the harbourmaster was unable to allocate another commissar to replace you. Knowing your reputation, heaven knows what Poliarkin got up to without you. He certainly had trouble with time-keeping as well as a temporary problem with his navigation system. Fortunately for you, his memory has got a bit sketchy of late but, if necessary, I'm sure I could give it a jog. In my experience, these unfortunate events are symptoms of a disease called smuggling, and as the FSB senior investigator in the port, that interests me a lot. You see, my crime statistics are relatively low at the moment and Moscow is asking me why I'm not arresting more people. They do not accept that generally the Oblast is well off and therefore people don't have to do any crime. They think people are well-off *because* of the crime. If that was the case, why would they need me to do my job? That's not good news for you, my friend. It means that according to the rule book I should lock you up for as long as I can. I wouldn't think that would be more than two years but even so, that's a bit of a stretch without a beer."

"Spare me the crap, Arbutsev. If you had any evidence, you wouldn't have to make a speech. I'm already bored."

The investigator grabbed the commissar's arm and twisted it up his back. A couple of the sailors spotted the minor disturbance and were about to intervene until the investigator flashed his ID card. Nobody registered his name, but all recognised the badge of the FSB, and turned away.

"I'm starting to think you have an attitude problem, Moscovoi. You know I don't need evidence to put you inside, suspicion and a crime form in triplicate is enough. Here I am, out of the goodness of my heart, spending time to come and see you in this fleapit with an offer which could just change your life. I really think it's time you paid attention."

Moscovoi's hostility remained in the eyes but evaporated from the rest of his body. He gestured to a nearby empty table.

"So what do you want to say?"

"I am requisitioning a trawler to go to sea for six days on a secret mission. I need a crew. Poliarkin will skipper and Anatoly, his bosun, is coming. Poliarkin seems to think you should come as well. Seems to have some idea you're a good guy to have around in a crisis."

"What crisis? How much?"

"You get to know when you sign up. Once you have signed, if you step out of line, I will bust you for treason and in that situation, if you are lucky, you would face the death penalty. I admit that's a negative way of looking at it. The other side of the coin is that your police record will be wiped completely, meaning that you will not have to answer for any crimes committed previously, regardless of the circumstances. I think it's a great deal for you. Perhaps the opportunity to start over afresh."

"If I sign now, will you piss off?"

"For now, yes. I am a busy man. But once you sign the form, I will be your boss. My first action will be to give you two days' holiday. Use the opportunity not to drink but to dry out. I will then contact you with arrangements."

"You said we'd be away for six days. Then what happens?"

"Frankly, I don't give a shit. Clearing your record for the sake of six days at sea is what this deal is all about. What's not to like?"

Arbutsev took a contract out of his pocket and a pen from his jacket.

Moscovoi added his autograph.

"Excellent," the investigator said.

"From now on, you must assume everything we discuss is confidential. We are going to the west coast of Denmark to repatriate a Russian citizen and collect a British man who needs medical treatment here. To do this we will need to pass through Danish waters and may be subject to a pilot's inspection. As the trawler's political officer you will have to deal with any enquiries at sea, which will mean explaining our presence in the area."

"Which will be?"

"Researching stocks and migration routes of Baltic herring. If you have the right paperwork, you will be believed, especially as we will not be dropping nets on the journey. You will need to ensure you are properly prepared and mark up some charts accordingly."

After the better part of an hour in the *Ded Pivko*, Arbutsev needed some fresh air and went for a stroll back towards his office along the Navy's Baltiysk number 8 quay, passing a destroyer and a frigate that appeared almost deserted, their crews clearly on leave. He was contemplating the complexity of the clandestine military mission which he would lead that would clearly constitute an incursion into a hostile NATO country, with national implications regardless of the outcome. If it succeeded, he would have achieved something more impressive than one of these giant symbols of maritime power was ever likely to. It was a humbling thought. He needed to carefully think through what military resources would be needed to support the mission.

*

Poliarkin hadn't explained to Arbutsev his role in helping Ponomariev to escape in the first place, and remembering the difficulty of fixing it, was privately amazed that he should find himself helping to organise his return. What did he care? He had earned good money in the process and now, with the deal he had made with Arbutsev, could look forward to enjoying it.

Two days later, in between a couple of short inshore runs into the Vistula Lagoon, he had done the fuel calculations (naturally overestimated) for the Danish trip and phoned Arbutsev to fix the order, before going below deck with Anatoly to discuss some modifications to create a private cabin for their expected cargo.

He was called back to the deck by a familiar but now unwelcome voice.

"Oi, Igor, what's happening?"

The voice speaking pidgin Russian belonged to Grigor, the younger of the Zanowsky brothers.

"Hi Grigor, what are you doing here? It's dangerous. The police will arrest you if they know you're around."

"Don't worry – I have a different passport and besides, I come here so often I think even your border guards regard me as a friend, in the same way I think of you. Every now and again, I think of the good trades we have done over the last three years. When I think of the money we've made, it makes me emotional. That is why I had to see you so soon after my last visit, I had to ask you to your face; what the fuck are you playing at? Stefan and I have been waiting to receive our money – you owe us two hundred and fifty thousand euros for our last delivery and we want it now, otherwise we will have to finish our business. Understand?"

He drew a line across his neck.

"I haven't had the opportunity to tell you but I have trouble with the authorities, they're watching me closely. They know I was involved in smuggling and have worked out Stefan is linked. I've had to give them some of the money to keep them quiet."

"Give? You'd better get it back; they can't have any evidence."

"This is Russia, my friend. The authorities won't give a fuck about the evidence. If it suits them, they just make the story fit the facts. I think it will be OK in a few weeks when some other event draws their attention. Then I can start to pay you, but for now I must lay low. So low in fact, they're blackmailing me into doing a secret trade for them."

"What?"

"The guy I had to give the money to is the FSB senior investigator here, Arbutsev. He is the one hiring my boat to go to Denmark to repatriate two guys – one is that bloke who you were helping to get out, Ponomariev. Apparently, he's coming back and I'm being lined up to collect him."

Poliarkin saw the surprise on Grigor's face. In fact, what he had said was possibly the only thing that could have shocked the Pole.

"When are you going to collect him?"

"Don`t know yet – I think in the next ten days or so. This guy, Arbutsev, has your money. Arbutsev is coming with me to Denmark."

"Text me the date when you have it. If I don't get the money by then, we will have to let Mr Arbutsev feel the pain of our displeasure."

Grigor now seemed in a hurry to leave, climbing out of the hatch onto the deck before purposefully walking down the quay towards the estuary ferry.

Despite the age of the smartphone, Baltiskya Kosa was still one of those locations that had the benefit of a public payphone. He used it to call the family's garage business office in Gdansk and spoke to his brother, Stefan. His news was not greeted with the surprise he had expected.

"I took a call from Winston last night. We've been asked to help out. One way or another we will recover our money and then double it. This will be a good trade for us."

*

Stefan called Winston back the following day.

"I don't doubt the quality of your work, Stefan, but if you're looking for a similar payday to last time, you've got to earn it."

"You're a tough negotiator, Mr Winston."

"Spare me the bullshit. I have a very specific job for you. In a few minutes you will receive a couple of pictures on your phone of the two guys the Russians are expecting to pick up. I want you to find me a couple of lookalikes to take their places. What you have to do is to put them in a particular place at a particular time. I will send you details in a couple of days. They don't have to speak English, and they shouldn't worry about being taken by the Russians. I will get them out, but they must look the part. I'm sure if you go to a modelling or casting agency you can find them. Tell them you are shooting a movie short or ad and what you are planning is a screen test. You are more than capable of making this work."

"And if I do?"

"Same terms as before. Payable in euros into your bank in Gdansk."

"OK – we'll get it done. But you will need to tell us more about when and where the substitution will take place. One of our associates will be on the boat coming down from Kaliningrad. His information is that they will set sail next Monday. An FSB senior investigator called Arbutsev will be in command."

"I've heard of him. Wasn't he the chap who was assigned to investigate Ponomariev?"

"That's right. He's on this mission to save his career. Now his bosses are blaming him for the defection. It looks like he has one opportunity to put it right."

"They must rate him to give him a second chance. Most of their people judged to have fucked up just disappear. I'll look into him and see if I can pick up any clues."

"Let me give you a head start. He owes our family business

two hundred and fifty thousand euros, money he confiscated on behalf of his employers which he siphoned off for his personal use. Given the prevailing rate of exchange I am only prepared to trade it for a bullet and that is extra to our fees."

*

Winston's next call was to Laidlaw.

"It looks as though your residential in Denmark is attracting quite a lot of industry interest, Gavin. I really wouldn't mind coming along myself, especially as I hear Chuck Barnes and Eve Grainger are involved. I think you need someone to spell out the realities of UK regulation before everyone gets too swept up in 'American corporate speak'."

"You're very well informed, Gerry – we've only just secured their participation. I do hope I can rely on you to take a positive approach. The reality for us is that we need to work with them. You know you would need to be in Denmark for next Wednesday evening and, given the transport connections, you'll need to be staying overnight and Thursday, too. I guess you'll make your own arrangements for flights, either Billund or Hamburg. According to Des Kelly, the food is OK, but the accommodation is, well, basic, I understand."

"I think I can slum it for a night, Gavin. I think Kelly's call is a good one. You will certainly get some work done. From what I am led to believe, it's a bit of a backwater – there aren't many distractions, apart from the local wildlife."

"So I've heard. He's got someone over there who is allocating rooms and organising everything. I'll put you on the agenda as WCJ from the Cabinet Office, and assume you won't wish to appear until Barnes and Grainger have made their presentations. As far as the accommodation is concerned, everyone is grouped together in little holiday lodges on the edge of a wood. I'll put you down for a VIP room. I think that means you don't need to share a toilet."

SEVENTEEN

ARBUTSEV APPEARED AT THE Baltiskya Kosa fishing quay at eight in the morning, just as the crews from the night fishing runs were going home. Poliarkin had not joined them for the last three nights as he had stayed in dock helping Anatoly to complete the B474's internal modifications necessary for the journey. Bunks had been added and the hold significantly reduced to allow space for fuel, supplies and as yet unspecified military equipment. A new extension had been built onto the wheelhouse to create a small office for Moscovoi and bunks for Arbutsev and Poliarkin. The roof space above was used to secure a heavy-duty inflatable and outboard engine, screened with marker buoys and emergency rafts. A casual observer would conclude that this was a fishing trawler which took the safety of its crew particularly seriously, offering them a choice of means of evacuation, depending on the circumstances, and somehow the amended superstructure contrasted with the peeling paint and rust of the bow. The office for Moscovoi was a precaution against a potential boarding from a Danish pilot, so that there was a place for a visitor to go to discuss charts without having to access other parts of the boat. The vessel was now ready and crewed with a mix of Poliarkin's people and eight military personnel, who were kept separately below decks.

Arbutsev had instructed that there would be no mingling with the trawler crew on the journey there and back. Their departure out into the Baltic was routine, other than the hour; two in the afternoon. The harbourmaster had cleared a route south normally reserved for Navy ships and the three deckhands set to work on routine cooking and cleaning duties. For them this would be an easier assignment than usual. No checking and discharging of nets, no freezing of fish or stacking of boxes in rough seas. The toughest jobs for them would be the systematic refuelling with jerry cans and helping to launch and recover the inflatable when instructed. Arbutsev and Poliarkin would spend their time in the wheelhouse focused on navigating their way quietly to their destination. The sun that had greeted their departure from Baltyisk was slowly submitting to a veil of high-level grey cloud as they moved away from the shore. The effects of the sea's swell became more noticeable to the uninitiated. It would be the job of the deckhands to deal with the inevitable vomiting that would follow.

*

The morning of his exit, his final departure from the family home in the Thames Valley, was bright and sunny. Sue had called her goodbyes as she left to have coffee with a friend in Abingdon before going on to the cash and carry for Miles. Des's flight wasn't until early afternoon, so he had given himself plenty of time to pack for the journey. There were several bags that would need checking in. The items were not filled with clothes and the like (where he was going he wouldn't need much) but were instead stuffed with documents and records. One bag was for Triore, with his whole life; bank records, savings accounts, mortgage details, tax references, health insurance, driver's licence, will, car registrations, and the rest. Another was handover documents with a complete list of lab bookings, experimental designs and test data. Whoever would fill his boots at the Lauriston would have some clear direction for the HCCVD project, but tantalisingly would not find any help or guidance for the interpretation of results. That had been committed to his 'Book of Secrets', which would be deposited with Pastor Glistrup. It was hard to reflect that everything he had done on this earth in the past forty years amounted to the contents of no more than three bags. It was remarkable to think of how much he had packed into his life – people he had met, places he had been. With the conclusion of his life in sight, and the prospect of his day in the celestial court of judgement, he had the feeling that he should have developed more of an understanding of the world, emotional intelligence, *wisdom.* The only thing he thought he had learned was to recognise that the same situations in life often reoccur, and that when he found himself facing decisions, he might be smart enough to reflect on what he had done last time and the outcomes it had produced. Being a scientist, he'd never been much good as a people person. The few friends he had were individuals who had persevered to form a relationship with him, not the other way round. Had it been worth it? Perhaps, in a couple of cases – Galina and Aldo were two – but these were based on professional ties between peers, not so much about personal contacts. The situation with Sue remained his biggest regret. It was like a slow-motion accident. He knew what was going to happen, but couldn't stop it. The psychological glue that had held them together had become brittle and snapped. A repair had depended on both parties, not one. It was now only about the past, not the present or the future.

He gave Milo an affectionate pat and doggie treat, and locked up, depositing the house key on a nail above the back porch. Cocooned in his car, accompanied by Mahler, he drove out of the gate for the last time, down to the village green and the post box outside Mrs Harris's village store. He pulled in, waved through the window at the proprietor and put the letter addressed to his wife in the post box. Perversely, although the distance from the post box to the destination address was around 300 yards, the journey he had sent the communication on would go via the main sorting office in Oxford, some twenty miles away. The collective machinery of the Royal Mail would ensure it would not be delivered for three days – ample time for him to have commenced his final journey.

*

Bannan was informed within the hour of the departure of B474. He had arranged to issue an observation notice to NATO shipping en route, to observe and track, but not to intercept the vessel on its journey, and to brief his opposite number, Soren Neilsen, from the Danish intelligence services, about the whole plan. The Dane had been initially apprehensive, but saw the logic of allowing events to unfold. This would be billed as a NATO exercise, allowing for Danish forces to collaborate and share information as necessary and, more importantly from Bannan's point of view, provide the authority for a small specialist Special Boat Service tactical team to operate on Danish soil. Central to their shared thinking was a commitment to manage the situation without any live firing. He had also received an email from Stefan with the pictures of two characters he had identified as Kelly and Ponomariev lookalikes. It was always difficult to make judgements from pictures alone but he thought the likenesses would be close enough for his purpose. Stefan had booked space on a campsite on the north of the island and would be arriving in the next twenty-four hours. Also amongst the early arrivals ahead of the Lauriston Residential was Chemmy Moore, who would continue to shadow Kelly. Although operating to clear instructions from Bannan, there was no doubt the assignment was one of the more exciting ones from her point of view, offering the prospect of observing Henning Triore once more; perhaps not as closely as last time, but nonetheless a more engaging target than most. The success of this trip depended more on her anonymity, so for her the accommodation was the back of the camper van she had hired. Kelly had been easy to pick up from her vantage point near the mainland roundabout. As she drove over the causeway, following him, she reflected on her experiences with Glistrup, and realised that Rømø had a unique charm that this apparently nondescript mix of pine wood, heather, marsh and sand didn't communicate easily to the lay visitor. She looked forward to returning in the future in her own time to appreciate the island's vibe at her own pace. Meanwhile, Kelly's first stop was St Clement's. He must have called ahead because Glistrup was waiting, judging from his dress, in pastor mode. They shook hands and Kelly gave him a large sports bag. They seemed to be engaged in a brief but animated conversation before Kelly waved his goodbyes and set off south towards Havneby. Parking at the Kro, rather than checking in, he walked towards the small harbour, and a warehouse which appeared to be owned by a wind turbine company, to the right on a spit of land facing out towards Sylt. Westergaard was there to meet him, alongside a woman and another man with clipboards. They went in a side door and emerged ten minutes later, minus the couple with the clipboards, deep in conversation. She wasn't too interested in the shed. Given the fact that a truck from an audio-visual firm from Esbjerg was parked outside, he had probably been reviewing arrangements for his residential conference. Westergaard took him back to his hired car and they set off slowly, Moore following at a discreet distance. They took the only route out of town to the west, the main access point for vehicles heading for Rømø's famous southern beach. Passing the community sports hall and tennis complex, the road was lined with upmarket wooden villas set back from the road, which Chemmy knew from her research were owned by another one of Westergaard's companies. They pulled into the one at the far edge of the development bordering a wheat field. This acted as a buffer to a line of pines she estimated to be half a kilometre further on, marking the start of the expansive southern sands. Already parked in the driveway was a black BMW 7 series and emerging from the house to greet them was Henning Triore. Her heart missed a beat seeing him again. What was she like? It had only been a couple of months since she had been in his bed, but just the sight of him brought back those deep-seated carnal feelings she thought she had buried. *Oh God, this is going to be a long few days*, she thought to herself.

The three disappeared into the house, with Westergaard leaving alone, forty-five minutes later. Chemmy's instructions were to stay with Kelly, but she couldn't see what they were doing from her parked camper in the road. She set off on foot to find a better vantage point. She found a ditch at the edge of the field on the far boundary of the property. From there she found a place overlooking the back garden and saw Kelly and Triore sitting at a table. Both were reading and swapping documents, and then Kelly appeared to be signing one. Most likely the meeting had started earlier, probably at the time Westergaard had left, now two hours since. Dusk was falling; Glistrup would probably be taking another party of nature-loving tourists to see the Black Sun, and Triore seemed to have had enough also. He collected the papers, put them into a briefcase and offered Kelly a sort of a man hug, which she took to be unusual in a client/customer relationship. He disappeared into the house, but Kelly remained. Was this going to be his new base for the next few days? As night fell, lights went on and blinds were closed. For tonight this was journey's end, and for Chemmy, time to find a corner to park the camper van. Walking back to her room on wheels, the BMW had gone and the driveways of neighbouring properties were empty. What she had not realised was that Westergaard had hired a whole row of the neighbouring properties to the Lauriston to host their delegates attending the conference, and the block would be full in the coming hours.

*

The next morning, Kelly had risen early to return to the turbine warehouse by the harbour. Even Chemmy was impressed by the exterior, now sporting the flag of the Lauriston, and within half an hour a coach carrying the delegates arrived. In the general melee at the entrance, it had been easy to get in to see the interior, which seemed surprisingly small considering the size of the building. A set, complete with stage, screen and lighting theatre, seating for around eighty and a separate break-out area for working groups, which looked as if it would double as space for coffee and lunch. As she would have expected, although relatively small-scale, it was clearly a quality production. Kelly appeared to be some sort of editorial director, running through the order of presentations and the agenda as well as greeting VIP guests. From what she could overhear, a late addition to the speakers' programme had been the Danish energy minister, who was to give a welcoming address. There seemed to be several important-looking people loitering as though waiting for instructions. Although the surroundings had been professionally dressed, they were sufficiently austere not to allow for a 'green room' space for speakers either to check their slides or amend their speeches. Miscellaneous excerpts of classical music contributed to the growing anticipation of the moment, as those arriving by coach received their delegate packs and coffee. Most were evidently new to the location, wanting to step outside to enjoy the sunny but breezy conditions before getting focused on the business in hand in the darkened warehouse. Others stared intently at their mobiles.

If there was to be a raid here by a foreign power, Chemmy thought, there must be an overriding reason. This place was not easy to find and relatively inaccessible, even from the sea.

That was somebody else's problem. Kelly was not going anywhere in the short term. A breakfast of coffee and pastries in the Kro across the harbour awaited.

She had not realised it but one of the figures walking around the warehouse at that moment was Sir Gavin Laidlaw, clearly impressed with the effort Des had gone to in pulling the arrangements together. A private residential conference away from the sometimes claustrophobic atmosphere of the Lauriston had been an innovation in itself, and this was looking good. He was pleased to notice the camera positions in place to record the event, a useful reference source when it came to impressing potential investors. From that point of view he was feeling confident about welcoming Eve Grainger, Chuck Barnes and Professor de Leonibus to the gathering. By loitering near the warehouse door, he wanted to make sure he was on hand for the photocall with the Danish energy minister, when the moment arrived. What he was unaware of was the considerable trouble and expense Gerry Bannan had gone to to manage the security arrangements. Laidlaw didn't realise just how important and sensitive the situation was, to have justified the participation of Winston Carter-Jones in person. He could not possibly understand HMG's nervousness about Kelly and his state of mind, let alone the risk of losing their new Russian acquisition, who would be paraded shortly in front of his VIPs.

The day went like a dream. The Danish minister spoke of his country's core belief and growing economic activity while protecting the environment, quoting examples of their small but diverse sustainable energy initiatives. The programme was good, the speakers excellent, the engagement of delegates exemplary. Sir Gavin lapped up the adulation of his colleagues. Ponomariev had given what he had judged to be a high-quality presentation of such clarity and detail that he had found it hard to fully comprehend. Kelly, too, had changed his tune, seemingly more outgoing, embracing change and the opportunities it would bring the institution. Grainger had spoken about the need for governments to cut regulation in the sector to boost investment in safety and productivity, Barnes about a new era in transatlantic scientific collaboration and de Leonibus about the importance of developing a meaningful global programme of remediation to challenge climate change. All the external speakers had arrived with their PRs, who were feverishly drafting press statements based on their speeches and, for just a short time, it seemed as though Rømø was the centre of the sustainable energy policy world.

Some of the VIPs had to leave that night, and as a result would miss out on the social and recreational side of the event to follow that evening, before the conference itself would close at lunchtime the following day.

Sir Gavin was still in his element, slipping off the stage at regular intervals to mix with delegates as well as taking the opportunity to say some personal goodbyes to the likes of the Danish energy minister and Eve Grainger in particular. Of the VIPs, only Aldo de Leonibus was scheduled to stay over. Laidlaw's best moments kept getting better and seemed unlikely to be topped by Chuck Barnes.

"Great show, Gavin, great show – send me a link to the coverage. There are a few guys in Washington who need to see this. By the way – I was thinking about what you said about how we get through all this regulatory red-tape crap in the UK. I think you may be right. A straightforward takeover bid for the Lauriston is a bit of a blunt instrument. We can be smarter than that. I know Hector is getting to work on a new proposition right now so I think we can look forward to some happy days ahead."

Winston Carter-Jones arrived for the last half-hour of the day's proceedings, deliberately waiting until he had heard Barnes had left. A meeting with Barnes in Rømø, he considered, would not be helpful in the present circumstances. Although Chemmy and Ifor were around, for the purposes of this exercise they were each doing their own thing. Besides, Winston had other things on his mind with the conduct of the proceedings in the next few hours uppermost in his thoughts.

*

Arbutsev was starting to feel his own adrenaline rising as the B474 continued on its way. Such was the steady progress of the vessel he had become accustomed to the rapid rhythmic knocking sound of the engine, which was no longer an annoying distraction to him. His chosen route, threading through the southern Danish islands, was always bound to attract the attention of the authorities and he was initially surprised by the lack of challenge. Maybe it was because they were continuing at a steady pace and not tracking in a circular movement, which would have suggested they had dropped nets. He knew the Danes to be mercurial people, who were more interested in fish rustling than spying, so perhaps they wouldn't be interested in some old tub paddling through their 'back passage' giving them the runs. Besides, as far as he was aware, there was nothing happening in Denmark that his bosses back home didn't already know about. But he was wrong. His hosts were just waiting long enough to ensure that the B474 wouldn't have the option of doing an about-turn and changing sea lanes before making contact. They had passed the island of Lolland when the first radio message was received.

"B474 – this is Sønderborg Coastal Command. You are in Danish territorial waters. Please state your business."

"Hello Sønderborg. This is B474 out of Baltiysk headed 157 north. Copy. Required to survey herring stocks southern migration with sonar trail. Over. Nets not deployed. Over."

"B474 this is Sønderborg. Copy. Require pilot check to board. Please acknowledge and confirm."

"This is B474. Pilot check not required. Charts and sonar working well. Over."

"This is Sønderborg. Under Danish maritime law, inspection required. Over. The pilot will intercept your location in thirty minutes. Out."

Poliarkin looked at Arbutsev.

"It was always going to happen," he said. "This is why you need Moscovoi. This is his show. Anatoly, get below and warn our guests to ensure their equipment is stowed below our freezer boxes and they are doing something useful like sharing a meal in the galley. Our commissar can give their man the official tour."

They didn't have long to wait before a cutter from the Royal Danish Navy approached and came alongside. Two crew came aboard.

"Good evening. My name is Nielsen, the Sønderborg pilot, this is Rasmussen, my navigation officer."

"Welcome. I am Moscovoi, ship's commissar. Please let me show you around."

"You seem to have a lot of crew for a surveying operation?"

"Not really. Each of our vessels carries a full crew regardless of duties. Most prefer the camaraderie of sailing together to staying at home with their wives."

"You're heading to the North Sea, surveying herring, right? Sorry for our interest; we are normally notified in advance when Russian shipping is passing, especially through the southern islands."

"I must apologise, Captain Neilsen. I think the notifying officer in our harbourmaster's office went on holiday without processing the paperwork. If you step into my office, you may see our official licence and charts."

Neilsen started to walk towards the wheelhouse. Moscovoi put his big frame in the way.

"Captain, all the documentation you need is at the back here in my office, please…"

He steered the two visitors into the small midships office, which even with the cold sea air retained the smell of stale tobacco, the perfect accompaniment to Moscovoi's alcohol-infused breath. The paperwork was duly checked and photographed by Rasmussen. He used a well-fingered but weighty porn magazine left on the commissar's chair to hold down a curled edge of the current chart, while Neilsen held down the other as he continued the exchanges with Moscovoi.

"It's unusual to be doing a stock survey halfway through the season."

"That might be true but our catches in mid-Baltic are well

down on last year's totals. We need to understand what's going on. We want to be sure that our neighbours are not taking more than their share. After all, the herring is prized in Russia as it is here in Denmark."

"The charts show you heading for the southern North Sea..." Rasmussen observed.

"That's right – we surveyed the north about three months ago. It would have taken us too long to have done it all in a single trip. Besides, we do not have credit facilities to buy fuel at Danish ports."

"Of course," Neilsen said abruptly.

"Well, Commissar, all appears to be in order. We will leave you to continue on your journey. Stay safe and good luck with the survey."

The two Danes descended their ladders back to the cutter, waving their goodbyes.

"That was a bit quick," Rasmussen observed.

"It's fine, if we'd stayed longer we would only have made them nervous. I saw everything I needed to see. Did you notice the amount of safety equipment they were carrying and a modern rib stored on the roof of the commissar's office? I reckon that could accommodate a football team. Russian trawlers are not noted for their safety and the rib must be worth at least the same as the vessel as a whole. These guys aren't into herring surveys, they are fishing for people. Now in terms of numbers, I think they have brought a team of maybe ten or a dozen. I think with those numbers they are probably all competent seamen and experienced with weaponry. We can now be sure to give them a warm welcome when they get to Rømø."

As the cutter moved away from the trawler, Moscovoi waved his farewell and was joined by Arbutsev.

"Well done. They seemed satisfied."

"The Danes are easy. Not like the fucking Germans, who go through everything."

"Do you think they suspected anything was wrong?"

"Not when they saw our licence. Your people did a great job in making that forgery. I can tell you that it looks better than most of the originals."

"I thought you were going to at least offer them a vodka before they went."

"No chance. These guys are too up themselves for that. It's a waste of a good drink. Especially when I need it more…"

Their journey continued to the same monotonous beat. Within hours, the B474 had moved north around the top of Jutland and had started the run south into Rømø. It was time to take the final briefing below deck.

It was a cramped space to hold a meeting but that was what the moment had required. He had prepared a board with maps and pictures on it for the Navy team to study and started the explanation.

"OK guys. A straightforward job by your standards. We are headed for this position, the closest deep-water point to Rømø, just outside the local territorial jurisdiction. You will be going ashore onto sovereign Danish territory, armed but without any identification. We must travel across about 1.5 kilometres of open country from the landing point here. This is a mixture of firm sand, dune, heath, pine forest and finally a wheatfield, to this property, number one, Sonderstrand, which is a holiday lodge. Once inside, we will collect these two men. We expect them to be compliant but if they prove otherwise, they are to be tasered and injected with Propofol, which will send them to sleep. They will be strapped onto the telescopic double stretcher we will be taking and then carried back to the inflatable for onward transfer back here. This is a stealth mission; therefore, it is unlikely guns will be required, but each of you has a pistol with silencer and the guard who stays with the inflatable will carry an AK-47 for emergency use only. Remember, what good looks like her. It is to get in, collect our targets and get out quickly and silently. Live capture for any of us should be avoided. If that looks likely, each of you knows what to do. Questions?"

One of the landing party raised a hand.

"Are we sure no one knows we are coming so we have the element of surprise?"

"Yes."

"And are we sure there will be no one else at this house when we get there?"

"Yes. We have an agent there now, who is supplying up-to-date information on what's happening on the ground. I cannot speak to him directly but he has the ability to send me messages if the situation changes. When we arrive at the house, I will make the entrance, after we have first surrounded and secured the property."

"Do our targets speak Russian?"

"One does; I don't know about the other. Besides, you will not have to speak. I will do the talking in English, so we don't make it too obvious who we are."

"What time do we go ashore?"

"I expect we will arrive on shore at 22.00 and be ready to enter the house at 23.00. We should be back here and on our way home by midnight."

*

Galina was relieved to have Ruslan home at their central Moscow apartment from Murmansk even if it was on a brief visit between tours of duty. In some ways they were luckier than most. Being in privileged positions they had access to computers and technology that allowed them to conduct their private conversations online. The recent business with Nikitin, which she had first started based on a personal favour, had grown in significance out of all proportion and dominated their dialogue, which was supposed to be more about managing family matters and keeping contact with the children, discussing their schoolwork, forthcoming holidays and looking after elderly relatives. She had shared her worries about the threat Nikitin posed to their professional careers and reputation as well as what she suspected to be the risk to her illegitimate child and academic prodigy, resulting from his promised re-integration into the national scientific community. It was a tricky situation which seemed to have emerged from nowhere and Ruslan had made time to carefully consider their options during his home stay. The choice was stark. They either had to keep quiet, letting Nikitin first bask in the reflected glory of, in effect, persuading the defector to return home to a very uncertain future and then blaming Galina for creating the problem in the first place, or remove the problem altogether. Apart from his wish to defend his wife's reputation there was a knock-on implication for him, too. Privately he was not going to stand for his own reputation being undermined by some ministry penpusher with a thirst for more power. If Nikitin regarded death as some sort of casual administrative exercise, Ruslan was used to dealing with it from a more practical perspective. He was a soldier, a hero, in several fields of conflict, some official, some not. It could be argued that in some unofficial cases he could be described as a murderer, but that definition could only be employed if he was acting outside the orders or interest of the state. In this case, he saw a direct link between his own situation and that of the state and he felt obliged to act. Nikitin was a dead man walking.

In Ruslan's line of work, once a decision was made it was not revisited; rather it would be implemented without delay. Nikitin's thoughts at the time were far from his personal safety but with Arbutsev and his mission, perhaps the most daring he had ever sanctioned. He had convinced himself that it would be successful, and he already imagined briefing his governing committee and the President's Office. In particular, he rehearsed his reaction to the president's personal adviser asking whose idea it had been to plan the initiative. He had resolved to be modest, but clear in ensuring his role was acknowledged. The evening rush in Moscow had passed. It was getting late and he was hungry. There was nothing to be done in the office until he heard from Arbutsev. Besides, when the information came through it would be patched through to his mobile.

Time to call it a day and go home.

Leaving the office, he took his normal route heading for the Metro for the Sokolnicheskaya line out to Prokshino. With his overcoat buttoned up against the chill evening air and his trilby pulled forward he looked like any other undistinguished office worker, blending into the street scene. It is often said that the small professional espionage community are often some of the easiest targets to shadow, especially on their home turf, as it never occurs to them that others would be interested in tagging them. That was true of Nikitin. If he had employed his professional judgement, he might have become aware of a thickset woman, following purposefully in his wake. She, too, looked anonymous by local standards, dressed in a heavy black and camel overcoat and brown fur hat, in her late forties, brandishing two bags of supermarket shopping. According to the information board, they had two minutes to wait for the next train. Soon the breeze of stale air and the whine of the train's electric engine announced the impending arrival. Nikitin, like many others on the platform, moved forward to ensure they were able to board ahead of the throng. Then life seemed to go into slow motion. Nikitin had moved to the edge of the platform and then naturally stopped to wait, only his momentum continued. The train was now slowing as it entered the station, but still Nikitin's momentum persisted. He had now overbalanced and was falling not to the ground but onto the track in front of the train. It was hard to anticipate the last sensation he would have registered – the hard impact on the live rail or the scream of two women behind, combined with a groping action of one seeking to prevent his fall. The train had stopped but had been unable to avoid hitting the man. Chaos ensued, with Metro workers rushing to the scene and urgent announcements on the public address system for passengers to evacuate the station immediately. News of the accident did not appear until the breakfast TV news bulletin the following morning.

No information was given on the man's identity, and the incident was blamed on platform overcrowding.

*

It had been a day that had completely surpassed Sir Gavin's expectations. An expertly curated conference, well presented, strong and relevant content. The perfect morale booster and there was more to look forward to tomorrow, with an opening address from Winston Carter-Jones, a series of workshops led by Jake Roberts and of course, the high point of the proceedings, his own closing remarks. Now was the moment to relax. The evening was split into three. Firstly, delegates had some free time to enjoy one of three leisure activities – a nature discovery tour, led by a local national park ranger, Maurice Glistrup, an impromptu tennis tournament organised by local club secretary, Marisa Kjaer, or sand-sailing with Nils Westergaard. After a three-hour break, delegates would return to enjoy a barbecue at one of Westergaard's holiday lets, with music, dancing, and fireworks. He himself would not be involved in any of the activities before the barbecue. He would go to his chalet to finish off his speech for the morning. Given the importance of the occasion, he suggested his senior team colleagues, all of whom would have roles in the workshops, did the same. Des had ensured the seniors had their own accommodation in lodges near to the venue for the barbecue, but for convenience had made sure he had confirmed the number one lodge, the one closest to the sea, had been reserved for himself and Ponomariev. In line with Kelly's plan to break down barriers of formality, a strict dress code had been issued to all, with the offer of a prize for the most dazzling outfit which could be judged as the most opposite to that individual's character. Setting the example, Kelly himself was distinctively attired in a pink T-shirt emblazoned with the slogan 'Shit Happens' and fawn chinos; his new colleague, slightly more conservatively, wearing an Arsenal football shirt and red tracksuit bottoms. The approach had not been understood by Werner Liebelt, but he had put it down to British eccentricity. He had settled for a Hawaiian short-sleeved shirt, cut-off jeans and flipflops. As his colleagues walked off down the road to their quarters, he hesitated, lighting a cigarette, and taking in the scene. An observer might have thought he had been taken in by the mini tennis tournament getting underway on the nearby courts, especially as this option seemed to have been the most popular choice amongst the young women delegates. In reality his attention was focused on the departing figures of Kelly and Ponomariev. He watched them disappearing into their lodge at the far end of the development. Although he was pretty sure from the brief glimpse of the accommodation list that Kelly had kept in the conference hall, he could not be certain no one else was staying in their chalet. He wasn't able to check without raising questions about his own actions.

He sent a text to the burner number he had been given before going to watch the tennis.

*

By nine that night, the Lauriston party was getting underway at the number two chalet and the beat of the dance music became more intense. Kelly had joined Sir Gavin in being impressed by Westergaard's organising ability. The number two chalet had the largest garden and was a perfect location for the party. With coloured lights and bunting, dance floor, band, DJ and bar it had all the ingredients for a memorable evening – just as Kelly had planned. For him it was a double celebration, a chance to mark a successful first conference, but also the end of his career and life. As Westergaard had organised everything he had wanted the team from Terminal to be present – only they would know his real purpose, despite 'Winston' Bannan's suspicions. Although he been invited to attend by Sir Gavin, Winston had also used the explanation of preparing for the following morning as an excuse to say he'd pop along later, assuming he'd caught up on his paperwork. Part of his catch-up involved a meeting at his chalet with Stefan and fellow resident, Williams.

When a blue X-Trail pulled up outside, Williams went to investigate.

"Mr Winston? I am Stefan – a great pleasure to meet you at last. Thank you for your payment. I have completed my side of the arrangement. I have my two actors outside and ready to go."

"Good – my friend here will show you around. You know what to do."

Bannan nodded to Williams, who left with the Pole.

Now, this was the moment of truth.

Williams directed Stefan down to chalet number one. The blinds were drawn but the lights were on inside. Williams let Stefan and his two companions in and went next door. The party was humming. He found Kelly and Ponomariev and whispered in their ears before shepherding them both outside and returning to the throng. Roberts, Liebelt, even Sir Gavin were deep in conversation with some of the younger laboratory technicians (not surprisingly, all female) and didn't notice their departure. Surprisingly, it was Roberts who first noticed their absence, some twenty minutes later.

"Hey, anyone seen Des or Guntis? I thought they were drinking at the bar?"

Williams intervened.

"Guntis has been going on all night about wanting to check his presentation with Des for tomorrow. I think he's getting a little nervous and just wanted to have it right. Think Des got a bit pissed off and went to do it just to get him off his back. He told me he'd come back to the party when he got it sorted."

Liebelt raised his eyes to the ceiling and disappeared inside. Williams, too, took the opportunity to take a break. Once in the toilet Liebelt sent a second text before returning.

"That's a relief! When do the fireworks happen?"

"Not long now. Eleven o'clock," Roberts replied. "Hey Werner, you see that girl Sally over there? She works on the first floor. Told me she wanted to learn German. Now is a great opportunity to give her a first lesson." He laughed and went to the bar to get another beer.

Next door, Williams had taken command.

"Look Des, Guntis. I haven't got time to explain now, but I work for the British government as well as the Lauriston. We have reason to think there is a grave and imminent threat to you, here and now. When this is all over, I will explain, but for now, I want you to do exactly as I tell you. First, get changed quickly. Leave your clothes in a pile over there. I am going to move you to a safe place. Don't worry about the guys in the next room, they are friendly and working for us. Get changed *now*!"

The urgency in Williams's voice didn't require challenge from either. A quick change of clothes and Williams shuffled them out of the back door. As soon as he heard the door slam shut, Stefan emerged to collect the clothes and told the two actors to put them on, then to relax and watch TV. Secret cameras were on to record the immediacy of the moment, which was part of their screen test. When the doorbell rang, all they had to do was act naturally.

*

Chemmy was starting to think Bannan had given her the most boring task on the mission – to watch Kelly. Much to her irritation, she had seen Kelly going into the party with Triore, Westergaard and the rest. It was clear they were having a good time. Even more frustrating was the thought that her colleague, Williams, was enjoying the experience first-hand while she was left outside, sheltering in the bracken and pine trees. As a professional watcher, she was trained to observe activities that ordinary people might miss, and her attention was first drawn by some unusual movement in the nearby wheatfield. Using night vision goggles to pierce the darkness she registered several figures – she counted seven – moving slowly but purposefully towards the first chalet. The fact that they were crouched, wearing black, made her dependent on their movement for detection and their progress was cautious and measured. If she needed to raise the alarm, she had one button to press on her phone. That sent a red signal to Bannan and Williams. It was just after ten past ten. Bannan had left his chalet as soon as Williams had sent the signal that he had collected Kelly and Ponomariev; now with the matching signal from Chemmy, it was game on.

Williams had taken his two charges on a circuitous route through the trees to the cabin that Bannan had just left, with his host and opposite number, Neilsen, to watch events from one of Glistrup's nearby nature hides in the woods.

The tension in the air was such that neither chose to question him about what was happening.

It was clear Williams didn't have time to explain.

The blinds were drawn.

"Stay here, and don't move until I tell you." The order was clearly understood.

EIGHTEEN

DESPITE ANALYSING THE PLAN in considerable detail, in the moment Arbutsev was as apprehensive as he had ever been. Was the prospect of a quality flat in Kaliningrad and the restoration of his apparently tarnished career sufficient reward for confronting the danger he was now in? The situation seemed weird. He was leading a clandestine operation in hostile territory, facing not a firefight but pulsating dance music. It seemed scarier than being under live fire. He drew confidence from his immediate surroundings, which he had memorised in recent days from his maps. Thus far, every feature and terrain encountered had been as expected. The thing that had unnerved him was the fact that this party seemed to be taking place just next door to the house his team were targeting. He was clear they needed to get in and out quickly.

He gestured to members of his team to fan out, with two going over the side fence into the back garden. The lights were on. Someone was at home. He had earlier received the green light from agent Lutz. Although he had seen pictures of Kelly and Ponomariev before, he had left them on the B474, so he would have to rely on Lutz's description of how they were dressed to get the right people. Even in this intense moment, he was surprised that he had not met Ponomariev before in happier times in the course of his duties in Kaliningrad. His team lined up to storm in, although there would be no attempt to smash through windows. This needed to be a quiet door entry.

He needed one guy in a pink T-shirt, the other wearing a red and white football top.

He rang the doorbell.

Inside, the two Polish actors smiled expectantly and stood up. Their audition was about to begin. The man in the pink T-shirt opened the door in welcome but immediately froze as he was tasered by the first trooper; the second burst forward to taser his friend. While the two victims had fits on the floor the third assailant administered injections, effectively turning the writhing humans into static lumps of cargo. Squad members five and six assembled a double stretcher and strapped and loaded the bodies accordingly.

Arbutsev did a quick check to ensure the place was clear, before the team moved out of the back door, passing the double stretcher over the back fence into the wheatfield.

The action had been swift and clinical and had won praise from Neilsen and the British SBS team, who were watching proceedings and staring at the stopwatch they had started from the moment the Russian team had landed on the shore. Neilsen was technically on NATO duty but, as a Dane, resented the fact he was under orders not to intervene on his home territory.

"I wish we could just take out these bastards," he said. Bannan smiled.

"We've had the discussion, Soren. We need to be smarter than them. They have already lost the game. The people they came to collect are safe – just let events take their course and nobody will be any the wiser."

*

Arbutsev knew he taken the route of least resistance. The taser was only for use in an emergency. He had chosen not to hesitate, collect the goods and get the hell out. As his team slipped into the shadows it was considerably harder carrying the load, some 180 kilos, the dead weight of two grown men. There was still a kilometre hike across scrub to the beach and in the dark it required all his concentration to check he was moving in the right direction. He comforted himself with the knowledge that once they hit the beach they would be able to make faster progress. They were departing just as a firework display was starting with flashes and bangs coming from behind them. It was clear to Arbutsev that no one was interested in what he was doing. Crashing through the undergrowth they had now reached the final copse of pine trees; the magnificent expanse of beach stretched out beyond. Even in darkness it looked impressive, but from here on, there would be no cover until they had met the inflatable rib and put to sea. If anyone was watching, this was the riskiest action of the lot, getting across the beach without being shot.

*

Chemmy knew that Kelly was now being supervised by Williams. If something looked as if it was going wrong, Bannan or Williams would call. Otherwise her work was done for the night. She felt tired and ached from her time grovelling in the bushes watching Kelly. The party was still in full swing in the Sonderstrand and had she not been on duty she would have loved to have joined but it was too late. So late, in fact, that as she walked up the road to where her camper van was parked, she saw a big imposing figure walking in the opposite direction.

Oh no, she thought. She knew from his gait who it was. Her hair was wet and matted and she instinctively dragged it across her face as the only means of disguise available. She looked down and walked by at pace on the other side of the road. Having passed him, she had a sigh of relief that she had not been recognised, until seconds later, she heard his voice.

"Excuse me, but don't I know you?"

She stopped momentarily and wondered whether to turn.

She heard him taking a couple of steps back towards her.

Now there was no choice.

"Carrie – it is you? What are you doing here? Are you all right? You look as if you've had a bit of a fright."

"I think you may be mistaken. My name's not Carrie and I'm on a camping holiday with a friend."

"You look as if you *should* be on a camping holiday with a friend. I'm sure if you were, you wouldn't look so stressed. Anyone would think you had been hiding in the trees with the red squirrels for a few days. Please let me walk with you into town. We can get you a room at the Kro and you can catch a shower – somewhere warm and safe."

Chemmy realised there was no point in further pretence.

"OK Henning – let's stop playing games. Yes, I am Carrie, but I'm not who you think I am, and you shouldn't know anything else about me for your own good. It's nice to see you again and I wish you well for the future but now, it's goodbye."

She continued walking until he put his hand on her shoulder.

"All right, Carrie, or whoever you are. I think we spent some important hours together not so long ago. So important that if you were an actor you couldn't have conned me when we slept together – that was real and so is this."

He took her in his arms and gave her the kiss, that special kiss, she could not forget. She didn't resist as all her natural desires swept through her again. She knew she was about to repeat her action in Copenhagen, which she had promised herself never to do again. Last time her action was premeditated, this time it was impulse.

"I haven't got time to check into the Kro," she whispered. "It's right now, right here in the woods." He took her hand and led her up a path between two of the chalets into the pines. Once more, they felt the electricity and urgency of the moment. She knelt in front of him, unzipped his straining trousers, and again gave in to her intimate private fantasy.

*

Having checked his phone, Williams had the 'all clear' to bring Kelly and Ponomariev back to the Lauriston party and past the spot where Chemmy and Triore had met minutes earlier. Only one person noticed their return, most of the revellers having other things on their mind and probably not realising they had been away. The colour drained out of Liebelt's face – the shock of seeing the two principals back at the party made him send a text to Arbutsev in full sight of all.

*

Neilsen had been monitoring Arbutsev's route back to the shore. The Russian raiders were getting close to their point of departure. He looked at Bannan.

"I have to do this now, for the sake of the Poles."

Bannan nodded. "Don't forget the other; one of the Zanowsky brothers will be out there, somewhere, lining up a targeted shot. Make sure your people don't take him out. Getting a share of the action was their price for fixing the substitutes."

Neilsen issued the instruction. "Engage to defend. Indirect live fire."

"Copy, control."

The staccato popping of automatic gunfire could be heard in the distance.

Closer to the action, Arbutsev's worst fears were being realised. They were being shot at with high-calibre weapons, in the dark with tracer fire coming in from the left and right and had no cover.

It was the original shooting gallery.

He had no choice but to wave his arms and shout, "Abort, abort!"

His men dropped the double stretcher and started running for the sea and the waiting inflatable. Their compatriot, who had remained to guard their inflatable, was the only one with an automatic himself. Instinctively, he loosed off a couple of rounds in reply, in order to demonstrate they had some covering fire power of their own, while his colleagues clambered aboard and pushed the small craft out into the surf, leaving the captured bodies on the beach.

Inexplicably, the shooting from the shoreline then stopped. For a split second, Arbutsev hesitated, staring from the shallows into the darkness towards the place where the double stretcher had been dumped, realising his mission was failing if he left without his precious cargo.

That was just long enough for a lone figure to appear, lit by the light of the moon, looking directly at him from the foreshore, and for a single shot to catch him in the leg. He grunted and went down in the water before being grabbed by two of his companions and pulled in, as their outboard sprang into life.

"Recover the bodies to Havneby and confirm. Out." Neilsen turned and smiled at one of his British NATO colleagues.

"I'm pleased we managed to conduct this operation with typical Danish efficiency without requiring your assistance." His comment generated some laughs and slow hand claps.

*

Walking back to his chalet, Bannan reflected on a bizarre evening. How an international incident had played out within a couple of hours, a hundred metres from a party with music and fireworks, in a sleepy Danish backwater. This would be a great story for his memoirs. But now the immediate priority was to get some sleep. He had a speech to give in the morning.

Williams checked him in and secured the doors.

Two people not heading for their beds were Kelly and Ponomariev. Professionally it had been a big day for them but for different reasons. They sat down with a bottle of Scotch. Even at this late stage, Kelly knew he could say nothing about the coming hours. Instead, they talked about the evening's events, which had created another special bond between them.

"I heard Williams say those guys were Russian special forces. Did you know?" Kelly opened.

"Sure. If you have done what I have, you become a target for life. Somewhere, somehow they will get you. I was only surprised they wanted to kidnap me. I thought a bullet would have been easier. And God knows why they wanted you as well…"

"Perhaps it was bad timing, I happened to be with you."

"Come on, Des. You don't believe that, after what the Saudis tried to do? Your friend Aldo was telling me all about it, earlier. I think you have scared a lot of people to get that sort of attention."

"Well, I'll be a bit less scary when I retire."

"Retire? Are you going to quit?"

"I think about it sometimes. I am tired. I have done my bit. It's time for a new generation of experts to take over and I think you're the man for the job, especially following your performance today. You did very well. Besides, Sir Gavin rates you. Whatever you may think, he's the boss, and if you don't cut it with him, you won't succeed. Just look at Jake – not that clever, but streetwise. He won't be promoted any further. He's got too many friends in Washington, and his sidekick, Liebelt, I've never got on with. He always seems to be close when something goes wrong. Be careful of him. Looks the sort to have some questionable contacts with some of your old bosses. He once advocated doing a piece of joint research with Ukraine with some ex-KGB people. Said it would demonstrate that we were all working for world peace. And then there's our Welsh colleague, Williams. I got him all wrong. Didn't realise he was a spook looking after you."

"Neither did I," the Russian countered. "I got the impression he was there for you. It seems like you're the one who needs looking after."

They laughed.

"Well Boris, it only goes to prove that, whether you are in Kaliningrad or Oxford, it's best not to trust anyone. Anyway, I guess we'd both better get some sleep. We've only got a few hours of the night left."

*

The following morning Sue Kelly took Milo out for a walk, stopping at the driveway gate to collect the mail before returning to the house. It was such a routine thing to do, that although she would recover the mail from the box, she would not look at it until she got back to the kitchen door. This day was much the same as it ever was, except that her attention was caught by a handwritten letter addressed to her personally in a very neat script which she instantly recognised as belonging to Des. Her curiosity was instantly piqued, so she opened it without delay, before screaming and reaching for her phone. With Des on speed dial, she wouldn't have to wait long before it would be answered. Listening to the ringing tone, she could hear the muffled sound of a phone ringing in the study. She instantly realised that Des had left it behind when he set off to Denmark. As panic set in, her first action was to call first, Miles and second, Abigail, to ask if they knew anything about their father's movements. Then, Willoughby, whose phone was on voicemail and finally, Gavin. Of course, Gavin would be there in Denmark. He too was on voicemail, but for his benefit she left a more detailed message. There was nothing more she could do.

*

It would have been too late anyway, even if she had made contact. Kelly had risen just before dawn after just two hours' sleep. He had to meet Westergaard at the harbour. He had a tide to catch. He had come dressed for the occasion: T-shirt, water shorts, plimsolls.

"Good morning, Des. So now the preparation is complete. Are you ready and willing still to take the walk of destiny? This is the very last time you will be asked. From this moment forward you will take the path of judgement out there on the water in the light of the new day, your final day."

"Yes Nils, I am ready. Thank you and your team for your kindness and thorough preparation. I know it is time to commit my future to a higher authority."

"Very well. If you walk round to the foreshore on the coastal path you will see a red and white marker post. That is your starting position. I will meet you there, just slightly offshore where the sea is deep enough to take the draught of this little speedboat. When you see me, start walking out towards the boat. I can promise you the water will barely get over your ankles to begin with. When you reach me you will wait for me to move the boat to another position. While you are walking, I am checking the flow of the sand so that I can direct you towards the area of greatest undersea current. When I drop my hand you will again walk towards the boat. Then you will start the final journey. I do not expect we will ever meet again, but I can only hope you find the peace you have been looking for."

Kelly began his trek to the starting point and looked out at the flat calm water, sprinkled with diamonds of light in the early morning sun. His anxieties of the past few months seemed to have fallen away. People, situations, regrets. What lay ahead might be scary; he felt he was in transition from reality to something new, strangely enthralling, that he knew sooner or later he would experience. There he was, confronting uncertainty and greeting destiny on his own terms.

If his vision was sublime at the start of the process, committing his feet to the Wadden Sea seemed ridiculous. He wondered what anyone who happened to be watching would think – a typically mad Englishman abroad testing the waters.

He remembered the advice he had been given. Not to rush,

but to walk forward purposefully in a straight line and maintain a steady rhythm and metre. Keep his eyes fixed on the horizon and the coast of Sylt in front. Commune with nature. Listen out for the sound of the gentle wind, the cries of the myriad of birds waking up to the day, that faint smell of seaweed, the taste of salt on his tongue, the sloshing of the water, and the caress of the ebbing current on his ankles. This was starting to feel easy, too easy. His mind was wandering. This was the nearest sensation man could have to walking on water – a truly surreal, almost biblical experience. He arrived at the second and final rendezvous with Westergaard in his small boat.

"Keep going – don't stop. This is it! The moment has come. Goodbye and God bless."

For the first time, Westergaard was now behind him. Kelly didn't look back.

The water was getting deeper now, up above his knee. The effort expended to lift one leg in front of the other was greater. Each leg felt as though it had doubled in weight. The sandy floor was now less firm, his feet no longer resting on the surface but starting to sink down. He was starting to breathe more deeply. The water itself seemed noticeably colder and from a brief glance down, more opaque. Yet the promise of the experience beckoned him forward – nature's sparkling diamonds of sunlight glistening with more intensity on the water, the coast of Germany starting to reveal elements of detail. He was beginning to tire but knew this was the very feeling that would undermine his objective. He had to keep going, step after step after step. The water had now reached his waist and walking had become a sort of a sideways wading movement. Suddenly his left foot connected with some object, a stone or similar, causing him to stumble, falling forward, the dark water embracing his entire body. His natural reaction would have been to swim. Swim to survive – but this was not what he expected. He remained calm and focused. He wanted the treacherous sands of the Wadden to swallow him up now and he thought it was happening. At that moment there was nothing to connect to. No means of controlling his movement. The current was pinning him down, pulling him down, water invading his mouth and senses, banging on his ears, snatching the light away.

Now life itself was in the balance. The judgement of the years was now upon him. The coursing flow was taking control. This was no moment of review with his life passing in front of him, as most survivors of drowning recall. Breathing seemed impossible.

His world went black and still the diamonds danced in his head.

*

The bleary-eyed revellers from the night before had made their way back to the warehouse by the harbour. Industrial quantities of coffee and pastries awaited them. The morning session at the conference would be important. The first hour would consist of two plenaries which would give them the chance to come round before a series of workshop assessments and the concluding address from Sir Gavin.

Despite the delegates arriving in time, the session had not started and was running late. Winston Carter-Jones was refreshed and ready to go. Two of the key players of the morning session were notable by their absence – Kelly and Ponomariev.

Sir Gavin was not looking amused.

"*Fuck*, I knew it was all going too well," he muttered under his breath.

"I suppose he stayed up drinking until God knows when. Ifor, could you go round to his chalet and give him a shake?"

Williams nodded and headed for the exit just as Ponomariev came into the warehouse, ashen-faced.

"Sir Gavin, I'm so sorry to be late. I've been looking for Des everywhere."

"What do you mean?"

"He got up very early, I don't know what time it was, but it must have been before dawn. He left me a written message saying he was going for a jog and he'd see me here later. I knew he hadn't come back to the chalet when I left fifteen minutes ago. I hoped he might have come straight here. He said if you were pushed for time to use this…"

He held out a memory stick.

"He recorded a spare copy of his presentation, anticipating that you would ask him to do it anyway before the conference closed. Perhaps you could run this for now? No one would know it wasn't planned."

"Yes, yes… time is moving on and we need to get on with it. Give it to the sound engineer and I will introduce it after Mr Carter-Jones's presentation – assuming Des has not joined us by then."

Sir Gavin had always regarded Kelly as a maverick figure and had been surprised by how, in recent weeks, he had become more compliant with his management requests. To this point, he had been delighted with Kelly's work in bringing the whole event together, but rather than being alarmed by his absence, he assumed Des was missing on purpose, to demonstrate to all that he was a critical component of the Lauriston machine, and they couldn't manage without him. Sir Gavin made a mental note to tackle Kelly in due course for his perceived poor behaviour, which could result in a disciplinary. He turned to Bannan to apologise. Maybe it was because his guest was appearing as the dapper civil servant, Winston Carter-Jones, that he was gracious in accepting the apology, even sympathetic.

"Don't worry, Gavin. I quite understand. He must have been feeling the pressure of getting all this organised. He probably needed a bit of time out. Besides, I think it was quite something that he went to the trouble of recording his presentation, just in case."

WCJ's presentation was as predicted, a mixture of

congratulation for the Lauriston team for the pioneering research, the contribution it was offering the UK economy and the risk of losing competitive advantage with international collaboration without safeguards.

His message: "The Lauriston is at a crossroads regarding its future and only your hard work and the committed leadership of your management team can ensure you achieve the world-beating results I know you are capable of."

It was then time for Des to be formally introduced.

Sir Gavin took to the stage.

"Colleagues… friends. Everyone knows that the name of Dr Desmond Kelly is synonymous with the work of the Lauriston. His early discoveries have established him as the world's leading expert on HCCVD – a technology whose myriad of applications we are only just starting to understand. As many of you know, Des's commitment to organising this event to plan our future commercial activities has been obsessive and collectively we have much to thank him for, in organising this, our first ever residential conference."

He paused, to accept then join the audience applause. He continued, "Unfortunately, despite his best efforts, Des is unavoidably detained this morning and cannot be here in person…"

A few with sore heads in the audience smiled wryly.

"…but it is the mark of the man that he had the forethought to record his presentation just in case we decided to syndicate it to our partners unable to be with us today. So thanks to the wonders of modern communication, please welcome a virtual presentation from Dr Desmond Kelly."

Kelly's face then dominated the big screen. The presentation began.

"Hello everybody – I've been a bit presumptuous in recording this before we travelled to Denmark and have assumed that

so far you have found this to be a stimulating and worthwhile event. Our executive director, Sir Gavin Laidlaw, should be credited for this as he was the one who signed off the plan, so thank you to him…"

He went on to detail the Lauriston's achievements in the past year and the opportunities ahead, before concluding:

"The reality is that our future prospects depend on securing the long-term funding which the government cannot supply. We must make international multilateral commercial agreements to prosper, and the big money we can expect to earn will come from defence industry research budgets. As a scientist, I passionately believe that the discoveries we have made should benefit the world community as a whole and should not just be shared with the highest bidder or bidders, and so I find myself at odds with the Lauriston's corporate view. I am an idealist, a purist. If I wasn't, we would not have made the discoveries we have. In recent times I have been pressurised into changing my views – to share our discoveries with not just our own government, but those of the United States, Saudi Arabia, and even Russia. You should know I am no traitor, no liar, but a man of principle. Consequently, I have rejected them all, and in so doing concluded that, rather than providing limitless energy and a primary tool for fighting global warming, the HCCVD technology should be suspended until such time as a credible way to share the knowledge in a global context is found. That is not the job of scientists, but politicians. But what I have learned is this. If global leaders are to be motivated to do this, they, the politicians, need to be incentivised. I have taken it upon myself to ensure this happens. Recently I have been diagnosed with a terminal condition which would have meant that very shortly I would have had to step down from my role at the Lauriston. The

realisation of my impending demise has led me to conclude that I must take control of how and when I die. Taking control means I have documented everything I know about HCCVD and deposited it in a secret place with instructions that it is not to be published for twenty years, a timescale which allows time for the political community to settle their scores and map out a unified approach to global warming. This will be the time for HCCVD, always assuming you won't have discovered something better, in the meantime. Taking control has involved my hiring the expertise to assist me to die in a sustainable way. As you watch this, I can report that this very morning, with a clear head and heart, I have willingly taken myself out to sea to drown, to be consumed by the shifting sands of the Wadden Sea. I believe that as you watch me now on screen, in reality I died a few hours ago, secure in the belief that my personal and professional life is complete. I am tired. Tired of the stress of managing an innovative scientific research project within predetermined timescales, tired of being sucked into the politics of greed and envy. I am old. I have reached the end of the road. The end of my journey. I don't think there is any way back. I am content, but for me, there is no light at the end of the tunnel. That is not the case for the Lauriston. I am personally delighted that Dr Guntis Karins has joined us from the University of Riga. Having trained under who I consider to be one of the world's leading experts, Galina Rustanova, at the prestigious Russian Academy of Sciences in Moscow, Dr Karins is the person who combines the knowledge, intellect, and energy to realise the ambition of the Lauriston Foundation. In the short time I have worked with him he already seems like part of the family. I would urge you all to reflect on the new asset you have in the team and offer him your full support. It's time for me to say goodbye. I wish you all every success in your future endeavours and I have been proud to have been part of the Lauriston story."

As Kelly delivered his concluding remarks, an eerie silence filled the warehouse; so silent, in fact, that the only sound was the wind whistling outside. His passionate and personal speech had stunned most of the audience who heard it, except for two; Bannan and Williams, who had long worked on the basis that Kelly wanted out; but although suicide was a possibility, neither had been certain he had the bottle to go through with it. Sir Gavin took a sharp intake of breath as he saw in his mind the value of the Lauriston's assets tumbling. Jake Roberts looked alarmed, not least because, after this bombshell, he had to lead the coming workshop session.

Sir Gavin lived in the moment and took to the stage once again.

"Well, like the rest of you, I had no idea about Des's news. We're here in Denmark until this afternoon, so we will press on with our scheduled work programme for now. In the meantime, we will report this to the police immediately, so that they can investigate what has happened. I should make clear, that despite what Dr Kelly has told us, there can be no confirmation of the situation until he has been found. Given the sensitive situation we find ourselves in, I would remind you that this matter will be treated as confidential and commercially sensitive and will be within the scope of the Official Secrets definition in your employment contracts. Jakeman, over to you."

He stepped down and walked over to Bannan.

"*Fucking hell.* He's blasted us all down the tubes."

"I think you should take your own advice, Gavin," 'Winston' Bannan replied.

"This is now an exercise in damage limitation. You need a holding position. Find out what has happened to Kelly and more importantly, what he has done with all those files he kept in his head. By his own admission they are out there, *somewhere*. It is clear to me that what he has said and done is no impulsive act, but something he's planned for a while. It will need methodical investigation and he has already given you a clue – you'd better put the Russian in as an interim to manage his portfolio."

*

It had been six hours since the B474 had started its return journey to Kaliningrad and the time was dragging. They were now in the Skaggerak, this time taking the shortest and busiest sea lane that would bring them back into the Baltic, passing into the Kattegat, then south under the Oresund bridge – Copenhagen to the right, Malmo to the left. Poliarkin was moving as fast as he could. Although he had a wounded man on board who required hospitalisation, he couldn't risk stopping at any port on the way for fear of being impounded. It was a tragedy of the geography which meant there were no friendly ports between their present position and home. He had no choice but to press on. Medical services on board were the responsibility of the commissar, Moscovoi. Poliarkin had ordered him to do what he could to make Arbutsev comfortable below deck. Although competent in first aid, Arbutsev's injury was beyond his abilities. The victim was being sustained on a diet of vodka and morphine tablets, and drifting in and out of consciousness. Poliarkin knew that one way or another he would be required to file the report on their mission and took time out with him alone to understand the story of what had happened. Little by little, Arbutsev recounted the experience.

"We were close to success. The information from agent Lutz was good up to the last moments. We got to our targets and sedated them. We got them back to departure point and then it went wrong. We were ambushed on the foreshore and came under heavy automatic fire. It was dark and most of the rounds went high. We were taken by surprise. Under that level of attack we had to pull out or else we could all have been killed. The others were back in the inflatable. I had hesitated, wondering whether we could just turn around and snatch the two bodies. I had seen a new message in from agent Lutz, which I was trying to read, when some bastard appeared on his own at the water's edge and fired a single shot directly at me. I went down and was fished out by the boys, but the phone disappeared in the sea, so quite what the message was I'll never know."

"So, somebody knew you were coming?"

"Yes, they must have done; we wouldn't have come under such a sustained attack without preparation."

"Agent Lutz?"

"I can't think of anybody else."

Poliarkin already knew the answer. He had traded information about the mission to rub out his debt to Grigor Zanowsky and the Gdansk mafia in the interests of future business. It was ironic that the missing money had in effect been stolen from him by Arbutsev to buy his Kaliningrad apartment. Now the investigator was paying the price. He found it hard to reconcile the description of sustained fire with the image of a lone gunman suddenly appearing to take a pot shot. The sustained firing suggested several people loosing off ordnance from separate positions. It was remarkable that none of them seemed to have hit a target and then suddenly, they stop, clearing the way for the solo shooter. Despite it being dark, Arbutsev had had a clear sight of the silhouette of his assailant, tall and thin, which certainly fitted Grigor's profile. Were they all part of a team? Did the gang responsible for the sustained fire stop when they saw the lone gunman, who was evidently not one of the raiders who landed from the sea? Did Arbutsev, clearly in pain, have a clear recollection of the timescales? The sustained shooters may have decided they had already done enough to foil the snatch. If Arbutsev had it right, who recovered the bodies from the beach? He didn't give it any further thought, having recognised that he was in enough trouble anyway. The information the skipper had collected would be offered to Arbutsev's people if he didn't pull through, and hopefully, that would tally with the military men's account when they got back to their unit. The fact that Arbutsev had lost his mobile phone concerned Poliarkin the most. This must have been the means to talk to his bosses in Moscow, who doubtless would be alarmed by the apparent radio silence since the mission had started its return journey. In thinking ahead, Poliarkin had almost missed one vital consideration. While on board, Arbutsev was in the care of Moscovoi. He was clearly aware of their mutual dislike. He called Moscovoi to the wheelhouse.

"You know that there will be all sorts of shit flying about when we get home as we failed to do the pick-up. I want Arbutsev to take all the blame. We were just conscripts, after all, and we need to get back to our normal lives without fuss. If Arbutsev dies before we get home, there will be real trouble for all of us. Understand? Your job is to make sure he survives, because, if he doesn't, you won't have anywhere to hide."

Moscovoi didn't answer. He didn't have to. There was anger in his eyes. He had been recruited as an insurance policy against the risk of being boarded by the Danish pilot and fortunately he and his charts were no longer required. His contribution had amounted to nothing else, until now. The new responsibility of keeping a wounded man, who he detested, alive for the next forty-eight hours weighed heavily on his mind. He nodded and returned to the chart room.

*

"Is that Sir Gavin Laidlaw? Hi – Hector Birnbaum from Maximum Power in New York. I have Eve Grainger in the office and have just finished talking to Chuck Barnes in London and Bob Kleiner in Washington. Eve tells me you've been running a very successful corporate planning event in Denmark, of all places! Smart thinking! As the polar ice sheet melts those Danes are gonna get a whole deal more important, selling prospecting rights in Greenland. If you have any useful contacts there, let me know. I think our president pissed them a bit by offering to buy it off them. I guess they'd much rather deal with you Brits. Anyway, maybe we can find a way of doing just that. We've been reconsidering our takeover pitch and have decided it would be better for all concerned if we set up a joint venture business to pool our research expertise. That way we can make a long-term financial commitment to the Lauriston, build the brand and focus on commercialising your innovations. We can each take a share of the intellectual property, while we will own the development risk. We could call it 'Lauriston MPI – Maximum Power Innovations'. Sweet eh? This way we can keep all the regulators out of our hair and get on with the business; it won't even affect our market valuation. I know there's a lot of speculation about what will happen with Kelly out of the way. Tell you what, if our roles were reversed, we'd be sweating it out in Wall Street right now, but this plan doesn't depend on that type of speculation. We'll even let you guys have a say about who is brought in to run it. One condition from this end, Sir Gavin, we need the JV to be based at Fort Bragg in North Carolina. It's our shop window and that's the place we need to be to get the big research bucks. So waddayah say? The president likes it and he's already said he's gonna talk to your prime minister, Barnes and Kleiner like it and I *love* it! Are we gonna get this thing on? I've got Eve here ready to get back on the plane to London with all the paper. Shall I send her to the airport? She could be with you in the morning."

Laidlaw had to hand it to Birnbaum. He saw he was at a low ebb and knew now was the time to strike. Besides, Laidlaw badly needed a win. He had lots of stakeholders, including several in government, who were not convinced the Lauriston could go on as a viable organisation without Desmond Kelly. The whiff of conspiracy and intrigue about Kelly's apparent suicide was still the subject of conjecture in the media world and the likely appointment of Guntis Karins, however brilliant, would only add to the story. The announcement of a comprehensive collaboration agreement with Maximum Power Corporation would steady the ship, reassuring nervous public funders and boosting its reputation.

"OK, I'll take a look at it."

"Great. I'll send Eve on her way. You've got my personal direct dial. Call me when you're ready to talk."

NINETEEN

SINCE RETURNING FROM DENMARK, Sir Gavin had been in two minds about heading over to the Kelly residence in the Thames Valley. On one hand, as Des's employer he felt a moral obligation to offer any assistance necessary to the Kellys to cope with their loss. On the other, the risk of his relationship with Sue being rekindled could lead to even more problems for him in navigating the future development and reputation of the Lauriston business. Facing the dilemma, he settled on a third way, a fudge. Yes, he would pay a visit, but would keep it short. He had dallied with the idea of taking a member of his team along as a chaperone but dismissed it as being 'over the top'.

He would go for a coffee; that would be all.

Arrival at the Kellys' seemed a strange experience in the knowledge that Des was unlikely to return. As luck would have it he had ended up meeting Sue on the drive as she was loading a tray of homemade pasties into her car to take down to the pub.

Momentarily surprised, her body stiffened as he approached and she offered a faint smile.

"Hello, Sue, I was just passing. I just wanted to check how you were and whether you needed any help."

He read her embarrassment. He continued, "I guess it's a bit soon to come round, but as Des's employer—"

Sue interrupted, "You thought you'd better show up. Well, as Des's employer, you should know that for now, everything is all right. I am helping Miles at the pub and Milo is getting exercised regularly on my trips there when I am not carrying food. Abigail is doing fine, thank you for asking, and is coming back from filming next week. We learned a lot when Abi was taken, about coping with uncertainty and who our friends really are. Des sent me a personal letter saying he was going away and might not be back. I called you in Denmark to get a message to him before he went and you didn't reply."

"I did react. I reported it to the police immediately and they are investigating. Des used an assisted dying service, which is not illegal there. We were too late."

She started to cry. Instinctively, he hugged her. Despite the circumstances, the familiar smell of her perfume was intoxicating, her body close to his, arousing.

"And how do you know he is dead? Where is his body? How can we have a funeral? How do you expect me to move on?"

He tried to comfort her. "They are searching the area where he disappeared, but apparently it's difficult, as it's filled with moving quicksand. I've heard it's possible they will never recover his body. Then I suppose there will need to be an inquest."

"Oh God. This is his revenge – to make me feel permanently guilty."

"Revenge?"

She pulled away.

"Yes, revenge – in the letter I told you about, he mentioned he knew of our affair."

Sir Gavin looked ruffled.

"But how? We were always so careful."

"The bloody security camera on the front door. He was able to watch it remotely on his phone. He kept a diary of your visits. The damn thing didn't seem to work properly when the house was burgled months back, but apparently, picked up your visits."

"He never said anything."

"He didn't have to. That's the man he is… *was.*"

He told her about Des's recorded conference presentation.

"He was strangely rational and matter of fact about the whole thing. He had certainly been planning it for some months, even before we decided to hold the conference."

He paused.

"Look, Sue, I understand this is all pretty stressful and it seems it has some way yet to run. It's probably best if we don't see each other while the situation in settling down. We don't need any unfortunate gossip slowing down the wheels of justice right now. Isn't your son lined up to be a witness at that murdered landlord's forthcoming hearing at the Old Bailey? That will certainly be making the news."

"I will be going to court to support Miles, but only because he's a bit nervous. He's not the accused, but this character Suker, the one on trial, has some Turkish mafia connections in north London and he's worried about being threatened for giving evidence. But I need support, too. I need you to be there."

"Yes, well keep me in touch as things progress and I'll see what I can do."

It was not the statement of support she was expecting.

"Don't dismiss me, Gavin, I am saying I need your help. You were keen enough to offer it when you were fucking me."

Laidlaw visibly winced.

"As I said, it's a complicated situation, and we don't need to do anything that will make it harder for any of us."

"Gavin!"

"I must dash, Sue. I've got a VIP visitor from the States in the office this afternoon. Keep me posted."

"If you walk away now, that's it. It's over."

Sir Gavin walked briskly to his car and blew her a kiss.

Her heart sank as she listened intently to the tyres of his car grinding the gravel on the drive.

*

It was rare these days for Williams to be called into the office south of the river. More surprising still that Bannan had called him in so quickly following their return from Denmark.

The Welshman guessed there had been some urgent development requiring action on his part.

"It seems that, one way or another, the aftershocks of the Kelly quake rumble on," Bannan began. "I'm sorry we were not able to prevent his suicide, poor bugger. He was clearly in a worse condition than we thought. I have to admit I was wrong about that. I thought this was just a front to get that overbearing Laidlaw off his back. But there we are. However, we did at least get the important part of the job done. We stopped any possibility of the Lauriston research falling into unfriendly hands."

"Does that include the Americans, sir?"

"That will be dealt with separately by due process. Our work with the Saudis and managing the Russian thing was well received by the prime minister, especially the fact that we have managed to protect our contractors in Gdansk, which will help us to keep an eye on what is happening in Kaliningrad. All that notwithstanding, I wanted to tell you personally about Chemmy. Yesterday I received her resignation from the service. Seems she has taken up with that Triore and is moving to Copenhagen."

"What? After that undercover stuff? How has she managed that?"

"I'm not sure exactly, but it will come out in her debrief. Apparently, she met him again in Rømø last week when she was technically off duty. I can't really interfere. She will need to be compliant with the OSA and my opposite number in Denmark, Neilsen, will have her on a routine watch list. Unfortunately, Triore may have a low moral compass in my book, but he and the rest of Westergaard's Terminal colleagues are clean. The implications for you are clear. If you receive any contact from her you are to report it. Secondly, you are to remain in your role in the Lauriston for the time being. We need to monitor how the situation with Maximum Power Corporation develops. Don't worry about Ponomariev. He is the only one who knows of your connection here, and has far too much to lose, even if he were minded to confide in anyone else. The Kelly issue will remain sensitive while it concludes, so regard this time now as winding down your responsibilities. I expect to pull you out altogether in around eight weeks from now, so if I were you, I'd be planning a get-away-from-it-all holiday before being reassigned." Bannan had decided it was time to close the Kelly case. Time also for Winston Carter-Jones to take a break.

*

Bannan had been wise to keep Williams at the Lauriston for time being, but perhaps not for the reasons he had expected, and the fall-out from Kelly's departure was still being felt. In line with his thorough approach to his demise, Kelly had written a personal letter to Ponomariev and slipped it into the Russian's suitcase before leaving the chalet for the last time.

Dear Boris or should I say Guntis (!)

I realise my sudden departure from the Lauriston will have come as a shock, but perhaps upon reflection, you will be more understanding. In my quieter moments, I have surprised myself with my actions. Given my medical diagnosis, the idea of taking responsibility for arranging my own death has been hard for me to come to terms with, but in the end the prospect became so compelling I thought I had to see it through. Voluntarily planning the end of life is a challenge – there is so much to do and say. As you know I love being organised and my goal was to avoid leaving loose ends before my departure. Sharing my sentiments with you was one such. I have to tell you how my experience of working with you in recent months at the Lauriston has been a personal joy. Engaging your professional expertise has been stimulating for me and added value to our work. Although, as you know, I am less keen on the military applications of the HCCVD technology, I have to concede your studies on missile propulsion have moved its practical application forward at least five years. Well done! It is hard for me to say, but in one sense I was glad you experienced personal persecution and harassment in Kaliningrad because, perhaps, without it you wouldn't have taken the risk to leave. Although you are not allowed to talk about it in detail, I am led to believe your private circumstances are resolved and that you are happy in your new home with us in Oxford. You have a stellar career ahead of you at the Lauriston and to my mind, you are the natural successor to me as research director. Sir Gavin is also aware of my view. So it would seem the future of the Lauriston is safe in your capable hands. Use the opportunity wisely, and don't look back. Be careful, though, I have reason to believe your colleague Werner still has connections with the old country. He may well be informing on your activities. The real reason why I have had to write to you is not just to say goodbye and good luck. I have discovered some even more important information by chance that you need to know.

You will recall some weeks ago that you shared a meal at my home with other members of my family. It was a rare moment when everyone was assembled in one place at one time. On that occasion you seemed to be more than a guest in my home. You felt like one of the family. One of my personal family. To my amazement I have discovered that indeed you are my son, from a relationship I had before I met my present wife. Your mother became known to you once you had left high school and enrolled in the Academy of Sciences in Moscow. Unbeknown to you, she became your professional mentor and tutor. She is Galina Rustanova. You were conceived as a result of a brief liaison we had in Vienna some thirty years ago. She gave you up for adoption to save her own career. We had stayed in touch over the years, and I only learned of the connection with you very recently. I have no idea how you will respond, but in leaving this life, I understand you had a right to know. Your mother does not know yet that I have shared this information, but I do understand her reasons for keeping quiet all these years. I met her in London recently. She told me of your upbringing with loving step-parents and recognised that your career was under enough personal pressure without having to deal with this situation. Now she is married to someone in the military with two younger children to look after. Looking back, when I first heard this news, I was as shocked as you are on reading this. I have to say, my relationship with your mother endured not because of you, but because we became professional colleagues on the international science mentoring circuit. I have taken the treasured memory of my short time with her in Vienna to my death. In my head it seems like yesterday. Have no doubt you were conceived out of an enduring love, not lust. I regret I took too many years to realise it. If fate brings you and your mother together again I urge you to be gentle. I have no doubt her intentions were good. Have a happy life!

Yours,

Des.

The Russian had kept the letter to himself now for over a week. He needed to talk to someone and, knowing of Williams's past, brought it to his door.

"Read it and tell me what you think," he said.

Williams studied it for a minute before responding.

"Wow! Who would have believed it? I didn't think Des had secrets like that. He's right about Liebelt. We are watching him. I wonder how he knew? Must have been your mum who told him. Has anyone else seen it?"

"No."

"What are you going to do?"

"Destroy it. My life here is just starting to take shape as a free gay man. My adoptive parents gave me the care I needed and worked night and day to put me through my studies. Rustanova helped me establish myself in the Navy, for which I am grateful, but that is all. I cannot care for her as a mother. Besides, if I had any doubt, this news only confirms that I was right to leave and, as Des said – I can't look back now."

*

Des had written one more final letter – to Galina. In some ways, this had been the hardest to write; he found it difficult to find the right way to talk to her, as she was an ex-lover, friend, confidante, and professional colleague rolled into one. He took a risk in writing it and committing it to the post. He could not be certain it would arrive or whether it would be scanned by unseen eyes first. He comforted himself with the idea that in the age of electronic communication the days of old-fashioned spying had gone. Would anyone pay attention to something as basic as an ordinary letter? Most espionage was conducted through sophisticated electronic hacking systems online, so in reality, his message was more likely to be intercepted if it was sent in an email. Besides, as his final communication he needed to demonstrate he spoke from the heart, meaning it needed to be handwritten. It had been penned from his study in the Thames Valley and posted before he made his final departure to Denmark.

In the moment his mood was taken by listening to Shostakovich's 'Chamber Symphony in C minor', a poignant piece, said to be inspired by the horrors of the Second World War. Combined with the setting of the sun, the view looking across his expansive front lawn towards the cluster of lights of the village centre and a tumbler of Macallan, it helped him to tune into what he considered to be the quasi-tragic soul of the Russian psyche, something he felt he understood.

My dearest Galina,

I am not used to writing letters so when I feel moved to do so you can be sure I have something important to impart. Writing to you is not a risk for me, but I have no idea about how that leaves you in receiving it. Also, I cannot be sure it will even arrive, but here's hoping!

I was delighted we were able to get together last month in London. As I left you that night, I reflected on times we have had dinner at sometime or another at conferences on almost every continent, over the past thirty years. Those times when our respective governments allowed us to meet and enjoy each other's company as ordinary people were, for me, stand-out moments, which rank alongside any professional milestone I have ever achieved. Our friendship has stood the test of time – transcended the ups and down of global politics. We have shared personal and professional triumphs and setbacks and I hope in some measure helped us both to succeed in our careers. You were gracious and caring when I first shared my personal diagnosis. It was a difficult thing to discuss and yet for some reason, I felt confident about sharing it. I drew strength from you to confront my situation, so thank you. Of course, I have been delighted to hear news of your family and happy that, despite the pressures, you have succeeded in forming a settled domestic life alongside your professional responsibilities. Although as you will recall, I was shocked to hear about Boris, I was also proud of the product of our relationship. He has developed into a fine man and an excellent scientist with the capability to eclipse us both. It demonstrates how strange life is and how coincidence can strike in unexpected ways. Another example of life's unpredictability was your offer to help me to recover from my predicament with the prospect of specialist medical treatment in Moscow as well as your idea of helping me to access it. I can only imagine how difficult it must have been to put your reputation on the line to be able to make the offer and the favours you must have cashed in to make it happen. There was a time when I seriously contemplated doing it. Coming to Moscow to get better – but then what? Trading my health for my professional expertise to be used against my own countrymen? Once I had shared my knowledge what would be left? A lonely old man with a husk of a brain, living out his days in some anonymous state tenement block? Certainly, no prospect of getting old with you. And then Boris, could I really expect to persuade him to return to Russia, when he had risked everything to escape? Could you have protected him from the retribution that would follow? 'A traitor returned'. Undermined professionally and personally harassed, if not killed? If the plan were to succeed, I would have had to tell him about his true parentage and even if I had had done so, I could not have any understanding of how he would react. No, although it was well meaning it would be impossible for me to accept your invitation, and it is with a heavy heart I say this, as I know this is likely to impact on your own reputation. However, even if you were half the woman I know you to be, in your quieter moments, I think you will understand. My worry is this letter will not arrive before the collection arrangements are instigated and therefore the initiative is doomed to end in failure from the start, but there is nothing I can do about that now. I am sorry. Now to the future. What future? I am approaching the end of the road – leaving for Denmark shortly to bring my life to a managed conclusion while I still have the ability. I have engaged an assisted dying service to help me. I am sure I could have procured a similar service in Moscow for much less cost!

But at heart I know when the time comes, I won't be so brave. I have chosen a relatively quick and painless route that leaves no trace. I will leave my thoughts behind, but nothing more. I hope you will take pride in our son's bright prospects. I have left documentation to support his case to succeed me at the Lauriston and am confident about his chances. Also, I have written to him as I have written to you. Part of my closure is to offer the benefit of my experience. That tells me that I feel obliged to tell him about his real mother in the hope, someday, somewhere, somehow you can both be reconciled. It is one of my final greatest hopes. So that is all. Maybe we'll meet again in a better place, whatever that may be. In closing you should know you have both my love and personal respect. I know I will miss you badly.

Take care!
Des.

The letter arrived at its destination but took a week to make the journey to Moscow. Too late to stop the snatch but in time to confirm the unexpected demise of Nikitin.

The conversation was brokered by the announcer on the Moscow One breakfast TV news reporting an accident the previous evening at Lubyanka Metro station.

According to the report an unfortunate passenger on the crowded platform lost their balance as a train was entering the station. No other details or explanation was offered but it did give Ruslan the opportunity to comment, while Galina was making porridge for the family.

"There you go," he said. "I heard on social media earlier it was Nikitin. Pity about that. Shows the risk of overworking. When you're tired you get careless. Bet he just missed his footing at the crucial moment. There's a lesson in that for us all. Still, I suppose that's one less thing to worry about. It only took the FSB a couple of hours to put a new man in his place – Commander

Yuri Orlov. He's a man experienced in being on secondment – a caretaker journeyman. He's no threat. He used to be big in the artillery forces before going to the GRU to run an efficiency drive. Apparently, he's already letting it be known he is to run an inquiry into Nikitin's use of state funds as an immediate priority. That means they'll cut the military honours bit from the funeral arrangements and downplay his importance. Doesn't look good for the establishment, if one of their own gets rubbed out, especially in such an everyday sort of way. It's a shame I won't be able to go. I'll have to get back to Murmansk by then."

Galina knew better than to enquire why Ruslan appeared to have become such an expert on the health of the FSB's director, calling to the children to come and eat breakfast. While she waited, she said, "It's probably for the best. I got a letter from my friend Desmond in the UK yesterday. He told me he had decided not to come, so the snatch would have failed anyway. If Nikitin had been in charge he would have implicated us to save his skin. Now he will carry the can for the whole thing."

She raised her voice. "Come on boys, your breakfast is getting cold, you'll be late for school!"

There was little point in talking to Ruslan further. To do so would be to betray her loyalty to her husband and her love for the Englishman who had sentenced himself to death *and* to heighten her guilt for losing contact with her first child, a defector, a 'non-person' who it was best not to mention anymore. For a fleeting moment, she realised she must have been crazy to think her plan to bring the father and son to Russia could have worked in the first place. Even if the mission to collect them had been successful, Des's comments in his letter were right. There was no future in it.

It was now time to forget Desmond, and their shared past of fleeting moments. This was the notice of closure of an important part of her own life. She would miss him.

*

The squally weather and the heavy sea had been improving as they tracked east. Poliarkin started to pick up the navigation buoys marking the approach to the Pregolya estuary. A flock of seagulls had arrived overhead assuming they would find some rich pickings. They were now on the final approach and despite the emerging hazy sunshine, try as he might, he could not help feeling anxious about the return. He had radioed his impending arrival to the harbourmaster's office and been told to go to his normal berth at Baltiyskya Kosa. At least Moscovoi had kept Arbutsev alive in the past hours and he knew a medical transfer was being arranged across the water to the hospital at the Baltiysk naval station.

Approaching the quay, their arrival seemed to have sparked some unusual activity. Yes, some of his temporary guests were gathering on the rails to wave to well-wishers on the shore, but the numbers waiting seemed to be bigger than those usually assembled to buy fish directly from the boat. He had expected the medical team but there was a large military cutter (similar in size to his trawler), crewed and ready, waiting in the estuary nearby. Normally when the B474 returned from a fishing trip it would be tied up to a couple of other boats and not directly to the quay. Today was different. Other vessels had been moved out of the way to make space for them to be lashed to the concrete posts on shore. The bosun revved the engines into reverse for a final time, the vessel vibrating and kicking out a noxious cloud of black smoke before dying to silence. Poliarkin knew, as the skipper, that he needed to send a signal to anyone watching that he was in charge. He made sure he was the first to walk the gangway to dry land. Meeting him were two officials, one clearly a naval officer, the other a woman in her forties in a trenchcoat.

"Skipper Poliarkin, we have not met before. My name is Lieutenant Volkov, Russian Navy intelligence. This is Investigator Anna Kuznetsova from the FSB in Kaliningrad. We have been fully briefed on your activities and your colleagues will all be detained for interview before being allowed to go home. We know you were retained by the FSB under the authorisation of Colonel Dimitri Nikitin, Senior Investigator Arbutsev's boss, in Moscow. I am sorry to report that Colonel Nikitin has met with an unfortunate accident while you were away and has been replaced by Commander Yuri Orlov, who has appointed Investigator Kuznetsova to represent his interest. I should say that nobody here is questioning your work, Poliarkin. In fact, even if you were unsuccessful in making the snatch, you succeeded in getting everybody back without leaving some embarrassing mess for us to deal with. So thank you. Nonetheless, there are some questions we need your help with, regarding the authorisation for the mission to take place, and certainly we will be talking to Arbutsev about this in more detail once we have him cleaned up across the water. His leg is a mess, he might lose it, but we will see. The patrol boat will take Arbutsev and our military team back to the naval station. Everyone else will go to the harbourmaster's office for questioning. Please excuse the guards, they are only here to check that we have everyone and that nobody is missing."

*

Two hours later Poliarkin and the rest of his crew were released and able to return home. He was pleased to have had the personal discussion with Arbutsev on the return trip so that he could give a full account of what had taken place. During his interview it was the woman who was taking careful notes; the Navy man seemed only to have a partial interest. Once they had decided they had squeezed all the relevant information out of him, the investigator came to the point.

"We have received instructions from Moscow to delist all public records of the mission. You will need to sign a declaration promising not to discuss the matter with anyone ever again. It will be as if the trip never took place. Failure to comply will make you eligible for arrest and prosecution. I think, Skipper Poliarkin, this will be of concern to a man like you. It is unusual to find someone of… your maturity without a criminal record. Quite an achievement in my experience. It would be a pity to leave a stain on your character at your time of life."

Poliarkin was relieved by the remark. It confirmed that Arbutsev had wiped the records as he had said he would before they set sail for Denmark.

He nodded his head vigorously in agreement.

"I'm looking forward to getting back to my life as a fisherman, once I have got the hold cleared out."

The investigator smiled at him.

"There's one final thing. As we are clearing the records of any documentation which relates to this case it also means that, from an accounting position, we cannot pay you for the trip. You have already had help with fuel and food, so I hope that is sufficient."

Bastards, he thought, these government people always fuck you over in the end.

*

"Is that Hector Birnbaum? Hector, good to speak to you. Gavin Laidlaw. I'm in my office in Oxford with Eve. We have got through the Heads of Terms and subject to diligence on your valuation and IP plus capital investment guarantees I think, as you would say – we have a deal."

"Great news, Gavin – how do you think it will play out with your government people?"

"There's a lot to like here. You have been smart and found a way through most of the regulatory stuff that would slow us down. I think the thing that will really sell it is what you are prepared to do to guarantee jobs in the UK. If we find ourselves sitting on a major US contract secured because of our technological advantage you know they will want a slice of the action on the manufacturing side."

"OK – I'll get Chuck Barnes and Bob Kleiner to take the president through it and he can take it up with your prime minister. What about the recruitment angle?"

"We have to be the 'best in class' at every stage in this game. On the research side over here, the logical appointment is to put in place Kelly's deputy, Guntis Karins, in that role. He has a brilliant mind and track record to match. More importantly, no one understands what Kelly was doing on HCCVD better than him. As far as our new joint venture is concerned, you need to put in place a high-profile figure with global credibility in the industry. The best guy out there now is the Italian, Professor Dr Aldo de Leonibus. However, I have heard he's negotiating with the Saudis on another big deal to run their nuclear regulatory organisation and I'm sure they are talking big bucks. If you agree he fits your profile, I wouldn't delay in tracking him down. It might be a good move to put Jake Roberts in as his deputy. That would allow Karins a clear opportunity to put his own team in place. From what I can understand, he doesn't rate Liebelt and wants him out."

"Yeah, I get it. Eve has introduced me to de Leonibus. I know a few people who speak well of him. I saw him present in Berlin a couple of months back as well and I think he's done a few seminars here in New York. Where's he based?"

"Last time I heard, Sofia, Bulgaria, but he's one of these people who is always travelling around the place so it might take you a while to get hold of him."

"OK, Gavin. I'll get Eve onto it. In the meantime, get your attorneys to mark up the drafts and I'll take a look. I think if this is gonna work out the way we want, you'll have to take a seat on the Maximum Power board, and it's probably sensible for Eve to have a similar role at the Lauriston. Think about it. I'm already getting excited about you and me doing a signing with your PM and our guy at the White House – that will really make the headlines."

In his enthusiasm Birnbaum dropped the phone. The buzzing sound on his desk-top speaker drew a smile from Eve. It was clearly

Birnbaum's way of making a point.

The prospect of a new influential transatlantic role as a director of an international energy conglomerate, running alongside his existing responsibility at the Lauriston, would be a promotion commensurate with Laidlaw`s status. Who knows? Potentially a seat in the House of Lords might be offered once the ink was dry on the contract.

TWENTY

LIFE IN THE THAMES Valley at the Kelly household was still far from normal, but there were signs it was slipping into a routine. The mystery of Des's disappearance was still unresolved and would remain so, until the coroner's hearing; and assuming there was no more news from Denmark, there was little more to be said. It was not a topic any member of the family wished to dwell on. The best way of dealing with it was to keep busy. Sue had largely suspended her social life to avoid being asked too many questions. Singing in the church choir and playing bridge had been dropped for the moment and was only countenanced in emergencies if the vicar was short of a soprano or if she was needed to make up a four; their places being taken by cooking and preparing lunches and evening snacks as well as acting as the Dog & Duck's front of house landlady. At first, she hadn't really liked the idea of the role, but as she became more familiar with the way Miles was running the business, she grew in confidence. The real advantage was being able to pursue a superficial social life from behind the bar which gave her an air of authority. Because she couldn't be avoided, locals would make conversation with her, but none dared ask about the absence of Des; rather they concentrated on observing and sharing their memories of Bryan. Her new life helped her not to dwell on past relationships, especially the betrayal she felt she had suffered by the egotistical Gavin Laidlaw, who had dropped her to save his career. Miles seemed to be liberated by his new job as the licensee, which had already provided him with an income broadly in line with his wages from his London job plus flexible hours to match. Already the change was generating a marked upturn in fortune with his social life and his regular commitment to a weekly night out with a different girlfriend seemed to be settling down into a routine.

Although he shared the concern about his father, Miles knew that practically there was nothing he could do to resolve the situation. Besides, his worries had been focused on his appearance as a witness at Suker's murder trial.

When summoned, his lawyer had warned him that the evidence presented in court might be slightly at odds with his own recollection of events. The Crown Prosecution Service had instructed that the circumstances leading to the offence, Suker's then unproven link to Abigail's abduction, was inadmissible for reasons of national security. The case would be presented on an unfortunate coincidence which, by chance, had led to Bryan and Miles entering the Topkapi Nights restaurant just after it had been ransacked by thugs, as yet unidentified. The case would be based on Suker's mistaken assumption that in some way Bryan had been responsible for the restaurant attack and his subsequent murder was in revenge. He had been coached to ensure his answers to questioning would be short, to the point and at all costs to avoid 'the temptation to engage in speculation'. It had gone according to plan. Attending court, he had seen Willoughby, who had seemed relaxed. After all, he had got the 'collar' and the evidence was undeniable, a fact accepted by the accused himself, who, in turn, had been advised to keep quiet in the expectation of a lighter sentence and perhaps early parole.

The outcome was predictable – murder was murder – but a term of twenty years was the minimum he could have expected.

Some way, somehow, Abigail had been kept out of it. No news was released regarding her abduction. Given the fickle nature of the press, much of the detail had been forgotten. Word on the street had picked up on whispers it was a put-up job to promote a new film, providing a platform to launch another young, attractive, and potentially bankable British starlet on the road to fame and fortune in Hollywood.

Like her mother and brother, Abigail had come to terms with the absence of her father and the likelihood that he was now dead. But she felt a sense of confusion because of the lack of information and a body. Without a body there could be no certainty about his death. Without a body there could be no closure, no funeral. But despite the problems of the situation the world was moving on, her life was moving on. She was now swapping life as a casual extra in a laundry commercial for that of a serious career in the movies. She had come into money as a result of her Middle Eastern ordeal and was able to use it to bankroll an otherwise unachievable dream to star in and produce an independent film that would establish her as a serious performer. If this went well, the prospect of auditioning for leading roles alongside some of the biggest names in the business would be hers, and she wouldn't have to take her clothes off to achieve it.

The movie world was competitive, like any other commercial activity, normally driven by the need to attract investment. This project was different. The issue here was not the money but the creative treatment. The money offered by the Saudi government was useful, but in the context of the project as a whole, insignificant. The challenge for her was to come up with a screenplay capable of attracting investment from members of the wider ruling family. To do that, the story line would need to be officially sanctioned and consequently, access to the exclusive locations in the country granted.

She had been advised that to secure the broad support she needed for the project from the Kingdom, she had to organise a glitzy launch event to set out the plan. It had to be impressive enough to attract some of the biggest names in independent cinema – directors, producers, actors as well as critics, journalists and photographers from the movie world. An evening weeknight event in central London was the settled option, and the BAFTA offices in Piccadilly the natural location. She had made a modest investment in PR with a promise for those attending to go on to a private room at the exclusive Sirocco nightclub nearby. With half her initial gift from the Saudi government committed, she had reasoned that she wouldn't miss the money she had never earned. Besides if her plan was successful, in the space of a few hours her budget would increase in multiples of ten or more.

*

Although many of the professionals she needed to work with from the independent cinema world accepted her invitation, few were known to the general public, and were not necessarily regarded as the type of box office material she needed to impress her potential backers. But luck seemed to be smiling on her. Logan Chalmers, a veteran Hollywood A-lister, was in town on a private trip and frantic calls from her party organiser secured his presence. It was a sad fact that Chalmers' presence would generate more attention than anything she could do or say, and the reality was that he understood the pulling power of his personal brand. Fortunately Chalmers was the type of star who remembered just how difficult it was to get into the business and offered to attend at no charge, partly out of curiosity, to understand what was happening.

He had taken for granted the professionalism of the presentation. The platform for speeches, the set for photographs, the management. Although modest by his standards, this looked like a project with the sort of backing he would be interested in. He made it his business to do plenty of pictures with this girl,

Abigail. He had no idea whether she could act, but hey, she was pretty, and he thought they looked good together.

He allowed her to introduce him to several of her guests, some with track records in movies he had heard of but not necessarily seen. Attending with his personal assistant in tow, he regularly called over his shoulder to her to "check this out". The girl was following him around, noting names and other necessary details.

With the need to get as much attention as possible, the focus of the event was to formally announce her movie project, and so she had decided to do it with the minimum of fuss. An hour into the gathering she took to the stage.

"Ladies and gentlemen. Thank you for taking time out to be here tonight. My name is Abigail Kelly. I am aware you have plenty of other things to do on a rainy Wednesday in central London. This show is probably a bit different to most of the others you attend such as private viewings or opening nights. We are here to announce a major new project, perhaps the biggest commission ever for a debutante star and producer. But before we unveil our plans, allow me to welcome a special and unexpected guest, direct from Hollywood, Mr Logan Chalmers. Thanks so much for coming, Logan – your support is appreciated."

The star nodded his acknowledgement.

"Something which is different about tonight is that many people here know each other but not necessarily me. It's hardly surprising, as I am just starting out on my career. And unless you are a fan of Magical Glo laundry powder, you may not have seen me before on any screen, large or small. My story is a simple one. I have wanted to be in the movies since I was in kindergarten and have never grown out of it, although I have always spent time trying to convince everyone I met who had any sort of link to the industry that they should hire me. The thing that makes me different, is that I have the opportunity to invest in my own talent. Not so long ago I came into some money unexpectedly and am using it to back my own career. I will be successful because I am good at learning from others and I am trying to surround myself with a team of winners that will get my project off the table and into cinemas across the country, and who knows, maybe beyond."

She was interrupted by applause.

"Anyway, if you are interested in me, I'm sure we'll get a chance to talk later.

"The news you need to know is that I am planning a new version of *One Thousand and One Nights* based on Scheherazade's final story of *The Three Princes*, with the legendary storyteller seductress, using never-before-seen locations in the Kingdom of Saudi Arabia. Considering the number of movie versions based on the books, dating forward from John Rawlins's iconic 1942 version with Maria Montez, to the 2000 two-part mini-series with Mili Avital for Hallmark, I will endeavour to bring something new and contemporary to this classic piece of Middle Eastern literature, reflecting the way these ancient stories are told in the region today. What we will deliver will be a classic piece of high-quality entertainment, new faces and talent, supported by authentic locations, which we expect will make a major contribution to boosting tourism to the Kingdom."

More applause, then an interruption.

"This is a great idea and I'm sure there is a market for a product like this. I, for one, have offered to direct it."

The shout came from none other than Logan Chalmers, who in one athletic jump alighted on the stage to applaud Abigail in person. His surprise outburst generated the greatest level of cheers so far. Abigail was briefly swept up with emotion before regaining her composure.

"I don't know what to say… wow! That's amazing!"

More applause.

"I'm not sure how to follow that except to say please welcome Mr Mohammed bin Shararni to speak on behalf of the Saudi government."

The Saudi had a short speech prepared but the intervention of Chalmers changed that. It was clear he felt the mood of the room.

"Mr Chalmers has just won the full support of the Saudi National Film Corporation for this project. I think it's time we all sat down and started scheduling dates for filming..."

The resulting cheers sounded more like a football crowd – bin Shararni had not witnessed an instinctive public reaction to any speech he had given previously.

He smiled broadly, accepting the adulation.

Abigail had more to say.

"Thank you all for offering your support for our project. In the weeks ahead we will be sending out a newsletter to keep you posted on our planning and announcing members of the production team. In the meantime, before we close, please forgive me a couple of personal remarks. I have to say I wish my dad, Desmond Kelly, had been here to witness this little piece of movie magic. Some of you will know I lost him just recently and he's really missed. I know he would have been so proud. But in his absence, one of his friends has given me the confidence to press ahead and believe I can make the impossible, possible. I am lucky that he is passing through London tonight from his home in Bulgaria... please welcome Dr Aldo de Leonibus."

Surprised and slightly ill at ease, he joined those on the stage. He moved to the microphone, briefly shaking hands with Chalmers and bin Shararni on the way.

"Er... Thank you, Abigail. It is a surprise for me to be here to witness your announcement. I, too, am mourning the loss of my dear friend, and fellow industrial scientist, your father Desmond. I can hardly believe it has been less than three months since we last met in Riyadh and I find myself in London by chance tonight, on my way to the States to take up a new position as CEO of a new research venture in the energy sector run by Maximum Power Corporation near Charlotte, North Carolina. It is ironic that when we were last together, I was on the verge of taking a job in Saudi myself, but for now my future visits will be restricted to limited external site inspections only. I must tell you, Abigail, that in this short time you have reinvented yourself from just another movie hopeful to becoming a big screen hot property! I should add that, in my experience, during my negotiations with the Saudis I always found them to be direct and honourable. With this in mind, I have no doubt this new Arabian Nights collaboration will be a major success. Thank you and good luck!"

In one move, de Leonibus had succeeded in momentarily wiping the grin off bin Shararni's face. The Italian had in effect cancelled their private recruitment talks about heading up their own HCCVD research organisation. He walked straight past the Saudi off the stage to general applause, leaving him transfixed in the spotlight on stage, locked into a fixed smile.

*

It was the wind that seemed to come to his rescue. He was lying spreadeagled on the surface of the water gazing up through eyelids swollen and made raw by sea salt, at the blue sky, pockmarked with fluffy cumulus clouds. There was a gentle swell, not enough to disturb his newly found equilibrium but enough to keep blotting his hearing as the waves continued to explore the inner recesses of his head. Had he had more of his body below the surface it was likely he would not have felt the cold, but he had woken in the middle of a battle for control of his arms and legs, the sea water forcing his blood to retreat to his core, leaving a numbness in its wake. He was immediately struck by the similarities between this new world and the one he had recently left behind. All he could see and hear were blinding lights and the gurgling of water. He had become a human raft, drifting without power to God knew where. The very current to which he had succumbed now seemed to have taken pity on him, supporting his weight and steering him with a sense of purpose. His mind had no control yet, but was starting to collect in sufficient information to make sense of his situation. Instinctively he tried to swallow but his throat was caked in so much salt it rebelled, convulsing, and inadvertently contorting him from a horizontal to a vertical position, his knees and shins suddenly connecting him with something solid beneath him.

Firm sand. He was in the shallows.

With his position changed, he now sought to understand his surroundings better. The light seemed unusually bright. He could barely make out the beach ahead with tufts of green behind. No trees or discernible landmarks except some square shapes – no, cars – parked some way ahead near the sedge-topped dunes.

Fucking hell, after all I have been through, I'm still alive, he thought.

I can see the shore, I can hear the cries of gulls, I can feel the sand, the wind on my face and taste the salt. Is this a new shore, a new beginning, or have I come back to where I started?

It seemed a colossal effort to get to his feet. He felt incredibly tall or else it was just the water level falling away. He was rocking, trying to control his balance, trying to get one step forward, then another. This was hard work but he knew he was making progress as the waves turned to laps, more of his body becoming exposed, feeling the wet of his clothes against his skin, and then he went down again on his face into the sand and back to the black oblivion from which he thought he had escaped.

The next sensation he experienced was being turned over onto his back. That piercing light had returned, his field of vision filled with a concerned woman's face framed by the light blue background of the sky. Her mouth was moving, as if speaking, but her sound was muffled and indistinct to his mind. And what's this? More water from a bottle crashing on to his face. A hand was now cradling his head forward, the neck of the bottle being forced to his mouth.

Flooding, flooding, choking, coughing – salt burning his skin.

The sideways movement of his head channelling the water away and into the sand. Now a noise. A noise from deep within him – a groan and a pain that felt like a cheese grater being pulled out of his throat.

*

"Come on baby, focus. Try for me." Yes, it was quiet, almost hushed, but he heard that and registered it.

Neither the woman's anxiety, nor the long brown hair blowing across her face, could hide the natural beauty that filled his vision. Now his memory was returning. He knew who she was. This was Margarita, his South American 'girl from Ipanema', someone who had lived partly in his imagination and his computer since they had met by chance months ago at a conference in Berlin. They had got to know each other through a mad private dialogue on Facebook, which had got out of hand. Initially it had started from a need on her part to increase her professional network as a means of finding a new job.

As for him, he had succumbed to the personal flattery from a fellow professional who had shown some interest in him, his life, and interests. Their random initial contacts had increased, partly because of her own lack of distractions on a research ship anchored off the Chilean coast. But for Des, the contact had acted as a pressure valve, the chance to talk about anything other than the day job, with some anonymous person who barely knew him and wasn't in a position to cause him harm.

He loved the privacy of it, the secrecy of their dialogue and the slow, growing intimacy of their exchanges. He had learned about her life; the sacrifices her family had made to get her through college in the States, her affair with a fellow engineer who had been killed in an industrial accident offshore, and a dalliance with a Danish lawyer. She shared her frustrations about the difficulties many women faced balancing their work and private lives and her certain knowledge that her own ability to build a happy family life would not be compatible with the responsibilities of her work.

To Des, Chile seemed so far away. What could he do or say that he would live to regret? The value in the relationship from his perspective was the honesty – frankness – that went with it. He told her of his life and his personal passions and regrets, of his former love in Russia, coming to terms with his end of life diagnosis, coping with his wife's infidelity, his fears about Abigail, his plans to hire Terminal to assist his natural, but untraceable, death. Kelly had been surprised that in some ways, through his long-distance relationship with Margarita, he had already started to apply some of the life lessons advocated by Marisa Kjaer and Maurice Glistrup. He remembered talking about sex with Kjaer and hadn't dared to explain how his deeply personal long-distance relationship with Margarita had moved to that level, ultimately with both having witnessed the other engaging in masturbation. God!

Masturbation at his age and condition! She had encouraged him, aroused him – kept telling him to live in the moment and value every second of life. Her words, her encouragement, her *passion* had stolen his soul. In the literal sense, they may not have had sexual contact, but in every other sense they had. It seemed so wrong, so unplanned and unexpected. If there really was an all-seeing God, he would not need to admit his guilt; it would already have been added to the charge sheet for the prosecution in the celestial court.

According to Glistrup's mantra, the fact that he was still on earth (or if it was heaven, it had an earthly feel to it) must mean something. Kelly had retained the gift of life against the odds. It must be embraced as a new beginning, a rebalancing. There was nothing left to explain to Margarita – he had told her everything, down to the detail of his planned final sea walk. She had asked when and where it would happen, telling him she would be waiting the other side of the water if he made it across. He had taken it as a joke. After all, the whole enterprise had been based on his certain and imminent demise. He had not given serious thought to the future if he didn't die. That is why from every other angle – commercial, domestic, and administrative, he had moved on.

There was nothing left of Dr Desmond Kelly, just a footnote in some soon to become dusty papers in a research library in Oxford and a secret vault on Rømø. He had allowed himself to get involved in a fantasy in Margarita's head. She would help him get a new passport; Irish, as it turned out. All he had to do was to send her a passport-approved portrait picture and collect it from a box at the main Lausanne post office when attending one of his private medical consultations in Switzerland. 'GHW' – Gerald Hogan Walsh from rural County Waterford – had been created, the very identity he had chosen to operate a local bank account to book his private hospital appointments and pay his medical bills, ostensibly to protect the Desmond Kelly brand. It had all seemed so ridiculous; cloak-and-daggerish. Then he had mailed it to her in Chile. Another mad action. What would she do with it, sell it to local drug runners? He amazed himself by doing what she had asked. What the hell! Then events had got in the way. He hadn't thought any more about it. Yet it was a distraction from the fears of what lay ahead for him from the health point of view. Not only had she told him she would be waiting for him, but had started to explain how she imagined them creating a new life together, working on a major nature conservation project in Costa Rica, free from the responsibilities of their respective jobs, and perhaps having a child, clearly a stated ambition of hers. He had to admit the whole vision was so unlikely that it was a means of mental escape for him and, perhaps mistakenly, he had indulged her.

The world had indeed gone mad. A beautiful young woman, in some ways still a stranger, had travelled halfway around the world to find him on a chilly but golden sun-kissed beach, offering him the type of personal comfort he had missed for so many years. He had not thought he would survive and certainly had not expected her to turn his fantasy into a reality by being here. Now he had the prospect of spending time with her, to better understand her motivation and expectations.

She helped him to his feet, wrapping a giant towel around his numbed body and supporting him to walk to who knows where, like some wounded soldier leaving a battlefield.

This was his future now.

He had reached the end of the metaphorical road, just to find a new signpost towards a brighter, but uncertain tomorrow.

He had to look forward, trust his instinct, and follow the direction marked 'Hope'.

Nothing else seemed to matter.

ALSO BY THIS AUTHOR:

"THE VALUE OF LUCK"
A lesson about getting to the top and staying there...

COMING SOON!

About the Author

West Yorkshire-based Martin Venning is a project communications and strategic investment adviser working in the property and construction sector with 20 years' experience engaging with businesses in the UK, continental Europe and Asia. He trained as a journalist as part of his undergraduate studies and writes for pleasure.

mvenning.net

Matador